YOU CAN RUN BUT YOU CAN'T HIDE

"God *damn*," hissed Harry Lefferts. "Talk about a long shot paying off!"

He and Paul and Gerd stared at the pile of coins Donald Ohde had spilled onto the tavern table. Spanish silver, most of it, the best c[...] plenty of gold pieces mixe[...] were probably adulterated, [...] [...]ttered.

They did [...] the tavern to make sure t[...] doubt there was a footpa[...] [...]avern. But by now, weeks after their arrival in Amsterdam, no footpad or cutpurse in his right mind—no gang of them, either—would even think of crossing Harry Lefferts and his wrecking crew.

"Time to get out of town, then," said Harry. "Before the storm hits."

Ohde frowned. "There will be no 'storm,' Harry. I can assure you that the Frenchman was most satisfied with the transaction."

"Who cares about him? Sooner or later, Anne Jefferson's going to wonder what happened to the *originals*. We don't want to be anywhere within miles when that happens. Trust me."

Paul Maczka looked skeptical. "Come on, Harry. She's just a nurse. Gretchen, yes, we'd be in real trouble."

" 'Just a nurse,' " Harry mimicked. "Yeah, fine—but she's a *West Virginia* nurse."

He started scooping coins and shoveling them into his money pouch. "Come on, guys, fill 'em up. I want to be halfway to the Channel ports before Anne figures it out, and we find ourselves in the middle of a down-time version of the Hatfield-McCoy feud."

"They did *what*?" shrieked Anne.

Baen Books by Eric Flint

RING OF FIRE SERIES:
1632
1633 (with David Weber)
Ring of Fire, ed.
1634: The Galileo Affair (with Andrew Dennis)
Grantville Gazette, ed.
Grantville Gazette II, ed.
1634: The Ram Rebellion (with Virginia DeMarce, et al.)
1635: The Cannon Law (with Andrew Dennis)
Grantville Gazette III, ed.
1634: The Baltic War (with David Weber)
1634: The Bavarian Crisis (with Virginia DeMarce)
Grantville Gazette IV, ed.

Time Spike (with Marilyn Kosmatka) (forthcoming)

JOE'S WORLD SERIES:
The Philosophical Strangler
Forward the Mage (with Richard Roach)

STANDALONE TITLES:
Mother of Demons

Crown of Slaves (with David Weber)

The Course of Empire (with K.D. Wentworth)

Mountain Magic (with Ryk E. Spoor, David Drake & Henry Kuttner)

With David Drake:
The Tyrant

The Belisarius Series with David Drake:
An Oblique Approach
In the Heart of Darkness
Destiny's Shield
Fortune's Stroke
The Tide of Victory
The Dance of Time

With Dave Freer:
Rats, Bats & Vats
The Rats, The Bats & The Ugly

Pyramid Scheme
Pyramid Power

With Mercedes Lackey and Dave Freer:
The Shadow of the Lion
This Rough Magic

Edited by Eric Flint:
The World Turned Upside Down (with David Drake & Jim Baen)
The Best of Jim Baen's Universe
The Best of Jim Baen's Universe II (with Mike Resnick)
The Dragon Done It (with Mike Resnick)

DEAD AIR
by Charles Jaco

Veteran TV correspondent Peter Dees—hard-living, wisecracking, hungry for a scoop—seizes upon a story that could rock the world. Deep behind volatile Middle Eastern borders, a madman is stockpiling a lethal arsenal of chemical weapons. And someone on the outside is helping him. But as Dees peels back the layers of intrigue, his sources, many of them friends, begin to die.

From Port-au-Prince and Cairo to the scorched deserts of Saudi Arabia and Iraq, Dees finds the conspiracy much deeper than he ever imagined. For it seems that everyone—even the U.S. government—is hiding deep, damning secrets.

Published by Ballantine Books.
Available at bookstores everywhere.

MONSTRUM
by Donald James

He hunts in a landscape ravaged by war. In a country haunted by its past and a city built on tears, he leaves behind the disfigured bodies of young women. No one knows who he is or why he kills. But now the serial murderer they call Monstrum is being pursued by a policeman who must find the truth: about his killer, his nation, himself—and the dark heart that beats within them all.

"Sophisticated . . . Thought-provoking . . .
I read *Monstrum* at warp speed
and with real pleasure."
—RICHARD NORTH PATTERSON

"One of the best books I've ever read . . .
My nominee for Thriller of the Year."
—*The Philadelphia Inquirer*

Published by Ivy Books.
Available at bookstores everywhere.

Grantville Gazette III

Sequels to 1632
Edited and Created by

ERIC FLINT

GRANTVILLE GAZETTE III

Copyright © 2007 by Eric Flint

A Baen Book

Baen Publishing Enterprises
P.O. Box 1403
Riverdale, NY 10471
www.baen.com

ISBN 10: 1-4165-5565-X
ISBN 13: 978-1-4165-5565-0

Cover art by Tom Kidd

First Baen paperback printing, June 2008

Distributed by Simon & Schuster
1230 Avenue of the Americas
New York, NY 10020

Library of Congress Cataloging-in-Publication Data: 2006028452

Printed in the United States of America

10 9 8 7 6 5 4 3 2 1

Contents

Preface

Eric Flint

Jim Baen died a month ago. I suppose that's a strange way to begin a preface for a collection of stories from my 1632 series, but it seems appropriate nonetheless. Jim was the founder and publisher of Baen Books. He was not only the publisher who bought my first novel, *Mother of Demons*, and twenty-two out of the twenty-four novels that followed. He was also the man who published *1632* and was enthusiastically supportive of the series that emerged from it—which includes the *Grantville Gazettes*.

Jim was willing to take chances that few publishers would. When I first approached him with the idea of producing an electronic magazine devoted to the 1632 series, and distributing it through Baen Books' Webscriptions service, he agreed immediately. And, after the first few issues of that magazine indicated there might be a substantial readership for such stories, he agreed to start producing the volumes in a paper edition.

"Let's see what happens," he said to me at the time.

What happened was a success that surprised both of us. We had decided to hedge our bets with the first volume, which only came out in a paperback edition. Coming out in a time when the market for mass market paperbacks has generally been terrible, we expected the book would sell perhaps ten thousand copies. Instead, it sold over three times that many, with an excellent 77 percent sell-through.

(Sell-through is a term in the publishing industry that refers to the number of books actually sold, of the total number shipped. The average for the industry is about 50 percent. To put it another way, most books sell only half the copies shipped. The first volume of the *Gazette* sold better than three copies out of four.)

Once he saw those results, Jim decided to issue the second volume in hardcover first, with a later mass market reissue. Hardcover editions have a much better profit margin for publishers than paperback editions, and they bring a lot more in the way of royalties to authors. But, of course, they're also chancier, since they're more expensive to produce and it's always possible that customers will shy away from the price tag.

"Let's see what happens," he said.

What happened with that volume, which came out in March of this year, is still uncertain. Not enough time has elapsed for net sales and sell-through to be solidly established. However, the shipping order was very good— about fifteen thousand copies. That's probably twice the average shipping order for novels, and three times the average shipping order for anthologies.

That was good enough for Jim to decide to produce the third volume in the series in hardcover also. That's the volume you're holding in your hand right now.

At the beginning of June, I called Jim on the phone and asked him if he'd be willing to commit to a fourth volume of the *Gazette* in paper edition. He was, and we made the deal right then and there. That volume hasn't been scheduled for publication yet, but it'll appear sometime either late this year or early in 2008.

Grantville Gazette IV was the last book I ever sold Jim, or ever would. On June 12th, he suffered a massive stroke from which he never recovered consciousness. He died on June 28th.

All things considered, I'm glad the last book I ever sold my friend and publisher Jim Baen was one of these.

Eric Flint
July 29, 2006

FICTION

Postage Due
⦅◎★◎⦆
Eric Flint

"You've got to be kidding."

Anne Jefferson looked around the table in the big dining room of the USE's embassy in Amsterdam, at each of the other people sitting there. Immediately to her left sat Rebecca Abrabanel, the ambassador of the United States of Europe to the United Provinces. Sitting next to her, at the end of the table, was her husband Mike Stearns. Mike was the prime minister of the USE, and had arrived in besieged Amsterdam only two days earlier, in a daring airlift that still had the entire city talking—as it did the Spanish army camped in the siege lines beyond.

He and Rebecca were holding hands, clasped on the table. To Mike's left sat Jeff Higgins and right next to him—directly across the table from Anne—sat Jeff's wife Gretchen Richter.

Finally, at the other end of the table facing Mike

Stearns and just to Anne's right, sat Adam Olearius. As of the day before, Anne Jefferson's new fiancé. He'd finally proposed, and she'd taken all of two seconds to accept.

"This is a joke, right?"

That was more in the way of a firm statement than a question.

Silence.

"This is a joke, right?" she repeated. Her voice rose with the last word, a firm statement transmuting into a real question.

"A *joke*. It's got to be."

Desperation was creeping into her voice.

Anne now glared at Mike Stearns, her glare almost instantly being transferred to the handclasp.

"Stop holding hands with your wife!" she snapped. "It's disgusting."

Mike's eyebrows went up a little. Rebecca's went up quite a bit more.

Anne's jaws tightened. "Fine," she said, through gritted teeth. "It's not disgusting, it's aggravating. But that expression on Mike's face *is* disgusting. We all know you're getting laid since you flew into Amsterdam in that reckless flying stunt of yours, Mike. You don't have to be so infuriatingly smug about it."

Rebecca's eyebrows came back down, and a very serene expression came to her face.

"You!" snarled Anne. "*That* expression is even worse!"

Rebecca smiled—very serenely—and replied:

"I will point out that I have also sat for a portrait, in the interests of the nation."

"Baloney! You just sat for that stupid portrait Mike

keeps in his office in Magdeburg so he'd be able to keep admiring you after you left for Amsterdam. Don't give me any crap about 'the national interest.' And—"

Her voice was rising again, as desperation returned. "—*you* didn't pose half-naked."

Across the table from her, Gretchen Richter sniffed. "Half-naked, nonsense. The proposal was clearly explained. By the time the portraits are finished, you will be modestly garbed in various banners. To be sure, Rubens and Rembrandt and the Hals brothers will see you half-naked while you pose, but so what? They're artists. They don't count. Besides, Rubens has already seen you half-naked, plenty of times. Half, did I say? Nine-tenths naked."

Anne's glare at Gretchen made the one she'd bestowed on Mike and Rebecca seem like a fleeting glance of mild disapproval.

"So why don't you do it, then? The whole damn world has seen *you* half-naked!"

Gretchen sniffed again. "Don't be ridiculous. Only the Spanish army camped outside in the siege works and maybe half of Amsterdam's residents."

"Pretty much all of the city's residents, sweetheart," said her husband mildly. "It was a very popular, ah, tourist attraction while it lasted. I think the only ones who didn't come for a look-see were some old crones, and some of the preachers. Well, a few of the preachers."

Jeff didn't seem aggrieved any, though, at the thought of tens of thousands of people having gazed upon his wife's naked breasts. Actually, he seemed a little smug about it himself. Given Gretchen's bosom, that was perhaps understandable.

"You didn't answer my question!"

Gretchen shrugged. "I offered. They turned me down." She gave Mike and Rebecca a dismissive glance. "They said I wouldn't be the appropriate model for the purpose."

"Not hardly," drawled Mike. "The Spanish would have had conniptions. So would the prince of Orange, for that matter."

His eyes grew a little unfocused, as if he were contemplating something in the distance. "Now that I think about, I doubt Gustav Adolf would have been any too pleased, either."

"Kings." Gretchen's tone was icy. "Wretches, all of them. That fat Swedish bastard is depending on the Committees of Correspondence to keep his new little empire for him when the fighting starts up again next spring. But God forbid he should admit it."

Rebecca cleared her throat. "As it happens, Gretchen, I did pass your offer on to the cardinal-infante. The reports I've received indicate that Don Fernando was rather intrigued by the idea. But, not surprisingly, his advisers were adamantly opposed."

Her eyes moved back to Anne Jefferson. "You, on the other hand, are most acceptable to all parties involved. Especially with Gretchen as the alternative. You are a nurse, after all, a healer. Not a revolutionary agitator with a reputation for being distressingly quick with her revolver."

"Nine millimeter automatic," corrected Gretchen. "I don't like revolvers. Rate of fire is too slow."

"It's a conspiracy!" wailed Anne.

"Well, sure," said Mike. "How else would you pull off a stunt like this?"

★ ★ ★

In a tavern not far away, four men sat around a small table in the corner, hunching their upper bodies forward in the way men will when they conspire.

"So he's agreed, then?" asked Harry Lefferts, the leader of the little group.

The man to his left nodded. Donald Ohde, that was, the Scot-born German who served as the financier for Harry's special team. Or the "dog robber," as Harry called him.

"Oh, sure. He's always short of money, and his brother Frans even more so."

"It'll take everything we've got in the way of specie," cautioned the man across the table from Harry. That was Paul Maczka. Like most of the men in Harry's team, he was of hybrid origin: in his case, part-Polish, part-Saxon. And, like every single one of them, an adrenaline junkie addicted to adventures. But he tended to be very conservative whenever financial matters arose.

Harry waved his hand. "It's only money. We're not giving up any of the essentials."

Ohde nodded. "I told Hals. No up-time guns, no dynamite, nothing. Just money." He sneered, slightly. "Artist. Didn't even know what dynamite was, I think."

But Paul was not one to give up easily. "You can't get food, shelter and transport with weapons," he pointed out. "Not unless we're going to rob our way across to England, which would be stupid. We need *some* money."

The fourth man at the table spoke up. "We'll have lots of money once the deal closes. Ten times what we've got now. More than that. Enough to turn this shoestring operation into something out of a James Bond movie. Too bad they haven't invented jet skis yet. We could afford enough for all of us."

Gerd beamed. "Imagine the sight we'd make! Blowing our way up the Thames thumbing our noses at King Charles' soldiers."

Gerd went all the way back to the formation of Harry's special team. So, of all the down-timers there, he more than any of them could claim to be an "old Grantville hand." But it hardly mattered. By now, all of Harry's commandos had seen plenty of up-time films.

James Bond movies were very popular with them. Almost as popular as *The Terminator*.

Maczka was still skeptical. "That stuff is hardly what you can call liquid assets."

Ohde shook his head. "I've already got the buyer. Three of them, in fact, but it'll be the Frenchman who outbids the others. Stop fretting, Paul. Two days after it's all over, we'll be rich and on our way to the Tower."

He paused a moment. "Well, *we* won't be rich. But the cause will."

He even meant it, and quite sincerely. Of all the odd things about Harry Lefferts' special unit, perhaps the oddest was their code of honor. Very flexible and fuzzy at the edges, but hard as iron at the center.

Mike Stearns had once remarked that it was all that kept them from being the most frightening pack of bandits in Europe. He'd made the remark to his wife Rebecca after one of his meetings with Harry, where he'd given Lefferts another "special assignment."

Mike had shaken his head ruefully, his hands cradling a

cup of coffee. "Harry Lefferts. I swear. I told him to be a little careful about the way he raised funds for the operation. I didn't want any CIA drug-dealing scandals."

Rebecca sipped from her own coffee cup. "What did he say in response?"

Mike chuckled. "Harry Lefferts. What do you think? 'Can't, Mike,' he said. 'Drugs ain't illegal in this day and age.'"

Rebecca nodded. "True. That must have been a bit of a relief for you."

Mike shook his head. "No, not really. Not when the next words out of Harry's mouth were: 'More's the pity. We'll have to figure out something else.'"

"Oh."

On their way back to Anne's residence, her hand tucked into the crook of Adam's elbow, she gave her brand-new fiancé an uncertain look.

"You sure you won't mind?"

"Oh, no," he said, smiling. "Leaving aside her indelicate phrasing, Gretchen was quite right. You'll be wearing a pair of shorts and a halter in this pose. Which is considerably more than you wore for Rubens in your previous sessions."

Anne's mouth twisted into a grimace. " 'Pair of shorts.' Pair of hot pants, is what they actually are. And that so-called halter they want me to wear is what plenty of people would call a bikini top."

After a moment: "Okay. Not on the Riviera, I guess. But they sure would have called it that back in West Virginia."

Her expression grew a bit grumpy. "The *real* West

Virginia, I mean. Not this screwy wild-ass version of it we've somehow turned into since the Ring of Fire."

After a few more seconds, she said: "Well, okay. I'll do it, then."

The sessions started two days later. As agreed, in a house in Amsterdam, this time, instead of the Spanish camp where Anne had posed for Rubens on previous occasions. Three out of the four artists were Dutch, after all. Easier for Rubens to join them, than the other way around.

Rubens didn't mind. He was a very experienced diplomat as well as an artist, who'd often served the Habsburgs in their foreign affairs.

He'd always liked Amsterdam, in any event. And, who was to say? If this latest of many complicated steps in the dance of state affairs advanced matters still further, he might someday be able to buy a house of his own in the city.

"Let's begin," he said. Without there having been any discussion, Rubens had assumed leadership of the little project. It seemed natural enough. Not only was he slightly older than the two Hals brothers, he was considerably better known and more successful. The chaotic habits of the Hals family left them usually just two steps ahead of the debt-collectors.

Rembrandt might have challenged the matter. By now, they all knew that in the future world Grantville came from, Rembrandt would be an even more famous artist than Rubens. In many peculiar and subtle little ways, knowledge of what *would* have happened was modifying social status all across Europe. Rembrandt was still very young—only twenty-eight—and had not yet created the masterpieces that would, three and half centuries later, rank him among the greatest artists of all time. But everyone knew he *would* be—or had been, at least, in another world, since there was no telling what would happen in this one. So, he already had most of the prestige of a master.

He'd confided to Rebecca once that it made him very uncomfortable. And he handled the problem by maintaining a stance of modesty that was sometimes almost comical.

So, he made no objection. In this day and age, Rubens was preeminent among them.

"Let's begin," Rubens repeated. "Anne, if you would be so good as to remain still and steady."

"Still and steady ain't the problem," replied Anne, somehow managing to talk clearly while barely moving her lips. "It's keeping this stupid fucking bimbo smile plastered on my face that's the problem."

There had been a time when the thought of using foul language in front of great artists would have appalled Anne Jefferson. But now that she'd come to know them, in their own time and place, she didn't think much of the matter. All things considered, West Virginians and seventeenth-century Europeans got along quite well. It was an earthy age, whose people were at least as rowdy and raucous as Appalachian hillbillies.

Standing at his easel, Rembrandt smiled and went to work. The Hals brothers had already started.

Not a word was spoken in the salon for over an hour. Then Dirck Hals paused at his labor, frowned, and muttered to his older brother.

"It's slipped my mind. Which banner am *I* supposed to be portraying?"

"You idiot," came the toneless response. Frans Hals lifted the brush from his canvas and pointed at one of the flags hanging from the far wall. "That one."

Three days later, it was done. The salon of the house was now crowded with people gazing admiringly at the four portraits displayed to one side.

Anne Jefferson was the model for all of them, a fact which was obvious at a glance. The American was most attractive, in the way that young women who are pretty but not beautiful are. Pleasing to the eye, but not threatening or intimidating, and with just enough in the way of irregularity of features to make her face distinctive and easily remembered.

"Perfect," murmured the cardinal-infante. The commander of the Spanish army and his aides had been given a safe-conduct for the day, so they could cross the lines and come into Amsterdam to see the portraits. By now, after the long weeks of what had become a very peculiar siege, not even his advisers had raised much of a protest.

A bit, of course. Don Fernando was, after all, the younger brother of the king of Spain as well as a cardinal and an army commander. From the standpoint of a hostage, as good as you could ask for.

But the man across the room had given his word, and he was the prince of Orange. Enemies they might be, but by this point in time there was also a great deal in the way of trust between Don Fernando and Fredrik Hendrik.

There had been many negotiations and diplomatic

advances, after all, of which this was only the latest. More to the point, the days of the duke of Alva and his massacres and the equally bloody Dutch responses to them were thankfully many decades in the past. Even the sturdiest Calvinist in Amsterdam, except for diehard Counter-Remonstrants, would allow that Don Fernando was a good enough sort, for a papist and a Spaniard. And most of the soldiers in the cardinal-infante's army would reciprocate the sentiment, with regard to the House of Orange. It had been a hard-fought war, but not a savage one.

Don Fernando's eyes lifted from the canvas he was particularly interested in, and met Fredrik Hendrik's gaze. "I might need a bit of help with the printing," he said, "once we're ready to begin producing large quantities. I fear that siege lines tend to be short of printing presses."

"Not a problem," said the prince of Orange. "I shall see to it you have the services of some of the printers in the city."

Graciously, he left unsaid the fact that only *Spanish* siege lines would be short of printing presses. Dutchmen would have plenty, anywhere they went, not being semiliterate jumped-up sheepherders who called themselves "hidalgos."

Don Fernando nodded and made a little gesture to his aides. Two of them stepped forward and took up one of the portraits.

"We'll be off, then. I think we can safely expect the service to begin . . . in a month?"

Fredrik Hendrik pursed his lips, considering. "In the United Provinces, certainly." A bit wryly: "There's not much left of them, after all, since you arrived. I imagine you'll be able to do the same in the Spanish Netherlands. For the rest—"

He shrugged. "No telling what Gustavus Adolphus will decide."

"No, not yet," agreed the cardinal-infante. "The great test of arms is still ahead of us, in the spring. But what about the other small principalities?"

"I've already raised the matter with De Geer, and I think Essen will certainly agree. Probably Duke Anton of Oldenburg, also. You'll have to deal with the archbishop of Cologne, of course. As for Cleves . . ."

He rolled his eyes, the Spanish commander almost immediately doing the same. Since the death of Duke Johann Wilhelm in 1609, and the passing of the inheritance to his sisters, Cleves had splintered badly.

"We'll manage something," said Fredrik Hendrik.

A week later, the end result began appearing. In Amsterdam first, of course.

"Marvelous," said the dye-maker, examining the sheets of paper with their many small portraits. "And you guarantee they will be accepted anywhere in the Low Countries? These in Brussels, for instance?"

The agent from the new postal service nodded. "And those from Brussels will be accepted here. As long as the blonde is portrayed, it doesn't matter which flag she's got wrapped around her. House of Orange colors, the cardinal-infante's colors, it doesn't matter. The stamps are all good anywhere that either Fredrik Hendrik or Don Fernando's authority reaches. That, for sure, right from the start. Soon enough, we expect other principalities to join in.

Who knows? Within a year, perhaps even the USE and Denmark and France."

The dye-maker chuckled. "That'll depend a lot on who wins the war. Still . . ."

The dye-maker's wife intervened. She'd been silent up to now, standing next to her husband and squinting suspiciously at the sheets of paper. "We want some of the glue thrown in. And a brush to apply it. Brushes are expensive."

"Not a problem. A pot of glue and a small brush comes with every purchase of a sheet. One hundred stamps to a sheet."

The postal agent pointed to one of the sheets spread out across the dye-maker's table. "They're already creased, as you can see. Easy to cut them out. We're hoping, within possibly a year, to provide them with some gum already pasted to the back surface. Just wet them a little—a tongue-licking will do it—and the stamps will adhere to the parcel on their own. No glue needed at all."

The dye-maker pondered the matter, for a moment. But not for long. The established method for using postage worked, yes. But it was time-consuming, for a busy artisan, to have to go to a postal agent and have him manually stamp the parcel with a seal and sign it. Something of a nuisance. This way, with pre-paid postage, it would be much simpler.

And less costly, too. Not only were the new "stamps" slightly less expensive than the existing postal rates, simply in terms of money, but they were also much less expensive in terms of labor lost. If the postal agent could be believed, and the dye-maker thought he could, there would soon be special boxes in place all over the city where a pre-posted parcel could simply be dropped off for delivery. Fifteen minutes work for an artisan's wife or apprentice—perhaps only five or ten—instead of two hours or more.

"I'll buy a sheet, then."

"Splendid. Which one would you like?"

The dye-maker's eyes widened. "I have a choice?"

"Certainly," said the postal agent. "I told you. Any of the portraits is valid. All that matters is that it's the same blonde. She's the nurse, you know."

The dye-maker and his wife nodded. Anne Jefferson was quite well known in the city. Almost as well known as Gretchen Richter, in fact.

"Well . . ." The dye-maker stood up a bit straighter. "We should take the colors of Orange," he said stoutly.

"No," said his wife. "That portrait, she's showing too much skin. And who's Rembrandt, anyway? Never heard of him."

She pointed to the sheet with Rubens' version. "That one. He's famous and most of our trade is with the south, anyway. The cardinal-infante's colors are sure to be welcome in Brussels. Catholic or not, the linen-makers there are better business for us than these tight-fisted bastards in Amsterdam."

"Done," said the postal agent, reaching into his parcel and hauling out a pot of glue and a brush. "Oh, yes, I failed to mention that the pots and brushes all come with the initials of the artists. Whichever one you'd like."

"Rubens, of course," sniffed the dye-maker's wife. "The Hals brothers are drunkards and ne'er-do-wells. And nobody's ever heard of this Rembrandt fellow, whoever he is."

"Rubens it is, then."

★ ★ ★

"You're feeling better about the whole thing, I see," said Adam Olearius.

Anne smiled. "Well, yeah. From what I hear, the stamps are selling like crazy. Hands across the border, and all that." Then, quietly: "If it'll keep a few more people from getting killed, it was worth it."

"Might keep a lot of people from getting killed," her fiancé mused, sitting on the divan next to her. "Well, not by itself, of course. But along with all the rest . . ."

He lifted his shoulder in a little shrug. "Hard to know, of course, as it so often is with diplomacy. It's always a gamble."

"God *damn*," hissed Harry Lefferts. "Talk about a long shot paying off!"

He and Paul and Gerd stared at the pile of coins Donald Ohde has spilled onto the tavern table. Spanish silver, most of it, the best currency in Europe. But there were plenty of gold pieces mixed in with the lot. Some of them were probably adulterated, but with *that* big a pile it hardly mattered.

They did not bother casting glances around the tavern to make sure that no one was observing them. No doubt there was a footpad or two among the crowd in the tavern. But by now, weeks after their arrival in Amsterdam, no footpad or cutpurse in his right mind—no gang of them, either—would even think of crossing Harry Lefferts and his wrecking crew. The only difference between the way they gauged the matter and Mike Stearns did, was that professional cutthroats knew that Harry & Company *were* the most frightening pack of bandits on the continent.

That they might be something else as well was irrelevant, from a criminal's standpoint.

"Time to get out of town, then," said Harry. "Before the storm hits."

Ohde frowned. "There will be no 'storm,' Harry. I can assure you that the Frenchman was most satisfied with the transaction."

"Who cares about him? Sooner or later, Anne Jefferson's going to wonder what happened to the *originals*. We don't want to be anywhere within miles when that happens. Trust me."

Paul Maczka looked skeptical. "Come on, Harry. She's just a nurse. Gretchen, yes, we'd be in real trouble."

"'Just a nurse,'" Harry mimicked. "Yeah, fine—but she's a *West Virginia* nurse. She's Willie Ray Hudson's grand-daughter, fer chrissake. Got cousins—first, second, third, you name it—all over the hills and hollers. At least two of them are serving in the Thuringian Rifles and another one is downright crazy. Marcus Acton, Jr. Got in a fight with him once. I won, but it was touch-and-go. Just as soon not do it again."

He started scooping coins and shoveling them into his money pouch. "Come on, guys, fill 'em up. I want to be halfway to the Channel ports before Anne figures it out, and we find ourselves in the middle of a down-time version of the Hatfield-McCoy feud."

"They did *what*?" shrieked Anne.

Mike Stearns flinched from the blast. "Just what I said. They finagled three out of the four originals and sold them to someone. For a small fortune, what I hear."

Anne's face was pale, her expression a combination of shock, outrage and fury. *"How did they get them?"*

Mike grimaced. "They just bought them outright from the Hals brothers. Those two are always strapped for cash. Rembrandt told me he let them have his for free, once they explained what they wanted it for."

"That stinking bastard!"

"It *is* a good cause, Anne. The one thing about Harry is that you can trust him to be honest. Well, okay, in a Robin Hood and Jesse James sort of way. He's not really what you could call an upstanding citizen. But he's not a thief, either. That money *will* go to spring our people out of the Tower."

The last sentence put something of a damper on Anne's gathering fury. She knew all of the people imprisoned in the Tower of London herself, after all. Two of them were friends of hers.

"Well, yeah, fine. But. Still."

After a few seconds' silence, she hissed: "One of these days, I swear I will kill that son of a bitch."

Mike pursed his lips. "You'll have to take a number. By now, the line's probably up to a hundred or so."

After Mike left, Anne turned to Olearius and he gave her a comforting embrace.

"At least Rubens didn't sell his," she whispered. "I'm glad for that. He's always been my favorite."

Adam said nothing, judging it to be an unwise time to explain that Rubens *had* sold his original. He'd sold it to Olearius himself, and for a token sum, once Adam explained his purpose.

But now was not the time to get into that. The portrait was safely stowed away, in a place Anne would never think to look.

There was no hurry, after all, given his purpose. Adam would tell her in a few years, when the whole incident had faded into one of those more-in-humor-than-anger recollections for his soon-to-be-wife. By then, they'd have children; and, like any mother, Anne would be thinking about her children's prospects.

Which would almost certainly be splendid. The future was always unpredictable, of course. But Adam Olearius was quite confident that in any one of the possible futures he and his wife would find themselves in, being able to bestow onto their children an original portrait by Rubens would mollify his wife. Especially *that* portrait, as famous as it would soon be.

By then, it would be worth . . .

Who could say? A very great deal, certainly.

He wondered, for a moment, what would happen to the others.

Richelieu pondered the three portraits. They were magnificent, especially taken as an ensemble. Three portraits by three great artists, each of the same subject . . .

To the best of the cardinal's knowledge, nothing like it had ever happened in the long history of art.

For a moment, he was tempted to keep them for himself. But, as always, duty triumphed.

"In the Louvre, Servien," he said firmly to his aide. "For the moment, we'll keep them here in my chambers. But once the work in the Grande Galerie is finished, we'll move them there. They'll form the anchor of the collection."

In another world, the royal castle known as the Louvre wouldn't become a museum until 1793, during the French revolution. But Richelieu, determined to see to it that the revolution never happened at all, had concluded that launching a museum much earlier would add to the grandeur of royal France. It was just one of many adaptations he was making to the new world created by the Ring of Fire.

"And the other matter?"

Richelieu continued his study of the portraits, for perhaps a minute.

"A good idea," he finally concluded. "No matter how the war ends. I have come to the conclusion that the more civilized the contest, the more advantageous is the position of France. This"—he gestured at the portraits—"was a very shrewd maneuver by our opponent. Best to respond quickly and in kind, I think, lest we seem churlish."

Servien nodded. "It will certainly please the city's artisans and tradesmen. It can take up to three hours to get a parcel properly sealed and certified."

"Yes, it will." Richelieu did not usually concern himself much with the sentiments of the merchant classes, since in normal times they carried little weight in the political affairs of France. But the war was not going as well as he had thought it would, and the king's younger brother Monsieur Gaston—treacherous as ever—was using the fact to undermine Richelieu's support in the aristocracy. Should the worst come to pass and a real crisis erupt, having the support and allegiance of the Parisian mob could be important.

"We'll have Georges de la Tour do the painting. I'll want the same model, you understand. Given the situation, Servien, that's essential."

"I'll see to the matter, Your Eminence."

Anne Jefferson sat at the same table in the embassy, staring at Rebecca. Mike was long gone from Amsterdam, by now, since the war was heating up again.

"You've got to be kidding."

"Not at all," said Rebecca. "The French are offering to pay for your transport"—she glanced at Adam—"and your husband's, and they'll put you up in chambers in the Louvre itself. It's mostly a royal palace today, you know. They're certain to be very comfortable quarters."

She made a little face. "Allowing for seventeenth-century plumbing. But you've been dealing with that here in Amsterdam, anyway."

"This is a joke, right?"

Pastor Kastenmayer's Revenge

$\langle\!\langle\odot\star\odot\rangle\!\rangle$

Virginia DeMarce

April 1635

Ludwig Kastenmayer would never forget the day. April 11, 1634, by the reckoning of these up-timers, who had adopted the pope's calendar. The day that one of them had stolen his daughter. It was the worst thing that had happened to him since Count Ludwig Guenther assigned him to the new parish of St. Martin's in the Fields after the Rudolstadt Colloquy.

The man should not even have been in Grantville. He was an officer in the military of the New United States and should have been in Erfurt, where he was assigned.

Jonas—Jonas Justinus Muselius, the youngest teacher at the Lutheran elementary school attached to the church and a friend of several of the up-timers—had said that he was on "R and R." Even after Jonas had explained it to

27

him, Pastor Kastenmayer found it peculiar. There was far more to do in Erfurt than in Grantville. Theological lectures by guest professors. Organ concerts. Choral performances. Sermons by visiting pastors. The man should have stayed in Erfurt for his holiday. Erfurt was a magnificent city. Kastenmayer had greatly enjoyed all four of his visits there.

That man should not have come to Grantville and, within less than two weeks, seen Andrea on the street, walked up to her, introduced himself, persuaded her to accompany him to a public restaurant for a meal, and—married her! Six weeks before the end of the school term at Countess Katharina the Heroic School next to St. Martin's, leaving her younger sister Maria Blandina to manage all of the youngest children by herself. Still, there were only eighty-three of them, after all. There had been little reason for Maria Blandina to complain so bitterly.

Barbaric, this idea that couples could marry in three days' time and without the consent of the parents. Especially when anyone who thought about it should have realized that the parents would not consent. The man was—well, ultimately, to put it plainly—

Catholic.

At least he hadn't insisted that Andrea convert to his church. That would have been the final embarrassment. Nonetheless, it had been difficult to explain to the consistory in Rudolstadt. Extremely difficult, to say the least. Better yet, they had not married in the Grantville Catholic church. Pastor Kastenmayer had derived some minimal satisfaction from discovering that St. Mary's forbade such an absurdity as manifestly disastrous mixed-confessional matrimony on three days' notice, even if the civil laws did not. They had married before the mayor at the *Rathaus*, the man saying casually (Pastor Kastenmayer had heard secondhand; he had not been there in person) that they "could get the religious stuff sorted out when they had time."

Additionally, Salome, his second wife, suggested that it was his own fault for not having arranged marriages for the daughters of his first marriage in a more timely manner. Indeed, she had commented that it would not be entirely surprising if Maria Blandina chose an equally unsuitable spouse. She hadn't *quite* said that the girls were both self-centered young snips with pretty faces . . . not . . . quite.

Pastor Kastenmayer had duly sounded out Jonas about Maria Blandina. It would have been quite suitable; the father of young Muselius had been his second wife's half brother. But he had received a courteous refusal. Too bad. God had blessed Pastor Kastenmayer greatly—five children from his first wife, all surviving (and the two oldest earning salaries, one as a city clerk and one as a junior pastor, which was also a great blessing). Eight children from his second wife, seven surviving. And, ah, of all those, currently, three sets of board, room, and tuition at the university in Jena; two sets of board, room, and tuition at the Latin school in Rudolstadt, and two boys still not old enough for Countess Katharina the Heroic. All on the salary of a parish pastor, with a bit of tutoring here and there. Salome had recently informed him that they were to be blessed again. *I am supposed to find a dowry for Maria Blandina just where?* he asked himself. He sighed most gloomily and considered lengthening his morning prayers.

But Jonas, although refusing the offer of a wife, had suggested an alternative. What he called a "payback."

Jonas felt very responsible for the remainder of the village he had led into Grantville. A few old people, a couple of young mothers, and quite a few children. Well, some of the children had been adolescents in 1631, and most of the adolescents had been girls. The older boys had stayed behind with their fathers to fight the delaying action against the mercenaries from Badenburg. The boys lay dead with their fathers, in a mass grave next to the burned-out church. Now, in 1634, the older girls were becoming—at least at the ages the up-timers considered suitable—marriageable. Also without dowries. The arable lands of Quittelsdorf had been removed to West Virginia, Herr Gary Lambert had told Jonas. At least, that was the up-timers' best guess as to where God had chosen to put their fields. God moved in most mysterious ways. If they had not fled from the mercenaries, they too, presumably, would have been removed to West Virginia. It had been a good day to work in the fields.

"So," Jonas had said, "if the Habsburgs can do it"—he quoted the proverb about "happy Austria" waging matrimony rather than war, in Latin, of course—"then so can we. We must ask '*die Krausin*.'" Margaretha Krause, widowed with three children, had gone into service as housekeeper and cook for a middle-aged American whose wife had been left up-time and shortly thereafter had married him.

Before the construction of St. Martin's in the Fields, be it known. Pastor Kastenmayer had had nothing to do with it. The man was not Lutheran. On the other hand, he was a skilled artisan with a regular position, owned a house, and did not interfere with her church attendance. He had allowed her to have their daughter baptized Lutheran at St. Martin's. Things could be worse.

"But," Pastor Kastenmayer had protested, "I do observe the truth that the different churches and their pastors of this Grantville appear to survive in this parity arrangement without excessive conflict. But still—if we try to pluck away their members. That will certainly cause offense. Which Count Ludwig Guenther does not wish to cause. They are his allies. He is part of their confederation."

Jonas cocked his head to the side a little. "More than a third of these up-timers belong to no church at all."

"You mean that they do not enforce attendance?"

"No. People who do not belong to any of the churches in the town. They are not only not Lutherans. They are not even *heretics*." The honest sense of scandal that had enveloped Jonas when he first discovered this was still plain to be heard in his voice. "But, anyway. We steal their men, but we don't steal them from any of their churches. How can the other pastors complain if we convert the heathen?"

From the perspective of his sixty-five years, the first forty-five of them spent among the feuding theologians of Saxony, Pastor Kastenmayer predicted grimly, "They'll find a way."

But it had been irresistible. He called upon *die Krausin*, now known to the Grantville public as Mrs. Burton Vandiver. He did not overreach. The weapon that God had forged to his hand consisted of, after all, a dozen quite ordinary village girls, even though they had been given two or three years more schooling in Grantville. His requirements were basic. He needed a list of up-time marriage candidates: just "no constant drunkards, no brawlers, no lazy louts who will expect their wives to support them."

One more year. Palm Sunday, 1635. Harvest time coming in the spring. He smiled upon his congregation from the pulpit. "Today we welcome into fellowship through the rite of adult confirmation . . . Herr Ryan Baker, Herr Derek Blount, Herr James Anthony Fritz, Herr Mitch Hobbs, Herr Michael Lewis Jenkins, Herr Errol Mercer, Herr Roland Worley . . ."

The men stood in front of him, closely shaved, their hair cut very short with the exception of Herr Mercer, who had grown his to a respectable length for an adult man since leaving the army, wearing "neckties" and, most of them, the semistunned expression of guys who have not fully analyzed the process by which they got themselves into their current situation.

According to Herr Lambert, the "neckties" were a good omen, indicating that the men were taking their oaths seriously.

The girls of vanished Quittelsdorf had done well in the service of their Lord. Indeed, one was also betrothed to the stepson of *die Krausin*, but that young man, like his father, was a church member elsewhere; another was betrothed to a colleague of Ryan Baker, but that man also belonged to an up-time church. Still, he had seven. *Seven at one blow,* he thought, as the story of the brave little tailor flitted through his mind. Four of the Quittelsdorf girls, prompted by Jonas, had even made their chosen husbands go back to school and get the magic "GED" before they agreed to marry. *Jonas was, after all, not merely a school-teacher, but their own former teacher, from their lost village; they listened to him.* Pastor Kastenmayer proceeded through the liturgy in a dignified manner, but part of his mind was on other things.

Things Could be Worse:
Ryan Baker and Magdalena Heunisch

May 1634

Ryan Baker had gotten out of the army—stupid amount of paperwork involved with that, it turned out—and gone for a beer. Where he had found the girl. Magdalena. He called her Meg—Magdalena didn't come off his tongue very well. Four hours later, he asked a little doubtfully, "Don't you need to go home, or something? Won't somebody be worried if you don't turn up? What about your mom and dad?"

She wasn't any more than five feet tall, if that. Narrow little shoulders, flat little chest, tiny little waist, a bit more in the way of hips, but not a lot. Now she crossed her arms on the table, put her chin on them, looked at the mug of beer he had bought her, and said, "Dead."

"Ah? Dead?"

"Father dead. I was little girl. Had stepfather. Dead when the soldiers came. Had brother. Dead when the soldiers came. Mother bigger than me. Strong. Worked hard. Stayed to fight the soldiers. Brave. Dead." She picked up the beer mug.

It was dawning on Ryan that there might be situations in the world worse than the one in which he found himself. He had never been particularly fond of Dayna Shockley, who had already been his stepmother for ten years as of the Ring of Fire. It wasn't that she was awful—just that if Dad hadn't married her, he would never have talked to the woman. But his mother was left up-time, so there hadn't been much option except to move in with Dad and Dayna after the Ring of Fire until he finished high school.

He graduated in 1633, did his basic-and one year in the full-time military, and really, really didn't want to move back in with Dad and Dayna now that he was getting out and had a job as a trainee at the Grantville-Rudolstadt-Saalfeld Railroad and Tramway Corporation.

Meg was continuing. "Things maybe worse. Have little sister. Half sister. Still alive. Lives with me. No—lives with Maria. I live with Maria. Maria is stepsister. All live in 'refugee housing' with Maria's aunt. She is alive, too. She has two daughters still alive."

She lifted her chin. "Things maybe worse. If everybody else dead, much worse."

Ryan admired her for being so upbeat about it all.

"Maria's aunt not worry where I am. Too much work, too many girls, too busy. I am the end one to worry about."

Ryan put his arm about her shoulders, in what he intended to be a friendly and comforting manner. She cuddled her head against his neck. Her light brown hair was slick and smooth. He realized that he had a key to Mitch Hobbs' parents' empty house.

The next morning, she was quite friendly and cheerful. Which was good, all things considered. She'd been a virgin and she might have gone all tearful on him. Instead, she climbed out of bed, fixed porridge, and said, "I go to work."

"Where?"

"Kitchen at Cora's. Peel vegetables. Peel fruits. Peel, wash, peel, scrub. Peel more." Her hands moved descriptively.

"Ah." Ryan paused. *What next?* "Ah, what time do you get off?"

"When done. Cora pays overtime." Meg beamed brightly.

"Ah. I'll be off first, then. If I come pick you up . . ."

He stopped rather awkwardly.

"We could go see Maria's aunt. Give her this address. Tell her where you're living now."

He wasn't one hundred percent sure of that, but he was pretty sure that Mitch wouldn't mind having him rent a couple of rooms. The upstairs in the Hobbs house had two bedrooms that you got to on a really narrow and steep staircase. Mitch probably wouldn't be using them after he got out. There was only one bath and it was downstairs, but at least there was a bath. Some rent would help pay Mitch's taxes. And Meg would be a *really* good reason not to move back in with Dad and Dayna. Once Dayna found out.

He thought he'd tell Dad first. Maybe let Dad tell Dayna. When he wasn't there.

September 1634

Maria Krause looked at her stepsister with exasperation. "You're urping in the morning because you're pregnant, that's what."

Meg nodded quite cheerfully. "*Ja*, okay."

"You're pregnant and you are *not* married."

"I told Ryan. He says we'll go to the *Rathaus* and get married right away. It's all okay." Meg was not about to admit to her stepsister that she had been happily surprised by her boyfriend's reaction to the news.

Walpurga Hercher said, "No!" Very forcefully.

Maria looked at her reproachfully. "No? She is lucky that she will not be suffering for what she has done. Why not?"

"Because it won't help Teacher Muselius's project. Pastor Kastenmayer's project. Magdalena is one of us. We must make our husbands Lutheran for them. If Magdalena just marries Ryan at the city hall, it won't help."

Maria's answer would have been better placed in the barnyard.

"She can always fall back on city hall if he won't go along with it," Walpurga conceded.

Ryan was very startled to discover that although Meg was (when not morning-sick) just as friendly, cheerful, and pleasant as ever, she didn't jump at the prospect of immediate marriage. Meg, truth to tell, would have preferred to jump at it, but she found Walpurga Hercher rather intimidating. So she said, "Want to marry by pastor. See Teacher Muselius. You be Lutheran."

It was weird, really. Hugh Lowe, the big boss at work, had thought it was a good idea to see this Teacher Muselius. "You might as well find out what you're letting yourself in for, kid. Besides, they outnumber us. They're most of our customers. It can't hurt us to have an in with them, when we're looking for workers and supplies."

April 1635

Ryan had quickly come to the conclusion that Pastor Kastenmayer moved through life at a stately pace. The confirmation instructions had been excruciatingly step-by-step. It looked like this wedding was going to be a prime example of what Hugh called just-in-time scheduling. Meg was so little, to start with. As the months went by, there had seemed to be more and more baby, with less and less Meg to go around it, like she was shrinking. He'd had the marriage license for three weeks, just in case she started popping before today. And he'd called the mayor, who had agreed to run over to the hospital and marry them off before the kid showed up, in an emergency.

He stood in the front of St. Martin's, his mind wandering as the liturgy flowed over him.

Dad and Dayna were here for the confirmation and wedding. Well, Dad came and dragged Dayna with him. They *never* went to church. Plus his sister, Sam, who didn't ever go to church either. Plus Dayna's two kids. Plus, somehow, Dayna's ex, LeVan Jessup, and his wife, who was German and went to church here, plus her kid and their kid. Teacher Muselius had been very glad to see them. He'd led them to one of the front pews, introduced them to several officers of the congregation.

If it's a little girl, Meg says she wants to name the kid for her mom. Heroically dead in the defense of Quittelsdorf and all that. Ottilia? *What do you call a kid named Ottilia? Ottie, nah. Tillie, well, maybe.*

At least she wants to call a boy after her brother, not her dad. David's better than Hermann any day. David's a sort of nice name . . .

Things could be a lot worse.

We're All Cousins, Somehow:
Derek Blount and Ursula Krause

May 1634

The circle around the Vandiver kitchen table looked at Margaretha's list. *Die Krausin* had outdone herself. Pastor Kastenmayer had expected her to select one up-time man per girl and start to arrange marriages. Two years of marriage to an up-timer had taught her that this would not work. She had a list with twice as many men as there were girls from Quittelsdorf. This had not been hard, even limiting herself to heathen men who were of a social class that might be expected to marry undowered girls such as these. Quittelsdorf had never been the largest of villages. By stretching the definition of "marriageable" from seventeen to thirty-five and including a widow, plus Rahel's stepsister who was not even from Quittelsdorf, her list of potential brides was still less than a dozen.

Ursel Krause was standing behind Margaretha, looking over her shoulder. Ursel's little sister Else, the youngest of them all, was standing on the other side of the table, looking mulish. There was a stubborn streak in Ursula and Elisabetha Krause. Of course, their mother was born Elisabetha Hercher. There was a stubborn streak in the Hercher family as a whole.

"I," Else said, "will not do it."

"You," said Margaretha, "have the best chance of all. You have had almost three years of school here. You speak English best. And—" She paused to evaluate the possibilities. "—you are prettiest."

In the words of the Lutheran catechism, "this was most certainly true." No voice rose to dispute this assessment. Else Krause had curly auburn hair and a set of teeth that a princess would envy. She also, thanks to the Grantville Chapter of the Red Cross, had a toothbrush and baking soda with which she cared for them.

Plus, Else—and Ursel, of course, since they were sisters— still had a mother to watch after her. *"Die Hercherin"* watched her own daughters a perceptible degree more carefully than she watched her husband's nieces, assorted more distant cousins, and the other girls who had fallen into her care since the day that Quittelsdorf burned to the ground and its fields disappeared. And she had let her own daughters stay in the up-time schools the longest. Too long, maybe.

"I know the one I want," said Else, "and he is not on your list, because he is not a heathen. A heretic, yes, but not a heathen. If I need to become a heretic to marry him, I will. Pastor Kastenmayer must do without me. That is final."

It turned out to be final.

Ursel, from behind Margaretha, reached down and put

her finger on the list. She wasn't as pretty as Else—hair more a reddish brown than auburn, and straight; body a little less well proportioned; nose a little less perfectly suited to the face on which it found itself. "I know *him*," she said. "At least, I already know who he is. If I can have that one, I will do it. If not, not. I will not take a second choice from this list."

That turned out to be final, also. There was a *really* stubborn streak in the Herchers, and *die Hercherin* had passed it on to her daughters in full.

But, perhaps, it was not just that Hercher streak. Barbara Conrath, only three months older than Else Krause, also with a living mother, also with three years of school in Grantville since the Ring of Fire, said, "Not me, either." Then she grinned at Margaretha, making full use of her innocent round face, wrinkling her pug nose, and making dimples. "I get Benton. I know he's not on your list. 'Sorry, Pastor Kastenmayer,' and all that sort of thing. I'll make Benton go back to school and get his GED before I agree to marry him, though. Promise. *Schwiegermutter*." She threw her arms around *die Krausin*.

Margaretha was startled. Barbel would be a fine daughter-in-law, certainly. In eight or ten years. But the look in the girl's eye indicated that she was not announcing long-range plans. And her stepson was not on the list because he, like her own husband, was already a member of an up-time church.

She sighed. This was not going to be as simple as Pastor Kastenmayer expected.

★ ★ ★

Ursel Krause worked at the Freedom Arches. Not because of any commitment to the Committees of Correspondence's ideology nor, in fact, because she had even the slightest interest in it. She had applied for jobs in several inns and taverns. She picked this one because she liked the idea of staying behind a counter where the customers couldn't grope the waitress's rear end. That was worth doing without "tips." Her mother had agreed.

Every morning she watched Derek Blount come in, get his breakfast, look up forlornly at the blank, black screen in one corner where there was nothing on TV at this hour, reluctantly pick up the newspaper, and try to struggle his way through the front page. Finally, she realized that he had just as hard a time reading it as she did. But??? He was an up-timer. He spoke English, after all. Why couldn't he read it?

Since she was still taking ESOL classes in the evening—that was why she worked the shift at the Freedom Arches that began at five o'clock in the morning—after several weeks of just smiling at him (direct smiles, not just the "here's your order" smile), duly authorized by Pastor Kastenmayer and *die Krausin*, she asked him for help with her English . . .

June 1634

By this time, of course, Magdalena Heunisch was living with Ryan Baker, so they would have met one another, anyway. As Ursel explained to Derek, "We are not all just from the same village. We are all cousins, somehow. I am not related to Meg, really. She is sort of out on the far end. But I am related to her little half sister, Anna. On the Krause side of the family, Anna is my first cousin. So we are connected. And Mrs. Vandiver is my aunt on the Krause side, so her children are my cousins, too. And Lisbet and Walpurga are her first husband's nieces. Plus, they're my cousins on the Hercher side. Their dad was my mom's brother." She paused for breath.

Derek had followed this discourse without the slightest trouble. He thought that it was kind of nice. After all, lots of people in Grantville were one another's cousins, too. The town had been around for a long time. In addition to his brother, Donnie, and the two German boys his parents had adopted after the Battle of the Crapper, he had one first cousin on the Blount side who came through the Ring of Fire, and three on the Stewart side. Plus, Stew and Lesley had three kids; Cherilyn and Bob had one, plus, now, two German orphans they had adopted after the battle at Badenburg. Plus, he supposed, Pam's kids would get married one of these days. They were both working down at USE Steel toward Saalfeld and both dating a couple of Frenchies they had met there—Walloons, they called themselves.

That didn't count the Blount and Stewart cousins who had been left up-time.

Derek found it very hard to imagine a world without cousins and family picnics. It was really nice that Ursel had a bunch of cousins, too. It sort of gave folks something in common. If you ran out of other things, you could always talk about what your cousins were doing. Especially what they had done that they shouldn't. Like Meg moving in with Ryan Baker.

That was where this conversation had started. Ursel's mom didn't approve. At all. Derek somehow figured that he could just forget about lucking out the way Ryan had. At least, with Ursel. And, right now, he was dating Ursel. Which sort of meant that he could forget about . . . He had a suspicion that he'd been given a message.

July 1634

Derek drew a picture on the Formica table with his finger. He'd dropped by the Freedom Arches to see Ursel on her lunch break. He was out of the army now. Since yesterday. He'd been supposed to get out in May, with the other guys, but they'd asked him to stay a couple more months. He'd said okay, but that meant that he'd missed getting on the crews when the roadwork opened up in the spring. He'd have to go see Mickey Simmons, he guessed, he explained to Ursel. Mickey was doing the training for the Department of Transportation now. See if someone had dropped out. See if he could get on. Roadwork was about all he was good for, out of the army. Not having a diploma. And it paid pretty good.

"Why did you drop out? Doesn't your family go to school? When they could?"

Derek looked a little uncomfortable. "Actually, Dad does have a high school diploma. And he wasn't real happy about it when Donnie dropped out first, and then me."

"Well, why did you?" To Ursel, the question seemed reasonable enough. Her view of school was that it had been easier than work, any day. She had been glad, when they first came to Grantville, that the people had sent her back to school. And that her mother had let her go. This would not have been necessary. She had already been sixteen, old enough to leave school by Grantville's laws, and her family had needed money, certainly. And it had been not the regular classes for the up-time students her age, so she had not met many of them. But still.

"School is great." Ursel's endorsement of school was unrestrained. That was why she kept taking the classes three evenings each week. "If I could, I would go to school forever and ever and *ever*." She threw out her arms, as if embracing the whole Grantville school system at once.

"Ursel, first of all, you've got to understand. One thing, Dad's *always* had a job. He's never been unemployed, not once. But jobs are sort of scarce around here, so we moved a lot when I was growing up. Not a long ways, but from Grantville to Fairmont, to Shinnston, then back to Fairmont, then over to Clarksburg for a while, then back to Grantville. May have been a couple more in there, but I remember those. So Donnie and me—we changed schools every time. Every time, the classes were doing something that wasn't exactly what we'd been doing before."

He looked down. "I can't read, Ursel. Not really. I can make out some words, but not to sit down and read something all the way through. So I couldn't catch up when we moved. If I stayed in a class long enough, I could pick up what the teacher said and do pretty good in the class discussions. Good enough to squeak by, even if I bombed every test. Which I did. But it got harder and harder. I was flunking junior year flat. So I quit.

"Dad? Well, he couldn't really say much about it—not too much—without upsetting Mom. She's a dropout, too, see. And we were just no good in school, Donnie and me. We're no good."

He went back to drawing on the Formica, not looking at her. "You ought to forget about me, Ursel. Take yourself back to school. Go all the way. Be a teacher. You could, you know. Then you could be in school 'forever and ever and *ever.*' Forget about me. I'm a loser."

July 1634

Derek sighed. He should never have mentioned teaching to Ursel. Never.

She had not forgotten about him. She had announced, "If I have learned it, you can learn it. The same way."

She had kept every damn work sheet from the remedial-and-ESOL program at the middle school. Every damn one of them. He wondered where she had found to put them, given how crowded the refugee housing was. She said that she had tied them in a bundle with string and hung them from a wooden hook that she nailed to the ceiling.

After a day working road construction for twelve hours, a guy didn't want to go to school. But a guy did want to see Ursel. And, on the nights she didn't go to class, there she was. Waiting at the Freedom Arches. With work sheets.

And, after the first week, with other stuff. On her lunch break, she had marched over to the police department, found Mel Richards, who had been her first teacher here in Grantville, and somehow got a whole set of lesson plans.

Then after the second week, she was waiting there with Mel. Mel was the child-protection officer now, but she still had that teacherly look in her eye. And a stack of stuff. "Look, Derek, I didn't get that degree in special education for nothing. It's just diagnostics. We're going to find out what's the problem. It's likely a learning disability, since Donnie has it, too, Ursel tells me. Bring him tomorrow, if he'll come."

Donnie came. Partly because he had this thing for Britney Yardley, and she had a high school diploma plus a vo-tech course. She was assistant to the lab technician at the methanol plant. He didn't think that a loser was in her plans. But mainly because they were meeting at the Freedom Arches. He had promised himself, the day he dropped out, that he was never going to go inside a school building again. He could handle talking to a teacher, but no way was he going back to school.

Mel Richards could live with that. There were a lot of people around who had had a bad experience with school. She had a little talk with Andy Yost and the Grantville Committee of Correspondence.

October 1634

It wasn't a school. No way. It was just an extra room, added onto the Freedom Arches. No school desks, no teacher's desk, no looming shelves full of threatening books. You could bring in your food; bring in your drinks.

No schedules. Just the regular tables and benches. Everybody did his own thing, when he had the time. Mel came in the evenings, after work, and wandered around, apparently sort of aimlessly. She'd sit down a few minutes, first at this table, then at that one.

Ursel practically lived at the Freedom Arches, now, except for the three afternoons and nights she went to school. From five in the morning till two in the afternoon, she dished up food. From three in the afternoon until the place closed at midnight, she dished up work sheets. And happiness. Since the day that Quittelsdorf died, her brothers Hans and Conrad along with it, she had never been so happy.

Until Walpurga Hercher reminded her sternly that she was supposed to be turning Derek Blount into a Lutheran, not teaching him to read his own language.

That night, she cried herself to sleep. When Derek came in for breakfast the next morning, her eyes were still bright red. She was so miserable. He could see it. "Hey, Ursel, what's wrong?" He'd never seen her like this.

Ursel looked at the morning manager, said, "Deal with it," came out into the restaurant part, threw herself into Derek's arms, and in the middle of many more tears, told him. Pastor Kastenmayer and *die Krausin*'s list and Teacher Muselius and catching husbands to make them Lutheran and all of it. It was a full confession. Ursel was spilling a really big bag of beans. Derek was glad that he had on his flannel shirt. It was a lot more absorbent than just a cotton tee would have been. A tee would have been drenched and once this was over he had to go back out into the chilly October wind and build a road.

Ursel cried herself out.

Derek said, "Aw, kid. Tell you what. Bring me this Shorter Catechism thingie. If I can read it now, I'll go talk to your teacher guy."

He could read it. Sort of. Not without Ursel's help, but he could read it.

The best thing, though, after he talked to the teacher guy, was that he found out that he wasn't really expected to read it. To memorize it, but not necessarily to read it. It would be fine if Ursel read it out loud to him and he memorized it that way.

Ursel reading out loud was almost as good as TV.

April 1635

So here he was, about to be confirmed and married. With all his family watching. Not just Mom and Dad, but Donnie and Britney, too. Britney wasn't a church member anywhere, either. Plus all the cousins. Pastor Kastenmayer and the teacher had been real interested in talking about cousins—that Cherilyn didn't go to church, and Bob had been brought up Catholic, but he had lapsed. Lapsed Catholics sort of appealed to Pastor Kastenmayer, it seemed. He thought that lapsing was a good thing for a Catholic to do. The pastor seemed willing to live with the fact that Mom's sisters were Presbyterian, and it was just Mom who had dropped out of the Presbyterian church because Dad wouldn't go with her.

Teacher Muselius was standing there, a little to the side,

watching the whole pew full of people. He looked more like a cat about to pounce than anything else Derek could think of.

Derek didn't think that reading was ever going to be his thing, but Mickey had promised him a promotion once he finished his GED. That meant that Ursel could go back to school full time after they were married.

Ursel would make a great teacher, some day.

They could have lots of picnics and family reunions, with all the cousins there. Their kids would have lots of cousins. On both sides of the family.

A Really Gloomy Tune:
Errol Mercer and Elisabetha Hercher

Late June 1634

Walpurga had an almost irresistible impulse to clean something. The several months of neglect that the poor house had suffered between the deaths of Mitch Hobbs's mother and father had not been helped by a couple more months with Ryan and Magdalena (how Walpurga hated that "Meg" nickname Ryan had given her) living there, and certainly not by the addition of two other young ex-soldiers.

She had heard that the army of the New United States required that soldiers keep their things very neat. Why did this custom not extend to soldiers who returned to civilian life? *Was it her problem to figure out the mystery? Probably not.* She sipped at her mug of beer.

In one corner, her sister Lisbet was demonstrating

something to the young man with the brass musical instrument.

"To dance to." Lisbet stamped her feet. "Dance like this. Can you play it?"

She grabbed three of the other girls and they linked arms. First to the right; stomp. Then to the left; stomp. Move in; stomp. Move out; stomp. Village dances had very little in common with the elaborate patterns of the court dances. The Hobbs house was far from new; the living room quivered under the impact of the girls' sturdy shoes. Walpurga winced. *The floor, the poor floor.*

Errol Mercer was grinning. "Yes, lady, I can play it. If you want me in your band, I'm in." He put the clarinet to his lips.

> *"Yes, sir, that's my baby;*
> *No sir, I don't mean maybe;*
> *Yes, sir, that's my baby now."*

Stomp, stomp, turn and stomp, stomp; stomp, stomp, turn and stomp, stomp; move in, turn and stomp, stomp, stomp. Ursel Krause grabbed Derek Blount and pulled him into the pattern. Lisbet clapped with utter glee.

Every Lutheran wedding in Grantville. She promised it to herself. Well, maybe not every one. Probably not if the pastor's other daughter got married, and maybe not the up-time Lutherans. But most of them, definitely most of them. This up-timer would be able to play every dance tune she knew, dragging the rest of her little band along with him.

★ ★ ★

Early August 1634

The dance band was getting bookings. Errol, on the theory that the lady was the boss, had firmly resisted all impulses to lay hand on Lisbet. Hitting on the boss would bring a guy nothing but trouble. His day jobs had never been anything to write home about—bagging groceries back home in Fairmont before he got caught up in the Ring of Fire; then two years as a soldier; now back in Grantville, basically as a stock clerk at Garrett's Supermarket. At least it worked with the band. Play in the evening; go to work after the dance; stay as long as it took to get the stuff out on the shelves for the next day; sleep, rehearse, or play in the evening; repeat. So he wasn't setting the world on fire—it beat blowing himself up with explosives, which had been his other post-army job offer.

Late August 1634

School was about to start. The group—it had become a regular *Stammtisch*—kept meeting at the Hobbs house; Lisbet's new band kept rehearsing there. The mothers and stepmothers who had survived the evacuation of Quittelsdorf didn't really like these gatherings, but then they wouldn't really have liked the barn dances and *Spinnstuben* the girls would have been attending with the Quittelsdorf boys back home, either. That's what mothers and stepmothers were for: to put on gloomy faces and look disapproving. Walpurga sighed. *How did they expect the girls to get these men as husbands for Pastor Kastenmayer's project if they didn't spend time with them?*

At Tuesday's rehearsal, Lisbet looked at Errol and announced, "I need a new tune. A really gloomy tune."

"Gloomy?"

"Yes. Like this one, but new." Lisbet launched into a series of musical notes that Errol, if he had happened to be Presbyterian, would have recognized as "Old 124th" from the 1551 Genevan Psalter. Since he was totally innocent of all connection with any established religious body, he just nodded his agreement that it was indeed a really gloomy tune. He picked up his clarinet and played along a bit.

"Mitch, this isn't a clarinet piece. Didn't I see a sax back there in the rec room one day?"

"Yeah, but I can't play it. That was my brother Arvie's. Ain't been played since he got out of band."

"*You* don't need to play it, man. I need to play something gloomy on it. I'm no sax player, but I can finger it."

Sax? Did that have anything to do with the Saxons? Meg Heunisch found that living with Ryan Baker perpetually confronted her with new and perplexing questions. The "sax" appeared in Walpurga's hands, bright and gleaming (she had polished it just the week before), and turned out to be another brass musical instrument.

Errol started fingering it, leaning against the right arm of the sofa and propping his boots up on the coffee table. Walpurga cleared her throat in a meaningful manner.

Errol didn't exactly ignore her—he didn't even notice her. He hitched the lanyard over his neck to help him hold the weight, placed the sax next to his knees (its bell extended to his right in front of the sofa, almost to the floor), put it to his lips, and started to produce a really gloomy tune.

He pulled it out of his mouth and started to make a rude comment about "how long has it been since anybody took care of this mouthpiece?" when he was severely jolted. The lanyard, thank heavens, kept him from dropping the sax. He found that he had a lap full of Lisbet, who was enthusiastically hugging and kissing him. It wasn't a particularly erotic hug and kiss, but provided him with full opportunity to determine that every one of her rounded curves was quite solid and not in the least flabby. She was deluging him with German, of which he got only "*wunderbar.*"

Then, without further verbal communication, he was being dragged by the hand out of the house and down the road toward St. Martin's in the Fields Lutheran Church. Which was okay, given how long it stayed light at night around here in summer, even without daylight savings time. They went around the church, up to one of the teacher's cottages, and Lisbet banged on the door.

Jonas Justinus Muselius could hardly believe it. The tune was perfect for the new hymn he had written, which the children of the school would perform. It was not too complex for them. It was not pitched too high, which had a tendency to cause untrained voices to squeak. It was ideal. Herr Mercer should play it with them, of course. But a musician was expected to be a member of the church. Perhaps Pastor Kastenmayer would make an exception in this case, however. A potential catechumen. A potential fiancé. A potential convert. He laid out his argumentation in the classic debate form as he hummed.

September 1634

The treble voices of the first- through fourth-graders lifted at the early morning service.

> *"We're sorry;*
> *Sorry for our sins;*
> *Sorry we have done so wrong."*

Errol Mercer on the saxophone carried them along, as the strains of "Moon River" rose to the bare rafters of St. Martin's in the Fields.

During the weeks after the children performed the hymn, Errol experienced a blinding revelation. Down-time Lutherans hired church musicians. They actually paid them.

He also discovered that singing a hymn to "Begin the Beguine" was no challenge at all to a congregation that could produce "A Mighty Fortress Is Our God" in its original irregular meter, a capella, if need be. St. Martin's didn't have an organ yet. It was delighted to have a clarinet and sax.

He stopped by the school every morning, after he got off at Garrett's. "Jesus *liebt mich, dass weiss ich.*" He was no church lady, but everybody knew how to play "Jesus Loves Me." It went over real good, too. *"Du bist mein Jesus, mein liebster* Jesus." Muselius wrote that one new for the kids, after Errol played "You Are My Sunshine" for him.

Lisbet said, though, that *full-time* church musicians must be qualified. First, that they must be Lutheran.

That, Errol figured, was doable. Muselius, the teacher,

said that it was very doable. He furnished Errol with a copy of the Shorter Catechism in English (he had forethoughtfully had a hundred of them printed in Jena, from a copy borrowed from Gary Lambert).

Church musicians must also, Lisbet said, be learned. He should return to school and get his GED. All boards of church elders were very impressed by pieces of paper showing academic qualifications.

He was less enthusiastic about that prospect.

But she kissed him.

Going back to school would be a lot more work than stocking shelves.

She kissed him again. "Going back to school will just be one year. Stocking shelves can go on forever. Do you want to do that?"

She kissed him a third time. "Or do you want to get paid for your music? More than our little band pays?"

By this time, Errol had a fiancée. He also had a sax, having traded his late grandmother's engagement ring with its tiny diamond to Mitch for it (at the time of the Ring of Fire, he had been wearing it in his left ear; the army made him take it out and the hole had closed up). Lisbet agreed fully that it was more important to have a sax than to have an engagement ring. Errol was therefore quite certain that Lisbet would be a perfect wife.

Lisbet would have been less sanguine about the trade if the result hadn't been that the ring went to Mitch. However, she assumed that if all went as one could reasonably expect, pretty soon Walpurga would get the ring, and Walpurga was, after all, her sister. But she didn't see any need to mention that.

March 1635

Errol set Jonas's new Good Friday hymn to "Mood Indigo." It caused a sensation. Well, at least it caused a sensation in the Lutheran churches of Grantville, Badenburg, Rudolstadt, and Saalfeld, plus assorted villages in between. It wasn't performed in Jena, Weimar, Stadtilm, Ilmenau, Arnstadt, Eisenach, Erfurt, and Suhl until the following penitential season. By 1636, it had reached Strassburg, Nürnberg, Leipzig, Koenigsberg, Copenhagen, and Stockholm. (See Muselius, Jonas Justinus, *New Directions in Lutheran Church Music, Jena: 1637.*)

April 1635

Errol obediently recited memorized passages from the Shorter Catechism in reply to Pastor Kastenmayer's questioning. In between, looking at the lineup while the other guys said their parts, he started to wish that he had never played in that "golden oldies" band in Fairmont before the Ring of Fire, because he was having trouble keeping his face straight. He just couldn't help suspecting that any minute now, Howard Keel's voice would start rolling in with the music from *Seven Brides for Seven Brothers.*

He wondered how a performance of that would go over with the down-timers. He thought he remembered all the tunes. And they had seven brides.

★ ★ ★

What Next?
Mitch Hobbs and Walpurga Hercher

June–October 1633

Walpurga Hercher worked at the MaidenFresh Laundries. That was her regular job and she liked it, even if the boss did yell at her for wanting to stop and remove every little spot and tiny stain. "Not commercially feasible," Frau Rawls said. "Look, girl. Get it in, get it washed, get it out. If they wanted that kind of finicky care, they would hire their personal laundress."

Walpurga found it distressing. She would like for every piece of clothing to come out of the tubs just the way it should be. But Frau Rawls was the boss. Some day, she would have her own house. With her own washing machine. And her laundry would be perfect.

Once upon a time, she had not been a "refugee." She had not been a plain village girl, either. When she was fourteen years old, she had gone into service in the town of Rudolstadt, as a maid in the household of the second *Buergermeister*, no less. She had learned about tile floors and chairs with legs that had been turned on lathes. She had stayed until just before Lent in 1631, when her father brought her home and betrothed her to Wilhelm Conrath. His father had died the year before the Ring of Fire; Wilhelm was the only child and needed a wife for the farm. It would have been a good match; they would have married in the summer. Now Wilhelm was dead and she was a "refugee" in Grantville, along with her sister, her aunt, and various cousins.

They always needed money, of course. There was rent. With so many of them, they needed a lot of food. Living in a city, if you needed more food, you could not go out to the garden and pull some more. You had to pay for it right away. Walpurga had decided that Garrett's Supermarket was best, so she shopped there.

She always took extra jobs, when she found them. The Hobbs job was on the "bulletin board." A woman was sick. Her husband wanted a cleaning lady, once a week. Walpurga gathered all of her recommendations and applied. They were all glowing. She had learned a lot during her years in Rudolstadt. When Walpurga Hercher set out to clean something, she *cleaned* it. Herr Hobbs, "Call me Joe," hired her.

Frau Hobbs, "Call me Gloria," looked really sick. But she was not too sick to stop worrying about a dirty house. Not in the summer.

It was an old house, the way the up-timers saw things. Not big, really. Not too big for a single servant to clean. Downstairs, a "living room," a "dining room," the kitchen, the bath, a funny room on the side, an "old porch," Frau Hobbs called it, that they had surrounded with walls and windows, that they called the "rec room." Two bedrooms. Upstairs, on a steep little staircase that started in the pantry, just two more rooms under the roof. But the carved woodwork. The hardwood parquet floors. The beautiful ceilings with designs on the squares.

Frau Hobbs just wanted her to run the vacuum over the surface and clean up the kitchen and bathroom. But the treasure trove in the kitchen cabinet and the pantry. The waxes, the polishes, the "spray bottles" with their magical contents. While Frau Hobbs was resting, Walpurga had managed to get some of the house really clean. The two rooms upstairs, the staircase, the extra bedroom downstairs. The ones that the gentleman and lady didn't look into anymore. They were almost perfect by the time she was done.

In September, Frau Hobbs was too sick to care. In October she died. Joe Hobbs didn't care about the house anymore. He thought that he was just letting the cleaning lady go.

He did not know that he was breaking a heart and ending a passionate affair. Walpurga mourned her lost love deeply.

April 1634

Pastor Kastenmayer was thinking about payback.

Walpurga was reading the obituaries in the *Grantville Times*. Herr Hobbs, "Call me Joe," was dead. The house? Walpurga's heart leaped. Would someone live in the house now who wanted a cleaner? "Survived by his parents, Ken and Ada Hobbs. Survived by one son, Mitch, serving in the army of the New United States, and two sons, Arvie and Burt, who were left up-time."

She read carefully. She compared it to other obituaries. She had Else and Ursel and Barbel, who read English much better than she did, compare it to other obituaries. There was no mention that this Mitch had a wife. There was no mention that Herr and Frau Hobbs had grandchildren.

If God were gracious, this Mitch would want his house cleaned.

However, it seemed that this Mitch was still somewhere else with the army. He had just told his grandparents to lock the place up until he got out in a couple of months. Walpurga found that out. She knew who Ada Hobbs was. She talked to Ada Hobbs sometimes when she bought food at Garrett's Supermarket. She mentioned to Ada Hobbs that she had cleaned the house, last summer, for "Call me Gloria."

Ada, who had not been looking forward to dealing with the mess that Joe had left behind during his last six morose months, hired her to clean it again.

It was a wonderful reunion. She had the house all to herself for three whole days. But the kitchen was a mess and the bathroom was worse. She had to scrape gooey stuff off the beautiful "linoleum" with a "putty knife," before she could even mop it. She hadn't had time to even start making the living room and dining room and the bedroom that Herr and Frau Hobbs had used perfect. She had hardly touched the "rec room."

May 1634.

The name was on *die Krausin's* list. Walpurga saw it. Neatly printed, right there on the Vandivers' kitchen table. Mitch Hobbs.

Walpurga promised herself that she would never be impatient during a church service again. She would never complain that Pastor Kastenmayer prayed too long, or preached too long, or reviewed the catechism too long. She would never complain that they sang too many verses of too many hymns. She would never try to skip church on Sunday. Maybe, she would even go on Wednesday. Perhaps, she would even attend Teacher Muselius's catechism review classes for adults on Saturdays.

Maybe all of them should go to church more diligently and take communion more frequently.

It was clear to Walpurga that Pastor Kastenmayer had, as the up-timers said, a "direct line" to God.

Walpurga was not at all sure that having Magdalena Heunisch live with this Ryan Baker in the upper two rooms of the Hobbs house counted as Divine Providence. After all, they were not married. And Magdalena was not a neat cook. Still, it ensured that she would meet this Mitch, even if he did not want a cleaning lady.

June 1634

Mitch thought it was really weird to be sleeping in his parents' bedroom. But that was how it had worked out. He had Ryan and his Meg upstairs, where he'd been living himself before the Ring of Fire. He was renting the other downstairs bedroom to Errol Mercer, right now. Once Derek Blount got out, he and Errol would go shares on that room. The bunk beds had been in there, and it didn't seem worthwhile to do all the heaving and hauling to switch the beds around. So here he was in a double bed in his folks' room. All by himself. Once he found a job, the money end ought to be okay. But he didn't know what he wanted to do. Not go back to hauling human manure for

O'Keefe's, that was sure. He hadn't been sorry to quit that job when the army had called for every able-bodied guy who could be spared three years ago. He hadn't wanted to re-up, either—couldn't figure out why Lew Jenkins and Jim Fritz did. It was the reserves for good old Mitch, from here on.

But he didn't know what he was going to do next. There weren't a lot of choices, even in a boomtown, when you were a dropout. But he was not going back to O'Keefe's. That much, he knew for sure.

Walpurga watched Lisbet and the Mercer man in the corner of the living room, fooling with the musical instruments. It was strange, being in the house with so many people. She felt like she ought to be cleaning something. Her fingers practically twitched.

Between the times when she watched them, she watched Mitch Hobbs.

Who said that he was looking for a job.

She had heard her boss say it so often, to people who came through the laundry. To people from whom she was trying to get "investment capital." Frau Rawls wanted to go away from Grantville, build more and more MaidenFresh Laundries in other cities. The boss wanted to move to Magdeburg. Her mouth opened. "MaidenFresh Laundries is a growth industry. Anyone who gets in on the ground floor will make his fortune."

The rest of them just stared at her. She ran through the rest of the spiel. She didn't even know that she knew it all. It even sounded like Frau Rawls, the way she said it. Then she blushed, and said in her normal tone of voice. "My boss wants to go to Magdeburg. She will need a manager for the laundry here in Grantville. Ask her. Frau Vesta Rawls."

What was that girl's name, anyway? Mitch asked himself. What he said was, "They don't hire dropouts to manage businesses."

"You have been in the army. Your grandmother works at a business, at the supermarket. I know her. Your grandfather is in the UMWA and that means that he knows the important people. You can go back to school. And clean laundry is important. Very important."

It turned out that Walpurga had memorized another spiel from listening to it so often. This was Frau Rawls's "sanitation prevents widespread epidemics and will save many lives" talk. She delivered the whole thing.

A sister less exuberantly extroverted than Lisbet would probably have been deeply humiliated. Even Lisbet was looking a little surprised. What would Walpurga say next?

Walpurga was saying, "Come tomorrow. I will introduce you."

Vesta Rawls was a little doubtful. But Mitch was a vet; they owed the vets. And Ken Hobbs's grandson. Not to mention that anybody vouched for by that spot and stain fanatic Walpurga was bound to be the right sort to take an interest in laundry, she guessed. Though he had never shown any sign of it before the Ring of Fire. Maybe the army had matured him.

"I'll try you as my assistant manager. Three-month probation. If you're catching on, then I'll try you as temporary manager when I go up to Arnstadt for a month. If that works, then for six months temporary while I go up to Magdeburg. But get yourself out to the Vo-Tech Center this afternoon. You're going to have to learn bookkeeping, at a minimum."

September 1634

The minimum of bookkeeping had turned into a whole GED. Mitch wasn't sure how, but first he had talked to the business teacher and the business teacher had talked to the adult-education coordinator and the adult-education coordinator had talked to someone in the superintendent's office. All the rest of them had all agreed that he could finish in a year, in his spare time. It was a done deal before he could even open his mouth. Listening to them, he had an awful feeling that the concept of "spare time" had just gone flying out the window. Where was the idea of spending his evenings nursing a beer in the Thuringen Gardens, eyeing the girls? He had dreamed of that, while he was still in the army.

Instead . . . He was increasingly aware that he was still sleeping single in that double bed. He also was developing this strange suspicion that Walpurga Hercher intended that he should keep right on sleeping single in that double bed. Meg lived in the house, of course, and her sister Lisbet spent a lot of a time there, rehearsing with her band. So Walpurga had plenty of excuses to be there. Talk about having your very own personal chaperone. Any other girl he brought in, somehow, only came once. And never got anywhere near the bedroom.

★ ★ ★

February 1635

It was ten o'clock at night. There was something wrong with the books, which Mitch discovered at six o'clock in the evening. He had stayed late at MaidenFresh and then later. He had pulled out his textbook from the Vo-Tech Center. Finally tracked it down. Then started to fix it. Finished fixing it. Management wasn't all it was cracked up to be.

The house was pretty near empty. Ryan and Meg were upstairs, he guessed—the lights were on. Derek was probably over at the Freedom Arches with Ursel. He'd passed Errol on his way in, walking Lisbet home. He'd just not bother to eat. Not bother with a shower. Just drop into bed. He walked into the bedroom and . . . Walpurga was what?

In his bed. Well, standing on it. Fully clothed.

"What on earth are you doing?"

She blushed. "Putting furniture polish on the headboard of your bed." She caressed the wooden curlicues. "It is so beautiful. I want it to be perfect."

He had never thought of Walpurga as sensuous before. All of a sudden, other things that people might want to have be perfect flashed through his mind. In connection with Walpurga.

Well, maybe it was not perfect. But it had been very, very nice.

During the months while Walpurga had been watching Mitch to make sure that he did not make an unfortunate choice of a wife ("unfortunate" being defined in her mind as "anybody else"), she had also been watching Mitch. She had concluded that marrying this man would be no hardship at all on his wife. Her reaction to his new initiative had been quite cooperative. Now she rolled over and started to play with the hair on his chest, twisting it around her finger into neat little ringlets. "On Sunday," she said, "I will tell Pastor Kastenmayer that we are betrothed and arrange for you to start confirmation class."

We are? Luckily, he hadn't said that out loud.

He thought a minute. He had a really strong feeling that if they weren't betrothed, this wasn't going to happen again. Not with Walpurga. His body was hinting that it really should happen again. Preferably fairly soon. Walpurga finished the first row of little ringlets and started on the second. He had a vague recollection that down-time girls were perfectly happy to sleep with their fiancés. His body filed a memo to the effect that whatever might be going on up at headquarters, at least one regional office voted in favor of getting betrothed to Walpurga Hercher.

"Where's your dad working?" he asked. Her mom had died three or four years before the Ring of Fire, but he knew that her father was around somewhere, one of the few men who had survived the massacre at Quittelsdorf. Because he'd gone to Rudolstadt, that day, to sell a donkey. Come back to find the bodies. Dug the mass grave by the burned-out church. Looked for the survivors for six weeks, before he found them.

But he hadn't stayed in Grantville, even though old Matthias Dornheimer had wanted him to. Walpurga's dad would never start over, not now. He had hired out as a hand on a farm, somewhere. Not too far away. "We probably ought to look him up and tell him, too."

"He is in Lichstedt. He is working for old Johann Pflaum. I will ask Arnold to tell him."

★ ★ ★

Pastor Kastenmayer didn't see how he could possibly get this young man ready for confirmation by April. He was starting much later than the rest of the class. They were many lessons ahead of him.

"His grandfather," Jonas Justinus Muselius said, fighting not to clench his teeth, "is in the UMWA. Trust me. I'll get him there."

April 1635

Mitch didn't have this stuff down anywhere near as pat as the rest of them. He was glad that they were reciting a bunch of it in unison. He mumbled. In a pinch, he looked at Walpurga, who was sitting in a pew angled sideways to most of the rest, mouthing the words.

"I believe that the Holy Spirit proceeds from the Father and the Son . . ."

I do? Do I believe that? Must have gone over it pretty fast in class. God of Walpurga, if you're out there somewhere, watching this, remind me again. What's the Holy Spirit and why do I care who he proceeds from? She? It? No offense meant.

Walpurga had assured him that it would be fine. Once he got the management of Grantville MaidenFresh Laundries down pat, they could go to Teacher Muselius's catechism review classes on Saturday afternoons and he could go through it all again, more slowly.

He could? Ye gods! What next?

★ ★ ★

And Some on Stony Ground:
Michael Lewis Jenkins and Sabina Ottmar

April 1632

Sabina Ottmar picked up the ten-gallon milk can easily,
swinging it onto the bed of the truck. And the next, and
the next. Her heavy skirts matched the rhythm of her
muscular arms. The last one in, she fastened the back of
the "pickup" in place with a stick rammed through the
broken latch and called "okay" to the driver. He took off
for town. She went into the milk shed to clean up. If she
worked fast, it would be done before lunch.

Sabina loved her new job at the dairy goat farm of Mr.
and Mrs. Manning Booth. She had to remember that.
Mrs. Booth. Up-time women had the name of their
husbands. There was so much to remember. She pulled
the kerchief off her hair, retied it, and started to wash and
sterilize the jugs that the truck had brought back from
town. The kettles of water boiling on the wood-burning
stove were heavy, but she could handle them. She knew
that many people laughed at her looks, but if you were
Sabina Ottmar, it was good to be tall and strong. You had
work to do and no one else would do it for you.

It was good that this work was so fine. The Booths
treated her as a fully qualified dairy maid, and paid her
accordingly. She had a room of her own. She ate at their
table. It was more than she had ever hoped for.

Sabina had never heard of a totem pole and probably
never would. But if there had been one in the village of

Keilhau, her family would have been at the bottom of it. By the time Sabina was old enough to remember, her father had been a landless day laborer. He had once had his share of the lease, true enough, but had lived as such a wastrel that he had been forced to sell it back to his brother. Then he had died, when she was only five. He had been drunk, of course. He choked on his food.

Her oldest brother, Heinrich, was twenty, then. He had been a hard enough worker—still was, for that matter. But he was in service to another farmer. He searcely earned his own keep. Not enough to support a mother, a quite young brother who was simple, and a sister much too small to be sent to work. Her second oldest brother—carefully, she walked to the outside of the milk shed and spat, where it would not mess the "sterilization" of the jugs.

Good riddance that he had gone for a soldier. Too bad that he had taken his miserable wife and children with him. Lucky he left before their mother remarried— otherwise he would have stayed, trying to get money from her.

They had eaten, after her father died, on the charity of others. When she was twelve, she had gone into service herself. For very little wages, so young, and the daughter of Martin Ottmar the drunkard. The worst of the work, the worst of the beds, the worst of the food.

The worst of the hired men.

God was merciful, however. He proved it. She was barren.

Seven years after that, her mother had made a very fortunate marriage into Quittelsdorf. Old Matthias Dornheimer, twice widowed already, just wanted a housekeeper. But he was a very respectable man who would have no breath of scandal. He picked a woman past childbearing and married her with all the banns called. He had taken in his simple stepson (who also was his godson, and to whom, thus, he owed a duty). But he had seen no reason to take in a stepdaughter who could work.

By then, though, Sabina had reached her full growth. Scarecrow thin, but tall. Arms and shoulders formed by the hardest of work in the barns and with the cattle.

Strong enough to take care of herself.

And treated kindly by her stepsister, the well-placed daughter of a prosperous farmer. Not loved, exactly, but not scorned. That had been, perhaps, God's kindest grace of all, that Rahel did not treat her as a slut. Though she must have known the things that had happened, at least by report. In a village, everybody did, of course. Keilhau was not far from Quittelsdorf.

Sabina's meditations continued. It was good to be working for the Booths. The cleaning crew in Grantville had not been bad, but she was very glad that the girl on the other farm, Staci Ann Beckworth, she was called, had told her about this job. She would be quite happy to remain in service on this farm for the rest of her life.

April 1634

Lew Jenkins had never been married; never wanted to be. He had been living with Staci Ann Beckworth, though, back when. Not that her parents were happy about it, but she'd been going through some kind of spasm about being adopted.

Then the Ring of Fire.

It seemed that people thought that he was just a perfect example of the kind of able-bodied man who could be spared to enlist in the army full-time. They broke up. Well, after he went into the army, she couldn't afford to keep up the rent on the trailer, not with what she was earning as a waitress at Cora's, and moved back in with her parents. Then she got notions, finished her GED, learned German, married a German farmer. Lew was pretty sure the guy had ambitions. Arnold Pflaum, his name was. Old Plummy. President of the Grange, he was now. Hadn't hurt him a bit to marry an up-time girl.

Of course, he was also wearing his feet off right up to the knees, running those farms. Farming sure wasn't a life that Lew had ever wanted. The army suited him fine.

Some of the guys in the army complained about latrine duty. Hell, before the Ring of Fire, Lew had worked for O'Keefe's. Every damn day was latrine duty when your job was pumping septic tanks and catchment basins. In the army, at least, you had some days that weren't.

Today, for example. He went back to work. Whole barrels of uniforms had arrived, with no sizes on them. And, once they had opened a few, no consistent sizing within each barrel. He was holding each piece up against cardboard cutouts of three different sizes of soldiers, then folding them into three different piles. He got to decide which of the three guys they would most likely fit best.

Responsibility Jenkins, that's me. He grinned. He even refrained from deliberately mixing up the piles with one another.

His sister, Bernita, would have been proud of him.

★ ★ ★

May 1634

Walpurga Hercher looked at the list of possible husbands that die Krausin had drawn up for the Quittelsdorf girls. She put her finger on Lew Jenkins's name and asked, quite simply, "Why?"

Margaretha Vandiver, once upon a time *die Krausin*, looked a little defensive and said, "His sister."

"His *sister*?"

"Yes." The older woman reached across the table and tapped the name on the slate. "Mrs. Walsh, the clerk at the post office, is his sister."

Walpurga reflected once more on the utter absurdity of this custom of a woman's giving up her own perfectly good name for that of her husband (and possibly, should she be widowed, for that of another husband, and yet another— how ridiculous). It made it practically impossible to tell how people were related. Had not God himself in the Bible said that Mary was the wife of Joseph? Not that she was Mrs. Joseph? Walpurga had no intention at all of changing her name when she married.

Margaretha was continuing. "They are good jobs, in the post office. Jobs that Germans can do. Just to read the addresses. It is easier for us to read the up-time handwriting than for the up-timers to read ours. To sort the mail, take the mail to where it goes. These can be done by people who do not have the strength for the mines or making the roads. We need to always know when there is a vacancy. Before they put up the hiring notice. To make sure that the best people are ready to apply. These are extremely fine jobs." She paused. "And he meets what Pastor Kastenmayer asked for. He is not a constant drunkard, not a brawler, not a lazy lout who will expect his wife to support him."

"He does not have a house. He does not even have a 'trailer.' He lives in the barracks for the army. He does not earn enough to support children." Walpurga wasn't even nearly finished with her litany of Lew Jenkins's defects as a potential husband.

Rahel Dornheimer looked up, motioned with her hand, and asked, "Is he handsome? Is he kind of man who attracts women? Who has seen him?"

"He is not handsome. Not hideous; not misshapen or a monster. But odd looking. His lower face is scarred—the skin." That was Maria Krause. The whole table chimed in.

"Is he young? How old?"

"Thirty years, maybe. It is hard to tell."

Rahel asked, "Would he be kind?"

"Who can tell, with a man?"

September 1634

"They want me to make this marriage." Sabina Ottmar looked at the other woman, who was nursing a baby daughter, "I don't want to make you unhappy, my lady. I don't want to make Herr Pflaum angry that I ask you. But I think that you, perhaps, would know."

Grantville was very like Keilhau in one way. People gossiped.

Staci Ann Beckworth, now very respectable and, by marriage, Lutheran, wife and mother, church member in good standing, looked down at her baby, then up.

"I was a fool when I was living with Lew, okay? I was wearing black leather miniskirts and spiking my purple-dyed hair with mousse."

Sabina looked bewildered. Staci Ann detached the baby—she was pretty well done anyway—and handed her over to the other woman with a burp rag. "Just a minute."

She went into the back of the house and returned with a little book. "It's my old album. I don't know why Mom kept this." She opened so Sabina could look. "Miniskirts; that's purple dye; that's flourescent green dye in this one. And overweight. Ye gods, I was at my low point. I'd mostly gotten rid of this by the first time I met you." She took the pictures and left the room again. To put it back, Sabina guessed.

"That was me, then." Staci Ann looked up. "I guess, to you, I looked like a little whore. But I wasn't. Lew was the only one, before Arnold." She chewed nervously on a finger-nail. "Lew had me at my worst, see. And, yeah, he was kind. Not just that he didn't hit me. He didn't even yell at me, no matter what stupid thing I tried. He'd make a joke of it. Or just go outdoors. There's no mean streak in him."

She sighed. "Don't get me wrong. Me being me, I'm better off with Arnold. For Mom and Dad and the farm and all that. Mom despised Lew. But if it hadn't been for the Ring of Fire—for the kind of kid I was then, I could have done a lot worse, and that's the truth."

"I am barren," Sabina said nervously. "I can't have children."

"Well," Staci Ann answered, "neither can Lew. His mom didn't believe in vaccinations, the stupid cow. Mumps. Junior year of high school. And a gossip in the doctor's office told someone, so it got out. She got fired, but it didn't do

Lew any good, by then. Not the way guys that age are. 'Little Lewie lost his balls.' That's why he dropped out, I think, the things they said to him. He's smart enough that he could have finished, God knows."

April 1635

Sabina looked at the line of confirmands. In an hour, she would be a married woman. With a cottage on the Booths' farm, newly built, where she would live. Where they would live when he was on leave. She had no dreams. She was marrying this man because it had been arranged for her. He was not being confirmed because she had charmed him into it. He was being confirmed because Staci Ann Beckworth had asked Arnold Pflaum to talk to him, and his sister, about being Lutheran.

Herr Pflaum had also acted as the broker for her, in making a marriage contract, along with the Booths. It was kind of them. Of course, that was the sort of thing that a village's mayor did. Herr Pflaum had never been to Keilhau, of course; he was from Lichstedt. President of the Grange in Grantville was not *quite* the same, but Herr Pflaum was also a church elder at St. Martin's. Herr Pflaum was very young for such responsibility. But he did it well. For many more than just the people from his own village, just outside the Ring of Fire.

Sabina was not fully happy about being married to a soldier. She was aware as anyone that soldiers run the risk of being killed. Now that she finally would have a husband, which she never expected, she would rather keep him alive. But Lew had gotten used to the army during the last three years. He didn't want to change.

So be it. She would live in the much-too-big cottage by herself.

Lew's sister, Bernita Walsh, watched from the unfamiliar pew. She was so glad that Lew was getting married now—that he'd have someone. She knew that she had sort of pushed him into it, after the idea came up. And after she had met Sabina. She'd been worried sick about what would become of him, ever since Doc Adams had told her about the cancer. She only had a few more months, maybe a year at most, maybe a lot less. Sabina would take care of him, now. And David and Ashley. She wouldn't mind going so much, with Sheldon already gone for nearly two years, if it weren't for the kids.

Staci Ann knew. And Arnold Pflaum. And Manning and Myrna Booth. Those were the only ones she had told. But the new cottage that the Booths had built for Sabina and Lew had two extra rooms.

Sabina would make a place for the kids.

Briar Rose:
Roland Worley and Rahel Rosina Dornheimer

October 1634

"Prickly pear," Roland Worley said.

"That is?" Jonas Justinus Muselius asked.

"It's a, umm, a cactus."

"And a cactus is?" Jonas's English was probably better than that of any other down-timer in Grantville, but this topic had never come up in his many conversations with Gary Lambert.

The conversation at St. Martin's rectory was interrupted by a hike to the high school, which had the nearest library, a visit to the *World Book* under the topic of "cactus," and a picture of a prickly pear.

Muselius grinned. "Oh, yes. We would agree. Her name is not just Dornheimer, you know. She is our own little *Dornroeschen*."

"*Dornroeschen*?" Roland asked.

"Thorny little rose." He started to tell a story.

Roland picked his teeth. He thought, he said, that he had heard this one somewhere.

They headed for the librarian's desk. Between Colleen Carson and Elias Kurtz, the answer was finally, "I don't think we have a copy, here in the high school library. You ought to be able to find one at the public library. Or at the grade school. It's a fairy tale. The English title is 'Briar Rose'— that's also called a wild rose, or sometimes a bramble. They're very thorny."

Roland obediently remodeled his perception. Rahel Rosina Dornheimer was a briar rose, not a prickly pear. Which didn't mean that any guy who tried to get close to her wasn't likely to get poked with something sharp.

July 1631–September 1632

At the time of the Ring of Fire, Roland was divorced. His

ex-wife had taken the kids and moved to Beckley in 1996. Leaving him, a guy from Denver, Colorado, in Grantville. With a job, true enough—he was a machinist, and a good one if he did say so himself. Nat Davis paid him pretty well. And a house that he could afford the payments on, given that Nat Davis paid him pretty well. And, since he'd been in, between '83 and '85, a pretty decent slot in the West Virginia USAR. All of which meant that moving would have been a real hassle, so he stayed. A perfectly healthy guy with a bank account in a town where not one of the available females really appealed to him.

Then the Ring of Fire.

Jackson hadn't activated him. He was more valuable where he was, in the machine shop. He stayed in the reserves. In a couple of months, Nat hired a regular cleanup crew. What with the apprentices to train and all the new orders coming in, it was a plain waste of his men's time to do that.

That was where Rahel had appeared, sweeping around his machine. Prickly little thing. Pointy nose like a cute Halloween witch—not the big hooked kind, but the little one like his kids had drawn, two sides of a triangle. Hostile. Not picking-a-fight hostile, but just keeping to herself. The only person she ever seemed to talk to was one of the other cleaning women, older than she was, and not much friendlier. Sabina, that one was called. Sabina the Scarecrow, one of the men called her; she was all gangly and awkward.

Then Sabina disappeared. That was the first time he'd actually talked to Rahel—he asked her where Sabina was.

"She got another job. Goat dairy. She is good dairy maid.

Better job than this." Rahel returned to her sweeping.
Rahel was protective of Sabina. When her father married
Sabina's mother, any number of people had taken it upon
themselves to tell the sixteen-year-old Rahel just what had
happened to her new stepsister after she was first placed
into service at age twelve. Some plain; some with embroidery. From that day onward, Rahel had never let a man
touch her.

A month or two later, Rahel disappeared off the cleaning crew. By that time, Roland realized that he wanted
her. The only thing that he couldn't figure out was why.
He wasn't given to introspection. It never occurred to him
that the fact that his ex-wife had been sugar-sweet the
whole time they were dating and turned indifferent the
day after she had the wedding ring on her finger had anything to do with it.

But he went looking. The new job Rahel had found was
working for Irma Lawler and Edna Berry, the two elderly
"plant ladies" who were no longer up to long, uninterrupted
days of labor on bedding plants and seed gathering. He'd
leaned on the fence. He knew better than to trespass on
her turf in that garden.

It took several months of fence-leaning on his day off
before he learned much about her. Her two brothers had
been killed protecting the villagers fleeing from
Quittelsdorf, so now she had her father, who was seventy-
five, and her stepmother, who was seventy-two, to take
care of. It turned out that Sabina was her stepsister. She
also worried about her widowed sister-in-law, who originally
came from a different village and was in Grantville with
three sons to bring up and no marriage prospects.

Roland asked her out. Rahel told him plainly that if he wanted a wife who would keep house for him, he would be doing a charitable act if he married her sister-in-law, Dorothea, instead. She introduced him to Dorothea and encouraged them to go out. After three tries, Roland concluded that Dorothea was a weeping drip, and not someone it would be any fun at all to have for a wife. But he did find her a job as a live-in housekeeper to old Edgar McAndrew and his sick wife, which gained him a few points with Rahel.

He thought. It would take the most finely calibrated device in the shop to measure progress with Rahel.

May 1634

Rahel didn't like the whole idea of having the Quittelsdorf girls go out and marry up-timers as a project. She also didn't like living in a big town, any more than Sabina had. But she needed the better money that she could earn in the city.

And if—*if*, mind you—she did agree to do this, she could ignore *die Krausin's* list. There was an up-timer she could marry. A much better-off one than any of those. She'd gotten to know Roland Worley pretty well. But—as she had repeated to him many times, "I'm a farm girl. I want to marry a farmer." She even said once, as she extracted herself from a more compromising position than was customary before committing herself to something irrevocable, "This is silly. It would make much more sense for me to marry Guenther Conrath, if we had the capital to buy a lease. Or Hans Guenther Hercher." Well, maybe Hans Guenther Hercher, if anybody knew where

Walpurga and Lisbet's brother was, considering that he quarreled with his father when he was almost twenty and left home in a temper. He hadn't been seen by anyone in Quittelsdorf for the last fifteen years. But, surely, Roland would not be interested in such petty details as the shortage of suitable and available grooms.

By that time, he had pretty well figured out what portions of her anatomy he could approach without getting pricked too hard. Advancing upon an ear, he asked, "Would they do this?"

Rahel was increasingly furious with herself. She suspected that it was very unlikely that either Guenther or Hans Guenther would ever do that. Lease or no lease. Present or absent. *She was beginning to enjoy this.*

July 1634

Rahel started piling on the objections. "You would not want to be a Lutheran." She stated it as a foregone conclusion.

"I might be willing to consider it. Depending on what it involves." Roland thought that he was seeing signs of a snowmelt, but he didn't want to ruin everything by moving too fast. Not even though, the way he was feeling at the moment, he was inclined to say, "Lady, if you would just go to bed with me, I would be happy to put on a clown suit and do somersaults in front of city hall if that's what it takes."

"Maybe Pastor Kastenmayer won't think your wife is dead."

Roland had made up his mind to marry his prickly pear Rahel even if this might involve a future as a Lutheran married to a female farmer, so he went over on his next day off and did an end run by talking to the minister out at her church and the teacher who did the translations. They both agreed that it didn't matter whether his up-time wife was dead or not, since they happily ascertained that he had been legally divorced from her before the Ring of Fire—and for a reason that down-time Lutherans thought was okay. It appeared that taking the kids and moving to Beckley was "desertion" and someone named Saint Paul had said it was a good reason for divorce. They seemed to put a lot of stock in Saint Paul.

Pastor Kastenmayer was very surprised to learn that Roland had never heard of Saint Paul, except for the city in Minnesota. The discussion had required a visit to the library in the high school. Pastor Kastenmayer hadn't truly taken to heart Jonas's discovery that many of the up-timers in Grantville were heathen.

Muselius borrowed a book of children's Bible stories from Gary Lambert and gave it to Roland to read. He figured that instruction had to start someplace. That seemed as good as any other.

Roland had heard of Adam and Abraham, though not in any detail. And Jesus in the manger. The rest of the stories were news to him.

October 1634–March 1635

"Of course you must learn it all if you are going to be a Lutheran." That was Rahel's reaction to his protest that the Shorter Catechism was really a bit much to expect a guy to memorize.

"Why?"

"Because when you are a *Hausvater*, you will need to teach it to the children."

If Rahel had children on her mind, that had to be a good thing. After all, there were certain prerequisites for producing children. Roland snaked his arm around her waist. His hand angled somewhat upward and to the left. She didn't move away. He kissed the pointy nose. She moved a little closer, which meant that the hand could start to investigate the region where her bodice met her shift.

Roland got to spend a lot of time discussing the Lutheran canon law of both divorce (established) and time displacement (unprecedented) with Pastor Kastenmayer and Jonas Justinus Muselius, whereas the other guys in the confirmation class just had to make the run through the Shorter Catechism. He wasn't sure entirely why. The question of time displacement and whether his wife would be considered dead if they hadn't been divorced seemed to fascinate Jonas and the minister. Pastor. He had to remember to call him a pastor. Lutherans didn't call them ministers or reverends or any other word he'd ever heard for it.

They even took him to Jena to meet some really big guns in the church. He didn't see quite why, since they'd already agreed that he was properly divorced. But they kept talking about Gary Lambert. And that it would be much better to get the principle established in a case that didn't involve Lambert.

Finally he figured out that Lambert's wife had been left up-time. No divorce. And that the daughter of one of the big guns wanted to marry the guy. Which the big gun thought was a great idea, if it was legal.

What the hell? If he could be useful to them, it was no skin off his nose.

April 1635

Pastor Kastenmayer was taking his confirmands through the Christian virtues of faith, hope, and love.

Roland shifted from one foot to the other and wondered where patience fit into it all.

Promises to Keep:
James Anthony Fritz and Maria Krause

April 1634

Anna Krause leaped off the school bus and dashed into the refugee housing complex. "Maria, Maria. Maria, is Magdalena home? Tante Elisabetha? Is anybody here?"

"I'm here, Anna." Her half sister, Maria, who worked the night crew at the bakery for the Leahy Medical Center, dragged herself up out of sleep.

Anna at fifteen. All legs and arms. Only starting to fill out in between them. Dressed in up-time clothing. Maria couldn't remember if she had ever been so young. Or what she had been like, if she was. How could seven years make so much difference?

"I don't know where Magdalena is, *Schatz*." Maria

shook out her shift. "At work, I guess. If Cora's is busy, she'll stay as long as she can get overtime."

"Franz says it would be cheaper for Cora just to hire another girl. Two at regular rates equals the cost of Magdalena, and she's only working one and one half times the regular hours." Anna plopped herself down on a hassock.

"*We* are getting the money for one and one half times the regular hours. *We* need every penny we can earn. Don't let Franz give Frau Ennis any ideas." Maria yawned. "Tante Elisabetha went to supervise the cleaning crew. *Die alte Heiderin* is sick. They took her to the doctor's office this morning."

"Godmother is sick?" Anna's face clouded up.

Maria cursed herself. She should have been gentler. Anna had lost all the bounciness that had propelled her into the apartment. "She'll be all right, *Pueppchen*. I'm sure of it." *No. I hope it,* she added to herself. Maybe she could bring the bounce back. "What were you so excited about when you ran in?"

Anna's face suddenly glowed. She pulled out a piece of paper. "Look, Maria, I won. From all the sophomores in the school, my science project was the best. They will show it in the lobby at the hospital. With my name on it. For two weeks. Will you come see? I know that Tante Elisabetha and Magdalena won't have time. But it's not far from the bakery and the lobby is open all day and all night. Please, Maria. Please come see it. Just for a few minutes."

Six o'clock in the morning. Time to get off work. Maria was so tired that she thought she might die, but she forced herself to make the walk to the lobby. Anna's project was there, just as she had said. With her name on it. She stood, looking.

Softly, behind her, a voice asked, "Do you understand what she did, Maria?"

She looked back. It was the nurse from the Low Countries, coming up on those silent white rubber sneakers they still wore inside the hospital, when they had them. She shook her head. "No, Nurse DeVries. I can read the words and sound them out. But I do not know what they mean. The other marks, the bars lined up, the circles divided in pieces. Those I do not understand at all."

"It's a study about children's diseases in the villages around Grantville. Which diseases come most often to which village. With this, with what she has done, walking from one village to another, taking records, using her knowledge of the local dialects to ask questions and gather information that up-timers cannot, our public health nurses can try to find out why. Why does a disease spare one village, but regularly return to another that isn't more than ten miles away? Franz helped her, but she did almost all of it herself. The study design, the information gathering, the analysis. She's done a wonderful job. A lot of students five or six years older couldn't equal it."

Maria turned back to the display case. She stood a few minutes more. "I can read the blue ribbon, Nurse DeVries. It says my little sister Anna is the best of all the students. Not just the best of the down-time students. Not just the best in the special program. The best student of all, in her class, for doing this. So she will not work in a bakery. She will not be on the cleaning crew. Not in the kitchen at Cora's. I will do whatever I need. So she can be a nurse like you or Frau McDonald. Whatever I need to do. I keep my promises."

May 1634

In the Vandivers' kitchen, Walpurga Hercher put her finger down on the next name on the list. "Take him off."

Margaretha Vandiver shook her head.

"He is a soldier. He has no house. He has a bastard child. No way is he fit to be a husband."

"The child, yes. That would be a problem. A big cost to him, on a soldier's pay. But the mother has married, now. To Friedrich Pflaum, Arnold's brother, that is. You know him. And Friedrich has adopted the child. A small price to pay, old Johann Pflaum figured, for the farm that Owenna Lamb will inherit. Especially since it is a girl."

They all just stood there a moment, thinking about the Pflaums. More than half of the arable land of the Lichstedt, the village where they lived, had gone to wherever Grantville came from, they supposed. The Ring of Fire had done that. But an up-time farm had landed where those fields had been. Owned as an *allod* by a man with only two children. So Friedrich Pflaum had married well. Old Johann, truth be told, had too much of a good thing, even before the Ring of Fire. Mayor of Lichstedt. Five sons, every one of them as healthy as a horse and ambitious. The other four not quite as ambitious as Arnold, granted, but still ambitious. True, he had held two leases, his own and his wife's half share. But it would have been hard for him to place all five boys as full farmers somewhere. Now . . . First

Arnold married an up-time heiress, then Friedrich. Heinrich was soon to be betrothed to Deann Whitney. It was very strange that most of the up-time men had no wish to be farmers. But lucky for Johann Pflaum. With the three oldest sons farming up-time allodial land, he would have a few years before he had to think about placing Lorenz and Georg. Time, the way things were going, for him to buy up the rest of the leases for what was left of the fields of Lichstedt. There wasn't enough land to support a whole village, now. The other families were drifting off, looking for work in the new industries. Some of the Lichstedter were here in Grantville. It looked like only the Schellenbargers, Johann's in-laws and nephew, would also stay there and farm. There was enough of Lichstedt left for two, or maybe three, full leases. With access to up-time equipment through Friedrich, Arnold, and Heinrich, three men would be able to do the work. It wouldn't take a whole village.

"All right," Walpurga said at last. "Forget the bastard child. Keep, 'he's a soldier' and 'he has no house.' How can a man with no house head a household?"

"Who are we talking about?" Else Krause tried to crane her neck around Walpurga's shoulder.

"What are you still doing in here, Else? You've already said you won't be part of it. Go away and play. Take Barbel with you." Margaretha was annoyed.

Instead of going, Barbara Conrath poked her head over Walpurga's shoulder from the other side.

"*Ach*, we can kibbitz. James Anthony Fritz. Never heard of him."

"What does 'seasonal employment' mean?"

"Just part of the year, I think."

"'Unemployed' is pretty plain." Walpurga was not about to let go of her view that this man was an unsuitable husband, even for a dowryless farm girl.

"Where did you *get* this stuff?"

Margaretha looked very prim. "I gossip."

"How old?"

"Thirty-two. Maybe thirty-three. I don't have a baptismal record."

"Who are his family?"

"He's an only child."

"Still, he has to have parents. Are they inside the Ring of Fire?"

"Yes, here." Margaretha picked up another slate. "Mother and father divorced."

"For how long?"

"Nearly thirty years. Neither one remarried. Father, Duane Fritz. Presbyterian. He is a certified nursing assistant at the 'assisted living' home. Mother, Garnet Szymanski. Catholic."

Maria Krause said, "Stop."

Jim Fritz had not written home, the whole time he had been in the army. His mother was not surprised.

Garnet had faced it a long time ago. There was something odd about Jim. Like Duane.

She shouldn't have married Duane. But she had never been a pretty girl. Thirty or forty years ago, she had, aside from the gray in her hair, looked pretty much like she did now. Which wasn't bad, for a woman in her fifties. It was sort of—expectable. The thick waist and sturdy legs hadn't been attractive on a girl in her teens or a woman in her twenties.

Admit it, Garnet. You panicked. Twenty-five years old. No husband, no children. Certainly no religious vocation.

Duane hadn't been a passionate suitor, but he had been there. Two years younger than she was. Not—objecting, really. She had done all the things right, for marrying a Protestant. Gotten him to sign the promises, been married in the rectory by the priest. Jim had been born sixteen months later. By then, she knew it was a mistake. When they went to things at her own family's, she had tried to tell herself at first, Duane was just intimidated a little by all the noisy Szymanskis and O'Malleys. That was why he went off into a corner and watched TV the whole time. But then they went to the Fritz picnic, up at the fairgrounds. His own people. He took a folding lawn chair and sat at the very edge the whole time. Drumming his fingers on the aluminum tubing until they could leave.

Duane wasn't crazy. Not the way most people around Grantville meant it. He did a good job working at the assisted-living center. He followed orders and memorized routines. He had an apartment. No one had ever called the police to complain about either noise or trash. He didn't wander around shouting in the streets. He didn't see visions or go through emotional cycles from high to low. He wasn't even depressed, in any clinical sense. But he wasn't normal. Not interacting-with-other-people normal.

Neither was Jim.

If she hadn't faced up to the truth and divorced Duane before there were any more children, she would have condemned herself as the world's worst mother when Jim grew up to be the way he was. Standoffish. Touch-me-not.

The older he got, the worse it got—he dropped out of school because having so many people, loud and rambunctious, in halls and classrooms, abraded him more than he could stand. He had gone to first communion. He hadn't been confirmed. Maybe she should have tried harder, but right then, working full time and everything, just getting him through school had been all that she could deal with. Not CCD on top of it. He hadn't been to mass in, well, years. More years than she wanted to think about. Fifteen, at least.

She had sort of wondered how he ever got close enough to Owenna Lamb to get her pregnant. At least, little Andie seemed to have been spared it. She was a cute kid. The down-timers seemed to be realistic about these things. Friedrich Pflaum had invited her to the adoption ceremony at City Hall. And to dinner afterward. She hadn't been forced to give up Andie altogether. Probably the only grandchild she would ever have.

Pflaum had invited Duane, too, but he didn't come. Jim just sent back the consent form, signed, witnessed, and notarized. No letter wishing them well. That wouldn't have been Jim, to send a letter or a note. Or even a card. It wasn't the sort of thing that occurred to him. He did what needed to be done. The little flourishes and trimmings that put the grease in the works of human relations were completely beyond him.

Thirty-one years now, as a divorced Catholic, toeing the line. With no letters from your son. It gave you a lot of time to concentrate on your career.

Garnet picked up another pile of papers to grade. Classes in health care at the Vo-Tech Center were crammed to capacity. Life went on. She really wondered how Jim managed to endure army life.

Jim Fritz liked the army. Things were reliable. You knew from one day to the next what would be going on. Basic training had been unpleasant, a hassle—too many people around, almost like school. But the sergeants told you exactly what to do and if you did it, you were okay.

Then, after basic, they put him here, at the supply base in Erfurt. It was a really good job. If it hadn't been for the PT part of it, it would have been great. For that, and for shooting, he had to get out with the other guys. Mostly, though, he spent almost every day in this little side room off the main warehouse by himself, putting things on shelves, taking things off shelves, sorting things into bins, and making lists of how many of them there were. They all had numbers, so he didn't have to worry about what they were, just as long as they were alike. Then he packed them up to send out. He had lists of how many to put in each keg or crate. Old Man Stull told him where to send them.

Dennis Stull, the civilian procurement head in Erfurt for the army of what had been the New United States, considered Jim Fritz one of the best finds of his life. The man had absolutely no curiosity. He didn't care what he sorted or what the parts might be for, where they came from, or where they went. Plus, he never went out with the guys and got drunk, or consorted with prostitutes who might pump him. Or, if he did consort with them, he wasn't likely to be chatty about it.

For R&D projects, Jim Fritz was the fulfillment of a

security officer's dreams. Jim Fritz had a lifetime career in this man's army, if he wanted it, as far as Dennis Stull was concerned.

July 1634

First, she had to find him. Finally, Maria went to the army headquarters and asked. The young man, boy, really, at the desk gave her the address. He smirked. She guessed what he was thinking—the man already had one bastard and was about to have another.

Let him think.

She asked for two days off from the Leahy Medical Center bakery. She was surprised to discover that she had been accumulating something called "leave time" for three years. Her English hadn't been very good, back when she was hired. Since then, she had never had reason to ask for more than her Sundays, so she never had.

She walked to the base where he was, all the way to Erfurt. She had gotten Ursel to use the telegraph ahead of time. He knew she was coming.

He didn't know why. Some things, she thought, were better explained face to face.

At least, she thought so until she was speaking with him.

He sat there. Perhaps he listened to her. But there was no face to face.

Until she said, "Look at me."

After that, he looked at her.

★ ★ ★

Garnet was surprised to hear that Jim would be marrying a German girl. Well, perhaps not all that surprised. A marriage without a lot of verbal communication required might suit him.

April 1635

Jonas Justinus Muselius had found an English-speaking chaplain at one of the many Lutheran churches in Erfurt who was willing to undertake the man's instruction.

Jim had seen no reason to come to Grantville for the confirmation and wedding. Maria had spoken to Herr Stull, who ordered him to. Orders were orders.

Garnet had been surprised to receive the nicely written invitation (Margaretha had finally found a use for Else and Barbel in this project). She had been even more surprised to discover that Jim was joining a church. Any church. Jim was not a joiner.

She came by herself. She was the only one of Jim's relatives who did. She was a bit uneasy about it—the rules for Catholics taking part in the services of Protestant churches had eased a lot since she was a girl, but she still had a nervous feeling that watching your son join one was stretching the limits. She got there early, in spite of being nervous. Or, perhaps, because of it.

The teacher introduced her to her future daughter-in-law, Maria Krause. Who had a teenaged girl firmly by the arm. And spoke English—fairly good, actually. "Frau Szymanski. This is my half sister Anna. She won the prize for the best science project last year. Maybe you saw it. It was at the hospital lobby then. She has won the prize again this year. It is in the lobby now. You can go see it."

From Grantville, then—not some girl Jim had picked up at the base.

"She is to be a nurse. I need for her to live in your house, not in the refugee housing. In refugee housing, there are too many chances for Anna to do what she should not." Maria turned and pointed. "Her other half sister. Other side of the family."

The girl appeared to be nine months and two days pregnant. She was sitting with Perry and Dayna Baker.

Maria said firmly, "I marry your son. You are our family now. Anna can live with you. It will be much better. Don't worry, I earn the money. Pay you. Rent, food, all. I work hard."

"Ah." It was clear that Maria had no doubts. Did Garnet want a teenaged housemate? Even one who won two science fair prizes? It appeared that she had been relieved of the decision. "We can talk about it. When? Next week?"

"Tomorrow." Maria was firm. "He goes back to Erfurt. In the morning. I go back to work at the bakery. In the evening. In between, I bring Anna to you. Not waste time."

Garnet had a relieved feeling. This, she thought, was a girl who could cope with being married to Jim. Having a Lutheran son was a small price to pay for that.

Maria watched, as the confirmation liturgy ran its course. Somewhere in her mind, carefully covered over so that she didn't have to look at it directly, was the thought

that in wars, soldiers on active duty get shot at and sometimes they get killed. Then their wives are widows.

But as long as he was alive, she fully intended to do her
marital duty honestly. Each month, she would take her
"leave time" and visit him in Erfurt.

Maria kept her promises. The rest was in God's hands.

April 1635

Confirmations completed, the congregation adjourned to
the porch for the weddings. And to the school courtyard
for an event that would probably rank as the party of the
year in Grantville.

But, as Pastor Kastenmayer watched the beer flow, it
wasn't enough. *I want*, he thought, *my daughter Andrea's
husband.*

The Sound of Music
❦★❦
David Carrico

*Franz Sylwester, one-time violinist in the chapel of
    the archbishop of Mainz
To Friedrich Braun, journeyman instrument
crafter
    for Master Hans Riebeck, in Mainz
On the nineteenth day of January in the
    year of our Lord 1633*

Greetings, my friend,

I am sure by now that you have despaired of hearing from your prodigal, but I promised you that when I found a place I would write to you. By the grace of God I now have that place, and so I keep my word.

Before I proceed further, I must confess to you. I am well aware that I was somewhat less than

*gracious to you and Anna in those dark days after
that snake Heydrich smashed my hand. Please mark
down the things that I said then to the physical pain
of my wound and to the spiritual pain of knowing
that I could never play again.*

The pen paused as images flashed through his mind:
sitting in the tavern that night, arguing with Rupert
Heydrich as to who was the better player, goading Rupert
and smiling as the rising choleric tide stained the other
man's face—the sudden eruption of the fight behind him,
being caught in the brawl and knocked to the floor—
scrambling to escape the flow of the struggle—the sudden
panic as someone stepped on his arm and pinned it to the
floor—the explosion of agony as the boot heel smashed
into his left hand, and again, and again, and again—the
serpent's voice hissing in his ear, taunting him as he curled
sobbing around his wounded hand.

"Was there no investigation, no judgment made?" she
murmured in his ear.

"No," he said, "it happened in the middle of the brawl,
and no one would come forward to support my story."

There was a pause, then came, "Do you miss it?"

"I will always miss it," he said quietly, "but as my friend
Isaac says, 'The Lord giveth and the Lord taketh away.
Blessed be the Name of the Lord.' Where God has taken
one gift away, he has given several in return."

*I am well aware that I am alive solely because of
Anna's tending me during the fever, keeping the
wound rot from claiming me. I am also well aware*

that I am alive twice over because of the gift of silver
that you and Master Hans added to the pittance the
Kappelmeister gave me when he turned me out.
That gift kept body and soul together until I
arrived at my current place.

I am also very ashamed of my churlish words to
you when I shook the dust of Mainz from my feet
as I set out on my wanderjahr.

Another pause, another flood of memories: burning
with fever and biting his lip bloody to keep from crying
out as Anna tended his broken hand; the weak-chinned,
slovenly Kappelmeister confronting him in his room—"I
have no room for a one-handed violinist. You must leave
these quarters by the end of the week. Here are your final
wages."—the hand slamming down on the table, and lifting to reveal two silver pieces and eight coppers—
Heydrich smirking in the background; bickering with his
friends as they tried to restrain him from leaving, finally
shaking their hands off his arms and snarling, "I will not
stay in the same place as Heydrich, and if you loved me,
you would not either! If you will stay, then stay, but leave
me go!"

"A little rude, were you?" brought him back to the
present.

"Aye . . . and with no cause, for they loved me well. I
only hope they still do."

I had not traveled many days until I had repented
of them, and I am heartily glad to now apologize and
ask your forgiveness.

I had no destination in mind when I left you, and so I drifted aimlessly from place to place. I quickly learned that just as there is no future for a one-handed violinist, there is actually little that a one-handed man can do to earn his bread. No Adel or wealthy burgher will hire a man to tutor his children who was crippled in a tavern brawl. The clerks we used to patronize need two working hands. The mercenary companies will not take a one-handed man. Even the common laborers we used to sneer at require two strong hands to wield mattock and spade.

I took up with a couple of traveling players for a few days, who advised me strongly not to sing, as my voice would make even a crow sound melodious! I seem to remember Anna uttering a similar sentiment once, although she was smiling when she said it. They were not.

They also lifted my ignorance and lowered my arrogance when I attempted to become a drummer by showing me that that art is more complex than it looks—and that even a novice drummer requires two good hands to learn his skills.

As each day passed in succession, the Lord taught me humility, until finally, after weeks of such tutoring I left my pride, my arrogance, lying in the dust of the road. Then it was that the Lord opened a door for me. I was sitting in a low tavern near a crossroads, not even in a town or village, nursing the only beer I could afford to buy. I was trying to stave off the moment when I would go out into the night to find a haystack or barn to sleep in, when I heard a peddler wishing that he could tell his sister in Hamburg that he was well, so she would not worry so. A conversation ensued, with the result that I wrote a letter for him and he bought me another flagon of beer and gave me a copper besides. As days passed, I served as scribe to more people who were unable to write—soldiers, peddlers, laborers—anyone who could buy the paper and ink and would give me a copper or two to put their words into a form that could cross the miles. And I was glad to do so.

It is perhaps an irony that these people that I used to ridicule turned out to be mostly good folk—rough around the edges, often; more than a little crude, absolutely; perhaps not strictly honest by the prince-bishop's laws, but mostly honorable by their lights. And even the biggest rogue that I met was likeable. I certainly never met anyone who compared to Heydrich for malice.

The coppers I earned as a scribe eked out the silver you had given me as I drifted south and west through Thuringia, but the work was erratic and my resources kept dwindling. When I arrived at Grantville, there were few coins in my pocket.

I had heard rumors of Grantville while I was on the road, but I passed them off as typical gossip exaggerations. You have probably heard the same rumors, and knowing you, you are even more skeptical than I was. Believe them. To paraphrase the closing words of the Gospel of Saint John, there are not enough books in the world to contain the wonders of the place.

"Laying it on a bit thick, aren't you?"

"Perhaps." He smiled, still focused on the paper. "Friedrich will shake his head at how credulous I have become, and Anna will be scandalized at the sacrilege."

The guards on the approaches to the town decided I was harmless and let me pass. My English was less practiced than I remembered, or perhaps their dialect was different, but I still understood when they directed me to the grandest tavern I have ever seen, perhaps the grandest the world has ever seen, the Thuringen Gardens. It is huge, and bustles both night and day. It was near sunset when I went there, hoping to find scribal work. I was very hungry, so the first thing I did was order the cheapest food they had. They brought me something called a sandwich, which turned out to be a slab of ham and a slab of cheese between two slices of bread, spiced to the point of burning with ground mustard sauce. A curious thing, but one you get used to so quickly that within moments it seemed natural to have a mug in one hand and this sandwich in the other, even my crippled claw, alternating bites and sips.

After I finished eating the fine meal, which had cost most of my remaining coins and left me only a few copper pennies, I looked around for those whom I could approach for scribing work. The more I looked, the more my heart dropped in my chest, for nowhere did I see the ragged clothing of those who would use my services. Everyone in sight was clean and well dressed, well fed and content. As the serving maid went by I asked her if there was another tavern in town, one for the common laborers. She laughed and said that this bunch was as common as they came. It was most odd, Friedrich, that she was clad in trousers in public.

I knew nothing of Grantville then, but at that moment I wondered what I had wandered into. If, as it seemed, there were no poor, no one that would hire my scribing, how would I feed myself? In the depths of my depression, I nursed my beer, wondering what I would do now, when suddenly a loud voice penetrated my head. And I do mean penetrated.

Memory rolled as the pen recorded.

"All right, it's Saturday night here at the Gardens, and tonight we have some entertainment. Preeeee-senting the world's greatest rock-and-roll, blues, and country-and-western band, give it up for Mountaintop!"

The man who had been talking stepped away from the tall skinny pole with the knob at the top, and another man bearing a most outlandish-looking device stepped up to it and said, "Thanks for the intro. Of course, we're the ONLY rock-and-roll, blues, and country-and-western band in the world. Anyway, we're going to kick it off tonight with a song made popular by Elton John."

There were five young men on this platform, surrounded by cabinets and very strange devices. Three of them were holding things that in some very faint way could be likened to lutes or Spanish guitarras, and they were gyrating and gesturing with them. One of them was pounding on a strange flat cabinet with his hands. The last one was sitting surrounded by a group of drums of different sizes and Turkish cymbals on poles, beating them all rapidly with sticks.

Friedrich, do you remember when we sat in the tavern and listened to that Swiss traveler talk about being in the Alps and seeing an avalanche pour down a mountainside toward him? That is what I felt like. They produced the most awful cacophony I have ever heard, a veritable avalanche of sound. Even now I hesitate to call it music.

If I concentrated, I could hear individual musical notes and tones, but it sounded like no music I had ever heard. It was definitely polyphony—there were more than one voice present—but there was no contrapuntal flow, no interweaving of parts. I could hear moments of tertiary harmony, but they were overwhelmed by seconds, fourths, and sevenths. It was harsh, it was discordant, it seemed like what an anthem from the infernal regions would sound like.

"Mmmph!"

"What are you laughing at?" he asked.

"Rock and roll, the music from hell. Remind me to explain that to you later."

Then one of the men started trying to sing, but it seemed to me that he was more shouting. The only thing I could understand was "Saturday night's all right for fighting." I thought surely I misunderstood, that they would not be inciting a riot.

"I don't know . . . with those boys, that's entirely possible."

"Hush."

This went on for what seemed like eternity, but I have been assured was less than four minutes. It was more than loud. It was so rhythmic and percussive it was like some obscene martial music. I felt it physically as much as I heard it.

Remember your worst morning after a night spent drinking. Remember how your head felt. Now, double that feeling. Double it again. That approaches how I felt—as if my entire being was throbbing with the pulse of the universe. And then suddenly—blessed stillness—for a moment, anyway, until everyone else in the tavern stood to their feet and began clapping and yelling and cheering and whistling.

I sat stunned. Shocked. Appalled. Soon the crowd quieted and the men began making noise again. Unable to move, I listened to several more bouts of chaos. Eventually, I made the astounding discovery I could become used to even this.

*At last they ceased, and began moving their cab-
inets and drums and cymbals from the platform.
The tavern returned to tavernish sounds—many
conversations, some laughter, but no chaos. I began
to think again about trying to find people for whom
I could scribe, but before I could stir, a young
woman sat down across the table from me.*

"Finally, we're getting to the good stuff."

"And we will get done with it sooner if you will quit
interrupting me."

Memory began to scroll again.

"Hey, are you all right?" Blue eyes stared at him in
concern. He blinked several times, opened and closed
his mouth without speaking, again, and finally said, "I
think so."

"Are you sure?"

"Yes," stronger this time.

"Okay, you just looked pretty dazed for a while there."

"I . . . yes, I was." Pause. "What was that?"

She smiled, and said "What was what?"

"The . . . what those men . . . that noise."

"Oh, you mean the rock music?"

"Music?" Heads turned around them at the volume of
that word.

"You're new here, aren't you?" Confused, he nodded.
"Yes, it is music. You know about where we're from?"
Another nod. "It's very popular music from our
time . . . up-time, we call it now."

"If that is what music will become, may God spare me
from it."

She chuckled, then said, "With that attitude, you must be a musician. Do you sing or play?"

Without thinking, he said, "Violin," then closed his eyes in pain.

"Can I see it? Your violin?"

Eyes still closed, he raised his crippled hand from his lap and laid it on the table.

"Oh, my God," he heard her say softly. Steeling himself, he opened his eyes, expecting to see horror and pity, and was almost unmanned when he saw an incredible empathy—she not only knew his pain, she shared it with him. "It looks recent. Some kind of accident?"

"No. A jealous rival."

The anger that flared in her face surprised him. Eyes narrowed to mere slits, she hissed, "That's just evil."

He shrugged. "I cannot disagree, but it is done."

"No wonder you looked so lost when you walked in. You've lost your cornerstone, haven't you?"

"Perhaps, perhaps not," he said slowly, then gave a small smile, "but I believe I must admit to a kinship with Job. I rely on the Lord, but I do have some questions I would like to ask Him." She laughed, and he was lost in the silver skirling of her voice.

"I'm Marla Linder. What's your name, wandering musician?"

"Franz. Franz Sylwester, from Mainz." He recovered enough of his manners to stand and give her a bow, hand over heart.

"Sit down, sit down." She looked at him closely, and said, "Mainz. Are you Catholic?"

"Well, enough so that I could play in the bishop's

chapel. But my best friends are Lutheran, albeit quietly so in Mainz."

She quirked her mouth a little, and said, "From the looks of you, you haven't had much luck lately, have you?"

"No. A one-handed musician has no . . . no means to support himself."

"Have you thought about learning something else?" She interrupted him as he started to reply, "I mean, learning to play something one-handed, like a trumpet?"

"The thought, yes, but . . . there is something to violin, something about shaping the music . . . molding it . . . that trumpeters cannot do, that only strings can do. If I cannot do that . . ." He shrugged.

"Hmm," she said, "I think I know what you mean, but you might be surprised." Someone called her name and beckoned toward her from the platform. "My turn. I have an idea for you. Wait here and we'll talk again after I'm done."

Her name was Marla. She talked with me for a short time, and then she went to the platform and sat down behind one of the flat cabinets. I steeled myself for more discord and chaos, and was surprised when a much more harmonious sound was heard. She sang several songs in something like a ballad style. They were nothing like our songs: tempi were very loose and meters seemed to meld from one to another smoothly; harmonies were still dissonant, albeit not nearly so much as "the world's greatest rock-and-roll, blues, and country-and-western band." Not at all structured like anything I had ever heard before, yet somehow intriguing.

Some of the songs were pleasing, like the lullaby she sang to a sweet baby named James. Others were disturbing, like the one where she was imploring someone about killing her softly with a song. The last song had me wondering what language she was singing in, there were so many words in it that sounded like English yet made no sense. Even the title was confusing: "I dig rock-and-roll music," yet it had not one mention of a shovel in it at all.

In some strange way, the cabinet she sat behind was some kind of instrument, but it could not have been because it was so flat and narrow that there simply was not room for any kind of works within it. Nonetheless, it produced a most unusual sound. In timbre it was somewhat bell-like, perhaps like bells struck with soft mallets. That does not do it justice; suffice it to say that it was a sound I have never heard before.

I took some comfort in the fact that if the Kappelmeister had been present he would have been gibbering; partly over the strangeness of what was being called music, and partly over a woman singing unaccompanied, albeit only in a tavern. In fact, that thought quite warmed my heart, and I was smiling when Marla returned to my table, claimed me, and led me out into the evening.

Friedrich, she found me shelter, and a place to

work to earn my keep. But oh so much more importantly, she took me to people who showed me a new world, a world of music that I thought I had been barred from. First she took me to the school. It is not a gymnasium—they call it a High School, and all the children of the residents attend and learn arts and sciences. And music, Friedrich, they learn music! There is a professor there, a professor of music. Herr Wendell is a master in command of his art. He teaches these students, these youths, to play music, and to play it with passion. These youth, they play all manner of reeds and horns and drums. Everyone calls them a band. (They are not, however, to be mistaken for the "rock-and-roll" band.) Except that sometimes Master Wendell calls them a symphonic wind ensemble. He does not lead from a clavier, Friedrich. Instead, he stands on a platform in their midst, and by his gestures he shapes them as a potter shapes the clay. He was the one who showed me how our polyphony changed over time to a new style of music he called homophony, and began teaching me how to understand its forms.

Friedrich, you will not believe what they can do, the flutes and reeds and horns they have! Especially the horns! They have finely made sackbuts—except they call them trombones, which I find to be an odd name. And they have trumpets and other horns of all sizes, all made with great artifice with an innovation called valves that allow them to play diatonic tones in all registers. They can even play chromatic tones in all registers! They are incredible! But most astounding of all is what they use in place of the harpsichord. Oh, Friedrich, there is an instrument called a piano, that is to a clavier what the finest flute is to the crudest willow whistle! All of this Master Wendell revealed to me over several evenings.

Marla also introduced me to her friend, Herr Ingram Bledsoe, a maker of instruments, who makes some small instruments; some, as he says, "from scratch," meaning they are crafted totally by himself, and some from "kits." This is another changed word in the Grantville dialect of English that Herr Bledsoe had to explain to me. His "kits" are not baby foxes. He showed me boxes of instrument parts that had already been cut out from the wood and metal, and explained that he was able to buy these from other people and then assemble them into the instruments himself. He had several harp "kits," and some guitarras also. It seems to me that using these "kits" would rob you of the pleasure of searching out and selecting the wood, and bringing out of it the very shape you wanted. In their old world, however, it seems that the ability to accomplish things quickly was important, and there is no doubt that putting together the parts that someone else has crafted would quickly give you a finished instrument.

He also repairs many of the instruments they brought from the future.

> *This next part is for Anna. I was in Herr Bledsoe's workshop one day when I made the mistake of saying that women had no strength for music.*

Memory again.

Marla looked at him, eyes narrowed, and said quietly, "Is that so?"

He knew her well enough now to recognize the warning signs, and said, "Well, so my masters taught me."

"Your masters were fools, but I don't expect you'll take my word for it. Tomorrow is the town Christmas Party. There will be a concert in the Methodist church. You be there," and she turned and stalked out. He turned and looked at Ingram. "Did I say something wrong?"

Ingram just laughed, and said, "Yep, you did. I'd be there tomorrow, if I were you."

Knowing what was good for him, he went to the concert. Once again, Grantville shocked him, and he spent most of the concert in a daze. First of all, over half of the choir of almost sixty people was women! And Marla was among them. Second, the player at the piano was another woman! Third, they were good! The women's voices had a range and a power and a timbre that the boys' voices he was used to hearing on soprano and alto simply could not possess. And the pianist was extremely accomplished, demonstrating to him the power of that instrument as well.

There came a point where Marla stepped out from the choir, and nodded to the pianist, who began a quiet introduction. The epiphany came when Marla began to sing.

"Ave, Maria . . ."

As she sang that beautiful melody, he was transported to another realm, lifting on the effortless soaring of what seemed to be the voice of a very angel from God. He closed his eyes, drinking in the splendor with his ears, seeming to rise out of his body while she sang. When the beautiful song came to a close, he was the first one on his feet, clapping with all his might, tears pouring down his face.

Anna, you were right all along. Women can be musicians, professional musicians, and can be just as good as any man. Marla is the proof of it. I grovel at your feet, as I groveled abjectly at hers after the concert.

Friedrich, there is more knowledge of music in Grantville than there is in all the courts and chapels of Europe combined! Knowledge of our music and its past and what music had grown into in their time. Master Wendell and Marla have shown me that within our generation the center of music moved north from Italy to Germany, and that Germany remained the center of the greatest music for almost two hundred years. They have devices that play music with no musicians (they say it is not magic, just superior mechanical arts), and I have heard the music of Bach, Brahms, Mozart, Haydn, Beethoven, Schubert, and so many others. I know those names mean nothing to you now, but they are giants, Friedrich, giants. There is so much here, so much to feed on. But it rests on such a slender reed.

★ ★ ★

One last memory unrolled. Marla turned off the device that had just finished playing *Die Kunst der Fuge* by Johann Sebastian Bach, and waited with Marcus Wendell while he returned from the heights that the order, structure, and innovation of the masterwork had transported him to.

"I seem to spend much time crying around you," he muttered, wiping his eyes with his sleeves. "Very unmanly."

She shook her head, and said quietly, "To me it's a mark of how great a heart you have for music, that you can be so touched by the greatest."

"This Bach, this master of contrapuntal art, he was born when?"

"He was . . . will be . . . that is, 1685, I think. He's the beginning of the German era of great musicians."

He sat with brow furrowed, thinking intently, and finally looked up. "Marla, this butterfly effect you explained to me . . . how because you exist here, now, that ripples of change have begun and that the future you knew will never happen, people will never be born . . ."

"Yes?"

"Is that true of Johann Sebastian Bach?"

Sudden sucking of air, twin expressions of horror on Marla's and Marcus's faces, twin exclamations of "Ohmigawd! I never thought of that!"

Friedrich, we need you. We need you and Leopold Gruenwald and Thomas Schwarzberg to join us here, you three and as many of the others as you can convince to come. For you, Herr

Bledsoe will teach you of how pianos are made, and how to repair and maintain them, and of guitars. For Leopold, Master Wendell will show him all the wind instruments that he has, horns of all shapes and sizes, flutes and reeds, and new forms such as the saxophones. We desperately need Thomas to help copy down all the music that is available on their devices before they wear out. We must preserve and spread our German heritage, our legacy that has come from a future that will never be. And last but not least, bring Anna, so that she can learn from Marla and the others and become the musician she so wants to be.

Oh, come, Friedrich! Come for the joy of it, come to become the renowned master the Lord means you to be, come because I love you and need you. Send word as soon as you can.

Franz set the pen down and leaned back in his chair. Marla wrapped her arms around his neck from behind, and said, "Will they come?"

"Oh, yes. Friedrich at least will come, and Leopold should. Once Thomas learns of all the new music he can learn, no one will be able to hold him back. If they come, others will come with them or follow soon after. And of them all, Thomas is probably the one we need most. He can notate any music that he hears, so he is the solution to preserving so much of what you have on the CDs and . . . records." He tilted his head up and she leaned down to kiss him. "Yes, they will come, and together we will learn and save your music." Remembering the "movie" she had shown him the day before, he grinned and said, "And the Grantville hills will be alive with the sound of music."

Other People's Money
⟪◔★◕⟫
Gorg Huff

I

When Sarah Wendell had agreed to go out with David Bartley, it had seemed like a good idea at the time. She had totally forgotten that she was months away from her sixteenth birthday. The Wendell house rule was no dating till sixteen. Remembering that little detail hadn't been a problem when other boys asked her out, as several had in the last few months. David had his own version of the Delia effect. You sort of felt you were more grownup if you did what the adults wanted. Mostly David's thing worked in business matters, but this time the switch between working out how to finance the twins' scheme and his asking her out had come too quickly.

On the other hand . . .

David wasn't allowed to date till he was sixteen either,

and he knew she wasn't. Knowing David, there was no way he had done it on purpose. It was kind of nice to know that she was as capable of making him forget that sort of thing as he was of making her forget them.

Similar thoughts occupied David's mind. In his anxiety over how Sarah would react, he had forgotten that it wasn't entirely up to her. Apparently she had, too. When you spent half your time running—well, helping run—what was rapidly turning into a multimillion-dollar business, you tended to forget that you weren't old enough to date or set your own bedtime.

David had spent most weekends since the merger traveling to nearby towns to set up Higgins Sewing Machine Company franchises. It was amazing the number of villages that dotted this part of Germany. It had come as a surprise since the Ring of Fire that the seventeenth century was so well populated. So a great deal of his time these days was spent sitting down with merchants or master craftsmen two to three times his age, explaining to them how to deal with *rent with an option to buy* payment plans and other intricacies of adding a sewing machine outlet to their other businesses. Then there were the two times he had had to revoke a franchise agreement because the holder didn't realize that they meant it when they talked about a policy of honesty and fair dealing.

He wasn't exactly in charge of any of that. Truth to tell, he was sort of Karl Schmidt's tame up-timer, sort of physical proof of Karl's up-timer connection. Still, he was involved, and did have a say. He got away with it in spite of his age because he was one of the magical up-timers, and because he always had at least Johan with him and usually Adolph or Karl to provide an introduction. He had also gotten away with it because he worked really hard at forgetting that he was fifteen when he talked business.

The fact that he was wealthier than his whole family had been up-time and had what amounted to his own man-at-arms didn't help with the bedtime business either.

All of that cut no ice with Grandma. He was fifteen, he was not allowed to date, and his bedtime was ten o'clock on weekdays.

Well, he had put his foot in it. It was time to talk to Grandma.

Delia Higgins was trying to figure out how much she could rob Peter to pay Paul. That damn warehouse was threatening to become a bottomless pit. Delia was honest enough to admit that it wasn't the warehouse itself that was the problem; it was the research money that she had showered on Grantville High School. Alexandra Selluci ought to teach extortion.

No. Delia admitted to herself that she needed to learn frugality. Her agreement to build the warehouse, her remaining dolls, plus her property had provided her with a drawing account that had seemed limitless. She had wanted to use concrete in building the warehouse and as much in the way of up-time building techniques as possible. She had wanted more than that: she had wanted a work of art, the best combination of up-time and down-time construction techniques possible. So she had gone to Alex.

Alex had been trying to make bricks without straw in

terms of helping to reorganize the chemistry department with half the teachers gone, more than half the students not speaking English, and budget constraints from hell. She had made it quite clear that she had no time for the next "harebrained project of Old Lady Higgins, Grand Dame of the Sewing Circle."

Delia, her blood up, had promised to pay for the whole thing. That had shut Alex up. She realized that Delia meant it, and could actually do it. Alex had brought in Ambrose Salerno. The upshot of it all was that the Grantville High Tech Center got a brand-new concrete research program, complete with structural engineering courses where the teachers were half a chapter ahead of the students, or sometimes half a chapter behind, and Delia had a great deal less money. She couldn't really regret it. The kids that had gone into concrete were phenomenal. They were about four to one down-timer to up-timer, about average for the high school. They wanted to build things. Great big things, dams, skyscrapers, and roads, and were willing to work at it.

Then there was all the housing that was being put up, driving up prices, and her two builders arguing over design and materials. Between it all, she had spent all her doll money and more before the dolls were sold. She had gotten the warehouse built, and if not exactly a work of art, it was functional, and very large. Unfortunately it was only about half full at the moment. It wasn't paying enough to handle what she owed.

David's deferential interruption was something of a relief. Wise Grandmother was a role she found much more comfortable than Hard-nosed Businesswoman.

His problem was a hoot. So much so that she had difficulty keeping from laughing. She managed because it was clearly so important to David. David had forgotten again that he was just a kid. Not a hard thing to do if you weren't looking at him. He looked like your typical fifteen-year-old in the middle of a growth spurt: all angles and elbows, dark brown hair, short in the up-time style, pale blue eyes that usually looked a lot older than they did just now.

Judy the Elder had been secretly pleased at Sarah's announcement. She herself had been a tall gawky wallflower in high school. Not dating till sixteen had not been a problem; getting a date for the prom had. It wasn't till college that she had bloomed.

Fletcher was neither pleased nor secret in his displeasure. His displeasure had several causes that he disclosed to his wife with great zeal. An unkind observer might even have said with satisfaction.

First, he had been hoping for a few more months of relative tranquillity before the horde of horny—and now mercenary—boys started making their runs at his daughter.

"Well, David isn't after her money," Judy the Elder pointed out.

Fletcher gave his wife a look that indicated more clearly than words that his mind was not relieved. Eliminating mercenary just left . . .

Well, what it left didn't bear thinking about.

Judy the Elder decided to let her idiot husband get through his rant, so they could discuss things rationally.

Second, David knew the rules and his ignoring them was personally disappointing. Fletcher had trusted David.

Judy still trusted David, and was quite sure that he had simply forgotten. It wasn't a teenage power play to show the grownups who was boss. For one thing, David generally worked fairly hard not to show who was boss. She held her peace. It wasn't easy, but she did it.

Third, especially in this latterday Dodge City that Grantville had become, family rules were one of the very necessary safeguards, not just to keep the kids out of trouble, but to keep them alive.

This was a potential crack in the wall. Their kids already had one unfair advantage in the generation conflict. Sarah already had a net worth greater than her parents and Judy the Younger with her Barbie Consortium was gaining. Wendell really couldn't pull out the argument "As long as you live under my roof." Sarah had the wherewithal to provide her own roof, and Judy probably could in a pinch.

Another good reason not to get angry when it wasn't called for, Judy thought, but she kept her peace and let the Bull Male protective father run down. Then they could actually discuss the matter.

As Judy the Elder calmed her husband by the simple expedient of letting him run down, Sarah was going from repentant to downright pissed. It wasn't like she was some silly Juliet sneaking off to get married, or commit suicide or whatever. She'd just forgotten that she wasn't allowed to date yet. She had told her parents and apologized. She had even been initially willing to call David and cancel, though she hadn't said so. Not anymore, however. Now it was a matter of principle. She paid the housekeeper out of her salary from HSMC, not that she begrudged that. Mom and Dad both worked for the newly formed Department of Economic Resources, which was important work, but didn't pay all that well. The addition of her income from HSMC elevated the family lifestyle from existing to comfortable. She wasn't a little kid. She had a job, and did her share.

Fletcher had actually calmed down a bit when who should call but David Bartley, the cad, the rake, the libertine himself!

Luckily David wasn't calling to entice the innocent Sarah to an illicit rendezvous in the woods, nor to run off to Badenburg and get married. He was calling to apologize, and to invite the whole family to the opening of *The Importance of Being Earnest*. That is, to have the date without breaking the rules.

Opinions on the proposal were mixed. Judy the Elder thought it an excellent solution, one setting a marvellous precedent for future first dates (an observation that caused Judy the Younger some concern). Fletcher, of course, saw it as barracks lawyering; a crack in the wall for all the boys out there that wanted to do, well, what he had wanted to do in his youth. Sarah really would have preferred a less conciliatory approach on David's part, but she couldn't help but admire the sneakiness.

It was a compromise that everyone could live with. Which left only the question: What to wear? The five women of the Wendell household—Judy the Elder, Sarah, Judy the Younger, Mrs. Straus the maid, and Greta the maid's daughter—went into emergency dress-up mode. Fletcher retreated to the home office muttering to himself.

In the English-German blend that the play was written in, a line would be stated in one language and then paraphrased in the other, to make sure that everyone got it. Sort of like the Shakespearean trick of using three versions of a line, one to the left, one to the right, and one to the front so everyone could hear it.

The playwright team that had written this version of *The Importance of Being Earnest* had used that trick to play with the audience. The play worked if you spoke English, it worked if you spoke German, but it worked better if you spoke both because there were subtle and sometimes not so subtle differences in what was said in each language. The effect was a two-language pun of some sort about every third line. That wasn't the only trick up the writers' sleeves. The lines were arranged so that if you spoke only English it seemed that the guys were being reasonably sane and the girls were total ditzes. But if you spoke only German the girls seemed fairly reasonable and the guys off the wall. If you spoke both languages, it added to the feeling that they were talking past each other. At one point, one of the ladies described herself in German as preferring the quiet life in her country estate of Ept to the social whirl of the big city. The English version of the line was "I'm still socially in Ept." It was all like that, a reasonable statement in one language followed by a groaner of a translation.

"So, David," Judy the Elder asked as they all walked

outside during intermission, "how is Master Schroeder treating you?" Bruno Schroeder was the master tailor in charge of the clothing for Karl Schmidt and Ramona Higgins's upcoming wedding.

"I got him to give up the diapers."

"Diapers?" Fletcher was still a little miffed about the nondate date, and quite ready to hear about David in diapers.

"Yes, sir. Those really puffy short pants they wear. They look like diapers; worse, they look like full diapers."

"So what did you have to give up to lose the diapers?" Sarah asked with a grin. She knew that Master Schroeder was trying to convert up-timers to down-time fashions, even though he claimed to be looking for a compromise.

"Embroidery. Bruno has found a way to use a Higgins sewing machine to do embroidery. Basically he draws the pattern in chalk and then sews along the lines. Apparently the king of Sweden had all this gold thread embroidered onto his wedding outfit. Karl's and mine aren't going to be gold, but they might as well be considering how much dyed thread costs. Anyway, we're both going to have our outfits embroidered up the kazoo. Mine'll be bad enough, but on Karl's you mostly won't be able to see the cloth for all the embroidery: trees, flowers, coins, even sewing machines, in every color he can get from Mr. Stone's dye shops."

Fletcher laughed. "I must be sure to bring my digital camera."

David rolled his eyes. "If you don't, someone else will, probably the newspapers. Karl is making a big deal of the wedding. It's Badenburg politics."

Badenburg had joined the new little United States, but mostly it was politics as usual in the city council. The new elections were scheduled for some months in the future. Karl Schmidt was the foundry guild master in Badenburg, but that was because he had the only foundry in town. He wasn't, or hadn't been, one of the major players. Those were mostly the large property owners. With the merger between the foundry and the HSMC, he had rapidly become the biggest employer in Badenburg. A lot more money was flowing through his hands. More people looked to him. There were also more voters, since the property owner restriction had been dispensed with. And, just to add the icing to the cake, Karl's upcoming marriage to David's mother, Ramona, would give Karl a prestigious close personal tie to the up-timers from Grantville.

"He's planning a try for either a seat on the Badenburg council, or perhaps becoming the first senator from Badenburg. The wedding is going to be a sort of promotional show to demonstrate how important he's become. He definitely wants the press there. I think he's caught on to what expanding the franchise means better than most of the others."

"Let me guess. He wants to show off his up-timer connections?"

"Yeah. He's hoping Jeff and Gretchen will attend. Especially Gretchen. She's become something of a saint to the refugees. In regard to status, up-timers are like the jokers in a deck of cards. Whatever status you need to make the set work, up-timers are it. Of course, not everyone buys that. Claus Junker has decided that we are all peasants and Jews."

"Claus Junker? Do I know that name?" Judy the Younger asked. She didn't like being left out of conversations.

"On the Badenburg council," Judy the Elder clarified. "This year he's effectively the bookkeeper for Badenburg. He also owns a fair bit of the rental property in the city." She had met Junker, and neither had enjoyed the experience.

"You've heard some of the things Karl sometimes says about Jews and thinks he's being fair and evenhanded?" asked David. "Listen to this guy for five minutes and you'll think Karl is a paragon of openness. Junker also disapproves of children being involved in business, and of lower-class people trying to act like they matter. Jeff marrying Gretchen has proven to him that we are all peasants, because no one of rank would be allowed to make such a marriage. Of course, that doesn't mean he won't do business with up-timers, if they are properly subservient in attitude. He's backing some guy that's trying to make microwave ovens."

"Can we do microwave ovens?" Judy the Elder asked.

"Not according to Brent and Trent," said David, "or our science teacher at school. Not for five years at least, probably more. Mr. Abrabanel could have found out for him. But ask a Jew? Not Claus Junker. I could have told him, but listen to a child on a matter of business, especially a peasant child? No way. Heck, if he had been willing to talk to anyone without looking down his nose, he could have gotten the four-one-one. The thing is, he's a Von something or other on his mother's side. So he figures that he must be smarter than anyone else."

"So why care?" asked Judy the Younger. "It sounds to me like he's getting what he deserves."

"Claus Junker can fall down a well for all I care," Fletcher said, "but what happens when a major player, or even a minor major player like him, gets publicly burned in an up-timer–down-timer deal? It could shut off the supply of investment money. We need investment capital."

"Not us so much, unless you count Mom's bathroom," David said.

"Grantville in general," Fletcher clarified. "Some of the projects that really need doing will take years to prove, much less make a profit. So how is your average down-timer to know what an investment is, what's a wild gamble, and what's an out-and-out con? When the microwave project breaks, it's going to scare the crap out of the down-time investors who have been throwing money at us."

"Not that anyone threw money at HSMC," said Sarah, still annoyed about the attitude the adult business community had shown toward HSMC in the early days.

"That's already changed and you know it. And it never was true in terms of down-timers," Judy the Elder corrected. She was getting just a little tired of Sarah's harping on the matter.

"I've been approached several times in the last few months, by merchants and masters who wanted to know what I thought of an investment opportunity. Actually, that's one of the things that is bothering me about this latest project of the twins."

David was interrupted by the end of intermission. They left the school parking lot where they had been chatting and returned to the theater to see the second half of the play. The play was quite good, and one more bit of proof that Grantville was already drawing talent like a magnet.

The Grantville High School Theater seated seven hundred and fifty people in tiered seating so you could usually see over the head of the person in front of you. It was acoustically designed and had a sound system and lighting. It was one of the places where the expensive-to-make electric lights were used. The combination made it probably the best theater in Europe.

It showed plays five nights and two afternoons a week, and was usually packed. The three theater and music companies that took turns using it had a deal with the school that included teaching and financial benefits for the school. The final curtain fell with foundling Ernst restored and engaged to his cousin, and his older brother Ernst engaged to his ward, and everyone prepared to live happily ever after. The curtains then opened again for the cast to take a bow and accept the applause of the audience. As the final curtain fell the audience started to file out of the theater to wait for the buses.

While they were waiting in line for their bus Mrs. Straus plucked up her nerve and asked a question that had been bothering her ever since she had gotten her job as the Wendells' housekeeper. "Why do you not own stock in the sewing machine company, Herr Wendell? Sarah is your daughter, yes? What is hers is yours, yes?"

"Ah, no. Sarah is my daughter, but that doesn't mean that I own what she owns. Her mother and I do have certain veto power till she's eighteen, but her property—especially what we call real property; stocks, bonds, land, that sort of thing—is hers. And, come to think of it, that's probably a good thing. Not everyone in the government has been quite as careful as I'd like about potential conflicts of interest, and in the job that Judy and I have, it's especially important. We're out there trying to sell the improvements Grantville has to offer to the towns and villages around the Ring of Fire. Things like grain silos, plows, and so on. If we owned an interest in the companies that made them, especially if we owned an interest in one of the companies and not in another, it would be a real conflict of interest."

"So what's your problem with Brent and Trent and their washing machines?" Judy the Elder wanted to know. "Do you think you'll have difficulty raising the money, David?"

"I can raise the money, all right. In fact, I'll probably have trouble avoiding it once news gets out. The investors are going to expect results though. They'll want a repeat of the sewing machines, with a quick and high payoff. It's not that I doubt the twins, but we have a reputation now. I think I've felt it more because I've spent so much time out there, where Grantville is still sort of a magical mystery. They look at HSMC—and, believe it or not, Mom's bathroom—and they want in. They don't care how much it costs. They want in. It's like owning a share in a Grantville business is a guarantee of a secure future."

"Ah," Judy the Elder nodded, "the light dawns. What happens when it blows up in Junker's face?"

"Right," David agreed. "The thing is, aside from his unwillingness to do business directly with Jews, Junker is considered one of the sharper men of business in Badenburg."

"They're still going to want in," said Sarah. "Never doubt it."

"You're probably right."

"The bus is here. Where do you want to eat?"

"I don't feel like the Gardens. How about pizza?"

Ramona Higgins was at that moment in her bathroom in Karl Schmidt's house. She was demonstrating to her betrothed husband one use of the massage table she had insisted on. Karl had stopped complaining about the cost some time before. At this point he was no longer complaining about much of anything. He was barely capable of moving. Now she looked around the room that had been added to Karl's three-story town house. It was eight feet wide and fifteen feet long. It had a hot tub in the end near the main house, a shower in the middle, and the massage table on the other end. The water tank was on the roof of the bathroom, against the wall of the main house. From there the water flowed down and then back up a little way to connect to the water heater attached to the new stove. The hot tub and the showers had faucets for hot and cold water. Of course, the stove was needed to heat the water, but the whole household could have a hot shower every night if no one hogged the hot water. The bathroom was really just one of the changes made with the "bathroom dividend," as David called it. There were the porta-potties, too. They had to be emptied by hand. But for that there was the dumbwaiter, so you didn't have to carry the loaded pots up and down stairs. It was all like that. The bathroom was the best they could do within the budget that Karl complained about so much. In Ramona's opinion it had all turned out to be pretty good. The house was crowded, and everything was used for several things, but there was a feel to it like things were going well. The neighbors were envious, and thought they were very modern. As much fuss as Karl made over the bills, he was sure quick to show off the results.

Adolph Schmidt didn't know whether to be pleased or really annoyed. His papa had been right. The latest offer for HSMC stock was for fifty-seven American dollars a share, except no one was selling. That was the least of it. They were making sewing machines faster than he had thought possible, and selling them faster than they could make them, at a higher profit than he had imagined.

His father's engagement to Ramona Higgins had made the family up-timer friends, people that they could sit down with over dinner or a beer and ask questions of. Through those friends and the knowledge they brought, the Schmidts had a small electroplating operation up and running. Jorgen was also producing fairly decent crucible steel. Steel was still an art, but it was an art backed by scientific knowledge, and the pours that didn't work could usually be redone.

The Schmidts had been hiring almost since the day of the merger, and, for the first couple of months, spending a lot more than they took in. Then things had taken off. They had made and sold sewing machines at a heroic rate. Rather than being supported by the foundry and smithy, the sewing machine plant was now supporting both and the research operations as well.

Papa's senior journeyman, Jorgen, had been told to research the making of crucible steel. Further, the journeyman had been told that the steel was his masterwork. Making the crucibles had turned out to be the hardest part. Now that Jorgen had found the clay and could make the pots, he could make what the up-timers called high-carbon steel. Recently he had started experimenting with other additives for greater strength.

Jorgen's masterwork was judged by Master Marcantonio, the up-time master metal worker. Master Marcantonio had made most of the machines for the sewing machine factory and had a seat on the board of HSMC. When he was judged to have completed a successful pour of high-carbon steel, Jorgen was declared a master steelmaker. Papa had set up a new company, forty percent owned by HSMC and thirty percent owned by Jorgen. The remaining thirty percent of the stock was held by the company to raise money and provide stock options for its employees. All of which meant that Jorgen could now get married.

Adolph hadn't been so lucky. He had been assigned electroplating, and he had succeeded sooner than Jorgen had with the crucible steel operation. Adolph's operation was turning out gold-electroplated iron and now, steel flatware at relatively low cost. They always carefully explained that the items were only gold-plated, but at the prices they charged, the customers didn't seem to care much. The gold electroplating kept the iron from rusting, and the product looked like solid gold. However, clever chemistry didn't make Adolph a master smith who was able to marry where and when he wanted.

Most of the major cliques in school were represented at the pizza parlor that night. There were several new groups since the Ring of Fire. In addition to the traditional jocks, nerds, and toughs, there was now JROTC or cadets, artists, and entrepreneurs. Like at any high school, there were those who fit into more than one group, with a different rank depending on the category and several subcategories.

David and Sarah were right at the top of the entrepreneurs, but from there they diverged. Sarah was also near the top of the brains, a subcategory of the nerds. David was somewhere near the bottom of the JROTC. Most of the boys, and more than a few of the girls, were ranked somewhere in the JROTC. There was also, as there usually is, a set of the elite: the most popular and successful from the other groups. Who was in that last grouping depended on who you asked.

There was cross-pollination between the groups, and different groups had different degrees of influence. JROTC was the largest and single most important group. Brains, though not universally popular, had gained some prestige since the Ring of Fire. Entrepreneurs were fairly high up, and for obvious reasons they rose to near the top as the students approached graduation. This had the effect of moving David up in the JROTC group and Sarah up in the brain group. It also placed them both just on the edge of the elites. So David and Sarah were greeted by many of their fellow students when they arrived. The fact that they were there with Sarah's family put a bit of a damper on things, but Fletcher and Judy weren't the only adult customers.

Judy the Younger was definitely in the elite at the middle school, and had friends in high school. It was through her that the nature of the evening was revealed. The technique of taking out the whole family was considered, and viewpoints were mixed. There was the added expense, of greater concern to most than to David Bartley.

Between the tickets and the dinner, the evening had cost over two hundred dollars. There was also the inhibiting presence of the parents, right there for the whole evening.

On the whole, it was a fun evening, the conversation was lively, and David and Sarah had about as much time on their own as they knew what to do with, though not so much as they wanted.

Guffy Pomeroy was not looking his best when Officer Gottlieb found him. Electrocution, followed by a couple of days to ripen before anyone notices, is not conducive to a tidy appearance or pleasant aroma. There was a variety of electrical gear scattered around the body. Apparently he had been a bit careless in hooking something up, and ended up as the line of least resistance through the circuit. Or at least that's how Officer Gottlieb understood it. She was an old Grantville hand, and had been a cop for almost eight months. She had seen a lot of dead bodies in her life, mostly before becoming a cop. This, however, was her first electrocution. It wasn't pleasant, but not nearly the worst she had seen. Not being all that conversant with uncontrolled electricity, she carefully did not touch anything. She called in and waited outside for backup.

Guffy had been a well-known character in Grantville even before the Ring of Fire. He was a get-rich-quick schemer, not exactly a con man, but not exactly honest either. Guffy had a knack for getting people to back his schemes, usually to their detriment. He'd done two years for passing bad checks up-time. Down-time he had claimed he was going to be the reinventor of the microwave oven and the microwave forge and so on. The rumor had it that his backer was a bigwig from Badenburg. Guffy had been a hard guy to dislike and was easy to trust, till you knew better.

Well, he was past trouble now.

By now the Grantville area had three papers. Two dailies, the *Grantville Times* and the *Daily News*, and a weekly business paper that called itself *The Street*, and had pretensions of becoming *The Wall Street Journal* of the seventeenth century. The *Times* tried for a responsible tone with thoughtful articles and a restrained style. The *News* was big on flash. They also differed on several political issues. The *Times* was owned and edited by an up-timer, the *News* by a down-timer. The *Times* was very big on treating up-timers and down-timers just alike. The *News* felt no such restraint. While violently egalitarian in most ways, it expressed the view that up-timer knowledge was irreplaceable and every up-timer death was a terrible loss to the whole world. *Daily News* editorials called for up-timers to be restrained by law from wasting their unique knowledge and abilities in risky endeavors. The *News* had quite a bit of refugee support for this position, partly because high-risk, high-pay jobs that up-timers weren't allowed to do would need to be done by down-timers. The two papers often got quite snippy with each other on the subject.

This was one of those times. Guffy Pomeroy had obviously been working on something important, which might well now be lost for all time. The *Daily News* rushed into print. The *Times* was slower and more cautious. It mentioned his death above the fold, but it wasn't the headline. The headline had to do with Badenburg politics.

What neither paper caught at first was the short-term economic consequences. Claus Junker had invested a medium fortune into the microwave project. It was mostly his own money, but he'd had some extra expenses lately and some of the city's money had found its way into the project as well. Claus was already nervous about the project after several unasked-for warnings. The only things that had kept it going this long were Guffy's gift of the gab and Junker's aversion to admitting he was wrong.

There was no backup plan, and no fallback position. Guffy had offered ironclad guarantees of success. But how do you sue a corpse?

In Badenburg first, then in other towns near the Ring of Fire, people were starting to wonder, *What happens if my up-timer dies?* That was the first blow. About the time that concern was getting back to the Ring of Fire, the *Times* published its response to the *Daily News* article. It contained a report of what Guffy was trying to do, why it wouldn't work, a guess about how much it had cost, and the conclusion: "While any death is tragic, in this case the most likely result is simply to prevent a continued waste of his investors' money." There was no Black Tuesday, but it was not a good time for the Grantville Stock Exchange.

In the midst of the slump came Karl and Ramona's wedding. The wedding was a circus. People came from all over, partly because Karl was becoming an important man, but also because it provided an excuse to travel to the area of the Ring of Fire and look at what was going on.

The day was bright and sunny. Badenburg's market square was festooned with banners and ribbons. Tables groaning with food were everywhere. More than a couple of fatted calves had met their fate. There were countless cabbages, squash fruits, flavored gelatins, and all manner of good things to eat. There were jugglers, dancers, musicians, and assorted other entertainers. Three battery-powered boom boxes playing tapes at full volume added to the ambience. Games and contests were available for children and adults.

Invitations had gone out to every employee and stockholder of the Higgins Sewing Machine Company, as well as to every prominent person in Grantville, Badenburg, and the surrounding towns. The wedding was a show of prominence. Not everyone who was invited came; but then, not everyone who came was actually invited. Children were playing everywhere; quiet conversations were shouted. The noise was deafening.

The wedding itself had happened that morning to control the size of the gathering. The wedding reception was costing more than Ramona's bathroom, and had involved Karl taking out a loan secured by some of his HSMC stock. Delia Higgins was not going to foot the bill for a city-size block party to launch Karl's political career. Just after the wedding itself, Karl had announced the endowment of the Badenburg School for Young Ladies. Endowing a school or other similar civic project was the traditional way of gaining the sort of social rank needed to sit on the council.

There were many conversations on all manner of subjects, but two main topics dominated the conversational landscape: the elections for Badenburg's senate seat, and the recent downturn in the Grantville stock market.

David, Sarah, Brent, and Trent were getting a lot of questions about the stock market, and questions about specific companies. They were all, pretty much, the same questions:

"What happens to the company if the up-time partner dies?"

And:

"Can this product really be made?"

All too often the answer to both questions was: "I don't know." Questions, delicately put, about the consequences of the kids being removed from the sewing machine company were met with a different answer. There were four of them, and even if all were gone HSMC would continue to produce sewing machines and continue to produce new models as needed. It was a bit humbling for the kids as they realized they really weren't needed at HSMC anymore. The designs for the Model Two were already set, while those for the Model Three were almost set. Their knowledge of manufacturing and the use of machines to make machines had already been imparted. They just weren't needed in HSMC anymore. It wasn't that they didn't have value; but other than their publicity value, they could be replaced by down-timers or an accounting firm.

Brent and Trent had not been shy about mentioning their argument over whether to build washing machines or small-scale electrical power plants. Brent and Trent, as time went by, had focused more and more on the mechanical aspects of the sewing machine project. Aside from a certain natural avarice, they had never been all that interested in the money. They liked the idea of being rich just fine; they just didn't care much about how that part of it worked. They cared about making things. For them the fun part was figuring out how to make the parts and fit them all together so that they would work. There was tremendous satisfaction for them in seeing the first proto-type working and knowing that there was something new in the world because of them. Aside from the sewing machines, they had been closely involved in producing the collection of the gadgets that together were known as Ramona's Bathroom. In that project, they had met most of the top craftsmen in Badenburg. Now they wanted to make something new and useful again.

Brent and Trent knew how clothing got washed here and now, and found the process horrible. They knew that with small electrical generation units, combined with some basic circuitry and small electric motors, appliances could produce a tremendous leap in both comfort and productivity for every household that got one. They had worked up the plans for both projects. The washing machine could be done fairly quickly with what they knew now. They could be in production before the regular school session started. The electrical power plant and motor factory would take longer, and cost more. They wanted to get started on one or the other. David and Sarah had been dithering on which one they preferred. The twins decided to force the issue by going public. They buttonholed merchants and master craftsmen for their opinion on which to do. So far the opinions had been divided along simple lines. If the craftsman would be involved in a project, that was the project they favored.

Sarah had been approached more times than she could count about the availability of stock in whichever new company the twins ended up starting. Sarah knew why she was getting the questions, too. She had been standing just a few feet away when Karl had been approached on the subject.

"Talk to Sarah," he'd said. "I have the sewing machine company to run, plus the foundry, the crucible steel, and the electroplating. Besides, I've had to become concerned with politics recently. There are things that Badenburg needs, like a sewer system. I just don't have the time, which is a shame. I've learned enough about both proposed projects to be sure they can be done." Then, with what Sarah felt was a rather overdone tone of self-sacrifice: "Badenburg needs a senator who knows Badenburg and knows what the up-timers can and can't do."

Sarah left Karl and hunted up the twins. She found them cornering another merchant to ask his opinion. Together they went in search of David.

David had snuck off to the Boar's Head, one of Badenburg's inns, to avoid the questions for a few minutes. David was just sitting down and grabbing a bite to fortify himself before venturing once more into the breach, when Sarah showed up with Brent and Trent.

Things were quite a bit different since that first meeting in the woods shortly after the Ring of Fire, when they had started the process that ended in the creation of HSMC. For one thing, in Badenburg they were recognized for their involvement with the Sewing Machine Company. As a group, they were known as the Sewing Circle, sometimes even to their faces. They were important people now. When David had entered the inn the owner had, rather more deferentially than David was actually comfortable with, offered him the best table in the place. Whatever the likes of Claus Junker thought, most people in Badenburg were convinced that up-timers were, if not actual nobility, at least as good as and probably better than the real thing. That was the basic attitude toward all the up-timers; but in Badenburg, that attitude was focused on the Sewing Circle.

When the rest of the Sewing Circle showed up at the Boar's Head, people noticed and it became a forgone conclusion that they were planning yet another way to make life in Badenburg better. The funny thing was, as uncomfortable as the kids were with that reputation, that was precisely what they ended up talking about.

"So, David, which do you think we should do first?" Trent asked.

"Have you been listening to what's going on out there at all?" David asked in response. "It's not a panic yet, but it could turn into one real easy."

"What?" Brent asked. "Everyone we talked to wanted to invest."

"Yeah, with *us*. And about half of those people were going to sell their stock in some start-up to invest in you guys because they know you'll get results."

"So? We're respected." Brent shrugged. "That's just the way it is in Badenburg. It's kinda nice for a change."

"Right. There're you guys, then there's Guffy Pomeroy, who bilked Claus Junker out of a medium fortune, and escaped to where the lawyers can't get at him. Right now, every investor in Badenburg is wondering whether he's invested with the right up-timer. Bunches of them are considering jumping ship, just in case. I've spent most of the afternoon trying to explain to them that you guys aren't really all that special, which ought to be obvious to anyone who's met you."

"Well, gee, David, if I'd known I wouldn't have wiped the drool off Brent's face before we talked to people." Trent spoke with some heat. "Then they would have known right off that we were Mo and Curly waiting around for the third stooge. That would be you, Sarah."

"That's not what I meant, and you know it. While you were getting 'How much can I invest,' I was getting 'Should I sell my stock in the mattress factory' or whatever else they were invested in. I've been running around saying things like 'Yes—to me, please. I figure I can get it at a bargain right now.' And Sarah, you need to need to have a little talk with your sister, by the way. Her Barbie Consortium seems to be taking advantage of the general nervousness and their presumed sweet innocence to sucker people into unloading stock on them at a fraction of what it's worth. I figure Judy the Barracudy is gonna be grounded for about two years when your dad finds out. It's not that she's ripping off the a-holes trying to take advantage of them. Guys that try to rip off little girls are despicable, and guys that try to rip of those particular little girls are stupid to boot. What bugs me is that they just might turn the nervousness into panic."

Sarah shook her head, caught between outrage and amusement. In the past year she had learned a lot about how her little sister and her gang operated. She wasn't worried about the Barbie Consortium taking a loss. They had acquired a down-time merchant, Helene Gundelfinger, to do the legal stuff for their little investment group, and she was very knowledgeable about the market and what companies were worth what. The Barbie Consortium provided information on what people were doing, and who was coming up with what. Sarah seriously doubted that there was anyone in Grantville better informed on what was going on in the Grantville business community than Judy and her gang. People should know better by now, but somehow everyone assumed the girls' questions were just innocent curiosity.

Then she caught up with what David had been saying. "Do you really think there could be a panic? Guffy Pomeroy wasn't even a stock company. That was just a private deal between him and Junker."

"I don't know. The Grantville Exchange has been dropping slowly for almost a week now. It's ready for a rebound or a crash. I figure it could go either way. I've spent most of the day being just a little too anxious to buy. Seriously, I could have gotten control of the mattress factory today without half trying."

"Maybe you should have. The only reason it's in trouble is because Mr. Jones is a horse's hind end." Sarah had received a couple of reports on Mr. Jones. He was one of the people who were convinced that only gold and silver could be real money. Both her parents and friends had reported on Jones and the reports weren't favorable.

"There are a lot of reasons why manufacturing beds is iffy right now," Trent pointed out.

"That's not the point. We need some way for down-timers to invest in Grantville safely without having to learn modern physics or electrical engineering."

"That sounds like a job for a mutual fund or an investment bank," mused Sarah. "But if we announce that we're setting up a mutual fund or investment bank it's going to do the same thing as the twins' whispered announcement of their new projects."

Within a few days it became apparent that David was worrying over nothing. The market had taken a bit of a shock, but wasn't really in any danger. David hadn't known that, and the twins certainly didn't. Sarah probably would have realized if she had given it a little thought. Certainly her parents knew, and so did her little sister.

The market was not in any real danger of crashing but waiters have big ears, and this wasn't the sort of place where they had zipped lips to go with them. True, the waitress's English wasn't that good, and she wasn't all that close—but she was very interested. From the waitress to her father, the owner of the tavern, the words "mutual fund" and "investment bank" were heard. From the tavern owner to a merchant he dealt with, the rumor was spread and proceeded to change. The first distortion said an investment bank would save the market, which was in more danger than people had thought. Then, as the rumor progressed, the story expanded until it encompassed both a mutual fund and an investment bank.

The story now circulated that the Sewing Circle, the people behind the Higgins Sewing Machine Company, had a plan to provide guaranteed safe investment opportunities.

They had intended to announce their new project at the reception, but had put it off because of the scandal surrounding Guffy Pomeroy. Then it became . . .

By the time the Sewing Circle heard the words again, it was a done deal. Stories were circulating that important people, such as the mayor of Eisenach, who wasn't at the party, had been aware of the new project for weeks and—not to be outdone—the mayor of Badenburg was also a member of the inner circle.

Fletcher Wendell and Judy the Elder Wendell were asked several times that day about mutual funds and investment banks. Not once were they told the context. It was assumed they had to know what Sarah was planning. Besides, everyone knew how careful they were about even an appearance of a conflict of interest. The questions were general. Their explanation of the function of mutual funds and investment banks raised the level of excitement. Gretchen and Jeff Higgins were asked about it several times, and explained that they didn't know anything. They further explained that they hadn't known anything about the sewing machine company when it was formed either. Their stock had been a belated wedding present. Delia Higgins was asked about it, and she assured the questioners that she had heard nothing about it. She was not believed. The Partows were asked, and were believed. However, the Partows figured it was just the sort of thing Sarah was likely to come up with. They knew the boys wanted to make washing machines, and small-scale electrical generation systems. The adult Partows just assumed that was how the two projects were to be financed. They said that they would probably buy some stock in the mutual fund.

It shouldn't have happened that way, not from a group of kids talking. Not even from kids who had started a successful business. But Grantville was a magic place. In the course of a year, Grantville had improved the standard of living in Badenburg and the surrounding towns and villages rather dramatically. Lots of people were more than a bit intimidated by up-timers. They felt a little less intimidated by the kids of the Sewing Circle. The kids were perceived as being more approachable. Consequently, they had been constantly approached and questioned on varied matters financial and mechanical. They were well thought of.

Karl Schmidt heard about the mutual fund from Frantz Kunze, who was his closest friend on the Badenburg council, and without question, the richest man in Badenburg. Frantz was wondering why he hadn't heard about it from Karl. Karl knew the kids of the Sewing Circle, especially David, well enough to be fairly sure that something had been misinterpreted. Karl and Frantz adjourned to a private place to talk it over. It quickly became clear to Karl that the mutual fund wasn't a bad idea. Additionally, several important people had already gone on record claiming to be familiar with the project. If it didn't happen, and soon, there would be a number of embarrassed and resentful people whom Karl didn't want upset with him right now.

Wanting clear information, Karl sent someone to round up the kids. David, Brent, Trent, and Sarah were happy to be rounded up. By the time Karl's messenger came looking for them, they were getting questions about mutual funds and investment banking that they weren't ready to answer. The questions weren't whether such companies would be started, but rather were inquiries as to when, and at what price, people could buy into the mutual fund and investment bank the Sewing Circle intended to start.

"So, David, what is this mutual fund everyone is talking about?" That was Karl's first question when the kids arrived.

"I wish I knew, sir. The first I heard of it was when people started asking me about it at the party."

"Remember, while we were in the tavern?" chipped in Trent. "Sarah said that what we needed was a mutual fund or an investment bank. Did you have something set up?"

"No!" she insisted. "I was just talking, trying to figure out safer ways for people to invest."

Frantz started to laugh. "It was the Boar's Head, wasn't it?"

When they nodded, he continued. "The Boar's Head gets most of its supplies from a moderately crafty merchant who gives them discounts for rumors. You children need to be a bit more careful where you do your chatting. Well, no harm done. Except some people who should know better are going to be really embarrassed, having claimed to be involved in a nonexistent company."

"That could be a real problem," Karl pointed out. "I need political support on a number of issues: the new craft of crucible steel, making my run for the senate, and the bathhouse guild is complaining about Ramona's Bathroom. Don't ask me why."

"I can explain it to you," said Frantz. "Basically, they see the writing on the wall. They're worried."

"That doesn't change the fact that this is the sort of embarrassment I don't need right now. So have your, what's the phrase from the Sherlock Holmes stories, 'Miller's Street Irregulars' . . . whatever. Have the Sewing Circle here start the mutual fund. It's probably a good idea, anyway. From what Herr Wendell told me, a mutual fund would be a good solid investment for people who lack the time, inclination, or talent, to pick stocks for themselves."

"It would be at any other time, sir," said Sarah, "but right now with people so scared about what happened to Herr Junker . . . We're afraid that a safe investment would actually damage the market just now."

"I sometimes forget just how young they are, Karl." Frantz smiled. "No, Sarah, it doesn't work like that. First, because you're drastically overestimating your importance in the scheme of things. People are nervous right now, but not *that* nervous. It would take a dozen Guffy Pomeroys to really damage the Grantville market. Yes, people are envious of Karl's success, and he is careful to give you credit because it reflects well on him and his marriage to David's mother. But do you children really think Count Guenther is going to be scared off by Claus Junker getting clipped?"

He snorted a little laugh. "I knew the microwave was a bad idea months ago. So did Count Guenther and anyone else willing to study the matter. Well over half the money in the Grantville market is invested by people employed by the company that issued the stock. *They* know how their company is doing. Higgins Sewing Machine Corporation is a good company, but it's not the only one.

I am sure that people have been approaching you about investing in your plans and no doubt some are asking about selling stock to you. Some people panic easily, and some of those, in their panic, are willing to take advantage of a child. My advice is do what Sarah's mercenary little sister is doing, and let them sell you their stock for a fraction of its worth. If you're short of cash, I'll back you."

Frantz Kunze had been caught between disgust and amusement as he watched Judy the Younger fleecing those who were willing to take advantage of the youth and naiveté of her little group of young girls. Personally, he was perfectly willing to deal sharply, but not against a child. He had been quite impressed by the older children's civic responsibility, no matter how misplaced it might be. Such an attitude should be rewarded. Besides, the mutual fund was certain to be a good investment. The children wouldn't insist on control as so many of their elders did. There was a tremendous amount of knowledge held by the up-timers, but no undue amount of business sense.

"No," he continued, "the addition of a mutual fund will not cause everyone to desert the market. Some, yes—but mostly it will be those who don't belong there in the first place. Besides, what you propose to do is simply to collect the money and invest in the various stocks that people are selling to buy shares in the fund. Your mutual fund will actually add confidence to the market, especially if some of your own money is in it."

"It wasn't a proposal, just a thought," Sarah protested. "We hadn't gotten anywhere near a proposal yet."

"I think we're about to, though. Aren't we, Herr Kunze?" David asked.

"Yes," Frantz replied firmly. "I think we had better have everything worked out before the mayor announces he has sold Badenburg to finance the project. It will save everyone embarrassment." He smiled a gentle kindly smile. "As a matter of fact, I have a young guest. He's a factor from Amsterdam, here to examine the rumored city from the future and give judgment on the truth of the rumors, and the possibility of investment. He's been here long enough to see that there is a great potential for both profit and folly. I think we should probably involve him. If the merchants of Amsterdam can be pulled away from their obsession with tulips, they may be a good source of capital."

"How would it work?" asked Trent. "I mean, I get the part about investing the money from lots of different investors in lots of different companies. But what do the people running the mutual fund get out of it?"

"I'm not sure," said Sarah. "A salary, maybe bonuses based on how well the fund performs, or a percentage of the fund? I think it would depend on how the fund was set up."

From there the discussion went into technical details of how such a business would be set up, and who would control what. Fletcher and Judy the Elder Wendell were sent for, as was the factor from Amsterdam, Kaspar Heesters. After much discussion it was determined that it would be an open fund. The fund managers would take up to three percent of the gross capital each year to pay any expenses incurred. There was some argument over the percentage, but Fletcher suggested that since it was unknown how large the fund would eventually be, and impractical to predict the percentage that might be needed with any precision, they should set it up so that the board could take less if it turned out that less was needed. He also suggested some sort of incentive to encourage the board to use no more money than they really did need. Bonus payments to the fund managers could only be made if the income of the fund was greater than the expenses.

To give it a stable base, the kids would put in some of their HSMC stock. Frantz would invest and arrange more from other sources in Badenburg and surrounding towns. Karl snuck out of the meeting to spend some time with his new bride. In passing he directed the mayor to the meeting. Informing him privately—where others could hear—that since the news had broken the principals were gathering in *(mumble-mumble)* and a servant would guide him.

Meanwhile, back at the rumor mill that the wedding party had turned into, the absence of the Sewing Circle, Karl, Frantz Kunze, and later, the Wendells and Kaspar Heesters had been noticed. The flurry of financial speculation went up a notch. When Karl collected the mayor and had him escorted somewhere, potential investors started lining up. Who got called first quickly became a matter of status. In minutes, everyone knew that news of the prospective business had broken too soon, and the principals were doing damage control. The inclusion of Frantz Kunze, the richest man in Badenburg, and Kaspar Heesters, a factor from Amsterdam, meant that the business was larger and better financed than expected.

The reception had been a big party, in fact the biggest

party held in Badenburg since the start of the war. Financial and social movers and shakers from as far as eighty miles away were in attendance. As the financial feeding frenzy gathered steam, Karl and Ramona slipped quietly out the back. They were not heard from again for a week.

Fletcher and Judy Wendell left the meeting shortly after Karl did. They had been asked their opinion on the project, and in general they approved of it, although Fletcher was concerned about issues of possible insider trading. No sooner did they reach the street, than they were mobbed. While they had strong opinions on the matter of conflict of interest, they didn't feel the need to mention that the new mutual fund had been born only minutes earlier. They satisfied themselves with refusing to recommend, officially, this mutual fund. They explained that, because their daughter was involved, any recommendation on their part would be a conflict of interest. When asked if they would be investing in it, they acknowledged that they probably would, and that was another reason for them not to tout it. They spent the rest of the afternoon explaining mutual funds in general.

Judy the Younger was very annoyed, heartily embarrassed, and ecstatically pleased all at once. The annoyance was because somehow, her sister, who couldn't keep a secret if her life depended on it, had not let slip one word about a mutual fund or an investment bank. She was embarrassed because her friends in the Barbie Consortium expected her to have the lowdown on the activities of the Sewing Circle. Heather and Susan had already made pointed comments about the lack of warning. She was pleased because the rumors of the mutual fund were causing some investors to sell their stock in good companies at ridiculously low prices, now that rumor said there would be a safe place to put their money. The Barbie Consortium was getting some amazing deals. Judy figured that the consortium would probably double its assets today. As far as the fund itself was concerned, she would tackle Sarah on that tonight.

II

Karl and Ramona had spent a lovely week in the best room in the best inn in Jena. Karl found that he liked the up-time custom of honeymoons. He was even considering making it an annual event, until they hit the city gate on their return.

It wasn't that disaster had struck in his absence. In a way it was the reverse. "Herr Schmidt, Herr Kunze needs to talk to you before you talk to anyone else. I was told to tell you that it is vitally important that you see him before you make any statements to anyone, on anything."

The nervousness of the guard bothered Karl. It seemed as though the guy was afraid Karl would have him hanged if he gave offense.

When they arrived at Frantz's home, Ramona was whisked away to talk to the ladies while Karl was led to the study, only to be met with: "You picked a fine time to wander off." But Frantz was smiling when he said it. "We've been working all week getting the fund organized. Have you seen a movie called *Other People's Money*? The Wendells have a copy of it. I've spent the week trying to convince the parties involved that it's the perfect name for the fund."

"I still say it sounds like we're putting up a sign saying 'We'll rip you off,'" said Sarah. "I think we should call it A Rumor of Wealth. That's how it started after all."

"This is what you paid the gate guard to direct us here for? To get my opinion on the name of the kids' latest project?"

"No, Karl. We got you here to tell you who has been involved for months in setting the project up, and the delicate negotiations about which of the investors would be on the board of directors. You'll need to explain that the mayor was asked to serve on the board, but like you, felt he had to decline due to his extensive responsibilities. Likewise, three council members, including my miscreant son, have declined the opportunity to serve on the board."

Said miscreant son, Bernhard by name, bowed graciously to his father without rising from his chair. "Speaking of miscreants, go ahead and sit down, Karl. Marlene will have your Ramona describing your wedding trip in detail for at least the next hour. Ah. Your face should turn red. All the suffering you've caused all the men of consequence in this town. That Karl Schmidt would become a figure of romance I never would have imagined in my worst nightmare. You realize that I will have to hear about your wedding trip for who knows how long?"

By now Karl's face was an interesting shade of red, a

sight David, Sarah, and Adolph never imagined seeing outside the heat of the foundry. The youngsters were having a certain amount of difficulty keeping their countenances bland. The idea of Mr. Schmidt as a figure of romance did not bear thinking about, especially for David and Adolph. On the other hand, Mr. Schmidt being teased was a rare joy.

Kaspar Heesters came to the rescue. "We have all the craft masters on the council, and about half the rest of the council as investors, and it worked out that each group would have one representative on the board. Herr Schroeder will be the representative of the crafts, and Herr Kunze for the patricians. There are several more from other towns in the area. In total there are forty-six initial investors including the Sewing Circle. About half are investing cash, the rest are contributing stock. The important thing here, Herr Schmidt, is that the names of those initial investors are secret. Not to keep people from knowing who they are, but rather to keep people from knowing who they aren't. This is to avoid the embarrassment to people who have claimed to be investors before there was anything to invest in. That includes most of the forty-six members, by the way. In exchange for that double layer blanket of discretion, they have made certain concessions we couldn't have otherwise obtained.

"The size of their investments is generally large. They have agreed to a seven-person board and to its makeup. The board will consist entirely of down-timers, but Johan Kipper will have a seat as the representative of the Sewing Circle. The Sewing Circle will not be required to quit school and work full time for the fund. The whole project almost foundered on that point. It was only the threat of exposure that prevented it. We brought you here because it was vitally important that you know what answers to give when you are asked questions."

"Very well. What did I know? And when did I know it?" Karl asked.

"Primarily, that it was long planned, and kept secret so as to avoid potential problems in the market. The secrecy was so that every effort could be made to insure the safety of the investors before any money changed hands. In other words, the way we should have done it," said David. "Instead, we're perpetrating the next best thing to a fraud in order to protect the reputations of people who should have known better."

"Yes, we are, and you know why too, or should by now. I've explained it to you often enough in the last week." Frantz wasn't smiling now. "These are important people. They don't take well to being made to look foolish. If what actually happened came out, they would be forced to deny it, and the only way that they would have any hope of being believed is if they blamed it on someone else— which would be you four and the up-timers in general. 'No I didn't pretend to be involved in a business that doesn't exist. I was told about the fund weeks ago. When they didn't get everything they wanted, the up-timers lied and tried to make a fool out of me.' They would have to follow that up with strong and public condemnations of the Grantville Exchange, and that would do all the damage you were afraid of. Nor is it always their fault. The mayor of Eisenach wasn't even here, but he would be made to look just as foolish as the others. More than half the investors never claimed any knowledge whatsoever. Several of them publicly denied it, but were not believed. Now enough! The disaster is averted, and will remain so. We all stick with the story."

The young, thought Frantz, not for the first time that week, *can be horribly self-righteous.*

"So how much money will you start with?" Karl asked. "I assume that there will be enough to start either the Washing Machine Company or the Home Power Plant Company."

That got a snort from Kaspar. The one thing this venture wasn't was underfunded. The Washing Machine and the Home Power Plant companies were to be funded, and as quickly as possible handed off to others so that the twins would be available to consult on other projects brought to the fund.

III

Other People's Money had rented, at rather great expense, offices in downtown Grantville near the exchange. Frantz had won the fight over the name.

David Bartley's secretary did not have good legs. His figure wasn't anything to write home about either. On the other hand, after a six-week intensive course he could take shorthand and was learning to type on a custom-made typewriter. He had been hired because he was conversant with down-time business practices, and getting that way with up-time ones. Leonhard was punctual, proper, and respectful. He was also something of a pain. He scheduled everything. The love of his life was a daily planner. At least that's how it seemed to David.

On David's schedule for today were a series of projects to make various things. There were two proposals to make refrigeration units. One of the standard type, though they wanted to use something else as a compression gas. The other was something called an *absorption refrigerator.* David had no idea how they were supposed to work. He flagged both for Trent to check out and put them in his out-basket. Sitting right there on his desk was an in-basket and an out-basket. Every day when he got out of school, he came here, to his office, to find the in-basket full and the out-basket empty. The really funny thing was, he sort of liked it.

He hated telling people no, but it was worth it for the ones he got to tell yes. Especially for the ones he got to rescue. There were a lot of ideas running around loose. That was the problem. They were loose. All too often, they were loose cannons.

A good idea is a dangerous thing. "Wouldn't it be great if" or "I can make one of those."

Sure, they could make one of those—but how many could they make, and how fast and how much would they cost to make? Thank god for Trent and Sarah. The sewing machine company could have gone that way if it hadn't been for Trent fussing over details and Sarah asking how much everything would cost.

A lot of it was thinking beyond the times.

You can do this because we could up-time.

You can't do that because they couldn't do it down-time in our universe.

Increasingly, the New U.S. was neither down-time nor up-time, but something new. There were things that could be done in the New U.S., things that would have been harder to do up-time because up-time there was already something that was better, or at least already established. Now they were at the start of an industrial revolution, with a road map that showed places to avoid as well as places to go. One of the classes that David was really looking forward to next semester was comparative history.

He picked up the next item. This was a proposal to buy into the little lightbulb shop a down-timer had set up. It was suggested by one of the backers. David had bought lightbulbs there but not many, because they were expensive as all get out. Perhaps a bit less hand-making and a bit more mass production could turn the place around. Another project for the twins, David decided. Brent and Trent were starting to get irritated. They wanted to start their companies, but OPM had been so flooded they hadn't had the time. Proposals cycled through David to the twins, to Sarah, then back to David.

Next item. "Leonhard, what the heck is this?"

Leonhard didn't even look up "It's a play, Herr Barkley. Proposals of a new sort are always passed up to you."

Ah. Battle begins anew, David thought. Almost from the day he was hired, Leonhard had determined that his role was to keep David from having to deal with silly ideas. The problem was Leonhard's knowledge of what David was coming to think of as "new-time" tech could do was lacking. He lacked David's grasp of up-time tech, and more importantly the new combination of up- and down-time capabilities. In his first couple of days as secretary, Leonhard had trashed a potentially profitable idea. When the applicant approached David, he had not known what was going on. Leonhard had almost lost his job over that one. Fortunately for Leonhard, two things saved his position. David had to have a secretary as a practical necessity, and having a secretary was part of the price of letting him stay in school. Leonhard was supposed to make David's time at work be more productive. The other thing that saved Leonhard was that he never actually threw anything away, no matter how silly he considered it. He filed it. So when David asked him about it, he had it quickly to hand, and no harm done. What was worse, for tools-to-make-tools reasons, the project wasn't practical to do it this year but David had hopes for next. The project had been moved from the silly file to the later file and Leonhard looked for new silly ideas to plague David with.

"Would you see if Sarah has a minute, please?" David asked. That brought Leonhard's head up. "If she does, I'll go over there." David picked up the next item in his in-basket.

"What's the silly idea that has Leonhard spooked this time?" asked Sarah when David stepped into her office. Sarah's relationship with her secretary was rather better than David's was with Leonhard.

"Actually, I'm not sure it's silly," said David. "Someone sent us a play written by Manschylius Schultheiss. I haven't read it, and wouldn't know if it was a stinker or a masterpiece even if I had, but it got me to thinking. You know how full the theater is all the time, right? And I've been hearing talk about turning the football field into an outdoor theater. It occurs to me that if we can find someone who's good at that sort of thing, we could spawn a production company."

"I don't know." Sarah shook her head. "It's pretty high risk, and it's not like we can make movies. That's where the real money would be. Maybe we can try it later, when we can make movie film."

"Okay, I'll have Leonhard send the guy a nice note saying we're not backing that sort of venture at this time, but may do so in the future."

"Have him send back the play, too. Maybe Mr. Schultheiss can get it produced somewhere else."

"Well, David," said Kaspar, "I'm off for Amsterdam, or will be by the time you get out of school tomorrow."

"How do you think you'll do?"

"Honestly, I have no idea. When I left Amsterdam, I was unconvinced that the Ring of Fire had actually happened. We had heard stories, but even from a normally reputable source they were hard to believe. I was sent here to find out what was going on. Seeing the ring of cliffs and the difference in the land—it's not the sort of thing you tend to believe without seeing it. So it's entirely possible that I will be no more than another of the 'normally responsible people taken in by whatever is really going on.' On the other hand, I am taking back artifacts to show what's here, and what you can make. When I left, there were vague rumors about a coming crash in the tulip market. Those rumors were mostly disbelieved. Partly because though there are rare breeds that bring good sums there isn't really a tulip market. Now, there probably never will be. I've been gone three months now. I understand that some up-timers, or their representatives, have gone to Amsterdam to try to make deals. Much of what I have to tell my family and friends may be old news by the time I get there. I'm as prepared as I can be."

Kaspar smiled. He really didn't find David all that unusual. In a number of ways, David was a younger version of himself, a young merchant under the guidance of older merchants. The guidance wasn't quite so overt here, because Other People's Money was using the success of the sewing machine company and the magic of the Ring of Fire as its assurance of competence and good faith. If there was one thing the Americans did differently, it was their willingness to let anyone play. The mutual fund was not really a new concept. Similar techniques had been used by Romans to finance trading ships. The difference was the way the thing was organized to let just about anyone who could scrape up a little money in. That was the attraction, and the danger, of the up-timers. They were willing to let anyone in, which meant they gathered support from the most unlikely places.

Hensin Hirsch recognized the two members of the Sewing Circle when they came in the front door. Brent and Trent were fairly famous among the teens in Grantville, down-timers especially, and by now it was common knowledge that their investment fund was starting up. What Hensin wondered was whether they were here to buy some of the lightbulbs his father made, or to buy the whole shop. He rather hoped it was the latter.

The truth was, they weren't doing all that well. Hensin's papa had been a master glassblower in Magdeburg before the sack. They had wandered into Grantville in August of last year. Papa had seen a lightbulb work, and been captivated.

The small lightbulb shop had taken a year of scrimping and saving, and money raised from three investors who had expected better results. The shop had two rooms; one occupied by finished lightbulbs for sale, and one in the back where Papa made the bulbs. They had a vacuum pump from an old refrigerator, and Hensin baked linen threads till they were carbon. But between the rent, materials, and the sheer amount of time it took to make each lightbulb, the price they had to charge meant sales were slow. They were barely making enough to feed themselves, let alone pay their backers.

"Master Hirsch wouldn't let us examine his shop. Trade secrets, and all that. As if we couldn't look up how to make a lightbulb in the encyclopedia." Brent was disgusted at a wasted afternoon, and it showed as he flopped into the chair. The chair was nice. Tooled leather, made with up-time power tools by a combination of up- and down-time craftsmen. It matched the other seven in the meeting slash boardroom of the mutual fund. "The son was all right. I think Hensin wanted our help, but his dad would barely talk to us. I think he was really afraid that we'd tell him how to do it better, and the idea of teenagers telling him what to do freaked him."

"Okay. I guess we don't mess with lightbulbs for right now. We'll look at it again in a few months," said David. "What about Gribbleflotz?"

"Herr Doktor Gribbleflotz," Trent corrected. "He is, believe it or not, related to Doktor Bombast. Apparently there really was a Bombast, and this guy is related to him. He's not really bombastic though, just sort of bitter and cynical. I felt sorry for the guy."

"So he's a nice guy," said Sarah. "What about increasing production of baking soda?"

"Hey, I never said he was a nice guy. I just said I felt sorry for him. He's a good tech, and innovative in his way, but no theoretician. My hunch is his title is his own creation. He's sort of desperate for recognition, and he really isn't interested in doing what he's doing. He just needs the money."

"If we throw some money and a fancy title at him, he'll probably do what we want," Brent added. "He explained enough about what he was doing so that I'm pretty sure we can chop up the process he uses into different steps and get all sorts of stuff. He doesn't understand the marketing or organizational parts very well."

Sarah snorted at that. In her opinion, Brent didn't understand marketing or organization at all. "So we get him a business manager." With the help of Herr Kunze she had gathered a small group of craft masters and merchants who had been introduced to up-time management practices. They were ready, willing, and able to come in and take over the management of companies OPM bought into where the people starting the business didn't know business. They were employed directly by the board in support positions, with the understanding that if an investment opportunity needed someone with their particular talents, they would have the first shot at it.

★ ★ ★

Frantz had been expecting this. He took his copy of the proposal from his desk. His office was in his home in Badenburg, a well-lit room on the second floor of his town house. The proposal was from Delia Higgins. She wanted to build a hotel on her property, fifteen stories tall. The bottom two floors would be shops and meeting rooms, the next offices, then the rooms for rent. The proposal specified the rooms would be large and luxurious, based on a room in a Holiday Inn, whatever that was. The top two floors would have a fancy restaurant and private residences. The thing that would make it all work was the elevators. It was the proposal he had been expecting, though not quite on this grand a scale. What he wasn't expecting was what the kids had done. David, in fact the entire Sewing Circle, had delivered the proposal without recommendation. No note on how it should be done, no suggestion at all as to whether OPM should buy into the project.

In a way, that fit the up-timer passion for avoiding what they called "conflicts of interest," a passion Frantz had noted was spotty in its application. Some up-timers were serious about it, others less so. He had expected a warning from the Sewing Circle to the board that they were close to the applicant, which might affect their judgment. He had gotten similar warnings in several cases where they were friends with or actively disliked the applicant. Not this deafening silence. Something was wrong, and he had his suspicions about what it was. Delia Higgins had spent a great deal of money directly and indirectly on her warehouse project. She had looked into brick, quarried stone, concrete, and wood construction. With each experiment she had spent money, the largest amount on concrete. Eventually she settled on fairly standard down-time construction techniques, with concrete pillars added for support. "What do you think, Leonhard?"

"Young master Bartley was less than pleased with the proposal. I know he's been concerned over his grandmother's financial situation. I was rather expecting him to support the project for that reason. It would give Lady Higgins a much-needed influx of capital. From the discussions, it doesn't seem in any way beyond the up-timers' capabilities. While none of the children are expert in construction, there is a certain amount of expertise available. I honestly don't see anything here that can't be done. I would have expected young master Bartley to have approved it for reasons of family, and the rest to do so for reasons of personal loyalty to both their friend and the woman who gave them their start." Leonhard was comfortable with his role as spy for the board of directors. He liked the children well enough, but they were young. They needed to be watched for their welfare, as well as that of the board. He did find them confusing in their attitudes.

Kaspar Heesters arrived back home in Amsterdam in August of the year 1632. He arrived by sea because the water route was more suitable to the volume of goods he carried with him. The goods had filled a barge. He had many examples of new products, mostly for his own household, and to act as examples of the goods that could be bought in Grantville. They were, for the most part, things that the up-timers could make down-time. Some, though, like the small generator were, so far, borderline.

David Heesters, Kaspar's father, was a bit shocked at the amount of stuff Kaspar had brought home. He had seen that his son was provided with fairly generous living expenses and funds for some limited investments, but the mission had been primarily exploratory in nature. When he saw what was in all the crates he was shocked. It looked like his son had not only spent all the investment money on fancy toys, but had indebted the house as well. The only thing that saved him from seriously embarrassing himself was the faith he had in his son's judgment. He didn't publicly disown his son as a mad spendthrift. He waited and asked. When he learned the prices of some of the devices that his son had brought home, he became even more concerned, but no longer that his son might have wasted the family's wealth. It was simply that it was hard to believe that so much, well, stuff, could be had for so little money.

Then Kaspar showed him the typed copies of the history of the tulip bubble. "There isn't a tulip market. Yes, certain rare breeds would bring money if their owners would sell them but a market in tulips is just silly. Besides the price offered for even rare breeds of tulips has been dropping in the last month."

"Yes, Father, silly, but nonetheless real. At least it would have been if not for the Ring of Fire. What would have happened without the Ring of Fire? Someone would have been a bit short of cash and gone ahead and sold some rare tulip bulb, the buyer would be offered more for it and would sell it in turn, and the tulip bubble would start. You know the price offered for the Semper Augustus was twelve thousand guilders, for ten bulbs of a single flower.

There would have been tulip dealers who bought them not through any interest in tulips but because they could, or thought they could, make a profit on them. That's how it would have gone, but the Ring of Fire did happen. There were rumors even before I left of a tulip bubble that would burst. Those rumors have caused people to be cautious about buying tulips, bringing the price down. If you have any, Father, you really ought to sell them. Because when this gets out there truly won't be a market for them."

"And where should we put our money, O sage of the future?"

Kaspar brought out the mutual fund prospectus. That took some explaining. "It works like this. I take a guilder and put it in the pot." Kaspar actually pulled out a shallow pot from one of the boxes, and put a small green printed piece of paper in it. The paper had the image of a stag printed on it. "Several other people put in what money they have for investing. The pot is then turned over to the fund managers to invest in various businesses. Each person gets shares in the fund that equal the amount of money they put in. Nothing new so far. People have been pooling their money to invest forever. But now comes the interesting part. The fund managers invest what is in the pot into various companies, and a few months later, those companies are worth more than they were when we started. But now some other people want to invest in the fund. How do you determine how much their money will buy? You take all the money and property the fund has and determine its total value as of the day the new person buys in, and divide by the number of shares outstanding. So, say there are a hundred shares and the fund is worth a hundred and fifty guilders. Each share is worth one and a half guilders. The new investor can buy shares at a price of one and a half guilders per share. The original investor doesn't lose anything because his shares are still worth the same amount."

"And when I want my money back?"

"You sell your shares back to the fund."

"Why shouldn't I invest my money on my own?" David Heesters was really just testing his son here. He understood the reason for putting money into other hands to have it invested. It always came down to expertise, time, or access.

"Would you have invested in four children who intended to build a machine that sews?"

"No, and I'm glad I didn't, because if they are selling that device for twenty-five guilders they will go broke quickly enough. It must have cost hundreds to make. Besides, even at twenty-five guilders, how many people can afford it?" But Kaspar was grinning most impudently. Clearly his son had expected the question and had an answer ready. David sat quietly and listened as his son explained. Other People's Money, it seemed, had in its management staff those same four children who had introduced not only the machines used to make the sewing machines cheaply, but the concept of rent with the option to buy, as a way of acquiring goods. This avoided the whole problem of usury, since the buyer was getting something, the use of the product, and the seller was not charging interest, but rent. The children in turn were supervised and advised by local men of consequence who knew the situation, and were themselves investors in the mutual fund, including his son.

Kaspar had made his first sale in Amsterdam. It wouldn't be the last. This was a good thing, because Kaspar had a list of raw materials needed by the industries of Grantville.

Brent brought the project to OPM. It was a mechanical calculator apparently invented by someone named Curta. Terrell, one of the kids in school, had brought it to him. It was something he had from his dad. He wanted to build the Curta calculators like the Sewing Circle had built sewing machines. The calculator was more complex. It not only added and subtracted, it multiplied and divided, and other stuff. It had about six hundred parts. Brent wasn't really looking forward to what Sarah and David would say. It was a well-worked-out plan mechanically, but only mechanically. In the whole proposal there wasn't one word about production cost, or sale price, or potential market. But he'd promised, so he sort of snuck it onto the agenda.

This wasn't the first time this had happened. They had been approached by most of the kids in school about this or that project. Mostly they had been able to say, honestly, that they didn't have the kind of money it would take to start up a company, that they couldn't sell their stock without their parents' permission, that permission hadn't been forthcoming until OPM, and even with OPM, Mom and Dad hadn't allowed them to sell it all, only two thousand shares each. On the other hand, each and every member of the Sewing Circle had a portfolio of stocks in kid-started companies, a few of which were doing all right. Now the excuse not to back the projects of their fellow students was in desperate need of a rethink. OPM was designed as a source of venture capital for new start-ups, as well as to buy stock in established businesses. The kids from school had apparently decided it was time to try again.

Oddly enough, David thought they could do something with this idea. "It's like a useful Faberge egg. Expensive as hell, pretty and intricate, but this one does stuff. There's a good excuse to pull it out and show it off. It could be the next best thing to having a computer in terms of status, better in some ways, because it works without electricity. Give a couple away to important people, and everyone who thinks they're important will want one."

"They'll need a manager," said Sarah. "A couple of engineering types will spend the investment tinkering. Do you really think we can sell enough to get back our investment?"

"Don't know." David shrugged.

"Have them build a couple of prototypes. Find someone important to give one to and then see how many people ask for one," said Trent, who had become convinced that the stupidest thing they had done in starting HSMC was not building a prototype.

"It would have to be pretty," David added. "What I would really like to do is have the case in glass but that's not strong enough. Gold-electroplated?"

Sarah entered the Higgins house wishing she was anywhere else. David was chickening out, so were Brent and Trent. Someone had to talk to Mrs. Higgins. Liesel took her coat and asked her to wait in the living room. The down-time servants were having a strangely civilizing effect on the hillbilly up-timers. It was less than a minute before Liesel ushered Sarah into Delia Higgins's sewing room where the original Singer sewing machine was shoved into a corner. Mrs. Higgins was working at a desk David had bought for her. Liesel quietly closed the door behind her as she left. This was horrible, the worst thing Sarah had ever had to do. After Mrs. Higgins had had so much faith in them and sold her dolls. David was a wimp to leave Sarah to do it. Except David didn't know that she was here, and would be mad when he found out.

"What's wrong, Sarah? You look like your dog just died."

"Well, Mrs. Higgins. It's, well, the thing is . . ."

"Have you and David had a fight?"

"Yes, ma'am, but it wasn't about this, or maybe it was. I don't know."

Delia looked at her with sympathy. "Sit down, Sarah, and tell me about it," she said, waving Sarah to a chair. "What was the fight about? You know teenaged boys can be fickle, ruled by their hormones. Has David . . ."

"No. Nothing like that," Sarah smiled for a moment. In that area, at least she had David well in hand. Then she remembered why she was here and the smile faded.

"It's the hotel. Isn't it? The fund isn't going to invest in the hotel?" Delia had gotten part of it.

"Sort of. Ah. Well."

"Well what?" Delia was impatient now. "Spit it out."

Sarah did, in a rush. "David doesn't think they should, and he's right. I'm sorry, Mrs. Higgins. If it was David's money he'd do it, you know he would. But it's not. It's other people's money, and not just big fat cats, but widows, and orphans, and working stiffs, and well . . . David delivered your proposal to the board, and Herr Kunze turned right around and said the board would go along with whatever David recommended. I think he figured something was wrong when David presented it with no recommendation. Now David's trying to figure out a way he can finance the whole thing himself so he doesn't have to tell you no, or put other people's money in a bad investment. He won't even let the rest of us help. That's what our fight was about, sort of. David is trying to run everything, take everything on. But he's right about the hotel. The warehouse was poorly planned and overbuilt, and we're all afraid that the hotel will be too. And the thing he really doesn't want to say is that it would be a good project, and a sure moneymaker, if you weren't . . ."

Sarah ran down, ready to cry. She hadn't meant to say that last part.

Delia was in too much shock to be in any danger of tears. That would come later. Delia Higgins was a capable lady, and a good woman. But this was a hard pill to swallow. She wanted to find a reason that Sarah was wrong. She didn't want to believe that her faith in David was not returned. But the pieces were falling into place, his hesitation on certain subjects, his recommendation that she check things with Judy Wendell and other experts. How, often when she did, those experts had explained some error she had made. And how she had recently mostly stopped checking, even when David suggested she should.

And Sarah's last words: *A sure moneymaker if you weren't* . . . If she wasn't what? In charge? Involved? Apparently, it wasn't the hotel that David had the problem with, but her.

"What is the problem?" Delia asked with precision. Much as some one might ask a doctor about the amputation of their leg.

Sarah sat mute.

"You have to tell me, Sarah." Still in that detached tone. "It's me, in some way, isn't it?"

"Yes, ma'am. It is." Sarah tried for Delia's detached tone, but didn't quite bring it off. "There is such a thing as being too generous. The money you've spent on the concrete program will be good for the New U.S., but in terms of getting the warehouse built, it was mostly wasted. The condos you built onto the warehouse to house the staff were a very nice gesture, and it's made you very popular with your employees. It was also a pretty expensive gesture. The deal you worked out to build the warehouse set things up so that no matter how much you spent on it you would pay and it wouldn't affect the other stockholders' income. Nice for them, but it means that you're not going to get back your investment for years. All that's okay, as long as it's your money you're dealing with, though it worries the people who care about you. David figures you'll have to sell as much as ten thousand shares of HSMC to handle the balloon payment on your loans come January. That's all fine. It's your money that you got from selling your dolls and trusting us. But the truth is, even there we got lucky. We really didn't know what we were doing. This last year has been a very intense business course for all of us.

Each and every one of us would do things differently now. Important things. Things that could have sunk the whole deal if we hadn't been lucky. If Karl hadn't fallen for David's mom we'd probably be struggling to stay in business right now. He wouldn't have had any reason to look for another option; he would have gone into competition with us. We needed someone like Karl, someone who actually knew how to run a business. Someone who wasn't making it up as they went along, or reading it out of a textbook they didn't really understand. Don't get me wrong. Karl needed us too, especially right at first, to show him up-timer tricks. I wouldn't bet on it happening that way though. Not now."

"So you're saying that betting on you kids was a bad investment?" Delia was almost bemused now.

"Yes, and if you ever tell Mr. Walker over at the bank I said so, I'll deny it," Sarah said, trying to inject a little humor into the discussion.

The party was a bit less successful than I had hoped, Kaspar thought, as he was seeing the last guest to the door. This was his public welcome-home party, and the one at which he had introduced the mutual fund. His family had invited the wealthiest people they knew, twenty-three merchants of means. He had shown the goodies from the New U.S. and described things that might be made in the future. Then he had talked about the OPM mutual fund. How it worked. What it had to offer. Sales had been less than expected, but everyone had taken a prospectus. This made Kaspar feel hopeful. *Surely they just need some time to think about it.*

Two days later he learned of the forming of another mutual fund. Then he heard about two more the next day, and two more the day after that. By the time of the next OPM party, there were five mutual funds available for purchase in Amsterdam. The funds specialized in shipping ventures, commodities trading, and even one in tulips.

That last was the one that bothered him the most. One of the topics of discussion had been the aborted tulip market. Now that the Ring of Fire had warned everyone, that market wouldn't happen. He knew it, and he was quite sure the fund managers of the tulip fund knew it. So why? Was the tulip fund a way to dump tulips, by suckering lots of people for a little rather than a few people for a lot? But why would they need to dump tulips? Was it possibly an attempt to start the tulip craze early? But that was silly. With the documents he'd brought there wouldn't be a tulip craze.

His father told Kaspar simply to make sure his name didn't get tainted with the tulip fund. *And how am I to manage that?* Kaspar wondered.

Kaspar was called in by the authorities shortly thereafter, to provide them with an explanation of mutual funds and how they worked. He spent two days being grilled. He stated for the record, his disapproval and suspicions of the tulip fund, but he ran into a problem. There was an important clause in the fund contracts that OPM and the tulip fund shared. For OPM it was what David called the "twins" clause and everyone else called the "Sewing Circle" clause. On that first day, when OPM was forming itself out of rumor and innuendo, the rumor that Trent and Brent would be financed exclusively in the production of washing machines and home power plants by OPM, had, like so many others become fact. So a clause had been inserted into the OPM contract that specifically allowed OPM to invest in businesses started or controlled by David Bartley, Brent Partow, Trent Partow, and Sarah Wendell, even while they were employed by the fund. Kaspar didn't explain all that. He simply pointed out that the youngsters involved were thought lucky as well as talented. They were a sort of combination of young Leonardo Da Vinci and rabbits' feet.

The tulip fund managers had put a similar clause in their contract. Actually, they had left one out. There was no restriction on the fund managers as to what they might, or might not, buy from, or sell to, the fund. This meant they had the right to buy and sell tulips, or anything else, to the fund at a price they set.

"Since the fund manager is both the buyer and the seller," Kaspar explained, "it's unlikely there will be much bargaining, especially since it's his money on the one side and other people's money on the other. Unless he's an unusually generous fellow, it's not hard to guess who is going to get the better of the deal."

The tulip fund managers had apparently not made a point of bringing up the missing clause when discussing their mutual fund with potential buyers. In fact, the clerk of the "inquisition" hadn't been aware of it till Kaspar had pointed it out. Kaspar showed them the restrictions on OPM board members. OPM board members could not sell commodities or stocks to OPM or buy them from

OPM. All investments had to be authorized by the board. A member of the board of OPM could buy shares in OPM or sell them, but that was about it. The possibility of sweetheart deals was there, but required a third party.

It took a few days before it became clear what the tulip fund meant. Its founders had apparently heard the rumors of the tulip bubble but had read them differently. They had felt that if it had happened it would happen, and decided to get in on the ground floor and sell out at the top. They had not considered the changes the Ring of Fire would make in the markets. When Kaspar explained the effects the Ring of Fire had already had, they had realized their error and decided that a mutual fund would be just the way to get out safely. What Kaspar found most remarkable was that they had called it the "tulip fund." They might as well have painted a sign saying "Come and be fleeced." His father was less surprised, and concluded that it was pure and simple arrogance.

When what Kaspar told them to look for was found, it made him both friends and enemies in Amsterdam. It had also defined him to the city as the acknowledged expert on mutual funds. That was not all together a good thing. It made explaining the special provision for the Sewing Circle harder, and some people assumed that since he could use a fund to defraud them, he would.

The tulip fund had not broken any laws, nor had its managers quite broken the contract. What they had done was sell their tulips to the fund at a nice profit for themselves. They had then sold their shares in the fund, leaving the other investors in the fund holding the bag of tulips. It had gotten them out of the tulip market at no financial loss. It had also pointed out the dangers involved in any investment where the people you're dealing with aren't honest. The tulip fund managers had been fairly selective in choosing their victims from those without a lot of political clout. But while the victims individually didn't have much clout, collectively they had some. The idea of a class action suit was put forward, but the fund managers hadn't actually done anything illegal. It looked like the outcome would be that the managers of the tulip fund would come out of it financially sound, but would never again be trusted to create and manage a fund. Their general reputations as men of business had also taken a hit, for which they blamed Kaspar Heesters.

Between the tulip fund and the resentment of the technical prowess of the up-timers, there was a segment of the Amsterdam power structure that didn't really like the New U.S. Kaspar spent quite a lot of time mending what fences he could. For a while it looked like mutual funds would be outlawed in Amsterdam. The other funds were more honest, though, and mutual funds were an excellent way of allowing people to invest with relative safety in ventures that they could not afford to participate in, or have access to, without mutual funds. The shipping fund and the various commodities funds came to his rescue. In a strange way, so did the attack on Grantville.

With the tulip fund and the other complications, Kaspar had already been home longer than he had intended. He wanted to leave the sales of OPM shares in his father's hands and return to Grantville with its movies and indoor plumbing. Then the rumors about Spanish troops on the move began to hit Amsterdam. Suddenly everyone was terrified that the up-timers, and more importantly, their investments would be wiped out by a Spanish army. Kaspar had a decision to make. He would be within his legal rights to insist that investors who wished to withdraw from the fund lose the loading. Loading is a fee charged when you buy into a mutual fund, and when you sell out of one quickly. Because of the distance and communication lag, OPM shares were bought in Amsterdam at a price dependent on the share price when the money arrived in Grantville, but they were bought when the agent received the money. Kaspar had already received the money, but he didn't insist that the panicky investors sacrifice the loading. Instead he voided the contracts and gave them their money back. He resolved to ride it out.

It was an especially difficult decision because of his second job in Amsterdam. He was buying raw materials. The idea was that he would use OPM investment money to buy things like lacquer, iron, silk, chocolate (if he could find any), and other supplies needed by the industry and consumer base in and around the Ring of Fire. The profits on the deal would go to OPM. By now Kaspar had bought quite a lot and contracted for even more. He had to go to his father and ask for help. He managed to convince his father that Grantville would survive.

Delia Higgins was sitting at her desk, explaining to herself, again, how she had been right in her decisions about the warehouse. Granted it was a lot of money, but she wasn't just thinking about the warehouse. She was trying to develop the infrastructure for building the hotel. The concrete program at the school was developing a group of young people who could make structural concrete, and form it into structures that would support tremendous weight. Hiring Michel Kappel was done both to get a down-time builder familiar with up-time building techniques, and as favor for Karl Schmidt. Claus Maurer was a master builder with more experience than Herr Kappel, but again, part of the reason for hiring him was to get him familiar with the available up-time tech. It wasn't her fault that they had fought with each other and with the teachers at the tech center and Carl over at Kelly Construction. Besides, materials were so expensive that the cheapest halfway decent material was quarried granite from the ring wall.

The radio, which had been quietly playing the morning music program in the corner, became suddenly louder. "Attention! There is an attack!" the radio blared. "Raiders, probably Croats, but we don't have that for sure yet, are attacking the high school and the town! Becky is at the high school." The announcer was clearly upset though not quite in a panic. "Chief Frost wants everyone from . . ." There followed a list of streets and locations to be evacuated and places for the people to go. "Everyone else who is not part of the reserves should arm themselves and stay secure in their homes."

Delia Higgins stayed in her home and listened to live reports of the battle on the radio. She thought about how stupid the fight over the hotel was.

When faced with the flat-out choice of investing in the hotel with other people's money, David had turned down her proposal. He'd then tried to finance it on his own, not even allowing the other members of the Sewing Circle to help. *And what did I expect him to do? David has always been a stubborn little cuss, and I've encouraged him in it more than most as long as it applied to Ramona or Karl, but when he looked at me, at my project and didn't approve . . . David's lack of faith in my judgment. Ha! That was his job. To use his best judgment and determine if a project could do what it claimed it could. He's just been trying to do what was right.*

In the weeks since Sarah had broken the news, Delia had made her displeasure known, but she and David had never actually talked about it. Delia had done the right thing. She had called the bank and put a temporary freeze on David using his shares as collateral for a loan, so he couldn't invest his own future in her hotel project. But she had done it for all the wrong reasons. She hadn't done it to protect David. She had done it to show that it wasn't the money that she was upset about, but David's lack of understanding of what she was trying to do. Now, with the Croats raiding the school, she wondered if she would ever have a chance to heal the breach.

Lauer Traugott was living and working in Kassel. He had been a tailor in Badenburg before the Ring of Fire, of moderate skill but good business sense. Now he ran a sewing machine shop and hardware store in Kassel, where he had relatives. Over all, he was fairly pleased with his situation. Among the attractions of his shop was the only radio in town. It had been pulled from a 1984 Ford that hadn't run for years before the Ring of Fire. It had a twelve-volt car battery and a pedal-cranked generator that provided power for it. It picked up the one and only radio station in the world, the Voice of America, or, as it was also known, the VOA. From a bit before dawn to a few hours after and again in the evenings around sunset, it reported the news and provided entertainment and education to anyone with a radio. Most radios were crystal sets, but his was a real up-time "transistor" radio. This morning the program was music and he was mostly enjoying this alone. Later this evening there would be a class in sewer systems, and his shop would be full of kids and some adult parents picking up some up-time knowledge.

"There is an attack!" the radio blared. Lauer sat entranced and frightened as the events and instructions unfolded. There was a vivid description of Chief of Police Dan Frost standing in the middle of the street and bringing the Croat charge to a crashing halt. There was less information about what was happening at the school. It was horribly frustrating. There would be a few minutes of what was going on in one place, then a delay while the announcer described and discussed what they knew of the overall situation, then a vivid description of what was going on somewhere else. The Spanish attacks on Eisenach and Suhl were proclaimed to be no more than diversions. By the time the radio cut off for the morning the attack had been repelled, but the number of casualties and amount of damage that Grantville had suffered was not clear yet. What was clear was that the attack would have been worse if a contingent of the king of Sweden's army hadn't shown up to save the day.

That evening, Lauer and a considerable contingent of

Kassel's elite were sitting by the radio when VOA came on the air. "Ladies and gentlemen, I am pleased to report that there were very few casualties from this morning's attack." The announcer went on to name every person killed or injured in the attack. It was a short list. One American woman and a few Finns killed in the actual attack, some woodcutters killed as the Croats snuck in, some injuries, not quite twenty names all told. "Two hundred and thirty-four Croat bodies have been found so far, and more than twice that number of injured have been captured." It was a terrifying thing. Three armies sent, two as a distraction, three armies destroyed, and Grantville not even hurt, just angered. The battle was discussed in some detail, and the anger at Wallenstein's Croats' focus on the high school was clear. Then things got vague. It was clear that something politically important had happened, but not exactly what.

The real news came the next day. Gustav Adolf, the king of Sweden, had led the Finnish rescuers himself. He and the President of the New United States had negotiated an alliance forming the Confederated Principalities of Europe. More, the New U.S. was to receive the administration of additional lands. Kassel would not be part of the New U.S., but it was part of the CPE. While all the details hadn't been worked out, the outline of the agreement said one thing clearly to anyone that would listen. The New United States now had a protector and the king of Sweden had a new ally, both militarily and economically. It would take the news a bit longer to reach Amsterdam, but it had traveled better than a third of the way instantly.

★ ★ ★

David Heesters was sitting in his office and fretting. Kaspar was worried as well, he could tell. It had been almost a week since the news of the Spanish army had hit town. When the message from Lauer Traugott arrived it was a surprise. David had never heard of the man. Well, the message was to Kaspar. Kaspar it turned out had met the man a total of once. Kaspar had received the message with apparent trepidation, read it, and passed it on. God, it seemed, would not allow Grantville to be destroyed or even badly damaged. It read like one of the Westerns Kaspar had told him of, with the cavalry riding to rescue at the last moment.

"You need to do something nice for Herr Traugott, son. He is a man who can think quickly and well." Hiring the messenger to make the trip was not cheap. Now, at least a few hours ahead of most of Amsterdam, they had the news that the expected attack had been thwarted, that future attacks were unlikely, and were even less likely to succeed and that the ease with which Grantville could reach new markets was greatly increased. All in all, the New U.S. had come out of the attack rather better off than it had been before.

Now for the important question, what to do about it? David Heesters had no doubt. He could get backing, based on this letter, to buy commodities whose value had fallen when the rumors of attack had started. When Kaspar had started buying things in the Amsterdam markets, the price of the commodities that Grantville needed had increased. When the rumors of an attack on Grantville and the up-timers had surfaced, the price of those commodities had fallen below what they had originally been. When this got out, prices would shoot through the roof. Herr Traugott's messenger was standing tiredly in the corner.

"Herr?" David Heesters asked, looking at the messenger.

"Fiedler, sir."

"I understand from the message you carry that you were promised a bonus of five guilders if the message reached us in good time and its contents were not discussed with anyone?"

"Yes, sir. That's what Herr Traugott told me. I haven't said a word about what the radio told us to anyone." Clearly Herr Fielder was a bit concerned about his bonus.

"Good man," David Heesters continued. "If you will consent to be our guest for the next two days and fill your mouth with the best food we can manage instead of gossip, I'm minded to make the bonus a full ten guilders."

Herr Fiedler grinned, showing some missing teeth. "I never was one for gossip, sir, and do enjoy a good meal now and again. Not but what the news we heard over the radio doesn't make a good story, but I'll be content enough to let others tell it for the next few days."

"Very well then. I may want to talk to you some more later. But for now . . ." He rang for a servant. "Show Herr Fiedler to the blue room, and see if you can come up with something especially nice for his dinner."

"So, Father, who do we ask?" Kaspar had clearly realized the situation.

"Not, I think, the tulip fund." David Heesters grinned at his son. "And we must move quickly."

They spent a few minutes discussing who to contact. They would need to tell some potential investors. Show them the message, and then find through them an agent who was not associated with OPM, and arrange for them to do the buying. Messages were sent quietly.

Herr Fiedler spent some of the next morning "gossiping" to selected friends of the Heesters. They had most of that day before another messenger arrived with a somewhat garbled account of the Battle of Grantville. By then they had most of the goods Kaspar was supposed to get. Then the merchants of Amsterdam started putting it all together and the orders for OPM shares started pouring in. It was all very exciting, and seemed, to many, proof of divine favor.

"I'd like to see Mr. Walker."

"What is this in regard to?" Jackie Lowry asked. Sarah Wendell had had run-ins with Coleman Walker before. Indirectly, when he had refused the loan to start HSMC, and later on directly, when she was negotiating to sell the paper on rent-with-the-option-to-buy purchases of sewing machines.

"A deposit."

"I can take care of that for you." Jackie didn't want another fight.

"Not this one." Sarah opened a briefcase and showed letters on parchment. Parchment was not a good sign. It was expensive and tended to be used only for very large transactions. The number of letters was not a good sign either. Jackie yielded to the inevitable and called Mr. Walker.

Sarah was suffering the financial version of buck fever as she strode into Mr. Walker's office. OPM was in danger of failing from its success. She needed Mr. Walker's help. At the same time it was a vindication.

Coleman Walker was a small-town banker who had been faced with a very sudden change of circumstance a bit over a year ago. He was also a stubborn man. The combination had had a few negative repercussions. In general he had done pretty well, first in setting the initial exchange rate, then in making a lot of very good loans. Coleman had a wife and two sons. He was a firm believer in the bunghole theory of child rearing: "Put them in a barrel and feed them through a bunghole." The standard bunghole theory says to drive in the bung when they turn eighteen. Coleman's version suggested the bung should be driven in about twelve and they should be let out to go into the army at eighteen. When they came back they would be people. Probably to everyone's advantage most of the family's child rearing was done by his wife. He had never been comfortable around children. He didn't have much faith in their judgment. Hadn't when he was a child, hadn't when he was raising his boys, and didn't now.

There was a grand total of one exception to that rule. Making that exception had taken most of the last year, and had not been a comfortable process. The exception was walking into his office. The fact that he had come to respect Sarah Wendell didn't make him fond of her. In fact she was an affront to many of his most deeply held beliefs. His explanation of Sarah Wendell was that she was a freak of nature, like a two-headed goat. But from what Jackie had said, she was a two-headed goat with money. And the Bank of Grantville needed money. The Bank of

Grantville now had two sections, the Reserve and the Bank. The Reserve determined how much money the Bank could loan out. The Bank part was getting close to the limit. Coleman didn't want to raise the limit because he was afraid people would lose confidence in the dollar. He was, however, fully aware of the need for more money. They needed money to finance the industrial revolution, especially the roads. Getting the products of Grantville industry to the surrounding towns and villages was expensive.

"Miss Wendell, I understand you have some deposits."

"Yes sir." Sarah smiled. "Herr Heesters' trip to Amsterdam produced rather larger investments in OPM than we had hoped for." She started pulling out the documents. Most of them were certificates confirming ownership of this or that product: lacquer, silk, chocolate, and other goods, each with an estimated value in guilders. Then she got to the one directly from Bank of Amsterdam, all properly set out, assigning ownership of a large amount of silver to OPM. The silver itself was still sitting comfortably in Amsterdam. But this wasn't the first such note the bank had received, just the largest. By far the largest.

Kaspar's trip to Amsterdam had brought a tremendous addition of funds to OPM, making it possible to invest in larger projects. In light of that and Delia's willingness to accept the aid of a financial manager, the hotel project with modifications was finally agreed on in late 1632. Brent and Trent never actually got to start their respective companies, not exactly. They ended up handing them off to friends from school and managers provided by OPM. The Partow Washing Machine Corporation, PWMC, used

Trent's designs and the Home Power Plant Corporation, HPPC, used Brent's, but though they did own stock they never actually ran either company. PWMC started putting out usable human-powered washing machines in the spring of 1633, about the time that Johan Kipper met Darlene Braun. But that's another story.

If the Demons Will Sleep

◖◉★◉◗

Eva Musch

There were still two hours until his appointment at the city hall. Istvan Janoszi was walking around Grantville at a rapid pace, watching it wake up on a Saturday morning. He had been thoroughly briefed before he came, so he knew that the pace of a Saturday should be somewhat different than the pace of Monday through Friday. Still, to some extent, the place bemused him. How could a city function without a marketplace? But it seemed to be that the market just spread throughout the town. Instead of gathering in one convenient, designated, and duly licensed spot, women were setting up their tables on the grassy spots around the houses—just on some of them, but not on all of them—and putting out their wares. Other women were gathering around them, prepared to bargain.

How did they find out who is selling what and where the vendor will set up? he wondered. From near one of the tables, a young child ran toward the paved street. A woman, heavy with late pregnancy, turned from the piles of secondhand clothing and said a few sharp words, calling her back. Istvan thought, almost, that he recognized the words. But no woman from his home village was likely to be here, among these Americans. It had been nearly twenty years since he'd been there himself.

He had never wanted to go back to that village in Slovakia. He walked on, deciding to take in the Saturday sermon at the Calvinist church before his meeting.

Two men came into the Leahy Medical Center. The receptionist knew the first man. He taught physical education at the grade school her two sons attended. Since she knew he was a Scot, she said, "Good morning" instead of "Guten Morgen." Then she asked, "May I help you?" And she beamed with pride.

"Wonderful, Maria, wonderful!" Guy Russell said with approval. "Your English is very good now. Just keep coming to the adult-education classes." From the confusion on her face, he concluded that this was not one of the answers that she had been taught to expect when she memorized her dialogues.

She repeated her question. "May I help you?" Then she tried the rest of her repertoire. "What do you want? Is someone sick? Is someone hurt? Do you have an appointment?" To her obviously great relief, the last question was the correct one.

"We have an appointment. We are here to talk to Nurse DeVries."

Several simple declarative sentences later, they were

sitting in a small office that Guy Russell was sure was a
cubbyhole, but which he had learned that the up-timers
called a "cubicle," waiting until the nurse came in. Mrs.
DeVries was not, he thought, perhaps the right specialist
for his companion's problem, but she had an inestimable
advantage over any other of the nurses in the hospital. The
man accompanying him was originally from Cleves, and
Nurse DeVries spoke Dutch. Indeed, she was Dutch.
There might be some hope of mutual understanding.

The man with Guy was named Endres Elstener. Or
maybe Andreas Aelstener. Or possibly Anders van
Aelsten. It had depended on the mood of the company
clerk: all three appeared on the records of the mercenary
unit to which he had formerly belonged and he answered to
them all, although he preferred the last one. The Grantville
Bureau of Vital Statistics found this very annoying. One
apprentice clerk sat there all day and did little else than
cut pieces of paper into rectangular slips, all the same size
to go in drawers, and write down the different ways to
spell the same person's name on them. Guy didn't know
how what official or bureaucratic alchemy they used to
decide which one was the "right" way. It would be too
complicated to ask.

Anders knew the teacher because his son, also, attended
the school. Nurse DeVries came in. Anders explained. At
first, his problem seemed simple enough. His woman was
within a month, he was sure, of delivering a baby. He
wanted to have an up-time midwife when the time came.
This would be the last baby, he expected. His Barbara
wasn't young anymore. They had been together a dozen
years, and she was no young girl a dozen years ago.

Between the ten-year-old in school and this day there had been four babies, born in camps and along roadsides. Only one still lived—a three-year-old girl.

"Just bring her to the hospital when labor starts" was Henny DeVries's first answer. "We always have a nurse midwife on call. Even better, bring her in for one or two prenatal checkups, first."

That was when things got complicated. "There can't be four walls," Anders said. "Barbara screams a lot when there are four walls around her." He looked at the nurse's expression and said defensively, "I didn't do it. I don't beat my woman. She doesn't need beating. Walls made her scream when I found her."

Up-time, Henny DeVries had been a psychiatric nurse. She didn't really want to contemplate the events in the unknown Barbara's past that might have brought her to the point of screaming if there were four walls around her and a roof over her head. "Where did you, ah, 'find her'?"

"In Bohemia. When I was fighting in the Crazy Halberstadter's men. She was by a roadside, with a shovel, trying to bury an old man. She wasn't strong enough to dig. I took the shovel and buried the man. Then I took her back to camp with me. She is my only woman. I am her only man."

"Full name?"

"Barbara Hartzi. Or Barbola Harczy? Maybe Harssy? Near that. I can't spell Bohemian. Anyway, I don't think she was born in Bohemia. Farther east. Maybe— *Ungarn*?"

"Hungary."

"Or maybe Transylvania. Perhaps Croatia. She knows what the village name was, but she doesn't know where it was. But she was not very small when her family fled into Bohemia. She was almost grown to a young woman."

Henny sighed, then asked, "Does she speak any German?" It was far too much to hope that she would speak English.

"She has learned some of mine—the Platt from Cleves. But she does not speak the German from around here," Anders replied.

Henny contemplated the problem of delivering a baby, outside of the hospital, to a possibly Hungarian woman who had, over the past ten years, learned to speak a little Low German, but would almost certainly forget it in the stress of hard labor. *We do not have problems*, she reminded herself. *We have challenges and opportunities*. Although, most of the time, she admitted that the Mormon women who volunteered at the hospital were worth their weight in gold, there were times that she wanted to strangle them. Those times were mostly when they recited that "challenges and opportunities" jargon!

Then something occurred to her. "If she can't stand walls, then your family can't be in the refugee housing. Where do you live?"

"In a camp. Up in one of the 'hollows.'" Anders smiled proudly. "I made it myself. I invite you to come and see. We have made a good home, my woman and I."

Henny looked at Guy. Guy looked at Henny. She asked, "Your woman? Or your wife?"

Anders frowned. "My woman. Who would authorize a marriage for such as us?"

Guy looked at Henny. Henny looked at Guy. "It's Saturday morning," he said. "I'm not doing this because I work for the school. I'm on my own time." Thinking, he added, "Cleves is Calvinist."

"Let's go, then." Henny stood up, the men following her. As she led them through the entrance, she stopped. "Maria. I am on call. I am not on duty. Clock me out for two hours, please." She looked at her wristwatch. "It is nine o'clock. I will come back in two hours." She checked as Maria recorded this on the chalkboard; then said, "Thanks."

Henny had been at the hospital, if not on duty, for three hours already. When she stepped outside, she said, "I do not believe this." The sun was shining. The sky was blue. The only clouds were tiny, white, and puffy. The breeze was warm. It was May. It might not last for long, but for this one day, it was spring. She whirled around in her white sneakers, clapping her hands. Then she remembered to go back inside, take off the sneakers, and replace them with heavy walking shoes. She cast a wistful glance at the bicycle rack, but there was no point in outdistancing the others. They walked.

Earlier that morning, the driver of the freight wagon that stopped in front of St. Mary Magdalene's Catholic Church had also been happy for the good weather. It was not fun to unload wagons in the rain. The crates that he brought were very heavy. It took four men to unload each one of them. Father Augustus Heinzerling, who signed for the delivery, had run back to the rectory for a crowbar and pried one of them open, right there on the sidewalk. His prayers had been answered: *Auserlesene, Catholische, Geistliche Kirchengesaeng* (Cologne, 1623). They had arrived safely, even though the press was outside the borders of the CPE, in enemy territory. Now he had enough copies of the most modern, up-to-date, and popular hymnal that the German Catholic church published to supply every member of the choir and scatter them out among the congregation as well. He could have danced for joy. He did jump around a little and give a few shouts. After all, it was spring.

Once the crates were all open, the freight wagon was long gone. Father Heinzerling didn't have four men to carry them the rest of the way, so he intended to leave the containers outdoors and carry the books a few at a time with the help of his sons. Unfortunately, Heinzerling discovered that while he was going for the crowbar, the teamsters had become too efficient. Two of the crates did not have hymnals for St. Mary's but books that clearly belonged to someone else and had been removed from the wagon by mistake. He thought about what to do with the others. The crates were very heavy. He called four men who were just walking past and had them lift them onto the pushcart that the parish used for moving tables and chairs. He pushed the cart down the street and out onto the highway. The Presbyterian church was on the outskirts of town.

Everybody arrived at their goal at once. Since the entrance was temporarily blocked by Father Heinzerling and his pushcart, Guy paused to take a good look.

The scene was very strange. The old church, covered with tar-paper shingles and with a peeling tar-paper roof, still stood where it had been for years, unchanged. Around it and over it, a new brick church was being built. Guy remembered that last Sunday, the outer shell of walls had been about as high as a man's waist. This morning, they were twice as high as a man's head and the bricklayers were up on scaffolds. The window openings had been carefully measured to match those in the existing church. Eventually, the windows with their precious up-time glass would be moved to the new walls and inserted, with the remaining openings in the larger building simply shuttered until the congregation could afford the elaborate finishing touches. After the roof was put on, the men in the congregation would carefully dismantle the existing church building, piece by piece, so that as much of the woodwork and flooring as possible could be reused in finishing the interior of the new one. The unusable bits would be carried out the front door, beam by beam, and made available to other people who needed building material.

Instead of a dying congregation of mostly quite elderly Free Independent Presbyterians, the Reverend Enoch Wiley now ministered to an extraordinarily mixed collection of parishioners that included nearly every variety of Calvinist in Europe. Henny DeVries, although she had lived in the United States for many years before the Ring of Fire, was Dutch by birth and Dutch Reformed. The Scots in Mackay's company had almost all been Church of Scotland and most of them did attend church when there was one available. There was an occasional German Calvinist, who, like Anders van Aelsten, came from one of the former mercenary companies. Occasionally, there were Swiss Reformed, of both the Zwinglian and Calvinist varieties (although Guy was not sure what most of them were doing in town, he had his suspicions). Now and then there was a French Huguenot, or a passing Calvinist exile from the Spanish Netherlands, or someone from the Calvinist churches of Bohemia or farther to the southeast in Europe. There were even, of all wonders, a few of the snobbish PCUSA-type American Presbyterians, although those mostly held themselves back or, worse, in the Reverend Wiley's opinion, went to the prayer services that had been organized by the Episcopalians.

After the Ring of Fire, the Presbyterians and their miscellaneous Calvinist adjuncts had outgrown the "yahoo shack" of Tom and Rita Simpson's wedding very fast. The Reverend Enoch found it glorious, at first. First, he had added a Sunday afternoon service that catered to those with ingrained objections to instrumental music and hymns not found in the psalter. Then a Sunday evening service. He had added a Wednesday evening service. He had added a Thursday morning service, with an after-school catechism class for the children. As the 24/7 industries got up and running, he had added the Saturday morning service, aimed at shift workers who could not both earn a living and keep the Sunday version of the sabbath holy, as well, which was followed by an afternoon catechism class. He was now, in May 1633, preaching or teaching eight times a week. At the age of sixty-two. And he wasn't getting any younger.

By January of 1632, the deacons and elders had approached the bank. By the spring of 1632, they had located an architect. By the fall of 1632, they had found a building contractor, although he had said that he had so many jobs that he could not start until the next spring. They had started digging for the new foundations in March. There was to be a new, much finer church. There was to be a separate wing with classrooms and church offices. There was to be a "fellowship hall" that would lessen the temptation of Presbyterians to have wedding receptions and other functions in places that permitted the serving of liquor.

Guy Russell found that last provision very, very odd. The temperance movement was not something that had influenced seventeenth-century Scots Presbyterians. But he donated to the project, nevertheless.

Guy had also suffered through fund-raisers. Yard sales. Bake sales. White elephant sales. Needlework sales. Ham and beans suppers. Pancake breakfasts. Guy did not care for this aspect of the separation of church and state. Overall, he thought, it ought to be done by a system of church finance. Certainly the Swiss and Germans who were serving on the Board of Presbyters insisted that it was much simpler just to let the tax collectors gather the tithes as part of their job and turn the proper portion over to the kirk. But the Americans didn't do it that way. Nor did the Scots.

And they needed the money. As Deacon Silas McIntire had said, in a rousing and inspirational speech to the congregation, "Folks, we've got two choices here. We can put our noses to the grindstone and do it all now in one fell swoop. Or we can track construction mud into church on our shoes for ten years while we work on it one little niggling bit after another. It's 'root, hog, or die' time folks, and I hereby officially move that we *root*." Even

Guy had voted to root after that harangue. Well . . . He had to admit that in an uncommon burst of enthusiasm, he had seconded the motion.

Gus Heinzerling was just as uncommonly happy to find that the Reverend Wiley was busy getting ready for the morning service, so that he only had to deal with Mrs. Wiley. He found her much more approachable. Much friendlier. Far less likely, in general, to start denouncing the pope as the Antichrist in the middle of a conversation about where to put two crates of metrical psalters that had come FOB from Edinburgh via Amsterdam. Completing the delivery, he waved cheerfully at the others and headed back to St. Mary's with his pushcart, looking like a man who had been delivered from dire peril.

Guy had been present at a few of the dialogues between Wiley and Heinzerling, so could make a good guess about why the priest looked so relieved. Guy actually rather enjoyed Reverend Wiley's denunciations of papistry. Some of them were so familiar that they actually made him homesick. Though not for long. Why go back to Killecrankie to listen to the minister denounce popery when there was a minister who could and did denounce popery quite adequately right here in Grantville, where Guy himself had a secure, well-paid, job?

For the first time, Guy realized that he was not a resident alien—he was an immigrant. *I should see about those citizenship papers,* he thought.

Inez Wiley turned her attention to the other visitors. "In plenty of time, I see, Guy," she said cheerfully. "The reverend should be right here any minute and we'll get the service started." Reaching into her tote bag, she pulled out a large, old-fashioned, brass school bell and rang it loudly. The church lacked a steeple and the down-time parishioners expected church bells. "The family hasn't come yet."

Henny raised one eyebrow.

"Ah, weel," Guy said. "I have another little task at the service here this morning. But," he said, turning to Mrs. Wiley, "first things first. This is Anders van Aelsten. He was brought up Calvinist. He works at the mine. He has a woman named Barbara. They have two children. They are expecting a third very soon. Henny and I think it's time for the reverend maybe to say a few words over them?" He smiled hopefully.

"If I had ten dollars for every time I've played 'Restore Thy Brother' since we landed in this century," Inez exclaimed, slapping the back of her hand to her forehead like a silent movie star, "I could pay for all the interior refurbishing of the church by myself."

"Aren't you happy to see them restored?" Henny asked. She was prepared to continue exploring this philosophical line of thought, being noted among everyone who knew her for extraordinary thoroughness, but first an extended family appeared from the left and then the Reverend Wiley appeared from the right. From the left, three exuberant children charged Guy, yelling "Hi, Mr. Russell! Good morning, Mr. Russell! Thanks for coming, Mr. Russell!" From the right, the Reverend Wiley solemnly shook hands and said, "God's blessings upon you, Deacon Russell."

They all proceeded into the church, where, within the

next hour, amid a congregation of Guy, Henny, and Anders, a few up-timer church ladies, miscellaneous miners and steelworkers with their families, a few catechism students whose parents had sent them early on the presumption that an extra sermon never hurt anyone, and one man whom nobody else recognized, the latest addition to the family of Heinrich Eichelberger and his wife, Catharina geb. Kraemerin, emerged from the baptismal font with the improbable name of Guy Angus Eichelberger. Improbable, of course, if the hearer didn't know that his godfather was Guy Angus Russell.

Occasionally, Enoch Wiley made an effort to be jovial. "Well, Deacon," he asked after he had shaken hands all around, gotten the stranger, whose name was Istvan Janoszi, to sign the guest register, and seen the Eichelberger family on its way in possession of a neatly filled-out certificate, "how many godchildren does that make this year? A round dozen? The kindergarten teachers should have plenty of little Guys to go around in five years or so."

"Ah," Guy muttered, seriously embarrassed. "Since January, it can't be more than four. The rest were last year. It's the school, ye know. The children come to know me, so I come to know the parents. With the refugees' lives being so overset, no aunts and uncles or old neighbors to stand as sponsor, they look to choose someone who has found a place in the town."

"Enoch," his wife interrupted. "Guy's friend is Anders van Aelsten. We have another family to regularize and restore to fellowship. Two children, with a baby due."

"There's a wee problem," said Guy. "His woman screams if she's made to come within four walls."

"Then," replied the reverend, "things are perfect. God moves in mysterious ways, His wonders to perform, Deacon Russell. Bring them tomorrow. The weather should be fine again. We shall dedicate the new building at the early service, even though it won't be—" He paused and looked at the partially completed walls and uncovered roof rafters. "—quite finished. Once the dedication has been completed, I'll perform the wedding right here, in between the old church and the new walls." When it came to restorations to fellowship, Reverend Wiley's philosophy was *strike while the iron is hot*.

"We'd better," said Nurse DeVries to Anders, "stop at the Bureau of Vital Statistics and get you a marriage license on the way out to your camp." The Bureau of Vital Statistics was open on Saturday in Grantville. For that matter, it was open on Sunday. The inhabitants of the town kept its staff very busy. "Inez, do me a favor, will you? Phone the hospital and tell them that the appointment that I scheduled for this on-call shift is going to keep me out all day and not where I can be called."

"Enoch can call them," the minister's wife answered. "I'm going with you."

Anders van Aelsten was rather confused. His English was still limited, but it was good enough for him to realize that a man who had come looking for a midwife was about to be handed a marriage license. Instead? Also? He was far from sure.

One thing, he knew. "First. I find Barbara. She is at the shopping. Miklos and Ilona are with her. Then we go."

★ ★ ★

They walked out of town on the highway, to a gravelled road. They followed the gravelled road up through the hills to a dirt road. They followed the dirt road to a path. They followed the path for quite some time. It took them forty-five minutes, but the others were catering to Guy's gimpy leg. The rest of them could have done it in a half hour.

Anders displayed his home proudly. At some point, early in its construction, it had begun with a wagon bed. "To think," he said to Nurse DeVries, "someone had just gone off and left it that way, hanging off the edge of the road. Just because it had almost splintered in half when a wheel came off and it fell. I was so lucky. Nobody had taken it for firewood yet when I came by."

He had hauled each half of the wagon bed up to his camp by fastening sledge boards to the underside, and carefully fitted the two pieces back together, splicing them and putting piles of stones underneath to hold it some distance off the ground to keep the wood from rotting. For the first few weeks, in the summer of 1631, the whole family had slept in that, with a canvas draped over the top on two stakes when it rained. They had already had the canvas.

But time had passed, and as Anders counted out pay-days, additions had arrived. The wagon bed itself now had three walls about eight feet high. Two of the walls had been topped by wedges, so the extra-large overhanging roof slanted and the water that fell on it, when rain came, went into gutters and then into a barrel.

Barbara glowed with pride as she showed off the barrel. It was wonderful to have a man who made a roof and a barrel to collect water, instead of making a yoke with buckets so his woman could carry water from the creek. It really was. In rather broken Platt, she told her visitors so.

Anders continued the tour. As an annex to the wagon bed, which now contained three well-stuffed straw pallets, not to mention, on the little girl's mattress, a neatly folded bright yellow acrylic blanket, he had built another three-walled shelter, placed at right angles, also with a slanted roof and a barrel beneath the low edge. For that, he had bought a—well, a something—that he had seen in an open shed in someone's backyard. Neither Guy nor Henny had the slightest idea what it might be. Inez knew: the grain bin and spout from a late 1940's Case combine. In any case, the grain bin, with one of the metal sides cut off and placed across the top, was now set into a base of rough fieldstones and had become a cooking stove, with the spout serving as the flue. It was, Barbara said, quite the finest arrangement she had ever had. It was wonderful.

The four walls problem? The fourth wall of the wagon bed shelter was a loose flap, made of the canvas, now folded three layers thick. Yes, it could be warmer in winter. But cold was better than having the demons seize upon his woman and cause her to scream so. Anders was firm about that. He had fenced a kind of courtyard, on the other two sides, so the wind did not blow the flap too badly. One fence, as high as the walls of the sheds and with an overhanging roof, protected their woodpile; the other was waist-high.

Switching to High German, Anders told Guy that he had told Barbara that the courtyard was for the safety of the little girl. And that, too, was true. But it was open to the sky and one side of it was low enough that Barbara could easily jump over it if ever even three walls became more walls than she could bear. Even though it had a nice gate, still, gates could be locked. Locked gates were frightening. His woman could jump the fence if she needed to. She was not locked in. Ever.

Guy was favorably impressed.

Henny DeVries was inclined to denounce the whole thing as scandalous. Before she could open her mouth, though—

"I," said Inez Wiley, "have seen worse. Far worse. In West Virginia. In the twentieth century."

Nurse DeVries kept her mouth shut.

"We can't possibly take responsibility for delivering a child under those circumstances. It's unsanitary. It's hopeless. There's no lighting. There's no backup. What if something went wrong during the delivery?" Henny DeVries was in full oration as they hiked back to town.

"If it comes to a pinch," Inez Wiley said, "I'll deliver the baby up there in the camp myself."

Henny stared at her, aghast.

"You don't know me, Henny. You and your husband haven't been here in Grantville all that long. I was born Inez McDow. I'm the youngest of eight—Ma was forty-three when I was born. She was born in 1900, she lived until 1987, and she was still delivering some babies up in these hollows when she was eighty. She started helping her own ma when she was just a girl. Her ma was born just a few years after the Civil War. I started helping her when

I was fifteen. That was 1958 or thereabouts. I kept on helping her till she quit—or was put out by the licensing requirements. Ask any of the older people in this town how many of them were delivered by Millie McDow. Just ask them. When you get to the younger ones who were born out in the country, after 1965 or so, ask how many were delivered by Inez, really, with Millie just sitting there giving directions. You'll be surprised."

Inez stopped in the middle of the road and took a deep breath. "You *don't* know us, Henny. I don't want to hurt your feelings, but, honestly, you don't. You and your husband had lived in Grantville for ten years before the Ring of Fire, but you'd never been to our church. The first Sunday you came, you were still 'Mr. and Mrs. DeVries' to everyone else there." She paused. "I don't want you to think that we're ungrateful for what you're doing—you, or Dr. Nichols, or any of the people who just got caught up in this by accident. But it's not the same as if you were from here."

"How long does it take to 'be from here'?" Henny asked.

She was feeling a little embarrassed. *It's true*, she thought to herself. *We—Arie and I—hadn't become part of this town. Although there were no Dutch Reformed churches at all in this part of West Virginia, we didn't go to the Grantville church. We attended a different Presbyterian church in Fairmont—one that was more, well, I don't even want to think "upscale." A little more cosmopolitan. A little more in line with our tastes and interests. A lot less, I guess I have to admit, hillbilly.*

"Well." Inez had continued talking while Henny was

thinking. "Well—probably about eighty years. That is, your grandparents were here, or came here. Your parents grew up going to the schools and churches around here, and making friends. You did, too. And your children did, or are doing, the same."

"Oh."

"And you know how it all fits together. Do you have a picture of the town in your mind? A map? Not how it's laid out on the ground and how the buildings look, but how it really works?"

Henny shook her head.

Inez picked up a stick. Drawing in the dirt, she started with what, for her, was the center of the world. "Here's us, the old members at the Presbyterian church." She drew a circle. "And here are all the other old-timers, no matter what—Church of Christ, Methodist, Baptist, and such." These circles all overlapped the first one. "Then there are the Catholics." This circle overlapped the others a little bit, but most of it was outside the remainder of Inez's drawing, which was starting to look like the production of a child who had gone wild with Etch-a-Sketch. She stared at it and muttered, "What I wouldn't give for a nice, new box of sixty-four different colors of crayons."

She drew a couple more small circles, out on the edge, unconnected. "We've always had some people who came and went, who weren't part of it. Don't think that I'm just talking about Tom Simpson's parents. There's that guy Mike Stearns brought in about computers. The people who were working on the new company that was going to start up. Those kind of people come and they go. At least, before the Ring of Fire, they used to go. Now they're stuck here. And even though I try to think charitable thoughts about them—they look at us the way the noble-men around here look at their peasants. Ignorant, unwashed, chickens to be plucked."

Inez looked down at her shoes. "But we need those guys. We need every single person in this town. No matter how much some of them despise the rest of us. Even if they don't think we're real people. Even if we have to put up with being humiliated to get what they can do. We've hired the construction firm guy to do the remodeling on the church. Because he can do it. He's put a business together. He has the know-how and he has the people."

"Humiliated?"

"I'm not saying that you would say these things, Henny. Or a lot of the other outsiders. But nothing happens in a small town that doesn't get back to other people. After Silas, and Guy here, and the other deacons went to Bob Kelly's office and signed the contract for the remodeling deal—after they left, he griped that he'd been reduced to taking a job from a 'committee of fundamentalist red-necks.' Shelby Carpenter was working there. She heard him, and don't think that she didn't enjoy repeating it. Big joke on the bluenoses, and all that. He's not," Inez continued, "nice." This was possibly the harshest criticism she could formulate.

Then, suddenly, she smiled. Standing in the spring afternoon's sun, she looked ten years younger. "Deacons!" she exclaimed. "I just knew that I'd forgotten something! Guy, I know that you had to miss the meeting yesterday afternoon and you were already gone when Enoch tried to call you today. We have the most marvelous news!"

"It did occur to me," Guy said, "that the minister seemed a wee bit perky this morning. Did the church inherit a fortune?"

"Gordon Partow came back from Jena with the man from Geneva." Inez looked at Henny. "Gordon is Andy and Grace's boy. You did know that Gordon had gone to Jena with Mallory Parker to teach English, didn't you?"

Henny shook her head.

"Well, Gordon's always been a good boy. But Andy's so ambitious and it's practically driven him mad that Gordon was sort of aimless, but he'll be fine now that he's aimed. During this colloquy thing the Lutherans had, Gordon met this Mr. Cavriani and told him how worried he was about our church not having anyone to take Enoch's place when—well, when the time comes, as God has ordained that it will come to all of us in due season. Mr. Cavriani said that Gordon should go to Geneva. Just think: the city where John Calvin himself lived and taught! To study. To be prepared, ordained, and sent back. He's going. Mr. Cavriani says he can work part time in his company's office to pay his way. He's sending him with a letter of introduction to his partner. If Andy decides that Gordon's just been sort of, well, incubating a divine calling without realizing what it was, they should get along fine from now on."

Inez drew a deep breath. "They came to the joint meeting of the elders and deacons to tell us about it. We were just sitting there with our mouths open. Then Charlie—Deacon Vandine—you do know him?"

Henny agreed that although she did not know Gordon Partow, she had met Deacon Vandine several times.

"Belva was there, sitting in the back of the room, waiting

for Charlie so she didn't have to walk home by herself after work. Charlie looked at her. She just gave a sort of half-smile and nodded. And Charlie said, 'We'll go, too. I'm fifty, but that's younger than Enoch here. The church is growing fast. I'll just stay long enough to get what I absolutely need. A minimum. Then we'll come back and help Enoch and Inez. That way, Gordon can stay long enough to get the whole kit and kaboodle."

Inez had turned her attention back to the overlapping circles. "Now, here you've got all the college kids who were at Rita Stearns's wedding." She drew another circle on the outside. "They're working hard, but they aren't really mixing, mostly. If you look at them, the only one who's matched himself up with a local girl is the Totman boy—he's engaged to Pris Berry." She drew a narrow loop, connecting this outlying circle with the main set. "Some might say that Laforrest up at the high school married a local girl, too, but he married Kristen Elias, and Dr. Elias isn't really quite from here." Next to the loop, she drew a small circle, overlapping both the main one and the college students. "Dr. Elias came from out of town, but he practices with Dr. Sims, who is from here. Kristen and her sister grew up here. You might say that they're on their way to being from here." She thought. "And the Curry girl married Laban Trumble." She drew another narrow loop. "But he died." She drew an X across that loop. "Aside from that, they're pretty much marrying one another. I talked to Mr. Cavriani about it. He says that it's like the Italian families from Lucca in Geneva. They've been there for seventy-five years, but they're pretty much still marrying each other."

Inez looked hopefully at Henny. "Do you see, sort of?"

Henny nodded. To herself, she was thinking that she'd only seen Inez as a frumpy woman who took minutes at church meetings and plunked out hymns on a tinny piano, Sunday after Sunday. She hadn't realized, not at all, that if Inez had been born to an affluent family in a midsize city in Michigan, instead of to a dirt-poor family in a dying town in Appalachia, she could have, maybe would have, ended up as a chief intelligence analyst at the CIA. Not the kind who listened to chatter from satellites. The kind who put it all together and briefed the Joint Chiefs of Staff.

Anders van Aelsten and Barbola Harczy, the "right" spellings having been determined by the Bureau of Vital Statistics, were married the following morning—as Andrew Alston and Barbara Hershey, since when the clerk asked, "Do you want those names in German or American?" as flatly as pre-RoF she would have asked, "Do you want fries with that?" Anders had expressed a preference for American. The deacons had hauled the piano out the front door of the old church building and onto the stoop, so there was music for the ceremony. Inez chose "Guide Me, O Thou Great Jehovah" to start the ceremony and "O, That the Lord Would Guide My Ways" to end it. She didn't want the guidance for them: she wanted it for herself. In between, she played "Restore Thy Brother" once more.

Since the first agonized cry from a subscriber—"Ouy you not write ouat I ouear? You write ouat ozzer brides ouear?"—Beryl Lawler had developed a completely standardized form for the reporting of weddings in the society

column of the *Grantville Times*. She had a flying squad of
young women and high school girls in each congregation
who took notes. When Susan Logsden turned these in to
the newspaper office, Beryl rested her forehead on her
palms and moaned.

> The groom wore olive green cargo pants and a
> red-and-brown plaid shirt. The bride wore a pair
> of orange maternity slacks topped by a long, full,
> boat-necked, black-and-white striped T-shirt with
> three-quarter-length sleeves. They exchanged
> halves of a coin. Official witnesses were Deacon
> Guy Russell and Mrs. Henny DeVries. The couple
> was also attended by their children, Miklos and
> Ilona. The groom, formerly with the count of
> Mansfeld's military unit, is employed at the mine.
> The bride is at home.

After church was over, Inez sat with Barbara and Henny
on a bench outside the Bureau of Vital Statistics while the
minister and Anders filed the record. She found out, in a
conversation mediated by Henny and by Miklos, who was
otherwise chasing his little sister around the parking lot,
that Barbara was really a rather sociable woman. She
found the isolated camp, although it was far preferable to
being seized by her demons, rather lonesome—and a little
frightening when she was there alone all day with the little girl. She had preferred her years of living in the train
of a mercenary army, where there were other women to
talk to, and other children about. Weather permitting, she
walked into town with the little girl at least one day a week

in order to see friends she had made there. If "the zoning" would permit it, she would much rather have a place to live in the town. But it wouldn't, so she was prepared to make the best of things.

She had also, it turned out, picked up a small amount of English. "Yard sale," at least. "Bargain." And "cute." She delivered herself of "cute" quite emphatically as she admired her daughter, all dressed up for the wedding in a little pair of chartreuse capri pants and a chartreuse-and-white checked gingham top with a machine-appliquéd daisy on the front, her hair held out of her face by two plastic barrettes. Barbara called Ilona over and demonstrated what she hoped to find at a "yard sale" most of all. Her current heart's desire. She pulled Ilona's hair back. "Ponytail maker."

Inez made a deal. She had ponytail makers at home. All but one of her granddaughters had been left up-time, but the ponytail makers that accompanied their passage through life, strewn around their grandparents' house, she had just gathered up two years before, tossed in a drawer, and forgotten. If Barbara would come to her for a prenatal checkup each week from now on, when she was in town, a ponytail maker would be her reward.

"You can do it, or someone else can do it," Inez said firmly to Henny, "in our garage. With the door up. Stop fussing about privacy. Anyone who stares in at a woman having a prenatal just has a dirty mind. I'll clean the garage."

Seventeen teenagers cleaned the Wileys' garage Monday afternoon. They scrubbed it with lye soap and sand, then hosed it down. It hadn't been so clean since the day it was built. It had a dirt floor, but that couldn't be helped. It was packed down hard. They swept it and threw a layer of sand on the top.

Nonetheless, Inez was glad that none of the fancy nurses came to do the prenatal the next day. Darla Bowers, the retired practical nurse who "helped out" in Dr. Adams's office, was "from here." She understood about garages with dirt floors and cabins in the hills. She had been born in one of those herself, a few years before Inez. She and Inez had gone to the same one-room country school together: Darla had been the "big girl" assigned to see that the first-grader Inez managed to walk safely back and forth. They were, in fact, cousins. Moreover, she had been born Darla Wild, and was a sister-in-law of Edith Wild who was going off to Prague to take care of Wallenstein.

Of course, it wasn't reasonable to expect people like Henny DeVries who weren't "from here" to know any of that—any more than they knew the other connections that kept Grantville's people in touch.

Darla suspected that Barbara was closer to delivery than Anders had thought. The first week, though, she agreed that she could go back to the camp.

"No, I definitely do not think that it would be a good idea for you to try to do a psychiatric evaluation." Inez was staring at Henny with horror. "Yes, I know that she gets seized by demons and starts screaming if she's closed in. But she can live with that. Her family can live with that. What good would it do if you stirred them up?"

Henny sputtered.

"She doesn't speak much of any language that you speak. You don't speak any language that maybe she can talk just fine. Do you know Bohemian? No. Do you know Hungarian? No. Anders isn't even sure that what she spoke as a child *was* Hungarian. I remember when our boys were over in that Kosovo place. It seemed like every time we listened to the news, there was some other language in Eastern Europe. Serbian? Albanian? Chinese? Who knows what she speaks?" Inez knew Grantville very well. Past the borders of her native county, much less her native country, her grasp of geography became considerably shakier.

"We ought to try to do something," Henny protested. "At least fix her up to the point that her family can live in a decent, heated house. What are they going to do with that poor baby, next winter?"

"Whatever they did with Miklos and Ilona," Inez responded pragmatically. "What do you want to do? Parade her in front of everyone who shows up in town speaking some language that we don't know, asking if they recognize the words that she says? If someone does, keep him here for a three-way conversation about psychology? You don't have any medicine to give her. Let sleeping dogs lie."

Inez suspected, however, that Henny wasn't inclined to let those napping pooches alone. She talked to Darla. Darla talked to somebody else whom Edith had met while nursing Wallenstein after his surgery. That somebody asked around among various political and business agents, the "men in Grantville" who represented potential allies and enemies, trading partners and rivals, and found one who was fluent in Hungarian. He agreed to talk to Barbola Harczy, later Barbara Hartzi, and now Barbara Hershey, to find out whether Magyar was, in fact, her native tongue.

"Oh," Inez said happily. "I've met him. He's come to church a couple of times."

After the second checkup, Darla didn't want Barbara to go back. If only she would stay in the Wileys' garage until after she had the baby, Darla begged, then if the baby should need assistance, they could take the little one right to the hospital. They couldn't do that if she was up at the camp. They promised to leave the garage door open. They called Anders at work at the mine. They called Guy Russell at the school. They even called Henny DeVries at the hospital. Barbara insisted on going back home. School was out. Miklos would be there. He could run to call Inez if anything happened before the next week.

"At least," Inez said, "stay here long enough to talk to the man who speaks Hungarian. You and Ilona can walk back up with Anders when he gets off."

"Hungarian? Why?"

"Anders said that you were Hungarian, he thought. Wouldn't you want a chance to use your own language again?"

"Not send me back?" Barbara started to panic.

"No, no, of course not. You are a citizen here now." Inez wasn't getting through. Miklos had run off to play. *Guide me,* she prayed. She didn't get guidance. But Barbara's water broke. Darla and Inez got very busy for a couple of hours. And Barbara stayed put, in the Wileys' garage.

★ ★ ★

Guy Russell brought the man who spoke Hungarian. He was middle-aged. He looked very inconspicuous. Not at all intimidating. He spoke to the woman on the pallet in the garage very softly, for quite some time. After the first few words, however, in his native, homely, Slovak dialect rather than Magyar. Then he offered to stand godfather to her fine new son.

That would be lovely, Barbara replied. It would be nice to have an old neighbor as sponsor. But they should ask Anders. She thought that Anders would agree. Istvan was a fine name, very fine. But if he did not mind, they owed much to Deacon Russell. Perhaps there could be two godfathers. Istvan Guy? Or Guy Istvan?

The man who spoke Hungarian and Slovakian was not hypersensitive. Two godfathers would be quite acceptable, he assured her. He left her to her rest and went to talk to her waiting patrons.

Most of what he had to say was aimed at Henny DeVries, even though there was quite a group gathered in the Wiley's living room.

"You asked if she had 'buried her memories,'" he said. "No, she remembers. She knows where her demons come from. She just cannot make them go away. So she lives with them."

Istvan Janoszi shrugged. "Her family belonged on the estates of Count Ferencz Nadasdy and his wife. Nadasdy died in 1604. There had been—tortures—before his death. After it, however, there was no control at all. There were complaints to the authorities. From the ministers at the local church. From the guardian of the heir. To the Hungarian Parliament. Directly to Emperor Mathias. But nothing was done until Palatine Thurzo intervened at the end of 1610 and confined the countess Erzsebet. Ah, immured her actually. Walled her up. Her accomplices were tried and executed, but she was not."

"The countess Erzsebet?" Henny asked.

"Elisabeth Bathory. The Blood Countess. Barbola was on her estate at Castle Csejthe—at her mercy—until then. Two of her own sisters from Catiche village were . . ." He paused, seeking the right words. "Among those chosen as sacrifices. Among the frozen corpses found outside the castle after the countess and her accomplices had taken them. Indeed, Barbola was chosen also. She was already caged. She had already been tortured and bled for several weeks. Bled to make the countess her cosmetics to keep her beautiful and youthful. If Thurzo had not intervened on the day that he did, she would soon have been as dead as they."

"I thought," Henny said, "that Elisabeth Bathory was a figment of the imagination of the people who write B-movie scripts."

Istvan had no idea what a B movie might be, but he did know about plays, scripts, and imagination. "The countess died," he said, "on August 21, 1614. Less than four years before this war broke out. The Defenestration of Prague was May 23, 1618. There are minutes of the investigation into the case. She left a will. She was very real."

Istvan paused a moment, wondering how to explain. "In the confusion after the arrests of the countess' accomplices, Barbola' and her father fled to Bohemia—quite illegally, of course. They were serfs. They belonged to Nadasdy's estates." He waved a hand. "No, do not worry. I will make no attempt to remove one of your citizens. She has been gone a long time. Perhaps the Nadasdys have forgotten her. She must have been in Bohemia for several years before she met van Aelsten."

He looked at them. "The countess is dead. Her former servant girl now has another fine son to join the older children. Let the demons sleep—for both women."

Istvan shrugged his cloak over his shoulder as he went out into the cooling night air. He was quite, quite sure that the Nadasdy family would cause Barbola Harczy no trouble. Among those who had brought the—problems—in Csejthe to the attentions of the authorities had been a young peasant in Catiche village who had found the courage to walk all the way to Bratislava and petition the young count's guardian to investigate the disappearance of his fiancée. The guardian had investigated; the young peasant had been taken into the count's direct service. A great magnate of Hungary had immense business interests to manage. It would have been a dereliction of duty on the guardian's part not to add a subject with intelligence and courage to his staff.

For all the years since Bethlen Gabor betrayed the Protestant revolt in Hungary in 1626, Istvan had been Pal Nadasdy's man in Prague. Temporarily, he was Pal Nadasdy's man in Grantville. The count, he knew, was far more anxious to rehabilitate his family's good name than to find one escaped serf. It was not easy to be the son of the Blood Countess: he would not take actions that reminded people. In any case, Istvan had no intention of telling him where she was. The count's staff included lawyers and tax collectors who were frequently overofficious in attempting to enforce his rights.

He looked back. Through the windows of the Reverend Wiley's house, he could see lights. The garage, where he knew that Barbola Harczy rested with her child, was darkened. He was Nadasdy's man. And his family, too, came from Catiche.

It is time, he thought, *for all of us to let our demons sleep. If they will.*

Hobson's Choice
⊱◈★◈⊰
Francis Turner

Cambridge, England
1632 AD

A hesitant knock at the door disturbed the summer afternoon of study and desultory argument.

"Who is it?" asked Thomas Healey.

The door opened and a skinny but well-dressed youth, much encumbered with baggage, stood in the dimly lit, cramped landing. Standing next to him was Jack Hobson, the college porter. After a pause, in which the youth opened and shut his mouth several times without managing to say anything, the porter spoke. "Gentlemen, this is your new lodging mate, Master Richard Abell. A fellow commoner."

This statement was not met with rapture by either of the current occupants of the room. Thomas Healey and his longtime friend, roommate, and fellow BA, Simon Gunton, had been rather dreading this moment. They had been alone together ever since their former colleague abruptly and simultaneously inherited a large estate and lost the paternal insistence on education. He had departed the cloisters of academia with no intention to return.

The duo had discussed the generosity of newly rich young men with John Smith, the college president and bursar. They pointed to the appreciation one might have for the little courtesies such as maintaining a place for him should he choose to return and so on. Unfortunately, it seemed that a new academic year wiped the slate somewhat cleaner than they would prefer. Now they would have to share their rooms with another young snot.

"If the young gentleman would care to acquaint himself with his new companions, I'll just put the baggage by the cot," continued the servant, as he prodded the young man into the room.

"Ah . . . yes. Good day, sirs. I trust I am not disturbing your studies excessively."

Simon Gunton decided to take pity on the new student. After all, it wasn't his fault. And at least he wasn't one of those sprigs of the nobility who considered the entire world their servants.

"Welcome, young Abell! I'm Gunton and that scowling visage's name is Healey. Don't worry about the scowl; he's always like that even with a pot of ale in front of him."

At that welcome the young man seemed to gain some measure of confidence. In short order he was able to shake hands with both Gunton and Healey, swiftly supervise the placement of his luggage, and escort the porter to the door while unobtrusively slipping a coin into his hand. Then he turned back to the others and suggested that after he had unpacked and ordered his belongings he would be pleased to purchase some ale while they acquainted him with his new world.

An hour or so later, Gunton and Healey escorted young Abell down to the quad. They pointed out the location of the important communal parts such as the chapel, the library, the hall, and, "last but most definitely not least," the buttery. From the buttery emerged, as if on cue, two more young men and a torrent of abuse for "idlers and wasters who have nothing better to do than sup ale and dispute rampant speculation and gossip fit for market wives while obstructing those with gainful employment."

Healey looked at the two and called out to one of them:

"Dunster, my good man, you have wrought ruin for us all this afternoon! We are now perforce required to mix with the common herd in an extramural tavern and expose ourselves to who know what licentious behavior—perhaps you would like to accompany us to make amends?"

The man to whom this was addressed—slightly older than his companion—shrugged off the blame with a cheerful smile

"By all means, Healey. It would seem that you have fallen upon hard times and are required to share your lodgings with a companion again—to wit this elegant young gentleman. I shall be pleased to accompany you, purely to ensure that you do not corrupt his morals with your despicable Arminian views." Turning to Abell, he continued, "I am Dunster, my companion is Saltmarsh. Contrary to the views of the honorable president, we are neither idlers nor gossipers as we will be pleased to demonstrate. Methinks the president has been discoursing with our master. As usual, he has discovered that magisterial might doth prevail over both bursarial budgets and presidential privileges."

Abell was in turn introduced by Gunton. The five walked out past the porter's lodge and across the street toward a door that had a peculiar fish hanging over it. This, Abell was informed, was a "Pickerel." He received the further advice that the Pickerel was the preferred tavern for the right-thinking students. It combined propinquity with decency. However, it was also noted that the Three Swans—the "bursar's other buttery"—was also a Magdalene tavern. It was owned by the Bursar and was known to have been bequeathed to the college.

The problem with the Three Swans, explained Healey, was the clientele. Since it was closer to the castle up the hill and at the corner of a busy crossroads, it tended to have nonlocal customers. The Pickerel served the bakers, brewers, and other trades that were packed into the maze of lanes between Magdalene and St John's College, up the river. Saltmarsh explained that this difference was important: due to the traveling nature of the Three Swans customers, it was unwilling to advance credit to its customers. The Pickerel was more accommodating. Since Saltmarsh was, as he cheerfully admitted, a sizar—an undergraduate who acted as a servant to reduce his tuition costs—Abell presumed he had often made use of this generosity.

They took their seats around a table in the middle of the room. As the junior, Abell insisted on paying for ale for all of them. "Marry, 'tis a small enough cost and one that will be repaid manyfold by your imparting such advice as may assist in my navigating the perils and monsters of this place."

Dunster took it upon himself to impart the first advice and introduced the redheaded maid who was distributing the beer. "This young lady is Elizabeth Chapman—Bess to her friends—daughter of our host. She is critical to befriend, lest you wish to expire from unquenched thirst. Like her regal namesake, she is mistress of her realm and prone to banishing courtiers who displease her."

Abell looked on with bemusement as the young woman—surely not more than a year or two older than his sixteen—bantered with Dunster and Saltmarsh, threatening them with unspeakable punishments should they corrupt the morals of this handsome young gentleman. He felt compelled to intervene to stop the unaccustomed compliments.

"Mistress, I fear you do me too much honor. My father is no more than a London merchant, not even a guildsman. My family keeps on telling me that I spend far too much time reading and not enough time at any activity that might improve my frame."

"Is that so?" Bess responded. "Well, you are in good company here. Both Dunster and Saltmarsh arrived here as miserable sizars with no more meat on their bones than a February cow. Now Dunster is an honorable BA and while 'tis true that Mr. Saltmarsh is still a sizar, there is considerably more of him than there was a year ago. But I'll spare your blushes. I must be away to bring sustenance to others."

Bess left them and they fell to discussing families and

origins. This led on by turns to discussion of the college, both its people and its religion.

". . . now I am myself much taken with Bishop Laud's view that excessive simplicity is a false modesty and as much a sin as outright popery," expounded Healey. "The master is much of my opinion. We do not have the Romish trappings in chapel but neither are we as plain as the Genevans or their fellows across the river as Sidney Sussex might wish. Rituals help bind us to God and we can show our devotion by decorating God's house at least as well as our own abodes. Mr. Dunster, as I well know, does not agree with me on this point but yet we are willing to sit at the same table and debate the issue. You will find this is usual within the college. We are united in our detestation of Rome but in very little else. We manage to get along without too much disharmony. Indeed, the main source of disharmony is not theological but one might say etymological. To wit—do you prefer your Smith to be spelled with an 'i' or a 'y'?"

Abell looked a little confused at this.

"Our master is Henry Smyth," Healey elaborated, "with a 'y'. He was formerly a sizar at Trinity and more recently is my lord Howard's chaplain. He is a man of some power and influence within the university and the land. Despite that he is not, by any means, well connected within this community of Mary Magdalene. He has been master merely five years. Our bursar and president, on the other hand, is John Smith with an 'i'. He has been bursar since the early years of the reign of King James and has stood by this college in thick times and thin. And all that time he has been becoming richer and more critical to the smooth running of the college. Indeed, one suspects he had rather hoped to be master himself upon the demise of Goche.

"Now the two have had numerous battles over this and that," he continued. "The fellows are eternally split between those who favor the present wealth and favor of the bursar and those who prefer the master and such future favors as may come from him and his patrons. We juniors, even those of us with a degree, must therefore navigate between the Scylla of one and the Charybdis of the other. Any junior who provokes a confrontation had best be prepared for subsequent sanctions."

There were nods of agreement from the other seniors at this summary.

Saltmarsh added, "Of course, as a fellow commoner you won't be meeting the bursar as regularly as a sizar. But any serious transgression against the statutes will mean that you will have the pleasure of an interview with the same man in his other guise as president. When you do so, do not under any circumstances claim that you had leave from the master lest you become the cause of yet another battle. As they say: When great men fight, the causes of their wrath are likely to get trodden underfoot."

After a thoughtful pause, Abell spoke up. "Sirs, you have well repaid my investment in ale and I thank you. Perhaps we might move onto more philosophical matters? My father and our neighbors have argued endlessly about this new place in Germany—this Grantville—with its Americans and their peculiar ideas—"

Gunton snorted and broke in. "Oh, come on! Surely you don't believe all that rubbish. It's just an excuse for the Habsburgs to explain why they are losing to the Swedes!"

"Pray pardon, but I have met one who has been there. The royal physician, Dr. Harvey, did return from there upon one of my father's vessels and we did sup with him in London. The place most certainly exists and they do assuredly speak some kind of English and not the Dutch of their neighbors. Dr. Harvey had some part of a book which was printed on shiny paper and had images in colors that were like life. He would not let us read the text. He said His Majesty should choose who might have that privilege. Even so, the images were so real it was like looking through a window. He did show us a copy of a portrait of Queen Elizabeth that I have seen with mine own eyes. It was as if the artist had painted it, save that the page was completely flat and too thin for paints. I cannot say that—"

This time it was Saltmarsh who interrupted. "So is it true that they come from the future? Or are they merely wizards from Cathay or somewhere?"

"Dr. Harvey said he could not be sure whether they came from *our* future or not, but that he was sure they came from *a* future," Abell said. "They knew too much about people and places they could have no direct interest in or knowledge of, he said. They treated him well because in their past he had done some favor to their ancestors some years from now. But he said that they also told him that because they had come here the future would change so that he wouldn't do the same things. That doesn't make sense. Surely you either do something or you don't."

"Ha, ha, Dunster!" said Healey. "That's one in the eye for you predestinationists! Consider, you could find out what you did and then do something else. Think of it—you could do mighty deeds in a history that never happens! Perhaps you go to heaven there and are damned here. Or do you think that you will be allowed to choose which life to use when you come to be judged?"

"My dear Healey, restrain yourself. The doctrine of pre-destination is not yet wrecked. Even should there be two histories why should one not be blessed or damned equally in either? The events may be different but the soul will be the same and the soul will behave in like manner. But there is surely a simpler solution. Mayhap these Americans have been placed here on earth by the Almighty to provide a lesson to us all. They might think they had a history before they were here but the Omnipotent Almighty could surely cause them to come into existence with memories should He wish that. After all He created food to feed the five thousand, creating bread and fish from nothing. If He could do that with bread and fish, why should He not be able to create people? As Creator, He did create this world once, why should He relinquish the power of creation today?" Dunster paused smugly at this point, secure that he had comprehensively demolished Healey's arguments.

After a pause Gunton brought up another point. "Whether or not they prove or disprove predestination, since we are assured they exist they do challenge a number of other beliefs. For example we are told that they have no religion, that they welcome anyone—Christian, Jew, or heretic—that they have no kings and no respect for the established order. Surely this is greater import. Luther challenged the authority of Rome and the result has been more than a hundred years of bloodshed to free ourselves from the tyranny of Rome. Now these Americans challenge the authority of monarchs and nobles everywhere. How much blood will be shed to prove or disprove this?"

Abell had no idea about the causes of wars, but that reminded him of something else. "Not only that, they let women do as they please. Dr. Harvey said that even some of their soldiers were women! Not to mention their governors. Why, their leader is married to a Jewess who seems to have authority in her own right."

Utter silence reigned as this was digested.

"Well then, perhaps you are right, Mr. Dunster," spluttered Healey. "Surely the Almighty has placed this Grantville upon the earth to be a modern-day Sodom and Gomorrah. It may be an object lesson to be destroyed. Perhaps it is a warning to us of the limits to humanist reform and rationality. A place that denies the differences between the sexes is surely as depraved as Sodom and Gomorrah and as destined to eternal damnation. Why, the place must be a very bedlam of false prophets in the first place. Governed and defended by women? Well, hubris seems almost too kind a word for it! I just hope that its inevitable collapse does not presage the collapse of Lutheran Protestantism as well. It seems that the most likely cause of its destruction will be a Catholic army."

Healey's voice had risen in volume as he voiced his outrage and his words were clearly audible to the tavern's queen. This Bess, perhaps in memory of the namesake she had been compared to earlier, was unwilling to hear her sex denigrated without complaint and rushed over to make a defense.

"How can you say that? Why, you, along with all true Englishmen, admire Queen Elizabeth. If she can rule so well, why cannot another? And what, pray, is so special about soldiering that it should be restricted to men? As many a would-be cutthroat has discovered, a woman can wield a pistol as well as a man!"

Healey was not to be dealt with so easily and ignored the earlier warnings of the price of Bess's displeasure. He vehemently responded, "One good queen does not mean much. Think of the actions of her sister Mary and the chaos caused by that other Mary, queen of the Scots. Recall the pernicious influence of the Medici ladies upon the kingdom of France. It is perhaps a harsh truth but such is the way of the world. The evidence seems clear; most women are too driven by passion and emotion to rule justly and wisely. I believe the same holds for other crafts. Soldiering is not just a matter of killing. It also requires discipline and steadfastness. 'Tis the same reason women cannot be educated beyond a certain level. As gentle creatures, they do not have the fortitude to continue in the face of constant adversity. For a short period passion may overcome their usual properties, but passion cannot be sustained. In the long term all of us remain true to our essential properties. The property of woman is to nurture, while the property of man is to strive."

As Healey paused for breath, Dunster took up the baton. "My colleague is right. To be sure, women can show courage against adversity but it is passive. She does not strive to overcome but merely submits, with or without complaint, to her fate. A woman's virtue is constancy, to remain true to her own. A woman may be roused to defend her children. She may even sacrifice herself for them, but that is surely an example of the nurturing instinct. To be a soldier, to be a scholar, to be a ruler requires more than passivity. It requires that one be willing to push against the limits, not accept them; to conquer the passion and direct it inward. It requires self-discipline and that is not something that can be learned."

Bess was less than impressed with these arguments.

"Oh, really. Scholars! How do you know? Have you ever in fact tried to educate a woman? Or do anything other than leave her in her current state?"

Bess answered her own questions. "Of course, you haven't. Because everybody knows that women can't do that. Well, now, in this Grantville we have a place where people don't know that. And according your friend, Abell, when women are given the chance they can actually do these things too."

She paused for a moment then continued, "Healey, you gave all these examples of bad queens, but you seem to have forgotten the large number of bad kings. Kings who are as capricious, as poor rulers as any queen. I'm told half the princes of Europe are drunkards and most of the rest arrant cowards who hide behind privilege and never lead their subjects. And as for education, recall that many of the colleges in this town have been founded or refounded or supported by women. Why, we even have a Queens' College! If women can found colleges, why should they not also benefit from them? 'Tis well known that some noblewomen have private tutors and learn a great deal. Why should they be any different to your own sisters? I wager we could fill a college of women and there would none of the idlers that call themselves fellow commoners!"

Abell felt obliged to defend the concept. "My lady, I have the honor to be a fellow commoner! I certainly have no desire for sloth. I fought my father to be permitted to study. He wanted me to lead traders to Muscovy and other icy wastes."

"No doubt you will be the exception that proves the rule," Bess responded. "I think I recall that all your colleagues, even those now graduates, did in former times express themselves most forcefully about the lack of scholarly devotion of most fellow commoners. Gilded popinjays who pretend to scholarship and whose only virtue is that they provided employment for impoverished sizars was the consensus reached last Michaelmas, was it not?" Bess smiled sweetly at Healey and Gunton, who had the grace to look somewhat abashed. "If memory be one of the keystones of serious scholarship, then I think I may perhaps be a better scholar than either of these."

Gunton tried to defend himself. "Now then, Bess, we were not claiming such was an immutable law of God, merely that in our observation this was the usual case. A lad who has overcome paternal disapproval to study is entirely different to one who has yielded to paternal desires to claim a learned, if not clerical, son."

"If that's the case, why should women be any different? If women actually had the opportunity to attend university you would see whether or not women were passive. It's hard to be active when there's an entire world insisting that you not behave that way. I still say that the main reason women are claimed to be unable to be educated is because no one has ever tried."

"But what point would it serve you to attend a university?"

Healey asked. "What could you do with your knowledge? Most graduates intend to use their learning to become pastors. Even within the university it is required to take holy orders to proceed. No woman can be a priest."

"I've never understood why a woman can't be a priest. It doesn't matter, though. Not everyone is a priest; there are lawyers, physicians, philosophers at the least." Bess turned to the youngster. "Tell me, Abell, what do you propose to do with yourself once you have gained the learning that you desire?"

"I was hoping to study medicine as did Dr. Harvey. Before he spoke of Grantville I had intended to travel to Padua to study anatomy, but now perhaps I should go to Grantville instead. They have more knowledge than Padua and they aren't papists."

Dunster thought of the garbled tales and rumors that had been circulating in Cambridge. "Admirable sentiments, and I wish you the best of fortunes in your endeavors. If they are not warlocks or devils you will indeed be better in Germany, at least spiritually. But have you considered the physical risks? Germany has been fighting for years and an army could loot the place in a day. 'Tis true that, at the moment, Gustav Adolf is on the ascendant and these Americans have allied themselves with him. But Magdeburg was sacked only last year, why should Grantville be any better? Still you have some years to go before you need make up your mind. Perhaps things will be more peaceable then. And perhaps by then we will have more information from visitors about what this place really is."

Bess wouldn't let the conversation get sidetracked this

way. "Well, then, you are not apparently planning on becoming a priest! Is there any reason why a woman should not become a physician? And kindly don't bother to talk about the possibility that our delicate sensibilities cannot stand the sight of blood or death. I've probably butchered more animals than all of you put together. And while this inn is a lot quieter than the ones nearer the castle, we've seen plenty of tavern brawls here and worse! I misdoubt I'm the only woman who can say likewise—just ask any farmer's wife."

Saltmarsh, a farmer's son himself, had some sympathy with the barmaid but still felt obliged to point out the problems with her argument. "Perhaps, in theory, a woman might be capable of the physical acts required of a physician but there is still the delicacy of discussing a patient's health. A man would be most embarrassed to talk about such things to even his wife, let alone some strange woman. Other physicians would be likewise. Still, even were that obstacle overcome I don't see what good it does us to argue. No woman would have enough Greek or Latin to read Galen or any other of the ancients. She would be unable to become properly trained. There are enough men who pretend to be physicians, and many of them are, at best, half-trained quacks. We don't need females added to the mix."

Bess and Abell simultaneously tried to point out the flaws in that one.

"Your rhetoric is unsound—that a woman cannot—"

"That argument chases its tail . . . go ahead, sir. Methinks we have found the same flaw in the logic."

"Thank you, milady. First 'tis claimed that a woman

should not be educated because she can do nothing with it, then you do reverse your claim and state that a women cannot become a physician because she hath not the education. The correct logical deduction is surely that if a woman were to receive appropriate education then she could be a physician. Your statement that the world does not lack for bumbling quacks surely brings home another truth that echoes the previous comment about fellow commoners, namely that many men show limited desire to push the limits and strive against passive acceptance. We cannot directly deduce that since many men appear to have womanly virtues that the reverse is true. However, it seems not implausible.

"Consider Dr. Harvey's notorious treatise on blood and circulation. Despite that it is counter to the wisdom of the ancients, it follows directly from countless observations made over the period of a score or more years. Perhaps the same applies to women and education."

There was a thoughtful pause as Abell's elders considered and accepted the logic of his arguments. The pause was followed by the shuffling of feet and straightening of clothing that indicated a desire to quit the field of battle while still able to retreat in good order. Murmurs of "must be getting back now, must *mumble mumble* before *cough*" and the like followed apace. Indeed, Abell was left behind to settle the account while the others rushed the door at a speed that was only just dignified. Bess shared a conspiratorial grin as she gathered up the tankards.

"Mr. Abell, you seem to have discommoded your seniors with an ease that belies your years. Pray return often that we may attempt more such victories."

Abell, realizing that two of these seniors were his roommates and fearing possible reprisals, seemed less happy

"Oh, never fear," Bess added. "Healey will be using our arguments next week to trap anyone he can. Dunster pays little attention to anything beyond books and etchings and Gunton will forgive anything that he can use to make a puritan look like a fool. In Magdalene, debate and rhetoric are diversions, not serious."

In his relief at not having blighted his Cambridge career in the first hour, Abell was moved to generosity toward his new acquaintance.

"You know, if you had the desire, mayhap we could try and see what you could learn. I'm no tutor but I have the books and . . ." He stopped, unsure what Bess would think of his offer. Perhaps it was condescending; perhaps she would think he made it for other, improper, reasons.

Bess seemed to understand his hesitation for she smiled at him. "Why, thank you, kind sir. I fear there are many demands on my time, but mayhap we can find some spare moments here and there. My father will look askance at me if I continue to dally with you, so be off now. We'll discuss this further anon."

A few days later Abell had become familiar with the routine of life at Magdalene. He had been assigned one of the fellows as a tutor, had his first tutorial, and been farmed off to his roommate Healey for day-to-day tutoring. The weekday started early with a lecture at six in the morning, followed by chapel. Chapel was followed by breakfast at about eight o'clock. That was followed by a second hour-long lecture. As a fellow commoner, Abell was free of communal commitments after the end of that lecture until hall in the evening. He was merely required to spend some hours being tutored by Healey. Since it was still summer neither he nor his roommates had trouble getting up before six, as dawn was a good hour earlier. However, he was warned that this would become considerably harder as the year progressed.

Healey and he had come to the arrangement that they would spend the mornings studying together and thus in the afternoon he was on his own. The first two or three afternoons he had spent with Gunton and Healey, wandering amongst the printers, booksellers, and other scholastic suppliers in Cambridge. He purchased the items he had not brought with him. On the fourth day, a Saturday, he was told in no uncertain terms that he was on his own. Healey reminded him that, despite it being market day, failing to show up to hall would be a bad start to his college career.

Healey and Gunton then left him in their room to consider his books and possessions while they left for some nebulous destination that did not require the presence of juniors. After half an hour the Euclidean task he had been set by Healey had been completed and ten minutes later he was bored. As he contemplated the long beverageless afternoon of soul-searching that would be his lot if he remained on his own in his room, he also realized he had very few options available for socializing. All his seniors would be occupied with their own tasks and unlikely to wish to converse with a sixteen-year-old.

The two other fellow commoners were also at least two

years older than he and had made it clear they were not interested in befriending a junior whose father was a lowly merchant. The only other juniors he had been introduced to were all sizars and thus would be working. That left the queen of the Pickerel, though she'd most likely be working harder than the sizars, it being market day after all. On the other hand, he could go to the Pickerel and drink a tankard of ale and then explore the market on his own. It certainly beat sitting alone.

As he was walking past the porter's lodge he heard a cry. "Master Abell! Sir!"

He looked around and saw the porter, Hobson, who had helped with his bags on the first day. He was waving a letter.

"Sir, I was just coming to give this note to you."

Abell took the note, thanked the porter, and stepped back into the court to open it. It was clearly a reused scrap. His parents, who were snobby about such things, hadn't written it, then. The letter was short and written in a simple hand with a grasp of spelling that was more eccentric than normal.

> *Sir,*
> *If you were series inn yourr ofer mayhap we cold beginne thise afternon, I hav som tim at libertee. I hop that does not disterbe your studdees*
>
> *Bess*

It took him no more than a moment to shove the letter into a pocket and rush out of the gates and across the street to the Pickerel. He opened the door of the tavern and looked around. No sign of Bess. But how could he ask for her? Everyone would think he was looking for her for, ah, other reasons. As he stood just inside the door and pondered what to do, a serving maid came up to him.

"How can I serve you, sir?"

He gulped and blurted out, "I was looking for Mistress Chapman. . . ."

"Right you are, sir. If you are Master Abell then she told us you'd be along. Pray sit in this booth here while I fetch her."

A few minutes later two foaming tankards of ale arrived on the table and the redheaded person who brought them sat opposite him.

"God gi' good day, sir. Did you fly on wings? I did but give Hobson the note mere minutes ago."

Abell blushed and stammered, "No, no, I was, err, 'twas . . . ahh, I was just about to step out of the college when he saw me. In fact I was thinking of coming over here, I hadn't forgotten. But I had thought you would be working hard on market day."

"And you a merchant's son? Think you a moment: we are not by the market, nor even close. Our regulars are the tradesmen behind us who are all at their market stalls now. This evening we will be busy, but during market hours we are not so full." Bess paused for a moment and then, in a tone of voice that was totally different to her normal self-confident manner, she asked, "Are you really willing to teach me? I'm not sure I really want to be a physician, you know. I just want to do something more than serve ale all day. . . . I mean I do want to help people but maybe I could do something else. I just don't really know what."

Abell took refuge in a swig of ale while he tried to think what to say, reflecting on his own recently finished school days.

"At the beginning I do not think that signifies. No matter what you wish to do eventually, the first stage is clear. You must learn to read and write better in English. You must learn to read and write Latin and possibly Greek. Beyond that I suspect that theology, divinity, and ecclesiastical studies are not of use. On the other hand, you wish to travel. As well as Latin maybe you should learn French and, if you intend to go to Grantville, High Dutch would be of use. Natural philosophy and mathematics are probably also useful, but until you can read Latin you will be limited to the more basic forms of arithmetic."

He paused for a moment. "This could take a long while, you know. How much time can you study each day? Schoolboys take six or more years to learn little more than Latin, Greek, and arithmetic."

It was Bess's turn to think. After a while she replied, "I think you have the heart of the matter. I shall start with Latin and methinks that learning Latin will itself help my reading and writing of English. Once we have overleapt that hurdle, 'twill be time enough to choose the next. As for time? That is a harder problem. For the nonce I may be at liberty for an hour or two most afternoons, and if I can convince my father, mayhap he will excuse me from some of my morning chores. If one of the maids leaves or we have more custom in the afternoon I may have to halt my learning for a while."

She stopped for a moment then continued. "What do I need other than time? I can borrow a slate and I can find paper and ink if need be. You said you had books, but I have a few savings. I could buy some of them, if you tell me what to buy. And where can I study? This room can be a very bedlam, my room is too small and you cannot teach me there. It would be improper. . . . I think I must ask my father if we can use his cubby but that means I must say why."

Bess paused again. Clearly much planning and strategizing was taking place in her brain. "If you are to be my instructor you must meet my father and be approved else all is hopeless. However, if he approves, my learning will have his support and that will make it much easier. But we need not rush this, for failure would spell disaster. What else do you recall of Grantville that we may tell my father to whet his interest? And what about your background, since he will undoubtedly wish to know more about my instructor?"

They fell to a long discussion of what might be interesting to an innkeeper about a place from the future and its revolutionary concepts. Of course, the fact that their knowledge was at best secondhand and more often little better than rumor and gossip didn't help. Religious tolerance and the lack of Puritans and their disapproving manner seemed good. As did the female ruler bit, especially the fact that she was not American but apparently a Dutch or maybe English Jewess. The solid tradesman roots seemed to be Abell's best feature. If a humble merchant could educate himself and his sons, why not a tavern keeper's daughter?

The fact that Bess's mother had died in a plague some years back, along with both her brothers and one sister, leaving just herself, one younger sister, and her father seemed useful. Her father had shown no desire to marry again, so perhaps Bess could act *in loco filii*, as it were.

". . . or should it be *in loco fratris* since you are acting for your brother? Yet you are acting as his son so *filii* . . ."

Abell seemed to be getting sidetracked into forests of grammar and philosophy. His future pupil soon brought him back to the true path, though.

"It doesn't matter whether its *filli* or *fratis* or even Philip or Frederick, since I'll never learn the difference unless we convince him! But I think we have the right idea. Convince him that in Grantville a daughter is as good as a son and that in time here will be likewise."

She looked around and, taking a deep breath to calm herself, walked over to the kegs and the man sitting beside them. At first sight he bore little resemblance to his daughter, but a closer glance shaved off about thirty years and considerably more pounds and showed the relationship. Red hair had darkened to brown and a hard life had roughened and thickened the features. But the nose was the same: a bit too large for beauty but not disfiguring.

"Pa, can you come over here? I'd like you to meet Master Abell."

"I was wondering whether you would want to let me meet your new lad. Seems a bit young for you, mind."

"Pa, he's a fellow commoner at the college, just arrived this week. He's got a proposal for you."

The two of them returned to Abell.

"So, my daughter says you arrived here this week and already you're proposing to my daughter? I knew fellow commoners were better than sizars or pensioners, but that's fast work. Might even be a record were I minded to accept. A record for the brevity of your life as a student, that is. You do know that the king and the chancellor do not permit undergraduates to marry and especially not to townsfolk?"

Abell went bright red. But Bess, being more used to her parent's often crude sense of humor, just raised her eyes to the heavens. "'Tis nothing of the sort. He is both a scholar and a gentleman. Sit down and restrain your attempts at wit. Abell, this is my father, Mark Chapman; Pa, this is Richard Abell, fellow commoner at Magdalene."

She paused while they shook hands. "His father is a merchant who trades with the Baltic and of course he hears all the news from there. When he first came here on Wednesday, he was telling us all about that new place, Grantville, and how different it is. Anyway, we got into an argument about women because in Grantville the women are treated no different from the men. The girls can go to school or university just like their brothers can and they can own their own property and one of their rulers is a woman and—"

"So, let me guess. You have somehow trapped this poor boy into promising to make a little Grantville here—a utopian Granta Village as it were. And I further guess that you wish to be the first female resident of Granta Village? A place where you won't have to work all day in a tavern."

Mark Chapman may have looked a stolid dull-witted person. But, as the prosperous tavern itself testified, there was quite a brain tucked behind that dull exterior—a brain that, moreover, had experienced his daughter's wheedling ways for some eighteen years. Sometimes his daughter had a tendency to overlook that and try to be too

devious. But she recovered quickly, showing that she had
also inherited those quick wits.

"That's not quite true. We were arguing about whether
women could really learn anything and I said the only way
to find out was to try it and Abell said that he'd be happy to
try and teach me. Today we were discussing how we should
do it and then we thought we'd best beg your permission.
But I don't want to stop working in the tavern, or even work
less; I just want to rearrange things a bit. If I can swap a
couple of chores with Margaret I can find some free time
in the mornings on my own and most afternoons are free
anyway so I can take an hour or two then to be taught by
Abell. Think of it! You'll be getting an educated daughter
who can look after you properly in your old age."

"I fear I may be getting a daughter who is never satisfied with her station in life, but then I suppose I have
already got that. If I grant permission, at least you'll not be
bitter with me. Now then, sir, what do you intend to teach
this child of mine and how much do you expect to receive
as payment?"

"Latin. Latin and grammar, at first. And probably arithmetic and geometry as well. Ah, but I hadn't thought about
payment. I wasn't expecting any except maybe the odd
tankard of ale. Ummmm, we do need to have somewhere
private as a classroom, if that's possible."

"Cheap work man, aren't you! We'll have to see if we
can't do something better, though I'm not sure what
would be suitable. As for a schoolroom, I'm sure Bess has
thought of the cubby where I keep my papers and tallies.
So long as you don't harm them, that's most likely the best
spot. And maybe you should teach my daughter some

rhetoric, too. If I didn't have a heart of gold she'd have fluffed her chances!" With that, he got up and left them staring at each other.

"If I get a slate could we try the first lesson now?" asked Bess. "I'll get you another ale and show you the cubby."

The cubby was a poky room behind the kegs and next door to the kitchen. There was just enough room for a table and a bench as well as the shelves piled with tallies and miscellaneous junk. Abell sat himself at one end of the bench and thought hard about how he should start— verbs or nouns? verbs—first conjugation verb: *amo amas amat*—"I love; you love; he, she, or it loves," ah, no, perhaps on second thought better start with nouns and check that the grammar book has other example verbs. First declension noun: *mensa mensa mensam mensae*, much safer. Need to explain cases and parts of speech—subject in the nominative object in the accusative—better start with English words today, explain subjects, verbs, nouns . . . and she had to learn to write better. *Ha, I can dictate things and she writes them down!*

Just then Bess came in, closed the door behind her, and grabbed a slate from a pile of apparently unused ones. She sat at the other end of the bench, arranged her skirts, and looked at him. Abell gulped and began.

"I think 'twere best if we begin with English grammar. Since you need to practice your writing, you have to write down everything on the slate. Start with these two: 'the dog ran' and 'the dog chased the cat'."

> *thee dogge ran*
> *the dogge chaysd thee kat*

★ ★ ★

"Sentences in English have a subject, a verb, and usually an object. Subjects and objects are nouns—that means things. Verbs are actions. The subject of both sentences is the dog. The first verb is *ran*. The second verb is *chased*. The second sentence has an object, which is *cat* . . ."

By the time Mr. Chapman poked his head around the door to ask Bess to start work in the tavern they had spent a couple of hours. Bess had written more than three slates worth of sentences and learned about adjectives, adverbs, prepositions, tenses, and most of the other parts of speech.

"Shall I come again tomorrow afternoon? Yes? In the meantime I'll give you some homework. Write down and then find as many parts of speech in this:

"In the beginning was the Word, and the Word was with God, and the Word was God.

"The same was in the beginning with God.

"All things were made by him; and without him was not any thing made that was made.

"In him was life; and the life was the light of men.

"And the light shineth in darkness; and the darkness comprehended it not.

"There was a man sent from God, whose name was John.

"The same came for a witness, to bear witness of the Light, that all men through him might believe.

"He was not that Light, but was sent to bear witness of that Light.

"That was the true Light, which lighteth every man that cometh into the world.

"He was in the world, and the world was made by him, and the world knew him not."

She began writing.

inn the beginyng was the worde and the worde was withe godde and the . . .

Neither Healey nor Gunton were back when Abell returned to his room. He found his old grammar book and his copy of *De Bello Gallico*. What about a book to practice reading English? The Bible, of course. He thought frantically about whether he had seen a Bible in the tavern. Well, he had his own for tomorrow and no doubt Bess could buy one if they didn't. This was going to be much harder than Euclid! He wondered if he could share the chore. Perhaps someone like Saltmarsh would be willing, though he might not have the time.

Then Abell wondered if he should tell anyone. Obviously telling his tutor or any of the fellows was out of the question, but what about his roommates? What about Dunster? And, assuming he made some other friends amongst the new intake of pensioners and sizars, what about them? Would they keep it a secret? Would they think he was actually doing something else with Bess?

He recalled the jesting reference made by Mr. Chapman to the king and the chancellor. It was no laughing matter. The king had modified the university statutes twice in the last three years to make marriage between students and town girls essentially impossible. The penalty for improper behavior of this sort was to be sent down in disgrace, generally after a flogging. Best to not mention this to anyone unless asked, he decided.

As time went on the routine became fixed. He taught on Sundays, Tuesdays, Thursdays, and Saturdays for between two and three hours. And he tried to make sure that Bess had homework to do every day except Saturday. They fell into a routine, Latin on Tuesdays and Thursdays, English and arithmetic on Saturdays, Bible reading (and writing) on Sundays. They started with the Gospels and moved on to Acts after a few weeks. Once that was finished they moved on to the Old Testament, choosing by preference the passages with stories in them.

Bess had improved her English literacy sufficiently that she was starting to read other books for pleasure and she managed to get her hands on Lady Wroth's romance, *The Countess of Montgomeries Urania*. Abell was a bit unsure of the propriety of this book. It had caused a major scandal when it first appeared some ten years ago and was still notorious despite, or perhaps because of, the attempts to suppress it. As for Latin, she had managed to move beyond the flagrant guessing that is the hallmark of most beginners. While her sentences lacked grace and complicated constructions, they were generally grammatically correct. Although they still read Caesar, Abell had decided to introduce her to Cicero and his *De Oratore* as a way to kill two birds with one stone.

Abell was unsure whether her success was due to his instruction or her innate ability but he was very impressed with her progress. There was no doubt in his mind that Bess was as able a scholar as the average student. While she did not exhibit the genius that someone like Dunster displayed, there was no doubt she also did not act as stupidly as some of his other companions. Had she somehow managed to disguise her femininity, he had no doubt she could have held her place in any of the classes that he himself was attending.

Healey and Gunton had never asked him what he was doing during those afternoons when he was teaching Bess. Since they, and others such as Dunster and Saltmarsh, were regularly in the Pickerel, they could surely tell that Abell was well known there. They may also have noticed that he never seemed to have to pay for his beer there and seemed to know everyone serving there better than might be expected. However no one asked and he did not volunteer the information.

Early December 1632

Abell had begun to make friends with the other sizars and pensioners who had come up at the same time. He had more in common with them than with the other fellow commoners who were older and far less interested in studying. Abell, possibly partly inspired by the diligence of his own pupil, had been studying hard. His Latin, originally good, had become excellent and he reveled in the Aristotelian logic, textual analysis, and geometry. Theology was of less interest to him but he picked up enough of it to keep his seniors happy. With the winter break approaching, he was looking forward to seeing his family again, as were most of his fellow students.

One afternoon a little more than week before the end of term, the original five, as well as a couple of pensioners called Gale and Markham, were gathered in the Pickerel. As usual with such student groups, the conversation had shifted into the endless debate about Puritanism and Sacramentalism. Dunster, as always, was leading the assault on Laud and his vision of "a church as scarlet and debased as that of Rome with none of the excuses of precedent that might excuse the Romans." Healey, on the other hand, was giving as good as he got, complaining of the disorganization of the Puritan fringe "who cannot agree on anything save the evil of Rome and the dreadful possibility that people might wish to have fun."

While the rest looked on and made occasional points, Dunster and Healey proceeded to pick apart each other's arguments without bothering to answer the criticisms of their own. Since the debate was clearly not going to be resolved that afternoon—past experience indicated that it would never be resolved any afternoon—Gale decided to try and widen the debate by appealing to Bess to adjudicate in her role as queen of the Pickerel.

"Your Majesty, good queen Bess, I do beg your indulgence that you may pass judgment upon these two and thus restore peace to your realm."

"I cannot pass judgment but I declare that it is indeed time for a truce. I would have thought you would have learned by now: *de gustibus non disputandum est* or better, *de persuasionibus non disputandum est.*"

The table was shocked into silence. Abell, of course, was torn between the pleasure of seeing his work pay off and terror that he would be unmasked, but the rest of them were amazed. Not at the Latin tag itself—their own conversation was littered with such—but the fact that a tavern girl could not just quote a tag but amend the tag to make it more appropriate. True, a scholar might have chosen another word in place of *persuasio* but that was quibbling. It was almost as if an animal had spoken.

"Well, that was easy," Bess said. "Is there anything else you lack?"

"Whu . . . Where, ah how, did you learn that?" stammered Saltmarsh.

"I read it in a book lent to me by Master Abell, if that signifies."

All eyes on the table turned on Abell, who went bright red. But a few months of college had given him a lot more self-confidence.

"Do you remember that first day when we argued about Grantville and women? I thought I'd lend her my Latin grammar and primer and a couple of books so she could see what she could do." All true, but not mentioning that he'd also spent a large amount of time teaching her. "It seems Bess has packed quite a bit in the last few months. Mayhap you recall your logic of that day, Saltmarsh? 'Tis like Grantville itself, not so easy to subdue as one might assume. First Tilly, then Wallenstein. Life has not been good to Catholic generals in Germany."

Saltmarsh did indeed recall that day, as did Healey, Gunton, and Dunster. They recalled the town of Grantville and were all now diverted to consider the recent news from the continent. Despite a raid on Grantville itself, the Americans and their Swedish allies had trounced both the Spanish and the Austrian Habsburgs in separate battles in the past couple of months.

" 'Twas disrespectful, though mayhap fitting to Luther's memory, that the papists were burned out of the Wartburg. And Spaniards, at that. I hear the Americans were pitiless toward the Inquisitors. I wonder how they enjoyed being burned instead of being the ones doing the burning."

"But yet the Americans were merciful to the soldiers, whom they certainly could also have kept trapped within the inferno. I think no demonic sending would have been able to withstand such a temptation for slaughter, ergo our fears that Grantville was a devil's snare seem misplaced."

Bess was confused about something

"Pray, why was the Wartburg so fitting?"

Dunster was only too happy to explain. "Wartburg and the town of Eisenach were a home for Martin Luther, the father of the Reformation, for some years. Hence having the Jesuits burned out of there is a meet revenge for their martyring of so many Protestants."

"Now that is clear as day, though it leads me to another question—and I know well that this may lead us back to point where I intervened but I shall chance it nonetheless—why do we have so many disputes over religion? Whether Puritan, Catholic, Anglican, or whatever, we all believe in Jesus. You do all state the creed together and as I understand it the Catholic creed is the same excepting that it is in Latin. Why, then, is there so much debate?"

There was a short confused outburst as about five people started to answer at once, with Healey in this case eventually managing to take the lead.

"The simple answer is that we believe that the Devil has corrupted the Romish church. We can all respect the early church of Rome, and even in some of the more recent centuries 'tis undoubted that many devout Christians served the church. However, the power of Rome is such that it has attracted those who do not care for spiritual rewards in the world to come but rather seek temporal influence today. The worst corruption of all was that to which Luther did address his ninety-five theses—namely the selling of indulgences. Theologically this completely reverses the teachings of Christ for it, in effect, claims to let a rich man buy his way into heaven.

"Although this is not the only error that the Romans fell into, it is illustrative, since this biblically unjustifiable practice, as with so many others, had the effect of increasing the wealth and influence of the bishops, cardinals, and pope to such an extent that they can wield temporal power in this world. Further, the distractions of temporal power mean that the Roman church no longer concentrates on teaching the word of the Lord but prefers to keep the population in ignorance and superstition while frightening the better off to give their wealth not to the poor but to the church.

"The aim of the Protestant Reformation—and that is what we all agree with—is to return the church to its true form where it has not been corrupted by the temptations of rule and influence. The reason we subsequently argue is that the Lord was not as clear in his desires for this world as one might have wished. Hence churchmen must seek to interpret the scriptures and pray that we receive guidance. Our human frailty means that we are often unable to interpret what guidance we get.

"At its simplest, the Calvinist doctrine believes in stark simplicity if not poverty, with each congregation responsible solely for itself. To a degree, those of us who are less radical sympathize with that view. However, we believe it is an ideal and not something possible in an imperfect world. The problem is that such an ideal church faces many difficulties in this world. For us, the sacraments and symbols of the church serve an important purpose in bringing the ignorant to Christ, teaching them about the meaning of Christianity. Bishops help us organize the church so that we can be more effective in our message; whereas the Calvinists believe that they lead the church to repeat the errors of Rome."

There was a thoughtful pause while the various students considered whether there was anything to add and for Bess to think of a new question, which was forestalled by Dunster. "A masterly summary and one that makes clear why you are mistaken. Are we idealists then? Perhaps, but we should strive for our ideals and not accept the imperfections of the world. It is such as you who permitted the corruption to start in the Romish church. No doubt each step was justified in the name of expedience and no doubt compromise seemed better. The road to perdition is paved with good intentions. Better that we reject that road from the start than hope that we can stop before the end."

Bess found something to say in response. "Sir, methinks

your idealism will deter many of those who might otherwise repent. Any man who has lived a life of sin, nay, any man who has merely lived a life without particular regard for the church will hesitate to come to a church so austere and unwelcoming. Surely, if you wish to convert the world you must make it such that people will willingly join?"

Dunster was unused to arguing with people who did not have the grounding in theology; it made him unsure of himself. But he could tell this woman was shortly going to be asking him about predestination and he could also tell she wasn't going to like the answer. If he was going in that direction, best to be quick about it.

"The church should not seek to make itself attractive to sinners. We believe that not everybody can find Christ and not everybody will go to heaven. Since God is omnipotent and omniscient he knows well what acts we shall all perform. Hence we are *ab initio*, elected to enter heaven if that is our destiny. Moreover, we need not concern ourselves with those who are not of the elect, since they are in any respect doomed."

Just as suspected, Bess was unimpressed by the concept.

"That seems not only most inequitable but also removes the possibility of free will, which would seem to make our lives meaningless. What gains someone to strive to do good works or to live a God-fearing life if they go to hell anyway? If God has already decreed what happens, wherefore are we placed on the earth to act out our doom? 'Tis as if we were mere actors in a play!"

Abell wondered if Dunster would fall back on Calvin's claims that the wicked receive their just deserts while the elect are saved through God's mercy. That didn't seem promising, though, and Dunster tried a different counter argument.

"No, 'tis not so simple. We cannot guess the mind of God. Mayhap we are all destined to be part of the elect; however, we cannot know that and we should not give up."

"That seems contrary to the previous claim. If we should act then surely we should strive to convert those who do not believe and thus make the church attractive to the sinful and ignorant in the hope that they repent."

Dunster was positively not enjoying this. However, he fumbled for a way out.

"I think you should read Calvin's own words in the order in which they are written rather than dart from point to point. The books of his writings are in the library, I can show them to you."

He ground to a halt realizing there was a slight problem: such books were not permitted to be removed from the library, indeed they were chained to the shelves, and women were of course not allowed in the college. However, after considerable debate, other members of the party agreed that between them they could smuggle Bess into the library the following afternoon.

The next afternoon it all seemed to work like clockwork. Abell met Bess with a spare gown and cap to go over the male clothes she had borrowed. Her long red hair was gathered up under the cap so from a distance she was not obviously female. Hobson, the porter, had been suitably distracted by Gale asking him some involved question to do with the upcoming vacation and other members of the group were ready to call "cave" (look out) if a fellow should appear in the court. Dunster and Abell between them found the books and helped translate when Bess got stuck. Dunster was amazed at Bess's grasp of Latin, but even so, it was hard going. The more so, since Bess seemed determined to make sure she understood it all and did not miss a single nuance. Suddenly, they heard a "cave" hissed from the window. Before they could do anything, the library door opened and in came the Bursar.

There was no way to hide it. President and Bursar Smith had caught two members of his college consorting with a woman, a tavern wench no less, in the college library. It was a scandal! It spread around the college and then all Cambridge like wildfire, with the details becoming more and more sensational with each retelling. True, one of the college members was a fellow commoner and that sort of thing was expected, one might say almost required, of fellow commoners, but the other was a BA, one respected, in certain circles at least, for his scholarship and piety.

Of course, the more salacious rumors paid no attention to such quibbling details. Indeed, one rumor named them both as fellows and claimed that Smith had walked in to a scene of witchcraft with the naked witch having her way with both of them simultaneously after having performed some black magic. For some reason, the true story as told by all three of the guilty parties, namely that the woman was being shown John Calvin's writings on predestination, was utterly dismissed by those who heard it.

From the point of view of the defendants the only redeeming feature of the whole affair was that it was a

purely internal college matter. It was to be dealt with by
the college, thus ensuring a speedy judgment and preservation of some privacy, as well as the hope that familiarity
might also breed leniency. The fellows meeting to discuss
the case two days later was held in the hall with the fellows
seated around the high table and Abell and Dunster
standing before them. Healey and Gunton had been
asked to attend as witnesses and were seated at the end of
one of the long dining tables.

It was a frosty but sunny morning and the fire behind the
high table had taken the chill off the room. Surprisingly, the
master himself was in attendance. This was unexpected as he
tended to leave such disciplinary matters to the president;
presumably the rumors surrounding the case had made
him decide he had best hear the truth at firsthand. The
meeting began with the president describing what he had
seen.

"I entered the library and saw three people gathered by
one of the stacks. I greeted them and paid them no mind,
intent as I was upon mine own business. However whilst
I searched for the volume I desired, I thought again upon
whom I had seen. Dunster and Abell I recognized, but the
third person was unknown to me. Moreover he was wearing a Magdalene gown and cap and hence could not have
been a visitor from another college. I curtailed mine own
researches and walked around the stacks to again examine
the three.

"Upon closer examination, I saw that the third person
was undeniably female, albeit dressed in male attire. I
swiftly established upon enquiry of the three that she was
Elizabeth Chapman, the daughter of the landlord of the

Pickerel Inn. Naturally, I did enquire wherefore she was in the library wearing such a disguise and was informed that she was reading for herself the homilies and letters of John Calvin wherein he expounded his doctrine of predestination. I called Hobson and required her to depart the college in his charge. Subsequently, neither Abell nor Dunster has changed their claim and both have suggested that Healey and Gunton might provide some verification of it."

One of the fellows, John Howorth, a friend of the president and Abell's tutor, took up the role of chief interrogator. He began by requesting that Dunster explain himself.

"The previous afternoon a party of us—I, Abell, Gunton, Healey, Saltmarsh, Gale, and Markham—had repaired to the Pickerel for refreshment. Whilst partaking of such refreshment we did discuss diverse topics and our debate became heated. Gale made bold to suggest that Mistress Chapman adjudicate in the name of peace, upon which she did declare truce if not judgment by stating *'de gustibus non disputandum est'* and then correcting that to *'de persuasionibus non disputandum est.'* Naturally, such an apt tag from such a source did cause some consternation and we did enquire how she had come upon it. Abell and she explained that Abell had lent her his Latin grammar and vocabulary as well as his Caesar and Cicero.

"The discussion then moved on but Mistress Chapman remained a part of it. During subsequent debate Mistress Chapman did ask numerous questions about the doctrine of predestination and the elect to which I regret that I was unable to provide satisfactory answers. I reflected that were I debating such with an undergraduate I would not hesitate to refer such a one to the source, namely the writings of Calvin. Then, since it seemed that Mistress Chapman had sufficient Latin, I thought it would be to her advantage if we could manage the same thing. Abell concurred and we determined that, since the works were to be found within the library here, we should contrive some subterfuge to permit Mistress Chapman to read the texts. Abell elected himself to be her linguistic assistant while I guided her to the appropriate passages. While her initial questions were answered, exposure to Calvin's teachings awoke further questions and we failed to note the passage of time until we were interrupted by the president."

Howorth began to cross-examine. "It did not occur to either of you to ask for a special dispensation?"

The true answer to that—that they were sure any request would have been denied out of hand—was not one that should be mentioned. Dunster attempted a diplomatic evasion.

"Of course we should have done so. However, I regret that we felt that time was of the essence, since the term is to end so soon, and thus acted on our own initiative rather than waited for approval of a request."

"And as a result you have caused this college to be enmeshed in scandal as should have been obvious to one of the meanest intellect let alone someone who has a BA. To me the lack of such a request is indicative of the implausibility of the tale. I should like to hear some evidence to corroborate your story."

Both Abell and Dunster indicated that Healey and Gunton could be witnesses to the tavern debate. The two were asked to come forward and give their stories, which in turn they did. Their statements did indeed match that of Dunster. Both agreed that Bess had indeed used a Latin tag to end the initial debate. Healey stated in part that he had begun the discussion of the various forms of Protestantism as a result of a question from Bess and that once debate had moved on toward Calvinist doctrine he had let his colleague Dunster expound since he was well acknowledged to be wiser in such matters. Gale, Saltmarsh, and Markham were mentioned again as sources of additional corroboration. Howorth then moved on.

"You say that Mistress Chapman was able to construe the Latin of Calvin. I, and, I suspect, my colleagues, do find that hard to credit. You say she had only been given a couple of books concerning the tongue?"

Abell answered, "She did not comprehend every word. Dunster and I must provide the meaning now and then. However, she was well able to recognize the grammatical constructions used."

"And how long ago did you give her those books?"

"'Twas shortly after I came up, that is to say in August."

"And you claim that a tavern wench, whose education is most probably limited to a crude literacy in English and with little enough practice at that, is able to learn Latin to such a standard within four months without recourse to anything save a schoolboy text or two?"

Abell realized that this was crunch time: in order to make the truth believable he must detail some of his teaching, but that seemed likely to cause other problems for him. Still, at least it would help extricate Dunster.

"Well, she did ask me numerous questions. I did spend some afternoons guiding her."

"So you stand here and admit that rather than concentrate on your own studies, you did consort with a tavern wench upon numerous occasions? Where pray did these liaisons occur?"

Healey nearly burst out at the unfairness of the first part of that question. Abell had been a veritable paragon amongst fellow commoners and indeed his tutor had used him as an example to embarrass some of Abell's seniors. A witness of indeterminate guilt and low rank does not comment uninvited upon a rhetorical question, however. For Abell it was the second part that was the most delicate. Any whiff of previous impropriety could cause immense trouble. The fact that he had indeed begun to have feelings about his pupil that would be deemed inappropriate was just an incidental detail that complicated the whole mess. This was not something that Abell felt he needed to mention.

"Sir, Mr. Chapman permitted us to use his small room behind the main tavern room wherein he does keep his tallies as it had the wherewithal for learning. Mistress Chapman did her studying there and I did assist her when I was asked." The fact that this was every day was again something that Abell did not feel obliged to mention, but he could feel the ice cracking all around him and wondered how to proceed. That thought was swiftly put aside by the tempest his previous statement unleashed from the bursar.

"And what of the impropriety? We are a Christian institution and require clear moral behavior from our members. Consorting in private with tavern wenches is counter to these principles. You are an undergraduate at Cambridge, here to study and improve your mind, not to dally with trollops in taverns. Nay, worse, it seems that you are a very viper in the nest of this college. Not content to neglect your own studies to frolic with wenches, you also incite your betters to do likewise. It passes understanding how you might think that such a tale should be credible.

"I know not what you were doing in our library but I misdoubt that your pedagogical talents are such that you can teach an innkeeper's daughter to do anything other than count her pence and lie down for you! Perhaps as a fellow commoner you think you are above the disciplines of your fellow students, but you will learn otherwise. To begin with, you shall be gated until you have satisfied your tutor as to the progress of your own education and I trust the master will find some other punishment for the egregious lying that has accompanied your trysting. Indeed, was it up to me I would consider whether this college would be better off altogether without your disruptive presence."

"But I . . ." Abell started to stammer a defense but before he could get far, one of the fellows intervened. Dr. Greene, that was.

"President Smith, are you aware that if Abell has neglected his studies his accomplishments to date fail to show this? I certainly recall hearing stories in the combination room about this paragon amongst fellow commoners who was more diligent than any sizar. Furthermore, as you know well, the Pickerel is a respectable tavern as such places go. Had we been talking about a maid from the Three Tuns, I too would be skeptical. Incredible as it may seem, I am inclined to believe that the story is accurate in outline.

"I do confess I find it hard to credit the description of Mistress Chapman's abilities to construe Latin. However, that does not signify. Abell, you should be punished for execrable judgment and for flouting the rules concerning behavior. Indeed for bringing such scandal upon this place. But these are the faults of youth that are to be expected and your intent was good. Do you have anything you would like to raise in your defense?"

Abell paused for a moment. "Sirs, I confess I had not thought of external appearances when I offered to assist Mistress Chapman. I had thought merely of the challenge she had set herself and of what I might do to assist. In that respect, Mistress Chapman has proven to be a most diligent student with as much determination to study as one could hope for. I do believe that the thesis proposed concerning the educability of women has been demonstrated correct without recourse to rhetoric or logic. Indeed, she is an example that inspires mine own studies and can feel nothing but admiration for her determination to obtain education.

"I regret that this diligent study seems to cause disbelief, but I submit you can verify my tale by interviewing Mistress Chapman yourselves. Furthermore, while I do humbly apologize to the college for bringing scandal upon it through my thoughtlessness and impetuosity, I do most strenuously deny that there is any basis whatsoever in the bursar's innuendo. Mistress Chapman and I have done nothing other than study together."

There was a pause while the fellows considered Abell's defense. Then Dr. Greene spoke.

"Indeed, young Abell, if you are so sure of your pupil's

talents mayhap we should confirm them. Although I do wonder wherefore she desires such learning. It will surely lead to frustration since she cannot hope to exercise her newfound knowledge in a tavern. However, that is perhaps beside the point. The education of such a woman is not of concern to us save that it verify or not your tale. Still, such a demonstration might cause the doubters to reconsider your tale."

The master spoke for the first time. "Dr. Greene, I feel you are permitting yourself to be distracted by minutiae. Whether or not the girl can construe Latin, the fact remains that young Abell has indeed brought disrepute upon this college and we must repair that damage, come what may."

"Master, I am fully cognizant of that," replied Dr. Greene. "However, the college may retrieve its reputation by either dealing harshly with the prejudged miscreant or by determining the truth and acting accordingly. I believe the accused is indeed guilty of nothing more than youthful thoughtlessness and it behooves us to take that into consideration. Especially when the former course might well deprive us of a worthy scholar."

What Dr. Greene failed to mention was the other reason why flogging and expelling Abell would be inadvisable. The possibility of receiving bequests from the family would be forfeit if Abell were no longer a student, but that was understood by all the fellows. As a poor college, Magdalene could not afford to alienate the rich and powerful. The bursar, however, was not best pleased with either the spoken or unspoken defense of the miscreant.

"Dr. Greene, I am somewhat at a loss as to why you.

persist in this rhetoric. The boy has admitted to consorting with an innkeeper's daughter over a period of months. This is not a suitable pastime for a student and is counter to all the statutes of college. If we do not punish such behavior decisively we ourselves are vulnerable to accusations that we are lax in our management of the college. Worse, we may be accused of conniving in the establishment of a den of iniquity rather than a college of Christian piety."

Given the rocky relationship between the Cambridge colleges and both the crown and the see of Canterbury, this was a fair point. While Magdalene was not the hotbed of Puritanism that some of its neighbors were, it was still liable to be tarred with the same brush in regards to its loyalty to the established church. Archbishop-presumptive Laud would be only too happy to make use of Magdalene's perceived sins as a stick with which to oppress the entire university.

The master, however, was more of a politician than the bursar, and was beginning to see an alternative approach that would at one stroke stymie the colleges' external enemies, retain the goodwill of the Abell family, and (last but not least) ensure that the bursar was put firmly back in his place. Even the master himself was unclear which of these three satisfactory results was more pleasurable.

"Bursar, I do acknowledge your concerns for the future of the college and they reflect admirably upon you. Your thesis is indubitably valid. However, I also feel that Dr. Greene has created a powerful antithesis. If falls to me therefore to ennunciate an synthesis agreeable to all. Here, therefore, is my decision. Firstly, the notion that you, young Abell, be gated is sound. You shall therefore remain within the grounds of this college for the remainder of this term and for the entirety of the next. Should you have need to leave, you must first receive permission from your tutor, Howorth, and also be accompanied on the trip by a BA, one of Messrs. Gunton, Healey, or Dunster. The bursar is correct. We are here to study in Christian piety and no matter your intentions, a tavern is not conducive to such an attitude. However, further punishment shall depend upon your pedagogical aptitude.

"Dr. Greene, since you were so resolute in the defense, you shall discuss with Abell the limits of Mistress Chapman's knowledge and shall devise an examination thereof the results of which you shall share with myself and Howorth. Should we agree that her learning is indeed as claimed, no further punishment need apply since Abell shall be proven to be more enthusiastic than wise. However, should the young lady not have adequate knowledge, we will consider additional steps in the light of our discovery.

"Finally, Dr. Greene shall enquire of Mr. and Mistress Chapman whether they wish her lessons to continue. If so, we shall ensure that they do so under circumstances of impeccable propriety. Master Abell shall conduct such lessons as desired in my lodgings where my wife and servants may oversee them. Such lessons shall continue only so long as Abell remains dedicated to his own studies."

The bursar was obviously not exactly pleased by this judgment, as the glare he gave Abell and Dunster showed. But he was not willing to challenge the master when he had spoken in such terms. The other fellows likewise did not demur and thus the session ended.

★ ★ ★

When they got outside Dunster, Healey, and Gunton were pleased that they had been almost ignored in the scandal over Abell's behavior. Abell was light-headed from relief after escaping the bursar's threats. Dr. Greene called Abell to come to his room and discuss what he had taught Bess.

The discussion got off to a good start since Abell began by thanking Dr. Greene for defending him and apologizing for the additional work this was going to cause him. The description of what had been taught did not take long and Dr. Greene shortly dismissed him. Abell's fellow under-graduates were less merciful than the master and teased him endlessly about his teaching Bess, mostly with some undertones of respect and admiration. This was pleasing to the ego even if the actual taunts were less so. What was not so pleasing was that a moment's thought, not to mention hints from his betters, showed that he had just made an enemy of the bursar. Thus it was with mixed feelings that Abell took stage to London to spend Christmas with his family.

Two days later Bess entered the college as she had been invited. Having been guided to the master's lodgings, she was given a table where she spent an hour and a half or so writing down her translations of Cicero's account of the activities of Dolabella as well as demonstrating her profi-ciency in arithmetic under the supervision of Dr. Greene. Finally, she was given a Bible and told to translate as much of the first chapter of Saint Mark into Latin as she could.

This was by far the hardest task but she took it in her stride and made a credible attempt at the translation.

While Howorth and Dr. Greene reviewed her efforts, she was invited to discuss her future tuition desires with the master. To her surprise, the meeting included a young woman of about her own age or perhaps a little younger. The young lady, it turned out, was the master's daughter and the reason for her presence was that the master was suggesting that Abell act as tutor to both girls simultaneously, thus permitting each to chaperone the other.

This was quite a development. It seemed to indicate both that the master believed that she would in fact demonstrate sufficient learning and that the master had decided to approve the venture. (The fact that he would end up with a daughter tutored for free was purely incidental.) Since everyone knew of the Smyth-Smith rivalry, that implied that the bursar was in the process of receiving another lesson about the powers and privileges of the master. Bess would have accepted almost any conditions, and the plan proposed was about as good as it could possibly get.

They discussed the details of the proposed curriculum and the amount of time Abell would be allowed to dedicate to teaching. Then Dr. Greene entered and reported that her Latin was "by no means fluent but entirely consistent with some months of diligent studies and showeth a dedication often wanting in our pensioners" and that "she has a solid grounding that wants merely practice to improve."

On that happy note the meeting broke up with an agreement that Abell's first official lesson should take place upon his return after Christmas. For Bess the official status of her studies was a Christmas gift worth more than anything else.

January 1633

For Richard Abell the Yuletide break was fun but over far too soon. He had spent a lot of time asking his father and other relations about news of Grantville, with mixed success. It was hard to separate the fictional from the factual and the politics made it even more confusing. Abell had to get a lecture on what a future age would have called realpolitik from his father before he began to understand the motivations behind actions such as French Catholic cardinal Richelieu's financing of the Protestant king of Sweden in his fight against the Catholic Holy Roman Empire. On the other hand he was allowed to choose a few of Grantville's wonder goods to amuse his friends. The majority of these were most peculiar, being made of something that seemed to be neither wood nor metal but something in between. His uncle told him that the American merchant they had obtained them from had told him that this material—something called plastic— could not be made again for many years. Still, the clear bottle was extremely convenient for travelling since it was less fragile than glass, and the "ballpoint pen" was far superior to quill and ink. On the other hand, it was the pamphlet that he had a feeling would be most controversial, despite it being clearly just advanced printing. Entitled *National Geographic* and dated October 1998, it was utterly fascinating and something that he knew he could share and discuss endlessly with all his Cambridge colleagues and friends.

His father had also shown him the female mannikin with its radical clothing, which he rather thought Bess would like to see. However, this was not to be. Not only was this the sort of good that could be sold for enormous sums of money, there was no chance that this could go anywhere that it might be discovered by a strict Puritan and destroyed. As he rode on the Hobson stage back to Cambridge, Richard thought he'd like to see Bess wearing an outfit like that. He also wondered about the name. Did "Barbie" mean barbarian? Or was it something to do with cutting? And nurse? The costume didn't seem really suitable for looking after children. Despite the developed chest, he didn't see how she could suckle a baby without taking off almost the entire costume. Somehow Richard knew that even Americans didn't do that!

The news from the continent was mostly good. His family's trading journeys to the Baltic were unthreatened so far. The situation in Germany seemed more positive than not for the Swedes and their allies, with the possibility that the Baltic might once more become a source of grain. But, despite that, there was no sign of peace, which meant that disruptions to trade could be expected at any time. Indeed the success of the Swedes and Americans seemed likely to goad Richelieu into more direct action—something that did not bode well for southern trade. So far however, despite the rumbling mistrust of Spain, the English seemed to be maintaining neutrality and thus able to trade with all sides. Business was booming, not just in London but also in all the other ports where the family had operations from Boston to Southampton. The only fly in the ointment was that it seemed the Americans were spreading some sort of subversive organization, something called Committees of Correspondence, which threatened to overthrow kings, princes, and the established order. His father's circle wasn't precisely in favor of King Charles and the House of Stuart, but they were definitely against disorder since that tended to ruin trade and hence, more by default than otherwise, were against revolutionary new ideas such as those of the Committees of Correspondence.

This had led to a bit of an argument because Abell himself had become somewhat infected with the Puritan zeal at Cambridge. Not by any means as extreme as some, but despite rooming with Healey and Gunton who were certainly not Puritan, he had come to respect the scholarship and philosophy of his more Puritan friends. Magdalene was not particularly radical and its Puritans were more tolerant than many. While they disapproved of theaters, cockfights, gambling dens, and the like, they were not inclined to force their beliefs upon all. Dunster, Saltmarsh, and others like them had inspired much of his dedication. Their willingness to look beyond the class, position, and accepted wisdom when evaluating people had undoubtedly influenced his willingness to teach Bess. But when you got down to it, Puritanism was rather revolutionary and antihierarchical, which meant that in some ways it was not a million miles from the aims of the Committees of Correspondence.

Of course, "Puritanism" was a fairly broad label. The more radical parts would be frothing at the mouth at the idea of toleration. Particularly toleration of other religions and perceived works of the Devil such as drunkenness, debauchery, and the like which, according to Abell's father's comments, were precisely what toleration meant to the Committees. But the rest, the bits that didn't directly involve religion, they were very interesting and would appeal to any sort of Puritan. Abell was imagining telling all the news to his friends over ale in the Pickerel when he remembered that he had been gated. No more Pickerel. No more late nights wandering the streets of Cambridge. No more lazy afternoons on the common or poking around the market. Well, that was no great loss seeing as it was winter. Still, at least he would be seeing his friends again and presumably teaching Bess since he had no doubt she would pass whatever tests she was given.

By the time the stage arrived at Cambridge it was full dark. The cloudy, drizzly, gray, short winter's day had given way to a still more miserable night. Needless to say, Magdalene was inconveniently far from the Hobson stable and not on the London road, but the promise of a few pence had convinced the driver that he could do the detour. Abell was not the only person to do this. By his calculations the driver had made a good florin from the various travelers who had equally disliked the idea of finding their way through the dark wet streets.

Abell was almost the last person on the stage, just a couple of members of Jesus college remaining. The unloading of his trunk was swiftly managed by the driver, who deftly and unobtrusively pocketed his gratuity. The Magdalene porter equally efficiently moved it to his room. Abell would have liked to have gossiped a bit with the porter but the evening hall was imminent and he had to grab his robes and run. The advantage of being a fellow commoner was that one ate far better than the other students; and, of course, being at high table one had presumably more learned discourse. But, Abell reflected, the disadvantage was that one was visible if late and, while eating, the fellows could be remarkably biting about the behavior of junior members of the college, even, perhaps especially, when those juniors were seated at the same table.

However, as it turned out, apart from an occasional snide remark, the fellows were more interested in discussing the political situation, especially as regards to Thomas Wentworth. Since Abell had just arrived from London and since his family was believed to have reasonable connections with the movers and shakers in the kingdom, he was pressed for news and each tidbit he divulged was discussed over and over.

London rumor had it that not only had Wentworth been recalled from Ireland but that the king intended to promote him to high office and honor. The reasons for this were less than clear and provided the high table with an entire course of speculation. Abell suspected, but did not repeat his suspicion to his tablemates, that this had to do with the mysterious pages Dr. Harvey had brought from Grantville. The next course brought more speculation, this time about what Wentworth would do with his new powers. It was notable that the more Puritan-leaning parts of the fellowship seemed the most worried. Until recently, the sacramentalist Laud had not had notable success in reversing the Calvinist trends within the university or amongst the gentry, despite having the support of his monarch. Laud was not precisely known for his tact and diplomacy, nor did he yet have the power to enforce behavior across the land. Wentworth, on the other hand, was considered by all to be far more vigorous. If he decided to come down on Puritanism, that would be much more serious.

As the meal drew to an end, Abell was asked about events on the continent. The Confederated Principalities of Europe and the religious tolerance of the Americans were of great interest to the fellows. Anglicanism and Lutheranism were different in certain critical ways, not least because of their different origins and political situation. But, as one of the fellows noted: "Our two churches are forever plagued with the determination of the righteous course as we seek to navigate between the Scylla of Rome and Charybdis of Geneva. Oft it seems that every doctor of theology—nay, every bishop and curate—must be a captain making a different course."

Abell mentioned that the Lutherans around Grantville had already encountered problems of precisely this nature and that the Count of Schwarzburg-Rudolstadt was to hold a colloquy on how to satisfy the various factions of a faith. He also mentioned that Grantville itself seemed willing to tolerate any faith, even Jews and Papists. The latter was merely confirmation of previous intelligence, but the colloquy was both new and of great interest and must therefore be debated at great length. For Abell, who wished to talk with his own friends but was constrained to remain at high table until they had done the topic to death, this was exceedingly frustrating. Finally the discussion wound down and Abell was able to make his escape. To his frustration he learned from Hobson the porter that his friends had all decamped to the Pickerel. But, reflecting that it was an ill wind that blew no good, he satisfied his urge to gossip by conversing with Hobson.

"Hobson, may I enquire if you are related to that Hobson who is the university carrier?"

"Aye, that I am. 'Tis not too close a relationship. My grandfather was uncle to old Hobson, he who did become the carrier, and who died but two years past. He was a sharp one, that. I recall my grandfather telling me that even as a child he was always looking for a way to get a coin or two. He became carrier with but one wagon, more a cart than a carriage, and his stable began with the worst collection of broken-down old nags you ever did see. Why, my grandfather said that anyone else would have sold them to the tanners!"

"Ah, yes, the notorious Hobson's choice."

"No, sir. Hobson's choice came when he first managed to obtain better horses. All the young gentlemen insisted on riding the good horses and leaving the bad in the stable to eat their oats. Afore long the good were ruined like the others and so Hobson did decide that henceforth all should be hired in turn. That is Hobson's choice."

"I am well rebuked and do thank you for your correction. . . . Pray tell me, how did Mistress Chapman fare in the tests?"

"Exceedingly well! The master was most satisfied and hath decided that you may instruct his own daughter as well as Mistress Chapman. Thereby, as is his wont, gaining some benefit for himself."

"Erp . . ."

A later generation of Englishmen would have described his reaction as "gobsmacked." He had never expected to have to teach anyone but Bess and certainly had not expected to be so closely involved with the master's household.

He thanked Hobson and wandered across the court and up to his rooms in somewhat of a daze, albeit a pensive one. He wondered what the master's daughter was like. Come to think of it he couldn't remember actually seeing her since the master spent most of his time in Peterborough where he was a canon and his family resided there for the most part. They had been to Cambridge just once while Abell was there, passing through on their way to visiting the earl of Suffolk at Audley End and had stayed tucked away in the master's lodge for a night to tidy up and get presentable before the final leg of their journey. Rumor had it that the master had been attempting to impress his patrons and had enlisted his wife and daughters in the scheme. Rumor had not reported whether this had been successful or not, or even how long the family had stayed at Audley End.

The next morning after chapel the master invited Abell to break his fast with the master and his family that "we might discourse upon pedagogy and the female sex." Thanks to his chat with Hobson, Abell was not taken aback when he was informed of the master's scheme and was able to make sensible enquiry as to the level of Mistress Smyth's education to date. The Master's wife was gracious but remote, apparently having a poor opinion of the whole idea. But his daughter was more enthusiastic. Perhaps things would not be so bad after all. Abell learned that he would be giving his first lesson that very afternoon and that he was excused from the second morning lecture to prepare. He proposed to teach the women something about geography to start with, since it was something that would be new to both and would not require special linguistic knowledge. Mistress Smyth, he had been informed, knew how to read and write in English and how to cipher but no one had taught her Latin or given her much to study beyond her schoolbooks. She seemed keen to rectify that and recalling his own experience he thought that perhaps Bess could help teach her Latin.

After the lecture was over, his roommates came back. They had come back quite late the night before and no one had been in talkative mood when they awoke. Of course, they asked him all about London and about the master and he found himself repeating much that he had said the night before at high table. He distracted them from the interminable debates about Wentworth and Grantville by showing them the bottle, the pen, and the *National Geographic*.

Both were extremely impressed. The clear bottle with a closing that did not leak was practically miraculous, being so light yet so strong. And as for the pen . . . well, had his father provided him with enough they would have thrown up their studies and gone into business selling or maybe just renting them by the hour to other students. No need to continually dip the quill in ink, no need to sharpen it from time to time. No danger of ink spills or blots or any of the other mishaps that were part and parcel of writing in 1633.

They insisted on writing something with it, and after some debate, both chose a letter home as the most satis-factory way to brag to the widest audience. Abell let them bicker about the pen while he began to study the *National Geographic* in detail. When he had flicked through it earlier, it seemed fairly straightforward, being just a kind of small book of illustrated essays, but closer inspection served to add confusion. The majority of the book was indeed essays on "Human Migration," "Women and Population," and so on, but the first and last few pages were more odd, a mishmash of pictures of confusing objects with little explanatory text, as indeed was the back cover.

What was a 4x4? A Jeep? Asphalt? And where exactly was the funny place called www.jeep.com? Not to mention the request to "call 1-800-925-JEEP." Was this a name? Or some slogan to be shouted in the air? A curse or a spell?

No matter. Abell decided that the *National Geographic* would serve very well as a text to study. Surely both women would be fascinated to compare the reports of navigators and explorers such as Sir Francis Drake or Sir Walter Raleigh with the maps and tales in the book. He decided that the story "Feeding the Planet" would be the one to start with. It had maps that resembled maps he had seen of the known world and had many pictures of agriculture that seemed more familiar—despite the odd-looking people—than the pictures in the other essays. Also, it was fairly short.

He paid a visit to the college library and located Hakluyt's *Principal Navigations, Voyages, Traffiques and Discoveries of the English Nation.* But he soon decided that it would be best to begin with simple copying of the essay. Later it would no doubt be interesting to attempt to identify the various places and nations of the *National Geographic.* It might bore Bess to just copy, but Abell hoped the subject matter would be sufficiently diverting. He needed time to determine the true abilities of Mistress Smyth and to come up with a plan for teaching her Latin while not boring Bess.

The lesson was interesting. Since the master's wife was present she decided to attend the lesson and her presence put a damper on the greetings between Bess and Abell. It took a few minutes for all to determine the best way that the two girls should share the *National Geographic* and there was a brief moment of tension as Mrs. Smyth inquired whether Abell was intending on teaching lewd, heathen, or heretical nonsense to her daughter. Fortunately, Mrs. Smyth was no great scholar and seemed willing to accept verbal reassurance without examining the tract in detail. The students, however, set to copying with enthusiasm and frequent discussions about the meaning of phrases and words.

The most thought-provoking were the simple numbers. Abell himself had trouble comprehending the scale of the world. The very first sentence was astonishing—how could it be that the world at the end of the second millenium was adding so many people per day? To the girls, for whom Cambridge with its five thousand or so inhabitants was a large town, the concept of millions of people was unthinkable.

Abell's London chauvinism took a battering as well. London, the only major metropolis in England, had a population measured in the low hundreds of thousands. It had grown, of course, and since Abell's family had from time to time imported grain from the Baltics—something that had ended during the current war—he had an idea of its rough size, which was perhaps a quarter of a million people. The idea that the population of London could be added to the world every day seemed unreal.

The shocks continued once the meaning of the word billion was determined. Surely six million million people was impossible! Further reading of the essay seemed indeed to make that number impossible since the numbers did not add up, but the overall impression was staggering.

Before they knew it they had spent three hours copying and discussing the essay and all three had practiced arithmetic with much larger numbers than they had ever done before. Inspired by the essay, Abell had asked his two students to calculate the amount of food and drink consumed in first Cambridge and then London in a day, a week, and a year. Bess was able to provide some basic information about the weights and quantities of food served at the Pickerel as a meal for different people as well as ale consumption, which helped to start things. Conversion of pounds, pints, bushels, barrels, and so on yielded much fun and there was considerable argument about whether it was possible to equate a weight of beef or mutton with a fowl or a fish and whether bread should be counted as a single item or as its constituent parts.

Unnoticed during this mathematical extravaganza Mrs. Smyth had left the classroom but the entrance of the master some minutes later as the final calculations of London's annual food consumption were being made did bring all three back to the mundane world. The master, however, merely indicated that they should complete their sums so they did so with alacrity. Then once it was complete he asked them what they were studying. Both Bess and Abell were somewhat shy, but his daughter was only too happy to launch into an explanation of population, food, and the *National Geographic* that was somewhat confused yet which got the essential points across.

The master let the joys of arithmetic pass him by and focused on the source. Literally, since he took it in his hand and studied the relevant pages minutely. He quizzed Abell on his understanding of the origin of the *National Geographic*, its meaning, and the world it depicted. Abell replied that it seemed that the booklet was a sort of combination of newsletter and encyclopedia. From the precise dating and other indications, it seemed that a volume was produced each month and that this was distributed to subscribers, which was rather like the Dutch *corrantos*, but the contents seemed more timeless and pedagogical.

The concept was itself briefly interesting to the master but he put that to one side and considered the booklet, its content, and its implications. This was almost certainly the first Grantville work to arrive in Cambridge—or Oxford, for that matter, he thought with added glee—which meant that he had a clear advantage in studying Grantville. Recalling the conversation in hall the previous evening, he could see that Grantville studies were likely to be politically sensitive yet philosophically and theologically vital.

Yes . . . sidestep the politics by analysing the geography of the world that Grantville came from. If you ignored its version of seventeenth-century history, you avoided the dangers of political entanglement while filling in knowledge that was of benefit. And if the scholars in Magdalene could do that they could profit from the interest.

Geography! Present this as good for trade, navigation and they'd get the interest of merchants, which means they get more fellow commoners and benefactions—perhaps a university chair . . .

But first things first. They couldn't print this as it was without a lot of tedious politics. They needed to get commentary, which meant they needed copies that scholars could analyze. So they would need copyists to start with, who needed to be reliable and controllable. And . . .

Had the master been an excitable Greek philosopher at this point he would have run around the streets shouting "Eureka!" But since he was a staid English academic, not to mention a halfway good politician, he showed no ouward sign as he turned his attention back toward the three youngsters.

"Young Abell, do you realise what a treasure you have brought this college? 'Tis like finding a new work from Plato or Socrates in the courts of Persia or Constantinople. Nay, more like a Herodotus or a Thucydides, yet no scrappy moldy manuscript heavy with the dust of centuries. Many scholars in this town would devote much time to 'read, mark, learn, and inwardly digest' this pamphlet, had they knowledge of it. I pray that you may permit dissemination of its contents." Then, seeing Abell's face darken, he swiftly elaborated, "No, I do not require that you give up possession of it, merely that you permit others to make and study copies. Perhaps your pupils might make the first copies on good paper during their next lessons?"

It was Abell's turn for swift thinking. Not for nothing was he the son of a master merchant. He saw that he had the chance to bargain some improvements to his terms of imprisonment. The result was five minutes of what was effectively no better than the haggling of market wives, though no one would be so crass as to make the comparison. At the end of it, Abell's bounds were somewhat loosened and it was agreed that he and his two pupils would make one clear copy each of the entire magazine with sketches of the images where possible and with plenty of space for marginal notes around each page. Moreover, in conjunction with the master and Dr. Greene he was to oversee secondary copying of the three original copies made by those undergraduates who needed punishment for minor offenses, and furthermore he was begged to request that his family endeavour to locate other similar documents that the college would itself purchase.

Finally, it was agreed that all this was to occur in confidence lest other seekers after knowledge become encouraged to bid up the prices. Abell wondered out loud whether the university was going to send a delegation to the Rudolstadt colloquy due to start in a couple of months. The master looked pensive and remarked that the college was undoubtedly going to send an observer or two no matter what the university decided, and then wondered out loud whether the Abell family business would be willing to provide assistance in this journey and perhaps connections at the destination.

Abell was able to confirm that such assistance was possible, even likely, assuming a certain amount of monetary compensation but that he could not of course commit his family to anything. On that note and with the master reminding everyone that this was not a suitable subject for casual gossip, the party broke up for the day.

High table that evening was an occasion for Abell to see his master's political capabilities in action. By the end of it even the bursar was looking forward to the increased prominence of, and anticipated accompanying prosperity for, the college when it became a center of Grantville studies and all the academics were keen to discuss and debate the past-future of Grantville as they learned more about it.

The next morning's second lecture was devoted to Hakluyt, Will Adams, Mercator, Dutch mapmakers and English explorers, navigators, and their works. To Dunster, Saltmarsh, Gunton, and Healey this was a clue and they mobbed Abell at its conclusion. He was less than totally forthcoming but did admit that, yes, it did mean that the master was becoming interested in Grantville. He also broke the good news that his gating had been eased such that he might visit the commercial establishments of Magdalene Street, so long as he was accompanied by members of college who had taken a degree.

Abell did show to his companions the *National Geographic* and some of the astounding figures in the article—such as the population figures. However what really hit home, in a way that had not with the girls, was the throwaway comment that yields of thirty bushels of grain an acre were considered terrible! Since all his companions were countrymen, they realized just what that implied about the yields of England of the day, which were between a half and a third of that amount in good years. Theology was one thing but all, whether Puritan or

Sacramentalist, were united in the realization that "agri-chemicals," whatever they were exactly, would be worth anything short of a pact with the Devil to the average English yeoman farmer. A college that was not particularly religious had found a cause.

It turned out that the master, rather than having to use miscreants for the secondary and tertiary copying of the essays, received volunteers from every section of the college. The bursar insisted that "this Grantville nonsense" should not permit laxity elsewhere, and indeed his point was well made. The college could have come in for some severe penalties if it were perceived to be failing in its primary duties. The master's insistence that loose tongues be eschewed was also well understood. It was not clear whether the copying and subsequent exegesis of a pamphlet from Grantville would be construed as subversive or otherwise improper by either the university or London, but it was clear that the best way to avoid censure was to avoid needless publicity.

Magdalene, a college already physically separated from its peers by the river, now turned in on itself even more. Meanwhile the master and the fellows made occasional casual enquiry of their counterparts in the university, canvassing their thoughts on Grantville and their (lack of) knowledge of the upcoming colloquy. The majority seemed vaguely aware and generally uninterested. Of far more pressing concern to all were the stories of the recall to London and ennoblement of Wentworth, and the date when Laud would become archbishop of Canterbury.

To the intense irritation of the servants, the hall was appropriated for hours each day for the copiers to copy and check. Each evening the buttery, the Pickerel, and the other local inns and taverns as well as student rooms reverberated with debate about places such as Bangladesh or Rwanda. The most frustrating parts were the pictures or "photographs" that were impossible to transcribe, but that showed all sorts of peculiar behavior and objects. Since neither Abell nor the girls were particularly gifted artists they were unable to render them well and decided to omit most of them from their copies and drastically simplify others.

It was surprising how much scholars could tie together, when they were trained in the interpretation of Greek fathers and ancient Latin writers. Dr. Greene, now with the agreement of the majority of the fellows, proposed a large master copy to be placed in the library on which small numbers could be written referring to notes and discoveries made by different people.

One of these, identified by one of the more mathematically minded students, caused Abell some relief: it seemed that the mysterious "billion" was merely one thousand million, what the French and Dutch mathematicians were calling a *milliarde*. But the population milestones at the start of the journal made him acutely aware of the tenfold increase in the world's population between 1600 AD and 2000 AD. In the Pickerel, the discussions were usually moderated by Bess, who was now treated by many students as an equal. To a college with numerous sizars it was understood that labor did not preclude wit and wisdom and Bess's neat copying and frequently apposite comments had earned her respect for her mind.

The number of notes and conclusions grew swiftly.

Each week the master and Dr. Greene reviewed progress. In terms of providing avenues for further investigation, the project was highly successful. Likewise, in translating and interpreting the written words. In terms of describing the sort of world that Grantville came from it was less successful, but by no means a failure. It was possible to determine some broad strokes of history, to comprehend some of the capabilities of the world's technology, but it was clear that there was insufficient information to determine how these things were done. Agrichemicals, to take one example, were clearly some more advanced form of manure but what they were actually made of was not explained.

Many of the essays were thought-provoking to put it mildly, with the essay on "Women and Population" being perhaps the most shocking. Firstly, in that it discussed subjects that were practically taboo such as contraception and out-of-wedlock births. Even more shocking was that it made assumptions about the capability and occupations of women in 1998 that were utterly foreign to seventeenth-century England.

The first caused great initial consternation. When he realized what the words he was transcribing meant, Abell had paused in shock and the master had likewise nearly banned his daughter from further copying. But it was the second reason that was the more insidious. Even the most devout and strict Puritan, as keen as he might be to educate his womenfolk, could recall Saint Paul's strictures about the subordinate position of women, yet the essay brought home in so many ways that Bess had been right. The Americans really had come from a place where women were permitted, even expected, to do any task themselves that they wished.

There were serious debates at every level from the master and his fellowship to the lowest group of sizars with earnest and devout proposals to halt this effort. Surely this was all the blackest of heresy! If nothing else, it was a warning sent by God to show the dangers of the broad path to hell. Yet the arguments were rebuffed in the main by the argument that warnings needed someone to make them. If, as might be, Grantville was indeed a dire warning, then what purpose was served by the devout not investigating the danger and making their findings known far and wide?

One other shock, almost as indirect and insidious as the position of women in society, was the lack of reverence for the church. It was not that future society was Godless, for there were references to priests and to religions of one sort or another. It was the attitude that a person's relationship with God was his own affair and not that of his betters. For the members of Magdalene, a college where the fellows were usually required to be ordained and the students in the main expected to become priests, the resulting lack of mention of Christian religion was a void that left them continually unbalanced. It was as if the handrail of a steep and windy staircase was absent. Yet, despite the lack of mention of public devotion, it was clear from the news of the upcoming colloquy that these Americans were neither atheist nor heathen and that their rulers did care for the spiritual well-being of their subjects. It was this that led the noisiest debates, as students attempted to explain how a people of undoubted religion could be subject to a secular government.

In early February, the master took some of the less

controversial parts of the ongoing exegesis with him on a visit to Audley End and thence to London. His reception was somewhat mixed and he took care to avoid the royal court and Lambeth Palace. However, despite occasional setbacks he succeeded in his aim, which was to obtain sponsorship from both his patron the earl of Suffolk as well as certain merchants including the Abell family and others involved in the German and Baltic trade for a party of Magdalene scholars to attend the Rudolstadt colloquy in April and to attempt to procure additional source material from Grantville itself. Abell's father produced money on the strict understanding that his son was not to be a member of the expedition. The boy needed to learn discipline and self-control, both of which would be better found within the cloistered walls of academe.

End of February 1633

One evening, the Pickerel debate was in full swing. The discussion had started with debate about the size and composition of the party that was to make its way to Grantville in the next few weeks. Although Abell was known to be out of the running, the rest of the Pickerel group were considered near the top of the shortlist for selection. It was clear that Dr. Greene would be the leader since he had been involved with the master since the beginning and the master himself clearly could not be perceived to be gallivanting off to watch heretical colloquies. Since much theology would be discussed at the colloquy and since Dr. Greene was no theologian—indeed, he was not even ordained as fellows were expected to be—some junior with a sound grasp of theological niceties would be required. Dunster and Healey were both in the running for this position as both were BAs and generally considered strong scholars. However, unless rumor had failed to accurately describe the paucity of funds for the party, it was somewhat unlikely that both would be welcome as party theologians. Rumor said that Dr. Greene would name just one scholar for his theological expertise, the master would name one member on behalf of the earl of Suffolk, and the expected choice was a new BA who had links to both the master and the earl.

Finally, the London merchants would also expect a slightly more practically minded scholar to be chosen. Discussion of "Greene's choice" and "London's choice" as well as the possibility that the "master's choice" would not be as predicted was inconclusive. As the evening progressed, the discussion moved on to what the expedition would find in Germany, whether the place would be as peculiar as rumor suggested, and then the theological points of interest in the colloquy itself.

A middle-aged and prosperously dressed man entered the tavern, peering through the dim light as if looking for someone. Bess excused herself from the debate and walked over to him. She was thinking that he looked familiar, yet was sure that he had never before been in the Pickerel.

"Sir, are you seeking someone in particular?"

"If you be Mistress Chapman, then I am no longer looking." At Bess's startled nod, he continued: "I'm told you are an authority on the place called Grantville."

"Why, sir, I think you do me too much honor. 'Tis true I have some passing knowledge, but the true authority is yonder gentleman." She indicated Abell.

"That would be young master Abell, I assume. Perhaps you have not remarked it, but there is one big difference between you and your companions."

"Aye, that I am but a feeble witless woman," growled Bess. The debate of late had moved back to the more misogynist interpretations of parts of Saint Paul's epistles and Bess was feeling bitter.

"Nay. That is perhaps a symptom, but my meaning is that you are not a member of the university."

"Wherefore does that signify?" Bess realized that she was gossiping to a total stranger. "And pardon my forwardness, but who are you?"

"I'm Thomas Hobson, the carrier." Bess realized then why he looked familiar. Not only was he cousin to the Magdalene porter, he was one of Cambridge's leading citizens.

"The reason it is important that you not be a member of the university," Hobson continued, "is that you should have divergent opinions of the importance of certain subjects. However, I am running ahead of myself. I have supped with the mayor and others of like station this evening. Our conversation did concern this Grantville and, after divers speculations, it did occur to us that our estimates might be of greater worth were we to have discourse with one better informed as to its situation. Then, while we debated how best to approach the scholars, I recalled that there was one other, namely your good self, that was knowledgable. Yet, this being the significance, likely not enamored with theology and philosophy but being of a more practical bent."

Bess nodded agreement. " 'Tis true I do weary of some of their endless debates about predestination or the tolerance of heresy."

"I did therefore propose that we extend an invitation to you, with the consent of your father, to share the fruits of your studies with us when it might be convenient."

Bess was initially rather abashed to be asked to lecture the great and the good of the town, but she led Hobson to her father and was eventually persuaded that she should speak for an hour or two in the morning on the following Sunday, three days later, followed by an invitation to luncheon. Her father declined to attend the whole talk due to the necessities of managing the tavern. But he did agree, after seeing the pleading in his daughter's eyes, that the Pickerel could survive a Sunday noontime without his presence and that therefore he could be present for the meal.

The next morning, stage fright set in with a vengence. Bess was intensely aware of her humble position. Add to that the requirement to stand up and lecture to an audience for the first time ever and on a subject that she was by no means confident of her knowledge. She was remarkably distracted during her lessons and absented herself from her tavern duties as much as possible to clean, mend, and fret over her best dress. This fretting over costume failed to divert her attention from the content of the talk. She was unable to calm her fears except by writing out slate after slate of facts and speculation

about Grantville, and endlessly fiddling with the order
that the facts should be presented.

Sunday dawned and Bess attended the early service,
matins, at the round church with unusual piety. She had
got herself into such a state of nerves that she had barely
slept the night before. Finally, as the service came to a
close, she achieved some calm.

> "O LORDE our heavenly father, almightie and
> everlastyng God, whiche hast safely broughte us to
> the begynnyng of thys day: defende us in the same
> wyth thy myghtye power, and graunte that this
> daie we fall into no synne, nether rune into any
> kinde of daunger: but that al our doinges may be
> ordred by thy governaunce, to doe alwayes that is
> rightuous in thy sighte: through Jesus Christe our
> Lorde. Amen."

The third collect seemed remarkably appropriate and
her "amen" after it was heartfelt. Whether through the
grace of God or not, she returned to the Pickerel feeling
more cheerful. The day helped her mood with the sun
shining on a crisp, frosty landscape and, after gathering
her slates and making a final inspection of her appearance,
she made her way to the mayor's house. It was hard to be
miserable in the sunshine.

As Bess arrived at the mayor's doorstep, the door
opened. Thomas Hobson and the mayor himself stood
there to welcome her. Hobson relieved her of the slates
while a maid helped her remove her outer garment. Then

the party trooped into the large parlor where about half a dozen men of varying ages sat around the large fireplace. With them were two women, one much older than the other.

The men rose at her entrance. She was first introduced to the mayor's wife and the elderly woman, a Dame Joan Jermy, and then to the men. She recognized Mr. Parker and the man named Sir Edward Jermy was clearly Dame Joan's son, but the other names rather passed her by. When they were all seated and she had been offered refreshment by the maid, she began her talk.

"Mr. Hobson did say that you were interested in the practical so I shall not discuss the origin of Grantville and the question of whether it is the result of divine providence or diabolical malice. We do know that the town seems to have come from the future, that its inhabitants are as human as we are and that they have many things, techniques, and capabilities that we do not. My teacher, Abell, has said that the king himself is interested in their tales of history but I have no real knowledge of that. Although there is much that we do not understand, many things they possess are not entirely new, but merely improved versions of items of today. They do still print upon paper and this paper is not greatly different from that of today, yet the inks are of all the colors of the rainbow and thereby are pictures called photographs printed which are like paintings in their color and detail. And from the pictures we see that some dress in immodest fashion or wear bright raiment while others are as dull and modest as the most devout Puritan. It is the same with farming. They grow the same food and in some places use the same oxen as do we, yet in others they do use things that we do not have."

Bess started to relax as her audience listened attentively and interrupted only with occasional questions that were entirely to the point. From time to time debate would become more general, but always they treated her as an equal if not a superior, deferring to her opinions. The arrival of her father at noon took her by surprise, and the discussions continued as they were led into the dining room. Bess was seated next to the mayor at the head of the table with Hobson on her other side. Across the table sat Dame Joan with her father opposite Hobson. While talking to the mayor and Dame Joan about this and that she heard Hobson telling her father that she was "a credit to her family, gender, and town." Bess blushed at the general agreement to this statement. After a while she plucked up courage to ask why these worthies were so interested in Grantville and why they had preferred to listen to her rather than to one of the professors or senior graduates.

Hobson answered: "I trust I am not demeaning your intellect, Mistress Chapman, to point out that, although many in the town derive employment from the university we do not have an especial interest in the actions of the university or the colleges save as a body. The career of one student or the writings of one professor are of little regard to the residents of this town, though I own that the chancellor and his court does regulate much of our activities. The university provides benefit to the whole land of England and likewise draws its members from the whole realm. As regards the town, the university cares little save that we meet its wants for sustenance and the like. No matter that I carry their correspondence and their persons within my conveyances, no matter that my fellow merchants do provide provender, apparel, furniture, and so on. We are merely hewers of wood and drawers of water and they do not take us into their confidence.

"Furthermore the learning in this university is not such as befits practical use. Our eternal soul may care about the doctrine of predestination but our physical body upon this earth depends on more mundane matters such as meat, bread, and ale. Battles may be fought to prove God's favor on a cause but the profit and the suffering resulting do make for the loss and gain of fortunes in this world. The university does concern itself with origins and causes, methinks profit for the town does derive from actions and results. Were we to beg the professors for their knowledge and they deign to discourse with us, they would spend half a day discussing origins and another one explaining how Grantville disproved this Roman heresy or that Swiss one whereas you have started immediately with discourses on fashion and on farming.

"I know not whether we can, or whether we should, seek to emulate their achievements. But without knowledge of what Grantville is we can never start. The crumbs of knowledge and scraps of wisdom that fall from their table are not enough. We burgesses hunger for more. Enclosures and draining of the fens cause unrest that affects us more than it does them. If there is revolt it shall be us who bear the brunt. We hear rumors of miracles from this Grantville but none saw fit to elucidate as you have done."

Bess had been thinking the same thing recently, but she

was well aware of the deficiencies in her knowledge and thus strove to dampen optimism about their new understanding.

"I am not sure that I have done much more than show a map with large portions marked 'Terra Incognita' or 'here be dragons.' We know that not all of their wondrous technology has come with them, but we do not know what they lack. At Magdalene many have striven to comprehend the one document that we possess, yet we do not understand it all. For farming, we know that they can improve crops with these 'agrichemicals' but we know not what they are save that some things called 'nitrates' or 'phosphates.' It has been proposed that these words refer to a sort of alchemy for farming, and that therefore agrichemicals are some especial sort of manure. But we know not what are nitrates or phosphates, nor how to make them. So how can this knowledge of vocabulary help us?"

Dame Joan smiled. "Why, child, you have further shown your good sense. Today has indeed served merely to draw an outline, nothing more. And I know not what we can do to improve on the outline unless we visit the source. I have heard that members of the college will soon be undertaking to visit this place. But I know that if they do they will not see fit to inform us of what they have seen, nor are they likely to interest themselves in matters that might benefit us. Thus I propose that we sponsor a witness of our own to visit and report."

There followed considerable debate on what the witness should endeavor to learn, not to mention the desirable characteristics of such a witness. Eventually, after the hypothetical witness had been required to possess the education of Aristotle and the wisdom of Solomon, not to mention being a master at every trade under the sun, Dame Joan looked at Bess and raised her eyes to the heavens.

"Gentlemen," she interjected, "just where do you intend to find such a paragon of learning? It falls again to the weaker sex to show sense. We should rather make a list of whom we trust that can voyage for a season and then see which is best qualified than otherwise."

Not that this note of sense did a great deal of good. It seemed no one could recommend a suitable underling and none of the principals were able to excuse themselves from their businesses for an extended period of time without facing ruin, or so they claimed.

It was Sir Edward Jermy who broke the logjam. "Mother, you have remained quiet throughout this discussion. Are you intending to hide your own light under a bushel? Of all the people around this table you are the only one who has leisure. I'm sure my brothers and I can manage all the manors if you are not too old to venture to Germany."

Dame Joan looked startled. "Surely you are just looking for an excuse to be rid of your interfering parent! Do you prefer that I not be available as witness in that rent dispute that will be adjudged this term?" Then, talking over his vehement denials, she added: "But I feel that leisure is not sufficient. 'Tis said 'You can't teach an old dog new tricks' and I fear that be the truth. With the best will in the world I doubt I could make head or tail of all this new stuff. And I'm sure you can yourself testify as to the quality of my writing—or, rather, its lack."

Then she looked at Bess. "But I could take a companion, one whom you have all praised as a 'credit to her family, gender, and town.' Mistress Chapman, would you be willing to put up with an old lady on a voyage to Grantville? Since you are already wise to much about the place, I propose that you are best qualified to be our witness. Where to elect there is but one, 'tis Hobson's choice—take that or none!"

She smiled at Hobson. There was silence as the idea was considered from all angles, but no one seemed to be complaining. Bess looked thunderstruck. Finally she squeaked, barely daring to look at her father to see if he approved:

"You intend for me to travel to Grantville?"

"It seems your wits are capable of some deduction," Hobson responded drily. "Indeed, as Dame Joan intimates that would seem to be the sole solution. If you so desire, and your father agrees, of course."

The innkeeper nodded his shocked acquiescence.

"Oh sir!" exclaimed Bess. "I am honored to be Hobson's choice."

Historical Notes

The Pickerel pub is still a pub today and claims to be the oldest pub in Cambridge, although I have naturally invented its landlord in 1632. All the academic characters are real and in OTL Dunster went on to be the first president of Harvard. (www.president.harvard.edu/history)

I have, however, taken the liberty to modify the status of Abell, who was just a pensioner, and invent a background for him. He did share lodgings with Healey and Gunton and in our time line was the cause of a vicious internal college fight, which ended up pitting Smith vs. Smyth, by hinting that both they and the college fellows were Arminians.

The famous Thomas Hobson died sometime in 1630 or 1631, but we know he had at least one son since he left a manor and estate in nearby Cottenham to his grandson and heir, also called Thomas Hobson (d. 1667). I have assumed that the intermediate son was alive in the 1630s, running the business and called Thomas, but have been unable to confirm any of these assumptions.

Dame Joan Jermy and the other townspeople mentioned are also real. Reading between the rather sparse lines, Dame Joan appears to have been a tough and determined widow by 1633 (and was indeed involved in a legal dispute).

Much of this story is based on the researches of Magdalene's current generation of historians, particularly those of Dr. Duffy and Dr. Hoyle and the official Magdalene College History to which they contributed. (www.magd.cam.ac.uk/about/history/past.html)

The third collect at matins is taken directly from http://justus.anglican.org/resources/bcp/1559/MP_1559.htm

—*Francis Turner*

Hell Fighters

⚪★⚫

Wood Hughes

I: The Mission

The monastery of Subiaco:
Home of the Order of St. Benedict

"Brother Johann? The fathers are ready."

Brother Johann closed the small book he was studying and rose, straightening his black robe. While he had been aware of the gathering of abbots, he had no idea why the assembled abbots of the Order of Saint Benedict in the region had summoned him to their chambers. He followed Brother Mark into the meeting hall, which was carved out of the living rock cliff that the monastery was built out of. As he entered, he recognized the five abbots and archabbots. Each represented congregations of Benedictine monasteries from Rome in the south to the

Bursfeld Union in Germany and had traveled to Subiaco to consult on the current crisis facing the faithful. Also seated at the table was Dean Bernard, of his home monastery of Fulda.

"Thank you for coming, Brother," Cardinal Subiaco, the host for this congregation, began. "Please be seated. The order has been blessed by the wonderful work you've done in the six years since the Lord called you here to tend to our archives and the Saint Scholastica Library. However, Dean Bernard has brought us most disturbing news from Johann Bernhard, abbot prince of Fulda. We thought it may very well provide a most important calling for you and your skills."

Cardinal Subiaco nodded to Dean Bernard, who began, "It's wonderful to see you again, Brother. It's been too long since we've broken bread in Franconia. Johann, have you been following the news from our home?"

Brother Johann pressed his glasses back into place and squinted. "Not really, Bernard. I have noted in some of the recent reports the reversals in the campaigns to reestablish the Holy Church in the area. Of course I am aware that the monastery at Fulda itself is now under control of the Swedes."

"Not quite the Swedes, at least not directly." Dean Bernard pulled out a small book and passed it over to Brother Johann.

The book was of a construction that Johann had not seen before. It was of cloth, worn but smooth, wrapped around some sort of hard material. The backing had silver printing in what Johann assumed was English. It read: *Western Civilization*. He turned the book in his hands and felt the smoothness of the edges of the pages between their covers, and noticed a slight gleam that he had not noticed on the thousands of books he had handled in his life.

Pressing his glasses back into position, Johann then carefully opened the front cover and felt the glossy paper of which the book was printed. Casting a quick glance of disbelief at Dean Bernard, he thumbed through the book. Then such an incredible sight met his eyes that his mouth fell open and he instinctively crossed himself.

There on the page was an engraving unlike anything he had ever imagined. The colors were so vivid and the engraving was so fine that he thought momentarily that the people pictured there would begin to move at any moment. Johann had seen the finest illuminations that the Order of Saint Benedict had collected in the nine centuries since its founding, but nothing to rival this!

As he turned the pages, Johann noted illustrations, engravings, and actual paintings of people, places, and the most incredible artifacts that he could imagine. Even the clothing on those in the engravings changed from the familiar to more and more bizarre as he flipped rapidly through this incredible book.

"Dean Bernard, where did this come from? It is . . . most unusual."

"Most unusual indeed, Brother. It came from a city in the Saale River Valley. While filing away your monastic reports, have you come across any references to a 'Grantville'?"

"As you may recall," Johann responded in a puzzled tone, "I was born in the Saale River Valley just west of Schwarza. I recall no village or town by such a name."

"That is our problem, Brother," Archabbott Monte Cassino, who represented the monasteries of the congregation of Saint Justina of Padua, broke in as he leaned forward. "Until some months ago, there *was* no Grantville in the Saale River Valley, or anywhere else in God's Creation. It appeared there, full blown, along with people and inventions and artifacts which no one has ever seen before."

Glancing over to Bernard and nodding an apology, Archabbot Monte Cassino continued, "Forgive me for breaking in on your explanation, Dean Bernard. But the urgency of the matter requires a more direct sharing of information with Brother Johann.

"Brother, this Grantville has become the ruling power in Thuringia and an ally of the Swede. It, not the Swede, now controls vast reaches of Franconia and has managed to put the forces of Tilly in panicked retreat.

"They claim to be from a future almost four centuries ahead of our time. They claim to have no idea how or why they were brought here to the current time and place. The book you hold in your hands is evidence of the incredible things that their merchants and tinkerers can do with the most exotic machines. These devices mystify the most knowledgeable alchemists and scientists that the Church has consulted.

"Even more puzzling, although they have made a devil's pact with the Swede Gustavus Adolphus, they seem to be perfectly content to allow followers of the True Faith to practice our religious beliefs. They attempt to make no regulation based on their leaders' faith and beliefs.

"Dean Bernard has brought it to our attention that our

brothers in Christ, the Society of Jesus, have managed to place observers right in the middle of Grantville. This was done openly, with no apparent repercussions or persecutions of these emissaries. There even seems to be a Roman Catholic Church with its own congregation and parish priest, also from this amazing future.

"Brother Johann," Archabbot Monte Cassino asked, "would you please read the passage marked in the book you hold?"

Johann again looked down at the marvelous relic in his hands and noticed for the first time a cloth ribbon protruding slightly from the edge. Opening to the marked page, he saw a passage marked with what must have been a quill pen.

Johann was horrified at the desecration of such perfection. Still he began, "The confiscation of Catholic religious property following the Treaty of Westphalia (1648) had been for the benefit of Protestant rulers alone. More than a hundred monasteries and countless pious foundations disappeared at this time. By the middle of the eighteenth century a new movement devoted to the destruction of monastic institutions swept over those German portions of the Holy Roman Empire, which had remained loyal to the Catholic faith. The supernatural character of the religious life was totally ignored; abbeys and convents were permitted to exist only after giving proof of their material utility."

"That's enough, Brother." Archabbot Monte Cassino paused and looked around the table. "For nine centuries the order has brought education, civilization and the Good News of our Lord's Passion to the peoples of

Europe and the world. Now we find ourselves still strong in the faith, but weakened. Only three centuries ago, our order numbered over thirty-seven thousand monasteries. If this book is to be trusted, by the end of this century, we will be able to count only five thousand. Our lands in Germany are under Protestant control. Bursfeld itself is under Lutheran control. The Hessians have looted the great library at Fulda. And now, the Lord has brought to us a clear vision of how the Adversary will triumph over our best efforts unless we open our eyes to whatever it is He is trying to show us.

"We are in a crisis, Brother," Archabbot Monte Cassino continued. "Your brothers in Christ, here assembled, believe that the Lord has brought this test to us for a reason. After much prayer and discussion, we believe that Grantville was placed near Fulda at the time of its greatest challenge just so we could learn what lessons our order may have passed along to this future generation, represented by Grantville. Thus we hope to have a light cast on the path the Lord intends for us to walk during this time of death and destruction.

"You, Brother Johann, are from the very valley in which Grantville is now located. You worked and prayed and studied for decades in the library of Fulda. You brought such a rationality to the organization of the books and journals and other papers there that your methods have been adopted by not only our monasteries," Archabbot Monte Cassino gestured to the other abbots around the table as he continued, "but by Benedictine monasteries throughout Europe. You were called here to help rediscover the knowledge that our Lord has revealed to our brothers that has been stored here since our founding.

" 'Listen, my son, to the precepts of the master, and lend the ears of your heart.' These are the words of our beloved Saint Benedict and this is the calling which we believe that God has chosen for you."

All the abbots and Dean Bernard stood and clasped their hands as if beginning a prayer. "Brother Johann, we, the fathers assembled, humbly request that you make a pilgrimage to this place Grantville, not to spread the Word, but to listen and learn. We fervently pray that the Lord reveal His purpose to you, thereby to the future of the order and how we may continue to serve the souls of humanity by His Grace."

II: The Journey

Johann had spent the night in his cell praying for guidance on how to prepare for this great adventure that God had ordained for him. When the first rays of light broke through his small window, he ended his communion with the Lord, crossed himself, and walked to his library.

Like the fruit that tempted Eve, the book lay on the table where he'd left it the previous night. The stories it held! Up to the current time, it seemed to be accurate or at least convincing that there might be truths contained that he had not been exposed to. But then it continued, page after page of horrible, mind-numbing events and wars. But most amazing of all, the ideas!

Thinkers, some just born, some not to be born for centuries, illuminated this future with such intriguing ideas and the results of those ideas. Some of those ideas were on a par with Aristotle, some on a par with Lucifer, but all contained promise and all contained traps.

Johann picked up the *Western Civilization* book and wandered over and laid it next to the *Lattanzio Sublacense*. That was the first book written, typeset, and printed in this very monastery by brothers and fellow Germans Sweynheim and Pannartz. They had brought the first printing press to Italy in 1464. That very press still stood in another room in the monastery. He was staring at what he had always considered the holy art of printing, on one hand 167 years in the past, on the other 367 years in the future. He glanced up and saw the cabinet in which he had stored one of the only manuscripts of Saint Augustine himself, the *De Civitate Dei*.

"Blessed Saint Augustine," he prayed, "please show me whether this Grantville is indeed a city of God or a city of the Devil."

It took several more days before he was satisfied that he had learned all that his mind could absorb from this book of one future and began his preparations. As a Benedictine monk, Johann led a very simple life. Leaving behind material possessions was not a problem. Brother Julio was ready to take over his responsibilities in the library. Johann devoted his remaining time to meeting with individual monks. He prayed with them singly or in small groups and then began his trip to his almost forgotten homeland.

During the weeks it took for him to walk across the

Alps, Johann had sufficient time to realize that this was truly a journey into the future and the past.

Grantville, of course, represented the future. But Thuringia . . . memories of his childhood in Thuringia, seemingly lost in the decades since he had been away, kept coming up at every turn. He remembered skipping rocks off the small pools formed in the meanders of the Schwarza River and chasing rabbits in the meadows of his father's estate. He smiled as he recalled the rich smells of the pastries his mother could bake in that beautiful, giant, solidly built German house that protected his family and in winter, the family livestock.

It had been years since he learned that his sisters Gretchen and Inga had died of the plague. They were the last of his family, other than himself, to survive the horrible devastation of the "Thirty Years' War," as the book had named it.

Johann shivered and pulled his black robes closer and adjusted his pack. It wasn't just the chill of the mountain air in this northern clime that caused that particular shiver. "I wonder if Herr von Schoenfeld is still alive?" he murmured.

When Johann had been a boy, it was von Schoenfeld who had introduced him to the joy of books. They held wonderful tales, vistas and horizons that he could never have even imagined. Books had opened a door that had led Johann inevitably to the great library in the abbey of Fulda, the greatest library in southern Germany.

There it was Brother Georg who showed him how to preserve those precious manuscripts in such a way as to make them last. It was Brother Georg who showed him the beauty of the order of knowledge that exists in a library, and from that in the teachings of God as revealed by Saint Benedict.

And when Brother Georg was promoted to the Church Triumphant some years later, Johann knelt before Abbot Johann Friedrich von Schwalbach and accepted his vows, converting from the Lutheran heresy to the monastic life of Saint Benedict.

III: The Arrival

After several days of following the road down the Elbe River Valley toward where the Saale River joined its flow, Johann began hearing a peculiar sound. At first he thought it might be his imagination, the soft *potato, potato, potato* sound, but soon he noticed it changing to a low rumbling roar in the distance. Occasionally he heard a high-pitched whirring sound that he could not identify either. Crossing himself, once again he offered up his silent prayer for protection and took care to keep within sight any convenient hiding spot along his path.

At the next bend in the road, he saw the source of his concern. There, in the middle of the road was a machine, yellow with a large box affixed to one end and what looked like an arm attached to the other. In the center sat a man in dress something like what Johann had seen in the incredible engravings in the book. Black smoke blew from the chimney of the roaring machine as the person on top did something with some levers. The arm moved!

There was a large scoop at the end. The arm and scoop

took a bite out of the ground beneath, picked it up, and tossed it to one side. Then it repeated the action.

Johann was so amazed at this that he was startled by the high-pitched whine, which suddenly started up to the left of the yellow machine. He pushed his glasses up the bridge of his nose in order to improve his vision and squinted. He finally located a man standing by a felled tree holding something that was tearing a hole out of the timber. After watching the actions of this small crew of men and their machines for a time, he decided that if he was to ever reach Grantville, he must get past this challenge.

Johann walked carefully toward the men and their machines. Another one of them noticed him and, putting down his device, picked up something that resembled a musket but was much shorter. In bad German, he yelled, "Advance and be recognized! Keep your hands in clear sight! Hurry!"

Johann raised his arms to waist height and turned his palms up in what he hoped the stranger would view as a supplicating manner, and continued his approach.

"I come to find Grantville," Johann said when he was within range of normal speech. "Would you rather speak in English or German?"

The stranger was now joined by a couple of his fellows. "Hell, Jimmy," said one of them. "This guy talks better English than you do."

"What's your business, traveler?" asked the one named Jimmy. "What brings you to the United States?"

A moment's confusion slowed Johann's response. He had read of this United States, but it was clearly on the North American continent at least 140 years in the future.

No matter, he quickly decided. "I am Brother Johann of the monastic Order of Saint Benedict. I come to see Grantville and find God's purpose in bringing it here."

The one that challenged him brought his short musket to his side and laughed. "Well, Padre, as soon as you figure that out, be sure to let me know. I've been trying to figure that one out since we got here!"

The men welcomed Johann and offered him water from a bright orange container. They shared their food as they talked about themselves and their home. They referred to this pause as something called a "smoke break." It must have referred to the machines being turned off, because the smoke had stopped while they broke.

Johann was more interested in the men than the devices they took so much for granted. There was a genuine air of openness and confidence in even the least of the crew members. That was combined with a certain sense of danger should some nebulous opponent ever cross their path.

After finishing his first smoke break, Johann got directions from the crew. He picked up his pack and blessed them to be safe in their work. Every man bent his head and one even made the sign of the cross as Johann finished his blessing. The road, from that point, became noticeably more level. It had a layer of crushed rock that had been packed in some way. Where washes had been there were now metal pipes to allow the water flow to go under the roadbed.

For the next several days, Brother Johann continued to pass the familiar sights of villagers going about their proper work. Farmers in the fields gathered what, to Johann, seemed to be large harvests of their respective crops. Also the occasional machine would pass Johann. They were operated by more of these "up-timers," or "Americans," as they called themselves.

Finally he reached the last leg of his journey. Johann turned up the "American road" along the north shore of the Schwarza River. As he walked along the improved road, he passed more and more large American construction sites on and near the riverbank. Amazingly, it seemed that Grantville must be very close to his family estate.

When he came upon several houses within sight of the road, he realized that he recognized them. One, just off the road, had a cairn of rocks in the field in front of it. There was a sign which read:

WE DON'T KNOW WHO THESE MURDERING RAPING BASTARDS ARE THAT WE PUT HERE. DON'T MUCH CARE EITHER. IF THERE ARE ANY MORE OF YOU OUT THERE, BE WARNED. THIS AREA IS NOW UNDER THE PROTECTION OF THE UMWA. IF YOU TRY TO HARM OR ROB ANYBODY WE WILL KILL YOU. THERE WILL BE NO FURTHER WARNING. WE WILL NOT NEGOTIATE. WE WILL NOT ARREST YOU. YOU WILL SIMPLY BE DEAD. WE GUARANTEE IT. GO AHEAD. TRY US.

It had been a neighbor's home. Johann clearly remembered the young boy he had played and grown up with. While he couldn't quite remember the name, he remembered the boy always liked to work with his hands, while Johann preferred to keep his hands on books.

Then it struck him. He turned and realized that the American road dove into a cut in the ground just beyond this neighbor's home. How could this be?

Johann dropped to his knees, as the personal price of this mission suddenly became crystal clear him. This was the very land that had been seized from the abbey of Fulda during the early days of the Protestant Reformation. It was the same land that then had been awarded to one of Johann's ancestors for service to his rulers. This very land had been taken by God to advance His will.

Grantville was largely on his very own family land! What a divine irony. Johann's older siblings and their families were dead. Johann himself had taken a vow of poverty and renounced his claim to the land and its income. Thus God was free to do as He willed, and He obviously had.

Johann ran his hand through his graying but still blond hair. He now saw that his entire life had been laid out so that this very event could take place. Like most who study the Bible, Johann had at times wondered what Moses must have felt like when he saw the bush that burned but was not consumed or what the bystanders at the grave of Lazarus had experienced when he walked alive from the grave. Now, for the first time, he really, truly knew.

He passed through the cut and stepped on the soft dark gray rock surface of the road beyond. Johann looked around in what now seemed a state of continuing amazement at the slightly curved earthen wall that stretched out from him in opposite directions. It seemed to form a clear delineation between what was then and what was now.

Steep hills rose and fell on both sides as he continued

into what the American road crew had referred to as the "Ring of Fire." He passed small houses and buildings set back off the dark gray road. He also passed less traveled, but similarly constructed roads, which made their way to their appointed destinations. Johann began to notice a smell. He had been in many cities and villages in his life and recognized the smell of soot from the wood used to cook and to warm the inhabitants. He had been into the smithies and hammer mills where iron was worked over coal fires with its unique gritty, sulfur, and metallic smell. Even though this was stronger than he had been exposed to before, there was something different about the smell of this town he was walking into.

There was not the smell of ammonia from the human waste that was a common part of city life to his experience. Not that German or Italian cities were the depositories of human waste that brother monks related from their experiences in England, but so many outhouses and waste collection vehicles naturally left their perfume as part of the background smell of a city.

More and more people passed him on the road. Some of them were dressed in that strange new garb of Americans; most were dressed in the normal clothing that he was accustomed to. Then some wore with mixtures of normal garb and either a cap with a bill on it or light, tight shirts with drawings or messages printed on them. There was an increasing diversity of vehicles as well. Mostly there were horse-drawn wagons jockeying for position in the flow of traffic. But, occasionally, vehicles like Johann had seen in the book at the monastery passed with a soft rumble from under their metal surfaces.

No one seemed fearful. At most, the inhabitants appeared anxious to get to wherever they were going. Nor did he notice any beggars on the corners. Corners that he noticed were not made of cut stone, but of some kind of molded rock material that looked as though it had been poured in a molten state, and had frozen in place.

On his right as he walked up one hill, he noticed a tall, solidly built man stretching on the front porch of a neatly kept white cottage. The man looked very sharply at him, and then, as if making some kind of studied judgment, smiled and waved.

Johann smiled back and, shifting his pack, waved, finishing with the sign of the cross.

IV: *The Grantville Library*

"I'd better get back before Heather starts imagining the bodies are moving again."

"Jenny, leave the poor girl alone. She was just jittery when she realized that the job she was assigned to at the Bureau of Vital Statistics was at the funeral home. Of course, catching you taking a nap in a coffin just might have been a bit much."

Marietta Fielder had known Jenny Maddox since they were kids. Although two more opposite personalities could hardly be imagined, they'd remained the best of friends throughout.

"The simple pleasures I have to give up just to get good help these days. I've still got that extra large coffin ready, just in case you get tired of your current bed."

Marietta laughed in spite of herself, "No thanks, I'm perfectly fine with my current mattress."

"Will you looky there," Marietta said, indicating the man walking up the ramp outside the picture window in front of the Grantville Public Library. "Is that some kind of a down-time guy in drag?

"At least he knows how to pick jewelry. That cross perfectly compliments the black gown." Both girls giggled as the door opened.

Marietta greeted the oddly garbed visitor. "Afternoon, sir. If you need any help, just ask."

"Thank you, Frau. May I please see your library?"

"Help yourself. I'm going to have to ask you to leave your backpack up here though. We've had some trouble lately with people taking books without checking them out. Are you looking for anything in particular?"

Brother Johann looked puzzled and pushed his glasses back into place. "I don't really know. I've never been in a library quite like this. Is this the only area accessible to outsiders?"

"Now you've done it," Jenny broke in. "Here comes the Public Lending Library 101 speech. If you two will excuse me, I need to go. See you tomorrow, Marietta. Nice meeting you too, Mister . . . ?"

"Brother Johann. I've just arrived in Grantville from Italy."

"Funny, you don't sound Italian," Marietta said.

"No, I'm actually from . . ." Johann paused. "Very close to here, originally. But I've been serving in the Benedictine library in Subiaco for some years now. I was asked to come here in order to learn what the Lord's purpose was in bringing Grantville to our time."

"Oh! Well then, Brother Johann, welcome to Grantville. You just arrived? You mean you really just got here and came straight to the library?" Marietta was taken aback, half wondering if Johann was pulling her leg and half excited about the possibility of meeting a kindred spirit. She had been initiated into the field of library science at an early age. As a third grader, Mrs. Yardley had noticed her reshelving the 788.12 section in the correct order. Then she had offered her an after-school job as a page.

Johann nodded. "Yes, Frau. I asked where the library was and a kind lady pointed me this way. Is this the whole of your collection?"

"Goodness, no." Turning to her friend, Marietta said, "Jenny, I'll see you later. Let me help this man."

After she and Jenny finished their good-byes, Marietta continued, "This is just the reference and noncirculating section. My name is Marietta Fielder. Glad to meet you. Now, if you will follow me . . ." She walked to the back of the room to a step up to an open doorway. "This section holds up to three hundred books and through there"—indicating another door where an even larger room awaited—"are another four hundred-plus books and, of course, fiction. Uh . . . Brother, are you okay?"

Johann was staring at the ceiling, mouth open. Marietta looked up and saw the fluorescent light fixture. The plastic cover had fallen out last week and she hadn't had time to replace it.

"That's called an electric light, fluorescent to be exact. It was an invention of the early twentieth century. You're going to see a lot of new things here, Brother Johann."

"Yes, this I've learned." Johann followed Marietta

through the rest of her tour. He also recognized the same love of books and the preservation of knowledge in Marietta that had consumed his life. He listened to Marietta's explanation of the concept of an up-time lending library and was introduced to some of the staff. He noticed the occasional empty spaces in the shelves, like missing teeth in an otherwise perfect mouth. His mind swirled.

"Frau Fielder, perhaps I should take care of my lodging arrangements before the day gets by, and come back in the morning to study your collection. Do you know where I might find quarters?"

"That's easy, if you have money." Johann nodded as Marietta continued, "You ought to go to see Huddy Colburn at Grantville Homes and Land. He's been handling relocations and housing for the emergency committee since the Ring of Fire. His office is back on Main and just a half block on the right.

"We open at eight-thirty Monday through Saturday and usually close at seven PM," Marietta continued. "Five on Saturdays. I'll see you in the morning, okay?"

V: Lodging

Huddy Colburn put the paperwork back in its legal file and laid it on the Done pile. *Be careful what you pray for next time, Hudson,* he thought, and grinned briefly.

The first couple of weeks after the Ring of Fire, Huddy had gone into the office once a day just to reassure his remaining agents that somehow everything would work out. Business had stopped and no one seemed to know what was going to happen. Then the Mike Stearns plan had kicked in. Just as he had done since coming home, Mike had taken charge. On the strength of his personality alone people had given up driving their cars, pitched in with planting every available square foot of land, turned out for defense drills, and did pretty much anything else he asked.

When the first wave of refugees hit Grantville everything changed. Mike called Huddy and asked him to take charge of making sure everyone had shelter by winter. That alone had put Huddy and his agents on a heavier work schedule than they had ever thought of in this hillbilly town. Then, with construction firing up to build new housing, Huddy had taken it on himself to teach his agents how to do a simple construction inspection. If the builder didn't pass, he could count that Huddy wouldn't let the people he was responsible for live there.

A few days later Huddy's cousin, Willy Ray Hudson, breezed into the office with his business partners in Thuringen Gardens. Willy Ray was looking for some help in drawing up a partnership agreement. All the lawyers were slammed with work, so Huddy pulled out the reference material he had. It was left over from when he put together the buyout agreement to purchase Grantville Homes and Land from Mayor Dreeson.

After that, Huddy became the semiofficial Grantville business broker. With all the entrepreneurs who had bubbled up since, that, too, had become a full-time job. As long as Huddy was busy, he didn't have time to think of Mary, or the other thing.

Well, Huddy ol' boy, you wanted to keep busy, so get

back to work. He picked up the next file from the bottom-less pile on the right side of his desk.

Huddy had just gotten the paperwork spread out so he could figure out what this deal was all about. The bell on his front door rang. Since Maxine was out running errands and the rest of his agents were out looking at construction sites or collecting rents, Huddy leaned his chair to the left to get a view of the thin blond man in a black robe walking into his office.

"So where are we going to put you, Brother?" Huddy reviewed the notes from his conversation with Johann. "Would you excuse me while I look through the available properties files? Make yourself at home, I'll be right back."

Huddy walked out and Johann looked around the office. As a follower of Saint Benedict, he and his brother monks led a spartan life with only the simplest of necessities. This man's office was anything but simple. It spoke of a life lived in full.

The desk was filled with stacks of files, each neatly labeled. The walls were filled with certificates of some achievement or the other, an old red bandanna, and a mis-shapen leather glove. More than anything else, there were pictures of smiling people standing in front of houses. Johann was surprised to realize that he recognized one of the houses and the man who had waved at him as he entered the town earlier today.

"Those are my families." Johann was caught off guard when Huddy reentered the room. "I helped every one of those folks to buy their first home. You help people your way, Brother; I help them create a better life in their own home."

"Herr Colburn, I saw this man earlier today," Johann pointed to the picture. "Who is he?"

"You saw him today? That's Mike Stearns, the head of the Emergency Committee. When he first moved back to Grantville and got active with the United Mine Workers Association, he was trying to buy his own home. Some kind of glitch turned up in his credit report and I helped him get it straightened out. Mike's been sending young members of the local to me ever since."

Huddy gestured with his left hand, which held a small stack of cards. "Now, let's go over what's available. I would just send you over to Saint Vincent's, I mean Saint Mary's, the local Catholic church. But Father Mazzare's been sending folks looking for shelter outside the refugee camps to me for the last couple of weeks. He's out of town this week, anyway."

Huddy sat back in his chair and flipped through the cards he held. He considered the information held on each card before moving to the next. One caught his attention and Johann noted that Huddy looked puzzled for a moment, and then slowly a grin formed on his face. "Brother, first you've got to understand that where we're from, real estate agents can't discriminate against folks due to race, creed, color, or national origin. That means that every property that is brought to us can't do that either. Does that make sense?"

Johann nodded.

"Okay, then. My church just finished rehabbing the basement and made repairs on the heating system. It has room for eight boarders, two of which are singles. It's just a couple of blocks from the library where you say you'll be spending the bulk of your time.

"So, Brother Johann, how do you feel about living in a Presbyterian Church?"

VI: Systems

"I'd say he's somewhere between a kid in a candy store and a guy trying to take a drink out of Niagara Falls," Gloria Maze commented, as she inserted her sorting rod into the large stack of punch-holed book catalog cards. She lifted some out of the bin and deposited them neatly to the back. "Every time I poke my head back there, he's somewhere else just examining the books themselves, not even looking at the contents."

"Well, what would you expect?" Martha shook her head. "He's discovered almost four centuries of advancement in every field of knowledge. It's a lot to take in at one time."

"Marietta, it's been four days, morning to closing time, taking a break only to say his prayers and he's not even looking at the knowledge. Just the books and the bindings. If I see him run his fingers across the catalog numbers on another spine, I swear I'm going to scream."

Marietta smiled. "Gloria, do you think he's figured out what they are? The catalog numbers, I mean."

Gloria stopped and looked at Marietta thoughtfully. "We're the idiots. He's never been exposed to modern library science, why would he have known? That must explain the sad look that comes over him every time he looks at the numbers on the spines. He must think we've defaced the books somehow but can't bring himself to accuse us of it."

"Well, it's high time to begin his education." Setting aside her catalog cards, Gloria walked into the stacks located behind the circulation desk and quickly found the two volumes she was looking for. Both women walked back to the main library room where Johann was sitting, studying yet another book.

"Brother Johann, do you have a moment?"

"Of course, my ladies," he said while standing up.

"Brother," Marietta began, "we thought this might be helpful to you."

The women laid the volumes on the table and stood on each side of Johann. Gloria motioned him to take his seat and continued. "Brother, these are the keys to the library. It's the instructions to the system that we use to keep the books organized so people can find what they are looking for. It's called the Dewey decimal system.

"These numbers"—Gloria indicated the numbers on the spine of the book that Johann had in front of him on the table—"indicate that this book is about geography. That's a nine hundred classification, see? It's also got the same number on the inside title page right here."

Gloria turned to the page and pointed to the "910.285" on the page. "There were several different systems for cataloging books depending on the needs of the library, but most public libraries used the Dewey system. You'll also see the Library of Congress number," she said, pointing to that number on the same page, "but since we don't use that system, we don't have any publications on how it

worked in our library here, or at the school libraries, for
that matter."

Marietta took over. "See, Brother, each hundred means
a different thing. General information is 000–099,
100–199 is where we store books on philosophy, 200–299
is for religion and so on. Then the tens digits mean what
subcategory the books fall under and so on. If it is 207,
that means the book covers education and research in
Christianity, 252 is where published texts of sermons are
kept, and 255 is where information on religious congregations and orders are kept.

"Why don't you look through these and if you have any
questions, just come up and ask us."

Johann was stunned. This was a true book on how to
find books. The letters he had written to other monks on
ideas to find order in their monastic libraries seemed the
scribbling of a child next to this two-volume set. Crossing
himself and saying a quiet prayer of thanks, he opened the
first book and carefully began to study this incredible
system from the future.

The next day was very hard on Johann. He kept to his
well-appointed cell (no, suite was more like it) in the
Calvinist church basement. As he prayed thanks for the
marvelous gift of learning about the new system, he
yearned to go back to the library even if it was Sunday.
When he heard the organist begin upstairs and the choir
begin to sing "Here I Am Lord, Send Me," Johann couldn't
believe that he was quartered here in the basement of a
Calvinist church.

Even more amazing, no one seemed to think anything of it. Well, the up-timers anyway.

Wilson and Witherspoon, the Scottish cavalrymen, certainly maintained their distance, and he occasionally heard them mutter "papist" at him after he passed on the way to the library in the mornings. But he also had seen the sharp, disapproving glances that a member of the congregation, John Furbee, cast their way when they began.

But day of rest or not, even during his prayers, Johann's mind kept coming back to this marvelous creation of Melvil Dewey. *This is just another cross I must bear*, Johann thought, as he redoubled his efforts to cleanse his thoughts of work while in prayer.

It was almost comical to the library staff, watching this black-robed monk adjusting his glasses on his nose, consulting the DDC21, and then hurrying off to one part of the library or the other. His eyes gleamed with excitement every time he located exactly what he had been hunting for. And the look of absolute delight when he found a book that was mis-shelved that he could move to its proper place! That was worth the price of admission every time.

When Gloria took him to the card catalog and explained the triple filing system it represented, she thought he would burst out into song, or whatever it was that monks did when they were excited. Johann went through drawer after drawer of cards, checking to make sure that a book filed under the author's name was also filed under category and subject.

It really wasn't mean at all, Gloria told herself, to have

Brother Johann reshelf the returned books for her. He obviously enjoyed it so much. And Orson DeBolt certainly didn't mind when Johann asked to help him clean up after hours.

Orson had been fussing over all the clutter and trash from so much more traffic through the library since the Ring of Fire. Now he felt that his prayers at the Church of Christ had paid off, even if they had paid off in the form of a Roman Catholic monk.

By the time winter's first snow fell on Grantville, Johann had a firm grasp on the contents of the Grantville Public Library and understood why so many books had been moved to the high school to form the National Library. He even suggested that several other categories of books might be helpful to the researchers over there, trying to find technologies to help them survive in the present era.

As he learned more of the organization systems created in this future, he was less surprised to realize that even these systems were recognized by the people of their age as being less than perfect. There seemed to be an irreconcilable difference between the Library of Congress system and the Dewey system. Later, he was browsing through some of the slick newsweekly magazines he had found stored away in boxes. Johann found tantalizing hints of a system that seemed to be in the early phases of creation that somehow was able to take nouns and phrases from every document and relate it to every other document with similar uses of the same nouns and phrases. These systems had odd-sounding names, even by up-timer standards, but one that had won some kind of award he had to read out loud to hear the sound. "Google."

How they did this, Johann had no idea, but he knew in the words of Solomon, "All streams flow into the sea, yet the sea is never full." Perfection does not exist, did not exist, and would not be found in the works of these Americans. The process of God's Will continued.

But he had no interest in the technology and gadgets of the twentieth century, beyond those incredible fluorescent lights overhead. Those allowed him to do his work in perfect lighting conditions, no matter what time of day or night.

The organization of the knowledge, he felt, still must contain the secrets the abbots had sent him to find. He read the Catholic encyclopedia and marveled at the various concordances he had located. Some of the Protestant sermons had rung true to him, and even the rulings of future popes had indicated that the Church of this future had learned lessons from the Protestant movement of his time.

He carefully quoted appropriate passages in his reports back to his abbot at Subiaco, with the requested duplicate message going to the abbot prince at Fulda. He knew that his colleagues there would print duplicates to distribute to the other Benedictine monasteries that had been notified of his mission, and to his Holiness the Pope. Therefore he was careful to cite only the most conservative of sources.

Then there was the TV! At first, Johann thought of television in the same category as the puppet plays you could find on a town square during market week. Then he saw Charlton Heston portraying Moses in *The Ten Commandments* and marveled at the parting of the Red Sea.

He was hooked!

★ ★ ★

Although he had not attended the town Christmas party, he watched the Rebecca Stearns show that night to catch the news of the party and the disturbance that had happened there. After all this time in Grantville, Johann still marveled. In a largely up-time Protestant town, filled to overflowing with down-time Catholics and Protestants of widely differing religious beliefs, a Jewish woman could speak so eloquently about the symbol of the first baby born inside the Ring of Fire on Christmas Day. She said it was a sign of the bright future that stood before them all if they just kept working and believing in this American dream of being united by a better future. Believing and keeping their faith in the ideals of the rights of life, liberty, and the pursuit of prosperity for all mankind insured a better future for them all.

As Johann wrote his report that night, he realized that he had been shown a light to guide him on his path toward fulfilling his mission. When finished, he rested peacefully.

VII: Hell

Woolly Snider had big plans for New Year's Eve. The mines had closed down for their weeklong holiday. Even with the emergency situation after the Ring of Fire, the mines still needed to perform regular maintenance. Woolly, as usual, had been spending most of his off time at Tip's, his favorite local bar. Tip Fisher had built a damn fine brewery out back, which along with the still he swore was built from the plans his grandpappy had drawn up, served a very tasty boilermaker.

Unlike the owner of Club 250, Tip was more interested in cheap labor that didn't steal from him than where or when they had been born. It also didn't hurt that Tip's had a new barmaid named Inga. She was one of those refugee down-timers and always seemed to be at Woolly's elbow when his beer needed refilling. Even though she didn't speak English too good, she always laughed and blushed when he flirted with her. She wasn't the prettiest thing in town but had big tits and a solid, but not fat waistline. As he was on the long side of fifty, Woolly wasn't as particular as he had been in his early years.

To tell the truth, which sometimes even Woolly did to himself, he had never been very particular about women or booze. Those two vices had gotten him into trouble more times than he liked to recall.

Grantville was having a hard winter, so it didn't surprise anyone when it started snowing around nine that night. Woolly, having started early, was fairly well tanked by then. When Joe Coonce, the bartender, announced he was going to close early, New Year's Eve or not, Woolly decided he had nothing to lose by asking Inga to come home with him. Even with the confidence that Tip's still had given him, he was more than a little surprised when she nodded yes.

After Inga finished cleaning up, they walked up the hill in an increasingly heavy snowfall, to his shack. The shack wasn't much from the start. However, because it was connected to a septic collection station, it was now surrounded by a large cluster of new emergency housing. Woolly and his neighbors had built this jumble just downhill from the unincorporated village of Deborah to house a lot of paying refugees during the winter.

Tents, plywood shacks with tar paper roofs, and every imaginable construction shortcut was represented in the cluster of buildings. They were tightly packed around the central toilet and water facility that had at one time been the workshop of Woolly and his neighbor. Who the hell cared if those assholes at the town housing office didn't send renters his way? There were plenty of Germans looking for any warm place to sleep in the middle of this winter.

Some time later, Woolly rolled over and pulled his covers off and sat up. *Not bad, old man*, he thought to himself. *Even after all this time, everything still works like it's supposed to.*

As he listened to Inga settling in to her nap, Woolly decided that this would be the perfect time to break out his last pack of smokes. After all, if this wasn't a good reason to celebrate, nothing was!

Woolly fired one up and lay back down and considered his good fortune. He went back over all the little things that had made the evening enjoyable as his eyes got heavy.

As he fell asleep, Woolly dropped the still lit cigarette onto the floor. It rolled to rest against a rag that Woolly had been using to clean the pistons of his car before he installed his new natural-gas conversion kit. It wasn't for some several seconds more that the ash tip came into contact with the oily rag, which began to smolder. A small flame sprang up shortly thereafter. It found fertile fuel in the newspaper that Woolly had pasted to the wall to cut down on the drafts from outside. The newspaper, in turn, put out a plume of smoke and carbon monoxide as it quietly burned away. Unfortunately, Woolly had also been collecting and compressing plastic containers, which also caught fire. This produced even more black smoke and gas. Next to ignite was a stack of more newspapers and a comprehensive collection of slick men's magazines. Woolly had bought these at a gas station by the interstate some time before the Ring of Fire. Now they erected a plume of smoke and were an additional source of carbon monoxide gas. In turn, the curtains engaged, all of which poured more smoke into the room.

Woolly and Inga coughed, but were much too intoxicated and drained after their horizontal exercises to realize that the smoke they were breathing wasn't from the cigarette. It wasn't until the flames caught the polyester bedspread on fire that Inga woke to a terrible burning sensation around her legs. She screamed and she jumped out of bed right into the middle of another burning pile of magazines. If her cotton slip hadn't been fully on fire by then, it certainly was now. Of course, the bedspread wanted to stick to her skin as she dragged it, all the while screaming. Now standing upright, breathing in nothing but smoke and carbon monoxide, Inga continued to scream in agony and run around the room looking for relief. It came with the loss of oxygen as she fainted back into the middle of the now fully engaged bed.

For the second time tonight, Woolly had gotten lucky. Awakened with a start by the sounds of Inga screaming, his heart seized and he died before he even felt the flames begin to lick his naked body.

By now the flames had reached a temperature of over 1800 degrees at the ceiling and between 300 and 400 degrees at the floor and had burned their way through the tar paper roof. Glowing embers were rising up through the heavy snowfall, which had the effect of muffling the sounds of Inga's screams from the sleeping families situated around the flaming house. Mostly, the embers died in the heavy snow. But a few made the most of the fresh fuel they had found in a pile of straw that was stored under the eve of one of the temporary plywood structures nearby.

The dry straw caught on and passed the flames to begin licking up the corner of the adjacent plywood wall where slept the First Christmas Baby of Grantville. Born just six days ago to Mathias and Anna Heydman, who had fled into the Ring of Fire area fleeing the approaching armies of mercenaries, little Mike Stearns Heydman was sleeping soundly in his mother's arms. His father was pulling the late shift cleaning up at the police station. At first the warmth of the wall felt good to Anna. She was unaware that carbon monoxide gas had already slowed her reactions. First, she became aware of the coughing of her child, and then she smelled the smoke. She became alert just in time to see the wall give way and fire flame through the wall and catch her and little Mike's bedding on fire. She immediately grabbed her child and pulled him to her as she tried to escape the danger but the straw-filled mattress was too dry and flamed up, catching the baby's cotton swaddling clothes even as she was pulling him away from the danger.

Anna screamed as she ran to take the baby to safety outside. The flames burned higher on his clothing and now singed her hands. Refusing to let go, but not thinking about anything but getting Mike out to dowse the flames in a snowdrift, she didn't reach the front door before Mike was fully engulfed in fire. The flame now jumped to her cotton nightgown. Her last conscious vision was that of her only baby screaming in agony, flames licking over his face and illuminating his huge, beautiful, baby blue eyes. The flashover effect as she opened the door with one foot ignited a huge fireball, blowing her and her baby out into the snow where they mercifully died.

Thanks to the barking of the dogs, nature's own fire alarms, the call came to the nearest volunteer fireman on duty twelve minutes after Woolly's cigarette lit the rag. However, by the time the first fire truck arrived, it was essentially over. Of the twenty-three families comprising 103 humans huddled together in this privately built emergency housing area, only seven families had escaped the evening unharmed. Four others had only minor scorch damage to the pre-Ring of Fire house that they shared. Three entire families, fifteen men, women, and children, were burned alive and the remaining six families had at least one member dead or with severe burns from trying to fight the flames, for a total of twenty-eight second- and third-degree burn victims.

VIII: Fulfillment

"Brother Johann!"

Johann had just entered the café where he regularly breakfasted when he heard his name being called. Looking around, he saw Huddy sitting in a booth by the window, gesturing at him.

"Brother, join me." Huddy smiled, pointing to the empty seat across from him.

After Johann ordered his usual porridge, called something else by the Americans, Huddy leaned back on his bench and began, "Good to see you this morning, Brother. I suppose you've heard about the New Year's Eve fire by now?"

Johann nodded.

"I told those damn fools not to build that slum, but they wouldn't listen. And Dan Frost—he's the police chief—had too much else to deal with to go out there and force them to rebuild it properly."

Scowling, Huddy continued, "I had Chief Matheny and some of his firemen over after they finished their shift last night. God, were they bitter. The rest of my up-time booze is now gone, but they needed it a lot more than I did. The whole thing was preventable if any of the building codes had been followed." Huddy looked down at his plate and drank a sip of his coffee. "I know you've been spending most of your time in the library, but I wanted to let you know that Reverend Wiley has been telling me what a wonderful guest you've been at the church."

"The reverend has been a most gracious host. Especially considering the religious views of my . . . this era." Johann adjusted his glasses. "Huddy, how did you all do it? I mean, how in such a brief time, did you Americans, up-timers, adjust so well to such an incredible shift in your entire universe?"

Frowning, Huddy responded, "I guess we just had no choice. In my grandfathers' day, Grantville used to be a much larger town with several industries and a solid economy. By the time of the Ring, the pottery business and the electronics assembly business were closed and the last mine had been shut down. Those of us who decided to stick it out must be survivor types. The outside world had pretty much kicked us out before we got moved here. Maybe we just figured that this is a second chance for us all."

Johann nodded and finished his breakfast as he considered what Huddy had said.

"Brother Johann!" Johann, startled by the familiar voice, looked up to see Marietta standing by the booth, wearing no makeup and cheeks streaked with tears. "Brother, you must come with me. I can't get Jenny to leave the mortuary. She just won't stop obsessing over those bodies."

Jenny hadn't slept in two days when Marietta returned with Brother Johann to force her to stop and rest.

"Those bastards! Those absolute bastards." Jenny broke into tears yet again. She thought back to the totally preventable event that had placed all those charred remains that were still waiting processing in her funeral home's basement. "They were babies, Marietta! Little children who had done no harm to anyone."

Between the sobs, Jenny hugged Marietta's large frame, which was like the oversize teddy bear her daddy had won for her at the state fair so many years ago. "There wasn't a thought given to fire in that whole . . . whole miserable pile of shit. What the hell do we have building codes for, anyway? If any greedy, damn fool can build . . . can build anything he wants to with no thought for safety?"

Marietta and Johann helped Jenny close up and walked her home. Once there, while Marietta helped her friend clean up, Johann prepared a meal, blessing all the ingredients to bring Jenny the gift of endurance during this trial.

As Jenny and Marietta ate, Johann found Jenny's Bible and read the unfamiliar interpretation of the wonderful words he knew so well. "Praise be to the God of all comfort, who comforts us in all our troubles, so that we can comfort those in any trouble with the comfort we ourselves have received from God. He has delivered us from such a deadly peril, and He will deliver us. On Him we have set our hope that He will continue to deliver us."

After Jenny finally dropped into a much-needed sleep, Johann escorted Marietta to her home. He prayed for her strength to continue to support her friend in this time of her trial. Then he walked back to his room. While walking over the swinging footbridge crossing the now frozen Buffalo Creek, he stopped. With the electric and gas lights of downtown Grantville largely behind him, Johann gripped the support cable and looked downstream. Then he turned his head up to the brilliant cold points of light steadily gleaming overhead in the clear black sky. Letting his hood fall to his shoulders, he just let his mind go back over the events of this journey upon which God had directed him.

His ancestors, his family, the land they had owned all too briefly, the friends he had grown up with, the beliefs he had followed, and the life's work he had chosen all seemed to be a giant puzzle picture in which he was just now starting to recognize a higher plan than he had ever imagined before.

"I am your servant; give me discernment so that I may

understand your statutes. Your statutes are wonderful; therefore I obey them. The unfolding of your words gives light; it gives understanding to the simple."

In the report Johann wrote that night he observed:

> Brothers, when I took on this mission I wondered if Grantville was a city of God or a city of the Devil. I am now satisfied that it is neither. Grantville and the people that came back into our time, their past, against their will, are the same flawed people that we all see around us daily. They love their children, honor their beliefs, and grieve over their misfortunes. Then, like all people, they ask for guidance, and go on with their lives.
>
> Grantville, this entire Ring of Fire area, is not a city of God or of the Devil. It is a city of Man.

The newly elected government took office and quickly put into effect a series of measures to bring in more local down-time builders to get as many refugees out of the unsafe housing as fast as possible. Congress also consulted with the officials of their member city-states to make sure that the building codes Grantville brought back with them met with the needs of the local communities. Finally, the government passed a law formalizing a building safety inspection process and levied stiff penalties for violations, with no exceptions.

As the people around him carried on with their lives, Brother Johann continued his mission. A paper drive had been put into motion to move as much as possible of the up-time old newspapers and magazines out of homes and into safe storage in the empty areas of the library. Over time the drive had pulled in stacks and stacks of every conceivable type of printed material.

Johann set out to try to bring all of it into the order as set forth by DDC 21. First, he sorted the various materials into piles based on how it was printed: newspapers, tabloids, and slick magazines. Then he started to organize each group by publication date and publication. After the major categories had been carefully stored away and the number of copies and condition of each had been recorded in the card catalog, Johann began to work on the miscellaneous pile.

He wasn't sure why he had chosen to glance through the contents of this particular pamphlet. Johann had long ago resolved not to worry about the exact contents of this massive trove of information until he had finished his organization of types of materials. But, while thumbing through the pages before him, he saw the words.

He had already turned to the next page when his mind screamed at him about what he had seen. He flipped back to the page. Yes, the words were there! "Benedictine" and "fire department."

Reading the article, he now noticed with a shock the black-and-white photograph of what must have been a fellow follower of Saint Benedict in his black robe and some others in what appeared to be slick, black, long coats of some kind and helmets with large protective brims extending from the back.

Johann couldn't help but smile when he saw the name of the Order of Saint Benedict Abbey. Not only had he heard of the saint, he had filed many documents from the congregation of the priests of the mission that had been founded by the French father only a few years ago. Here in Grantville, Johann had attended the Catholic Church that had been named for him, Saint Vincent de Paul, but post-Ring of Fire, had been renamed Saint Mary's.

Brother Johann was sure it was the angel's wings fluttering against his neck that caused his hair to rise as he adjusted his glasses and read about the effects of accidents or uncontrolled hazards, panic, fire, explosion, natural disasters, or hazardous materials.

"Created following the catastrophic fire at Saint Vincent in January of 1963, a combination of monks from the Saint Vincent Benedictine Monastery, seminarians, and college students has since served the fire protection needs of the entire Saint Vincent community."

Brother Johann dropped to his knees, crossed himself, and began a prayer of thanksgiving that only ended when he became aware of Marietta turning off the lights in the next room of the library.

In his cell that evening, he began the report that he had so often wondered if he would ever be able to write. Saint Benedict had founded his order based on the belief that the individual should sink into service to his community, to not draw undue attention to himself beyond others, and that obedience must be a path followed by those appointed to lead as much as those being led.

Above all else, there must be a time for prayer, a time

for rest, and a time of work and all these times must be considered holy. Thus, the Order of Saint Benedict in all ways lived by the central tenet of prayer and work.

The things that had been taken from the order and the Church in that other future were clearly just things. The estates and the wealth and the power were nothing compared to the Holy Word they retained and the simple life of the rule as written by Saint Benedict himself in the sixth century.

A life of quiet service, away from the confusion of the multitudes but at the same time in service to the multitudes was very much the way of the firemen that Brother Johann had carefully observed in action since the New Year's Eve fire.

Spending the entire day preparing for the call that would eventually come, and being ready when it did, this was the way of the up-time fire department here in Grantville. Brother Johann now believed it to be a fitting occupation for his order.

Brother Johann's report was circulated among OSB monasteries throughout Europe, just as its predecessors had been. It was read to the brothers over dinner, as was their custom. The brothers of each monastery prayed and thought over the information Johann had brought into their lives and, consulting with their respective abbots, found their answers one by one.

The crocuses had just begun to raise their blooms above the melting snow when the first two men walked into Grantville from the west wearing their black robes and carrying their packs and walking sticks. By the time leaf buds appeared on the oak trees in the Buffalo Creek Valley, the residents of Grantville no longer wondered at the similarly garbed men who singly, or in groups of two or three, arrived from all different directions, calmly walked into the town's fire station, and closed the door behind them.

CONTINUING
SERIALS

Euterpe, Episode 2
⚬⚬★⚬⚬
Enrico M. Toro

To Father Thomas Fitzherbert SJ of the
*   Illustrissimus Collegium Anglicanum in Rome*
From Maestro Giacomo Carissimi in
*   Thuringen Gardens, Grantville*
August 1633

Very Reverend Father,

I am sorry it took so long to write you again, but a journey through Europe in these days is everything but short and comfortable. Only after I reached my final destination could I spend some time to tell you in detail of my adventures. I only hope your students and the other teachers at the collegium will forgive me for the time I steal from your primary duty. Hundreds of miles on the road can fill a lot of pages and break a courier's back!

I haven't received any letter from you yet, but I'm sure I will in the next weeks. After all the letter must cover the same distance I did and only the Americans seem capable of traveling faster than on horseback.

We arrived in Grantville last night and we are finally getting some rest from the fatigues of the trip. We are hosted in a brand-new inn that is more clean and comfortable than any other place where we have slept in the past weeks. We may also dare to pay a visit to the bathhouse and enjoy the too often neglected pleasures of hot water and soap. Soon maybe we will enjoy some of the amenities of the twentieth century.

This town is so different from any other I've visited, so unique that it would take too much time to describe even my first impressions, but I promise to carry out this task in my future letters.

Today, as soon as we arrived we paid a short visit to the local church, but we plan to introduce ourselves in a more polite and thorough way to Father Mazzarre, Grantville's parish priest. Our goal is to make a good impression, but it's hard to have a respectable appearance so covered in mud and dirty as we were this morning.

We need also to start looking for a long-term accommodation. The town is crammed full, but I have the feeling that some American will help us.

As you have certainly noticed I said "we" and not just "I." Many things happened during this trip and I'm not alone here. Well, I think I'm confusing you, so I had better start from the beginning.

I left Rome very early on a hot day in June. It was the only possible way to avoid the traffic that jams the gates of the city when many people come from the countryside to sell their products.

As I told you in my previous letter, my travel companions were three German Jesuits all freshly graduated from the seminary and ready for their first assignment. The youngest of them, Matthias Kramer, was going to Innsbruck to teach in the local college. The other two, Dietrich Adler and Heinrich Schultheis, were directed to Wien, where the company has its headquarters for the Holy Roman Empire. Together with their servants, we had an armed escort of five horse arquebusiers detached from the papal cavalry. With their leader, the cavalier Ruggero Longari, they were remaining in Wien at the papal legation.

The coach we traveled in is a proof of the power and influence of your order, dear Father. It was entirely made of timber reinforced with bronze. Not only did it have glass windows and not just leather curtains, but six horses pulled it. Moreover the coach was provided, I have been told, with one of those new "swan neck" suspension systems that allows the wheels to make large turning movements and makes traveling easier for the passenger. Made to fit six to eight people, it was very conformable for just the four of us and I had planned to read as much as I could during the trip.

I brought with me a small library: a copy of Torquato Tasso's *Jerusalem Delivered*, that small but already so famous book titled *Lo Statista Regnante* written by Don Valeriano Castiglione, the two volumes of the *Advancement of Learning* by Francis Bacon, your recently printed translation of Turcellini's *Life of Saint Francis Xavier*. I found it very appropriate to bring along also a copy of Tacitus' *Germania*.

After all, Father, it is you who always said that reading a page or two in Latin every day keeps the mind keen and well trained. Unfortunately, as I will explain later, I didn't have many occasions to read.

Once you leave Rome, the Via Flaminia follows the Tiber valley for a few miles until Saxa Rubra where it begins its way among hilly countryside headed toward Civita. Many travelers, once on the top of the first hill, make a stop to rest in a place called Malborghetto. A very large inn has been built there, using the remains of a triumphal arc. The view from there is breathtaking. Under a blue summer sky, it looks like a Tiziano's landscape. One can see the whole Roman countryside and the last ridges of the Apennines surrounding it. Far in the background, one can see the whole of Rome and it is still possible to recognize some of its features like the Dome of Saint Peter, the *cuppolone*.

While we were relaxing under a pergola lazily eating food from a tray full of pears and pecorino, I saw a rider coming in haste up the road. He was somehow familiar, but only once he got closer could I recognize Girolamo Zenti. He was riding a very tall steed and was dressed like someone ready for a long trip. Thigh-high boots, a leather doublet, and a plumed large hat made him look very different from the artisan I met in his shop. The sword at his side and the two pistols on the saddle did nothing but reinforce the impression. My Girolamo looked like a dragoon!

Quite surprised, I began waving at him. I rose from the table to meet him along the way and I told him how startled I was to see him on the very same road.

"Well, Maestro, for the moment I can just say I had a

change of mind. I will explain myself later, once it is possible to have some privacy. I'm happy to have found you so early. At the collegium, they told me you had left at dawn. Thank God you are not rushing those horses! Besides, I'm afraid I have to ask you the huge favor not to introduce me to your friends as Girolamo Zenti. You'd better tell them I am Carlo Beomonte, a friend who needs to travel to Germany and would like to share the long journey with you."

I did as asked, but I was eager to know more.

The same night, when we were guests at the Rocca Colonna in Castelnovo, I met him in the castle's courtyard. He was sitting on a bench trying to stretch his long legs and watching the castle servants doing the last chores of the day. After some time, once he realized we were alone, he lighted his clay pipe and gave me an account of the latest facts.

Girolamo had spent the night before in Trastevere gambling in a tavern, a place notorious for being visited by the offspring of the Roman aristocracy.

One of them had spent hours playing dice with my friend. Playing and losing big money. This was a very dangerous and explosive situation. As you can imagine, the young noble didn't accept losing face in front of friends and accused Girolamo of cheating.

To make his words sound truer, the young noble hastily drew his sword, probably expecting that a normal commoner would have backed off. Instead my companion, maybe for having drunk too much wine, reacted by drawing his own sword.

"Probably I took more fencing classes than he did, or

maybe it was just surprise, but I ended the fight quickly by putting a few inches of steel through the young nobleman's shoulder. Nothing deadly, but enough to put me in serious trouble. It is never self-defense when the loser is the son of the marquis Casati.

"So, while my friends kept the young man's retinue at bay, I escaped as quickly as I could. While running home I realized I had just two options left: leave town that very same day or find refuge in a monastery and take the vows. I don't much see myself as a member of the clergy. Even if judged innocent by the police, I would have had to fear Casati's personal revenge."

Girolamo went home to change clothes and to take the pistols he kept in an hidden place together with his cash money and papers. Then he sneaked into his partner's home nearby and explained how he was forced to go away, probably to Naples, to escape the law. He had then spent the rest of the night hiding in a safe place in the ghetto.

With the day still young, he went to get the horse that he kept in a stable just inside Porta San Paolo. He had already begun his escape south when he recalled I was leaving for Germany. So, with a certain apprehension, he reentered Rome and paid a visit to the collegium. There he met Renato, S. Apollinare's sacristan who told him of my departure for Grantville a few hours before. Relieved to know I wasn't too far away, he went north following the Flamina until he caught me.

I objected that even if we made it to Thuringia it could be a long exile for him. But, quite confidently for a fugitive, he replied:

"Yes, I know it can be long. But if what you have told me

of these Americans is true, they will value a man more for his skills than for his birth. And that is a place where I'd be happy to live. I'm tired of licking aristocratic boots any time I want to sell one of my works. I'm tired of being unable to read the books I want or to live the way I want. I'm fed up with these aristocrats and their caprices! Considering how much I'm interested in these pianos of yours, there is no better place to go!"

I was seriously afraid he could have put himself and me in further trouble. But there is something in him I like no matter what. I find his careless approach to life quite enticing and his enthusiasm contagious. So I told him I was happy he would come along, but that he had to be careful. More troubles and he would have to travel alone.

He promised me I would not regret my decision. Beside some minor accidents, I may say he has been very discreet for the rest of the trip.

He had another surprise up his sleeve.

It happened just the morning after our talk, while we were getting ready to leave the castle. The three servants were loading our chests and the rest of the baggage on the coach roof. The driver, under his coach, was carefully greasing axles and hubs and our escort was letting the horses have a last drink. Girolamo was nowhere to be seen.

While we were about to send one of the soldiers to check if his horse was still in the castle stable, Father Matthias saw him coming from the village holding two saddled horses by the reins.

One was his courier, Rodomonte, and the other was a smaller, but not a bit less beautiful brown mare.

When I asked him about this new addition to our party, he answered that the mare was for me, if I wanted to accept it and if I could ride her. Then Girolamo added: "Maestro, I think that once we will be alone on the road, traveling by horse will give us some advantage in speed and agility compared to renting or buying another coach."

I pondered his words and I agreed with him. So I replied that I could ride. I wasn't a master of the skill, but rode enough to stay on the saddle while following a coach. My bigger problem, I explained, was that I had never traveled on a horse for long stretches.

"Well, you will learn! These are the perfect conditions to do so. I can teach you some tricks, and you can always rest on the coach from time to time."

When I asked him the price of the mare he answered, "Don't worry, Maestro. I plan to sell the horse once we have arrived in Grantville. I have yet to see a war zone where there is not a desperate need of horses. As a matter of fact I plan to make a profit. Anyway I need to abuse your kindness again as I need another favor."

"Please speak."

"The problem is that I'm not very good with languages. I can speak a few words in French, but that's it. I need to learn more English and German and I was wondering if you could help."

"That will be a pleasure to me. What's the mare's name?"

"I've been told it's Carlotta, do you like it?"

"Could be worse," I answered, while caressing Carlotta's nose.

I think we both enjoyed the possibility to use the road

as a schoolroom. We both had a lot to learn and all the time spent riding, talking, and prattling gave us the occasion to know each other better.

The more I knew him the more I felt that my early feelings about Mastro Zenti were true. He is quick of wit and tongue and has much more experience of this world than you would expect from a man of his young age.

He was born in Viterbo, where his mother's relatives are renowned wood carvers. His father, Achille Zenti, was a soldier, a *reiter* in the Pontifical Army. Girolamo speaks highly of him and he must have been a good man. Unfortunately he fell sick and died in 1619, when Girolamo was just twelve. His mother remarried soon and Girolamo was sent as apprentice in Rome to learn the art of wood carving and instrument making with another artisan. The same one who is now his business partner.

He admitted not to be the first country boy who had let himself be corrupted by the pleasures of a big town. Especially one so seducing as Rome. But, despite his introduction to vice and sin, his great natural talents permitted him to keep on his apprenticeship. So he became a journeyman at just sixteen and a master at twenty when he produced his first harpsichord.

Since then, work and his natural curiosity brought him to travel in other states, mostly in Naples, Tuscany, and Lombardy. Only three years ago, with his name already established, he came back to Rome where he purchased half of his former master's enterprise.

Girolamo's father wanted him to be a soldier, an officer maybe, so he started very young training in the science of soldiering. Since then he has studied with different arms masters wherever he went. His skill is such that, once back in Rome, he managed to be accepted in the sword combat school of one of the Alfieri brothers. Who, I have had explained to me, have improved the already deadly teachings of Ridolfo Capoferro, the famous fencer, and direct some of the most important salles of the peninsula. Both his pistols and his rapier, he told me, belonged to his father.

Like his lifestyle, I am afraid to say, his political and religious ideas are quite radical.

Once, while we were both enjoying the vapors of a good grappa, Girolamo's tongue got loose enough to tell me of Naples where he befriended one of the last scholars belonging to Brother Tommaso Campanella's circle. Eager to learn, he has been strongly influenced by the theories of the Dominican philosopher.

Even if today Campanella is a free man and a trusted advisor of His Sanctity, his students are still persecuted in the lands governed by the crown of Spain as they strongly reject the Spanish hegemony and domination in Italy.

So Girolamo, like Petrarca, Machiavelli, and many others before him, dreams of an Italy free of any foreign domination and united in a league of states. It is a dream that never became true and, I am afraid, probably never will.

Discussions and gossip, riding classes and languages learning didn't distract us from our primary goal, traveling.

For the first two weeks, we had been blessed by very favorable weather. Not too hot, and with some scattered rains that wet the dust on the road without making it too muddy.

The traffic on the Flaminia is never scarce. Mostly it consists of merchants carrying goods and farmers bringing their animals or their crops to the nearest town. We were well aware of the chance of worse encounters along the road. Maybe because of our military escort or because of the papal insignia painted on the sides of our coach, we never met any trouble.

The road is quite large and well drained. Two carriages can pass side by side and the grades and slopes are never too harsh even when crossing mountain ridges.

We crossed northern Latium and entered in Umbria. We crossed a great Roman bridge at Narni and slowly climbed the Somma pass, which brought us into the territory of Spoleto.

Spoleto, once the capital of the Longobard duchy, is a magnificent town. We stopped there to rest for a day at the guest quarters of the monastery of Saint Luke and found the time to visit the Towers bridge and the cathedral. We didn't neglect the rich food. The area is renown for its trout and famous black truffles.

In the monastery we learned of a local legend. The locals say that Pope Innocentius III, here on a visit, miraculously made a spring of icy water gush out from the cloister floor. This spring is said to be able to restore fully the health and stamina of any weary traveler who drinks it. It is superfluous to say we filled our bellies and our canteens.

The day after, just outside of Foligno, we encountered an infantry regiment going to Urbino. The old duchy has been the most recent addition to the Papal States territory, having been ceded to the Church by its last aging duke seven years ago. We managed to travel with the soldiers as long as possible. Our trip became slower, but even safer.

The Via Flaminia is an open-air treasure for any student of architecture. Along its way it is possible to see and visit hundreds of vestiges of ancient Roman buildings: tombs, bridges, theaters, road markers, and much else.

Two of them made a deep impression in me. One is the River Furlo Gorges, where the road has been completely carved into the mountain rock by the work of thousands, I imagine. In one place where frequent landslides made the road unsafe, the Romans carved two long tunnels into the mountain so that the road could be kept always open. The tunnels are used even now. It is an amazing show of the skill of the ancients.

One of the Jesuits, a lover of history, found it amusing to see the Pope's ragged regiment marching on such a road. A road used by the Roman legions to crush by surprise the army of Hannibal's brother at the River Metauro battle and by Narsete's Byzantines to intercept and defeat Totila's Goths many centuries later.

Povera Italia!

The other vestige is less impressive, being a simple stele placed in the market square of Rimini, the town built where the Flaminia ends and the Via Emilia begins. Simple, but of no less historical value. The stele says:

> *The dictator Gaius Caesar,*
> *having crossed the Rubicon,*
> *addressed his comrades-in-arms in the civil war*
> *here in the forum of Rimini.*

★ ★ ★

I don't know if the stele is real or a fake carved much later. Some claim it is fake, but I found it fascinating anyway.

Once it left Rimini, our road followed the Adriatic coastline toward Ravenna and Ferrara, in the lower river Po valley. Being so close to the mouth of the biggest Italian river, the area is filled with marshlands and swamps. It is a dreadful place, haunted by malaric fevers and pellagra caused, I've been told, by the terrible swamp fumes. Not even the night brought us any relief from the hot and humid weather. All the time, but especially in the hottest hours of the day, we were continuously attacked by armies of mosquitoes. Only the occasional winds from the sea brought us some relief.

After four days in such a miserable state we finally reached the nice town of Ferrara and could rest comfortably in the governor's palace.

The next day we crossed the Po on a *traghetto* and finally left the Papal States. After a fast inspection at the customhouse and after paying a surprisingly low tax, we entered the Venetian Terraferma.

It was in the low Polesine that we learned from other travelers of the destruction of the Dutch fleet in a great naval battle and of the Spanish invasion of the United Provinces. The winds of war were blowing again in northern Europe and we were traveling toward the center of the storm.

The news left us with a dark and gloomy mood that neither our fast pace on the well-kept Venetian roads, nor the security provided by the Capelatti patrols, nor the good hospitality we received in Verona, could lift from us.

The fact that we were traveling in an area full of refugees from the duchy of Mantua didn't help. That town was brutally sacked by an imperial army three years ago. More than one-third of the duchy's population was murdered or died from the plague brought by the imperial conquerors. This was the same plague that spread all over northern Italy. What was once one of the wealthiest states of the peninsula was reduced to ruins. As a matter of fact, it was the sack of Mantua and the fear of another 1527 that made His Sanctity's government hastily increase the defenses around Rome and add more troops to its armies. Venice seems the only safe place left in northern Italy. An island of peace in an ocean of war. Will it last?

Anyway, we decided to stop in Verona a little longer to make some small repairs to the coach before reaching the mountains. It was then that I discovered another of the many talents of which Girolamo is endowed. It seems he is possessed of a remarkable financial shrewdness.

Over the past five years, Girolamo has used a large part of his savings to finance a portion of some Venetian mercantile expeditions in the Black Sea. While very risky these expeditions produce high profits when the ships return, because goods are sold at many times the initial price. Reinvesting the profits the same way he managed to earn quite a sum. All this without actually touching a single coin, any operation being done in bonds secured by some of the most important Venetian banks. Once in Verona he came to know that the Nasi family has a branch open in Grantville. So he visited the Veronese branch of the same bank to exchange part of his finances for letters of credit to be used in the American town.

"This should be enough," he told me that evening while we were crossing Piazza delle Erbe and walking back to the inn. "I think I can buy enough supplies and tools to open a decent shop in Grantville and hire some helpers. I think I know where I can find the best timbers of the whole Alps."

The Alps! If God should choose a throne to sit while in this world, it would be there. Because there is no other place that sings more clearly of His power and of the beauty of His creation.

Once the repairs to our carriage were done and the coach ready, we left Verona on the road that we followed up to the Danube. The road follows the River Adige and it brought us closer and closer to the border. So, while the plains became hills and the hills became mountains, we left the Serenissima Republica and entered the episcopate of Trento, the southernmost province of the empire.

It took us two days of easy riding to reach the city where we received hospitality in the castle of Buonconsiglio, residence of the bishop prince. During the evening we had the occasion to admire in awe the halls where the council sessions have taken place and to learn more about the status of the war in Germany.

The Adige valley offered us a magnificent landscape that gave us true moments of joy. The river cuts a straight, deep dent in steep mountain ridges that are interrupted only by other, smaller valleys created by its many tributaries. Small, neat, and beautiful villages are scattered around the valley and many castles have been built to guard the road from higher ground. Our eyes did feast on the charming countryside: from the gentle slopes of the foothills covered with vineyards and chestnut orchards to the lush alpine grazing land: from the dark green fir forests to the gray rocky peaks of the mountains.

I loved the wine produced in these valleys. It's called Welschriesling and it is dry, fragrant, and fruity. A perfect companion to wash down the dust from our thirsty throats.

The valley is quite large south of Trento, but the further north we went the closer we came to the mountains. In the episcopate people still talk a strongly accented Italian, but, once past the small town of Mezzocorona, we finally entered the Tyrol with its German-speaking inhabitants.

Where the Adige meets the river Eisack we finally reached the town of Bozen, and ended the first part of our trip. Girolamo and I would follow the Adige to Meran and the Reschac pass, while our other companions would take the Brenner pass road toward Innsbruck. The weeks spent on the road together helped the growth of a sincere friendship among us. I remember fondly the laughter and the constant good humor of young Matthias, potbellied Father Einrich's passion for chess and Italian food, the sincere admiration and deep knowledge that Father Dietrich had for anything Roman. I hope that their trip ended as well as ours and I plan to write them soon to learn how they fared.

The day we separated, we woke up very early to celebrate a moving mass at the beautiful Church of Saint George. We felt it necessary to thank Our Lord for the safe passage He had granted us and to ask Him to make the second part of our trip as safe as the first. Only then, reluctantly, we separated.

The rest of the morning was spent in Merchants Road looking for two mules and two packsaddles to carry my baggage and other supplies we bought. Girolamo and I left Bozen in the heat of the early afternoon and reached Meran that night.

We had planned to travel to Schlanders in the morning and try to make Glurns the same day, but bad weather stopped us. When we left, the entrance of the Schnals valley, well protected by a grim castle, was on our right. Above the valley the sky began to turn black. Thunder and lightning started striking the mountain slopes all around us. We arrived in Schlanders barely before the squall line. Then rain, hail, and gusts of wind poured down the valley. We found refuge at the Gold Eagle Inn in the outskirts of the town and decided to stop for the day.

It turned out to be a good decision. Resting at the inn, we enjoyed a tasty amber beer and filled our bellies with some *obermoosburgkeller*—a pork shin roasted on the spit that is as delicious as its name is hard to pronounce. I decided to take my traveling spinet inside and, after the meal, I began tuning it (Girolamo made the process much faster) before I enjoyed myself trying to arrange some simple tunes.

In a short time I discovered I wasn't the only one with an instrument in the inn. Girolamo produced a flute he had hidden somewhere in his bags and an inn employee and another customer joined us with a violin and a Venetian guitar. After a little practice, our improvised ensemble began to get along quite well and we started playing. We began with some minuets and gavottes, then we passed to some old pieces of Francesco Da Milano and other popular ballads and we went on with some simple dances.

The innkeeper kept providing us with beer and food and seemed quite happy. As news of our improvised concerto reached the rest of the town, the inn became crammed full before dinner.

So much beer had his effects on us and I realized I had drunk too many mugs of it when I began to sing and roughly translate in German some lecherous lyrics written under false name by Adriano "the abbot" Banchieri.

I see already the disappointment on your face, Father. But it was a nice, fun, and innocent night and if I must spend more time in Purgatory for that so be it! After so much road we deserved some rest, I think.

During the concert we discovered that one of the musicians was traveling to Fussen, in south Bavaria, and we decided to cross the Alps together.

His name is Johannes Fichtold and he was returning back home after having finished his apprenticeship in Padua. He went to Italy to learn to build lutes and guitars the "Italian way," with the back of the lute constructed with many narrow ribs glued together. His family owns a lute maker's shop, and young Johannes is going to work back there.

Hearing this, Girolamo smiled like the cat who ate the canary. Fussen is the place where he planned to order the timbers he wanted to use in his new enterprise.

The next day, despite our hangovers and the muddy and slippery conditions of the road after the storm, we managed to go at a sustained pace. We began a more steady climb along the Vinschgau valley, riding in part through mountain forests and in part among cultivated fields and apple orchards. Above the village of Schluderns we enjoyed the view of the Churburg, a magnificent castle guarding the entrance of the Matsch valley.

Our morale was incredibly high, but we were abruptly sent back to the sad state of the contemporary world on our approach to Glurns. The town is a little architectural jewel in the crown formed by the Alps, but all its beauty was spoiled by a set of gallows near the east gate and by the rotten corpses hanging from them.

As we approached the gruesome scene, a group of soldiers wearing dark green uniforms and large hats told us to stop. They looked formidable with their very long muskets and an impressive array of blades.

"Jaegers!" said Johannes, while the soldiers came closer. "They are the local militia. Fiercely loyal to the emperor and incredible marksmen."

The soldiers asked for our passports and wanted to know where we were headed and the reason for our trip. Once satisfied by our answers one of them, who looked like their commander, gave us a warning, "The corpses you see hanging here are part of a band of bandits that are marauding this area. Deserters from what once was Tilly's army. Once on the pass, watch out for your lives. Unless," he added with a grin, "you can pay for the services of his Imperial Majesty's hunters."

"And how much would this service cost?" I asked.

"Three golden ducats for each one of you, two for the animals. Four expert guides will guide and protect you up to Nauders, the first town beyond the pass."

"*Sto fijo de 'na mignotta!* This is robbery!" said Girolamo, luckily in Italian.

"Please close your mouth," I told him. "I'm sure you are more than able to defend all of us. I don't want to have potential enemies ready to ambush us along the road and hostile militiamen behind our back. We can afford to pay and I am ready to do it. Dead people cannot waste money. That's a privilege of the living."

I was surprised by my firm tone of voice. And apparently so was he, because he managed to remain silent while I finished dealing with the sergeant. The next morning we would be escorted beyond the Reschen pass.

The fact that endless people since the beginning of the world have used this road is probably because crossing the pass is not very hard. But for a small slope before the village of Reschen, the road climbs its way gently along the hills and the mountains. Even the top part of the pass is surprisingly easy, as it maintains more or less the same altitude for half a dozen miles.

At the end of the day, after the long ride among woods and meadows, we made camp in an empty barn just above the little town of Nauders. We were tired, but proud of the progress we had made.

It may have been because of the presence of the Jaegers, but nothing bad happened along the way. I was quite wary of all those horror stories about travelers left with their throats cut in some roadside ditch.

The company of the soldiers was more pleasant than expected. These are not bloodthirsty monsters. Even if widely recruited as scouts by the imperial armies, they are mostly just hunters or woodsmen who spend part of their time defending their land and families. Not only did they not rob or murder us, as Girolamo feared, but they cheered us up with their numerous hunting stories and mountain tales. I particularly appreciated a story about a holy white steinbock who lives in the area, but this is not the time to tell it. Their knowledge of the land and of the flora and fauna is also extraordinary.

From Naders the road brought us to Landeck and from there it crossed many other valleys and small towns until, a few days later, we left the duchy of Tyrol and entered the Bavarian town of Fussen.

Fussen, built where the River Lech meets the Via Claudia Augusta, is apparently another of those numerous small towns scattered all along the river valleys of this mountain area. They all share common features: one or two thousand souls at most, a circle of walls, a small cathedral, and a small fortress. Even if the wars in Germany and in Italy have reduced the flow of travelers who pass by this town, what remains is enough to grant prosperity to their inhabitants.

What makes Fussen special is the fact that in the last fifty years it has become the home of some of the most famous lute makers of our time. The vicinity of the Alps with their huge reserve of valuable timber and the closeness to important trade routes make it the ideal place to build instruments that can be sold throughout Europe, from Spain to Poland, from Denmark to Sicily.

Once in town we received hospitality from Johannes's older brother Hans, a respected member of the lute makers' guild. The guild not only controls the sale of any instrument built in town, but also watches very closely the trade in timber, making sure that the best planks of yew, oak, cherry, and fir not leave the town.

"Oh, we will see about that!" Girolamo told me with a bellicose light in his eyes. "The guild member that can keep me away from what I want still has to see the light of this world."

As a matter of fact, the bargaining must have been harder than he expected because he more or less disappeared for all the duration of our stay in town. He was busy meeting guild members and the owner of the local timber mill, pleading, flattering, threatening, whining, and God only knows what else! But at the end he obtained what he wanted, a good number of planks of very good timber to be sent to Grantville in the shortest possible time. Only later did he tell me that he had been able to obtain the wood supply only by agreeing to enter the guild and to pay a huge annual sum to have such a "privilege."

I used those days to visit the town and its surroundings. I saw from a distance the Hohenshwangau Castle, but I far more enjoyed a visit at the small Saint Anna Chapel where I was struck deeply by some wooden panels painted with scenes of a dance macabre. That artifact seems made to direct our thoughts toward the precariousness of life and it seemed very appropriate for what I had seen in my first days in Germany. Here life is lived under a constant threat.

These people seem to have lost hope in the future. They appear to feel it is likely that the future will bring destruction or a violent death. This is a small, rich town, where everybody should be happy and busy enjoying the many gifts God gave them. Instead fear, no matter how well hidden, is the most common emotion among the locals. Fear of an army sacking and pillaging their pretty homes, fear of plague and famine. Fear of an unwanted war upon which they have no control.

After three days we left town. Girolamo was furious at the terms he had to accept to get his timber. Nothing seemed to cheer him up, not even the smart jokes of Johannes who had decided to come with us (with the blessing of his brother who saw profit in expanding his business close to the fabled Americans) and who seemed as eager as we were to visit the American town.

All kinds of rumors about war followed us all the way to Landsberg and then on to Augsburg. Somebody was saying that the kingdom of France had raised a huge army near Strasbourg and was ready to invade northern Germany. Others were saying that one hundred thousand Swedes and their fiendish allies were already across the Danube directed toward Ulm and Wien and killing everybody along the way. Someone hinted that it was the Spanish that were coming through the Valtellina and now were in Baden-Wurttemberg, ready to defend to the last man the Catholic population.

We learned to not give much credit to all these rumors. As a matter of fact, the only soldiers we saw at that time were a regiment of Bavarian troops training just outside Augsburg's walls.

In Augsburg we had another proof of the anguish Bavarian people were living in. While we were heading toward the Jesuit collegium, we were stopped in Maximilianstrasse by a large procession of people praying for the defeat of the Protestant forces. All the confraternities of the town, members of all the religious orders, seemed to have united for the event. The air was full of supplication;

religious songs and Kyrie were sung and statues of many saints and of the Virgin Mary were carried toward the cathedral, Dom St. Maria. Even having spent all my life in Italy, I had rarely seen such a strong display of public faith. My companions and I were so struck that we followed the procession until we saw all the statues enter into the beautifully carved gates of the church.

All the roads to and from Augsburg are full of refugees. Only the fact we were on horseback and able to leave the road in the most crowded sections made us move as fast as we did. Anyway it took us over three days to reach Donauworth at the confluence of the Danube and the river Wörnitz and to finally find the rival armies.

The town is at the border between Swabia and Bavaria, and is located along the last navigable point on the Danube. At the moment, Donauworth is in Bavarian hands and the big garrison and the heavy fortifications seemed to show the will of Maximilian's troops to remain here. However, the fact that Swedish soldiers were a few leagues away from the town walls didn't help our passage.

Our intentions were to cross the Danube in this place, but the situation didn't seem very favorable and we had previously agreed we should stay away from any army as much as possible.

We went straight to the wharves on the Danube to find a boat that could bring us down river toward Ingolstadt where we hoped to find better conditions. Only by paying a sum that left our purses much lighter did we manage to find a barge.

Our plan succeeded. We spent the night at the wharves and left at dawn. After a few hours on the river we reached Ingolstadt. From there we took a road that should have taken us straight into Nuremberg.

The second day along this road a squad of Swedish troops stopped us. With them was a man dressed in strange clothes who, when seen closely, looked as stolen from a forest during fall. If he is hidden in the wilds it must be very hard to spot him. The name written on those clothes, his strange German accent, and his even stranger weapon gave us other hints that he was a real American.

The Swedish soldiers are probably used to causing awe and fear in civilians like us. I'll never forget the puzzled look on their faces when we started to laugh! But we couldn't conceal our joy.

"*Cazzo* Giacomo we made it!" shouted Girolamo, colorful as usual.

"*Thalassa, thalassa, thalassa!*" I replied, my mind following strange paths leading to Xenophon's Greek army and its march to the sea.

We definitively had lost our decorum as we started hugging and patting our shoulders. Girolamo barely restrained himself from hugging and kissing the American on the forehead. The American stared at us like we were madmen.

Our feelings must have been contagious, because the Swedish troopers seemed less grim and the American, probably once he realized we weren't a threat, was smiling.

I removed my hat to him and introduced in English my friends and me. Then I showed him one of Mazarini's letters of introduction.

All this happened ten days ago. I would tell you more,

but my eyes are sore, my hands tired from so much writing, the ink is almost gone, and I need another quill. Just know that the rest of our voyage went quite smoothly and early this afternoon we arrived in Grantville. While I'm writing, Girolamo and Johannes are downstairs enjoying the local brews and, if I learned their habits well, also the local women.

Now the first part of our adventure is ended, but the hardest part of our trip has still to begin. Will we manage to do what we came here for? Will we be able to build good relationships with the Americans? Will Euterpe smile upon us? I don't know, Father, but I have all the intentions to try.

I hope I am in your prayers as you are in mine, always.

Your friend and student,

Giacomo Carissimi

P.S. What does "dude" mean?

FACT

Iron
(◦★◦)
Rick Boatright

The most dangerous mammal in North America kills over 130 people each year, and seriously injures another twenty-nine thousand. The most recycled material in North America was dumped in landfills until the late 1970s, but now, nearly 100 percent of that material contains recycled content.

The animal? The white-tailed deer. The material? Highway asphalt. Things that are very important are often common and overlooked.

Prior to the 1970s the question "What's the most recycled material?" had a very different, but just as surprising answer: Iron. Nearly 100 percent of all automotive iron and iron from construction debris, as well as over 80 percent of iron from consumer appliances is recycled. Iron doesn't have a memory. The girders and beams from the World Trade Center were sold to iron foundries, and will appear as buildings, refrigerators, and washing machines around the world. Over half of the iron used in the world comes from recycling.

In coming issues of the *Grantville Gazette* articles will discuss various problems facing the Grantvillers, including the "stainless steel problem," the replacement of the power plant, constructing boats and bridges and barges, making the steam engines to power those, reproducing the machine shops and building new machine tools, the chemicals industry, coke, medicines, surgery, anesthesia, clocks, navigation, and mapping. All of these face a common element in what the 1632 series authors and background researchers have come to call the "tools-to-make-tools" problem: iron.

In the early 1630s, just before the appearance of the Ring of Fire, the annual production of iron in the part of Europe that became the USE was about fifteen thousand tons. One hundred miles of main line railroad needs over twenty thousand tons of iron. The telegraph line from Grantville to Magdeburg needs almost fifteen thousand tons of iron. Small main line railroad steam engines need three to five tons of iron each, and "real" railroad engines run seventy-five tons. Barges, even small barges like the classic U.K. narrow boat, require six to ten tons of iron per barge. A fifty- by twelve-foot barge runs around thirty tons. Future articles in the *Gazette* will detail the rapid increase of iron and steel production in the USE. The projections resulting from the projects named in the 1632 books published by 2006 indicate that within two years of the Ring of Fire, European iron production will have to have increased by a factor of two to three, with a planned increase by a factor of ten by year five.

This leads to the question: what is so important about iron? Other materials like wood, copper, aluminum, plastics, and alloys including brass and bronze are all common. Why make such a big deal about iron? This article will attempt to place civilization's use of iron in context historically, and physically.

Iron is the fourth most abundant element in the earth's crust. The most abundant is oxygen, which isn't much good for building things. Next is silicon, which we use for computer chips, but not for bridges or boats. Third is aluminum. We do build with aluminum, but winning aluminum metal from the earth's crust turns out to be a very difficult prospect that requires the use of massive amounts of electricity. Most aluminum in the crust is bound up chemically in ways that make it very difficult to separate, even with twenty-first-century technology. Iron, on the other hand, comprises about 5 percent of the earth's crust, and can be separated from its ore with little more than fire and charcoal. Other metals used by civilization are very rare. Copper exists in the crust at sixty-eight parts per million. Lead is even more rare at ten parts per million. One driving force then that makes iron an important part of civilization is that it is common, and easy to produce.

Iron has some very neat properties. It is very strong. Pound for pound, iron was the strongest material available before the twentieth century. It is very workable. Iron can be cast, beaten, rolled and formed into almost any shape. Because it is strong, thin sheets of iron can substitute for thick, heavy layers of other substances. Iron can be flexible, and makes great swords and springs. Iron can be stiff and makes great cutting blades and hammers and tools. Iron melts at a very high temperature. Iron's melting point is more than twice the temperature of a normal open fire. Iron doesn't even soften in normal fires, so it can be used to contain fire and form stoves and pipes. Even when heated red-hot, iron retains much of its strength. No other single metal does all these things. Copper is ductile; it can be formed into all sorts of shapes, but it is soft. Bronze can be hard, but it is weak, and melts at a low temperature. Lead, gold, and silver are soft, and the latter two are so rare that we make money out of them. Iron is unique and has been the basis of civilization in Europe, Asia, and Africa for over three thousand years.

How do you produce iron then? First, select a rock with lots of iron in it. The iron will be bound up with oxygen. The best iron ores are nearly pure rust. They are little more than iron and oxygen. Most iron ore isn't of this quality, and contains varying amounts of silicon, sulfur, manganese, and phosphorus. Oxygen combines with carbon more strongly than it binds with iron. If you powder iron ore and charcoal or coke, and heat the mixed powders, the iron gives up a bit of its oxygen. The oxygen binds with the carbon to make carbon dioxide. In the simplest smelting process, crushed iron ore, crushed charcoal, and a little limestone or sea shells are heated together until they are red-hot. As this spongy mass, called a *bloom*, cools, pure pieces of iron are intermingled with leftover charcoal and the other chemicals left behind. The parts that aren't iron are called slag. The bloom would be hammered and turned and hammered and turned, and the slag would be squeezed out, and the bits of iron would come together to form *wrought iron*. *Wrought* means "hammered" or "worked." In the seventeenth century, there were hundreds of hammer mills scattered throughout Europe wherever a seam of iron ore coexisted with a stream capable of turning a wheel and powering a hammer. All the iron available in Europe in the seventeenth century started life as wrought iron. Wrought iron has a carbon content of around 0.02 to 0.08 percent by weight. This is important because the factor that is the most important in describing the strength and brittleness of iron is the carbon percentage. A very small difference in carbon results in a huge difference in the properties of the iron. Consider the next type of iron to be smelted.

If you take iron and carbon and heat it above red-hot (to about 1,200 degrees Celsius) something interesting happens. The iron begins to absorb the carbon, and starts to melt. The iron-carbon mixture has a melting temperature far below the melting temperature of pure iron (which is around 1,500 degrees C). If you make a tall chimneylike structure, and layer charcoal, flux, and iron ore in it, and pump air with a bellows through it so that it gets above the critical temperature, molten iron would run out of the blast furnace. The cast iron produced has 3 to 5 percent carbon in it. *Cast iron* is very different from wrought iron. It is hard and brittle. If you hit it with a hammer, it will crack or shatter. Microscopically, cast iron is a mat of fibers of iron crystals, iron carbide crystals, and graphite. It is very rigid and very tough. It doesn't soften much before it melts, and it cannot be worked by hammer and anvil into a shape like a knife, a sword, or a gun as wrought iron can. Cast iron was known in Europe in the Middle Ages, but was not used much beyond pots, pans, cannon, cannon balls, and bells. Casting iron was called *founding* and so businesses that cast iron are called *foundries*. Cast iron is perfect for making things that need to be very rigid.

Cast iron is not very expensive. Generally, items made out of cast iron are cast in sand. A wooden copy of the item is made, and sand is formed around the master. The master is removed, and molten iron is poured in. After cooling, the sand is shaken off and reused. Grantville will use far more cast iron than the Europeans were using before they arrived. They know neat things to make from it, like Franklin stoves, frying pans, and the Eiffel Tower. But for all its strength, cast iron is brittle. Guns made from cast iron fail because they are not elastic. They can't expand with the explosion of the powder and then spring back to shape. If they are not made very thick to withstand the pressure, cast iron guns explode after a few uses, so they have to be very heavy for their power.

Beginning in the Middle Ages, iron makers learned to transform cast iron into wrought iron by burning the carbon out. They would use a *fining* furnace, where they would break the cast iron into small lumps and heat the lumps with a stream of very hot air. The iron would melt, and carbon would burn out and the decarbonized iron droplets would sink to form a bloom below the hot zone. Then, they would forge the bloom just like they would in a hammer mill. Wrought iron made this way was more expensive than iron made directly from the ore, but the two-step process could be done with some iron ores that the one-step process was not effective for. This was expensive.

In the late 1700s, an Englishman, Henry Cort, developed another technique for transforming cast iron into wrought iron. Molten cast iron was poured into a stone basin in a reverberatory furnace and exhaust gases from a hot fire were run over the top of the basin. A worker with a long rake stirred the surface of the puddle of iron, and carbon monoxide in the gases would combine with carbon in the iron. The resulting pure iron melted at a higher temperature than the cast iron it was suspended in, so it would form semisolid bits of wrought iron. At first, these *puddlers* would gather these into a single mass that would be wrought like any wrought iron. Later puddlers would keep mixing the mass of iron, as it became more and more viscous. Skilled workers would recognize when the hot iron had "jelled" enough to have had enough of the carbon burned out of it.

Blast furnaces produced bulk cast iron efficiently, but the puddling furnace was a major bottleneck. The process was slow. It required huge amounts of fuel. Only very strong men could stand the heat, and work the thick, heavy liquid metal and tell when it was ripe to be withdrawn. Many attempts were made in the 1800s to mechanize the process, but they all failed.

So far we've talked about two types of iron. Cast iron, with carbon content over 2 percent, and wrought iron, with very little carbon at all, less than 0.1 percent. What about iron in the middle of the range? We know that wrought iron is flexible, and can be forged into all sorts of shapes. We know that cast iron is rigid and brittle. It should come as no great surprise that iron between 0.1 percent carbon and 2 percent carbon is intermediate in its properties. It is stiffer than wrought iron, but less stiff and brittle than cast iron. It has a higher melting point than cast iron, but less than wrought iron. Clearly, this is what we want to use to make stuff. Iron intermediate in carbon between wrought and cast is called *steel*.

Even today, the basic chemistry of iron is such that it is difficult to move directly from iron ore to steel. In 1632, we have to come at it from one end or the other. We can take wrought iron and add carbon to it, or we can take cast iron and reduce its carbon. Several techniques were developed in antiquity that resulted in steels of different carbon content and different microstructure. One common element is that all these were small batch processes that were labor intensive. Steel was very expensive.

The oldest known steels were produced by cementation. Sheets of wrought iron were packed with charcoal or other carbon sources in a closed ceramic container and heated red-hot (1,000 to 1,100 degrees C) for five to seven days. The carbon would be absorbed into the iron in the solid state. The process was very slow since the iron is solid, and the carbon atoms have to move into the spaces in the solid iron crystals. The resulting sheets of *blister steel* had very high carbon content on the outside, and very low carbon content at the center. The sheets would be forged and folded together to distribute the carbon more evenly in very fine layers. This process of heating and folding and heating and folding was very labor intensive. The result could be a blade that combined the best of both wrought iron and cast iron, with very rigid hard bits to hold the shape well, and very flexible bits to allow the weapon to flex. But it was difficult to impossible to make large forms like guns and cannon this way. In the 1740s Benjamin Huntsman developed a way to take the blister steel from the cementation process and melt it in a closed crucible with a special flux that grabbed up fine bits of slag to make a very pure *crucible steel*, but crucible steel is very, *very* expensive.

Smiths in India developed a different method of heating wrought iron pellets with organic material in sealed containers for long periods at high enough temperatures to get the iron to melt and the carbon to mix with the iron in liquid phase. This *wootz* process resulted in ultrahigh carbon steels (nearly 2 percent) with microstructures that mixed the pure iron and the iron-carbon complexes at a much smaller scale than could be achieved by the folding and forging process above. The resulting blades called "Damascus" steel had a combination of strength and flexibility that was unmatched until the twentieth century, but the process produced only small ingots suitable for knives and swords. The material could only be forged at low temperatures or the whole thing would literally fall apart as the steel turned into cast iron. This still didn't produce a steel capable of being formed in bulk.

The other way to produce steel is to reduce the carbon in cast iron. Smiths in China mixed bundles of cast and wrought iron together and forged and heated them to diffuse them in a manner similar to the cementation process describe above. Puddling furnaces can be run without removing the wrought iron pieces from the molten iron, mixing the result over and over until it is of a thickness and carbon content wanted. This was the first process that could produce *bulk* steel. The amount of steel that you could produce was dependent on the strength of the puddler and the reach of his rake.

Still, technological civilization needs cheap bulk steel. The first railroads ran on wrought iron rails. The passing trains bent and deformed the rails, and wore the edges so fast that on some busy stretches the rail had to be replaced every other month. What the world needed at the dawn of the railroad period, and what Grantville and the USE needs in 1632 and beyond, is cheap steel that can be cast into rail and cannon and other forms.

Enter Henry Bessemer.

In the first half of the 1800s, steam engines had become common, and it was possible to produce pumps that could move huge amounts of air at high pressures. Prior to this, smiths had been restricted to the air that they could move with bellows. Some of the bellows were very large, and operated by water wheels, but the pressure was limited and the flow intermittent. By the 1850s engineers had developed pumps that could be driven by steam engines and blow air continuously at high pressure. These were first used to increase the size and output of blast furnaces and resulted in a drop in the price of cast iron.

In 1856, Bessemer designed what he called a *converter*. It was a large, pear-shaped vessel with holes at the bottom that the new pumps could blow compressed air into. Bessemer filled the converter with molten cast iron and then blew air into the bottom, causing it to bubble up through the molten metal. The resulting reaction was very violent. The oxygen combined with the silicon and the carbon in the cast iron, and burned off into the air in just minutes. As the oxygen in the air combined with the carbon, the reaction gave off heat, and instead of freezing up from the cold air, the metal became even hotter. Bessemer converters are large. Small converters take charges of five tons of molten iron. This means that very large quantities of steel can be produced very rapidly.

Historically, it took twenty years to perfect the Bessemer process to deal with all the chemical intricacies of iron ore. Bessemer himself cheated by using pig iron from special phosphorus-free ore bodies in Sweden. But by 1876, the basic Bessemer process could handle most anything that was thrown at it, and vast quantities of molten steel could be produced. Finally, with the Bessemer process we have the ability to produce cast steel items in bulk like railroad rail, cannon, and beams.

The Grantvillers can cheat too. They already know about things like lining the bottom of the converter with limestone to scavenge the phosphorus from the iron. With the books and knowledge brought down-time, the Grantvillers should be able to skip over two hundred years of technical development and jump into the age of rail.

Iron production is very scalable. In the U.S., in 1847 460,000 tons of wrought iron railroad rail was sold at a price of $83 a ton, and 2,000 tons of steel rail at $170 a ton. By 1884, wrought iron rails were no longer made at all, and 1,500,000 tons of cast steel rail were made at a cost of $32 a ton. By 1900 the cost of steel rail was down to $14 a ton. Participants in Baen's Bar in the 1632 Tech conference have been following this process for several years as a team of Barflies lead by John Leggett have documented the growth of USE Steel in a series of monthly reports.

Informed readers will note that this discussion skipped over the Siemans open hearth furnace, which largely replaced the Bessemer process by 1900. The consensus of the iron folks in Baen's Bar has been that the Grantvillers do not have the details of the designs, or the material, especially structural firebricks and other refractories, to successfully build and operate open hearth furnaces.

The Grantvillers will have several techniques to make steel in a variety of carbon contents from very low to nearly cast iron. However, to get the most use out of steel it is necessary not only to create it with the right chemistry, but to treat it to the right temperature conditions.

Consider the following recipe: Take two cups of flour, two eggs, one-third cup of oil, three teaspoons of baking powder, one teaspoon of salt, and one-third cup of buttermilk. This recipe can produce pretty decent biscuits, or pancakes, or waffles (if you separate the egg yolk from the white and beat in sufficient air). On the other hand, overmixed, dumped into a pan, and placed into a 450-degree oven, you'll get an inedible lump. Similarly, the same iron/carbon ratio can produce a wide range of steel products.

The room temperature normal form of iron is called ferrite. If you have ever studied crystals, you may want to know that it's a body-centered cubic crystal. If not, what's important is that ferrite has few gaps. It's a "tight" crystal that can hold only a few hundredths of a percent of carbon. If you heat iron above 906 degrees Celsius it switches to a face-centered-cubic structure called austenite. Austenite is a roomier crystal that can hold up to 1.7 percent of carbon. But you can't hold your tool above 900 degrees Celsius forever. As the temperature falls, the iron atoms try to rearrange themselves into a ferrite structure, and the carbons get squeezed out and diffuse to carbon-rich zones. Eventually, as the temperature reaches 723 degrees Celsius, the austenite crystals are as rearranged as they will get, and the carbon stops moving. What's left is crystals of ferrite, interspersed with fine layers of iron carbide (FeC_3) This layered material is called pearlite and is the basis for high-strength steel wire and rope. The more carbon steel has, the more pearlite is formed, and the harder the steel is.

What happens if instead of letting the steel cool slowly, we plunge the red-hot newly forged tool into cold water, or brine, or a mixture of water and oil? There isn't sufficient time for the carbon to diffuse and form carbon-rich zones. The iron may "want" to switch to the ferrite form, but the carbon is in the way. The crystal lattice becomes very distorted. If you look at the resulting crystals under a microscope, the steel has a distinctive structure with interlocking needles of crystals. There wasn't time to form big crystals, and anyway, the lattice is so distorted that the big crystals wouldn't work. This series of interlocking needles was named after its discoverer, Adolf Martens, and is called Martensite. Martensite is very rigid, so martensitic steel is very hard, but stiff.

It is possible to just convert some of the pearlite in a steel into martensite by heating and then quenching just the working end of a chisel or drill bit. The technique of rapidly cooling a steel blade to make it harder has been known since ancient times. Swords in particular have many myths about the proper solutions, temperatures, and procedures for quenching. Once a piece has been quenched, it may be useful to increase its strength and flexibility by reheating it and holding it at an elevated temperature long enough to allow some of the microstructures to realign. This is called tempering. A temper is followed by a quench, or rapid cooling to make sure the outside of the tool is hard. Tempering is an art and science all its own in addition to the chemistry of the steel. With a clever combination of heating, quenching, and tempering, it is possible to make tool steels that can be used in lathes and cutters and drills to cut steels of the same chemistry that have not been "hardened." Tempering in lead baths, hot oil baths, sand, and tempering ovens are all treatments that will be available down-time.

So far, we've just discussed iron and carbon. It is possible to mix iron with other metals. In particular, in 1912 Harry Brearley produced the first stainless steels. Stainless steels are low carbon steels with 10.5 percent or more chromium added. They are resistant to rust compared to steel without chromium. They stain "less" than plain iron. Chromium atoms combine with oxygen to form hard, stable clear layers of chromium (III) oxide (Cr_2O_3) on the surface of the metal. Chromium atoms and chromium-oxide have compatible geometries, so the oxide packs neatly on the surface of the metal and stays attached well. On the other hand, iron oxide (Fe_2O_3)(rust) has a geometry that does not pack well against iron atoms, and so it flakes, or falls off the surface, exposing more fresh iron to the oxygen.

In chrome rich steels, if the chrome-oxide layer on the surface is scratched or disturbed, it quickly forms a new layer of chrome oxide, and protects the bulk of the metal underneath. That is why stainless steel is stainless. It's self-protecting, sort of. Note that the protection requires having oxygen available to form the protective layer. In oxygen-poor environments, or in low-circulation situations, stainless steel doesn't resist corrosion any better than plain steel. Also, in seawater, or in other situations where chlorine is available, the chloride ion attacks and destroys the chromium oxide layer faster than it can be formed.

The addition of nickel to the mix of iron and chromium can have even more interesting effects. Specifically, adding sufficient nickel results in the steel retaining its austenite structure at all temperatures. Among other things, chrome-nickel austenitic steels can be nonmagnetic.

Stainless steel, and its corrosion resistant companions will form the center of a full article in a future issue of the *Gazette*. For now, recognize that the Grantvillers know of only one source for chromium they can reach, it is going to be extremely difficult to mine, and lies near the arctic circle. Modern stainless steels may also contain nickel, manganese, niobium, tungsten, and titanium, none of which the Grantvillers will be producing anytime soon.

Iron, and more precisely steel, is central to the industrial expansion of modern technology. Few choke points in the development of modern civilization are pressing on Grantville harder than the shortage of steel. The expansion of iron and steel production will stress every resource: transportation, mining, construction, chemistry, lights, power, water, and manpower. It is a challenge they have little choice but to meet. Meanwhile, stranded up-time, I'm going to attempt to avoid hitting a deer while driving on an asphalt road in my steel car.

The Impact of Mechanization on German Farms
⁌❄⁍
Karen Bergstralh

What will happen when Grantville introduces nineteenth-century farm equipment to seventeenth-century farmers? Will there be a rapid adaptation of the new machines followed by a similarly rapid increase in productivity? Will this in turn lead to an equally rapid decrease in the numbers of farm laborers? What factors will shape the mechanization of USE farms and how will mechanization shape the USE? All these are questions that occur in the background of the 1632 series. This article attempts to explore these questions and make my estimates at the correct answers.

The seventeenth-century farming methods were labor-intensive and time-consuming, requiring large groups of people to plant, care for, and harvest the crops. Despite this, in normal times, the farming villages of Germany were producing enough food to support themselves and had extra produce for sale to the cities. Economically these villages ranged from very poor villages that barely managed to stay above subsistence level to quite wealthy surplus-farming villages.

One thing to remember always is that the early modern German farmers were not ignorant, stupid, illiterate, or superstition-ridden. Books and pamphlets on farming were very popular and widely read. While translations of Roman texts on farming were considered *the* authoritative texts, farmers did not slavishly follow the advice found there. Three-field crop rotation, not mentioned by the Romans, had been practiced for centuries by farmers throughout Europe. In this method each field was left fallow every third year. The village livestock grazed on the fallow field, fertilizing it with their dung. After harvest the village animals were set to graze on the remains of the harvest, again fertilizing the fields. Farmers might not know why it worked but they could see the results. The German farmers will be interested in Grantville's knowledge and machinery.

Disease and destruction has reduced the available labor in many areas. Add the pressures of the growing industries around Grantville competing for what labor exists and the farms will remain short of people to work the crops. This lack of farm laborers will be a driver for mechanization.

Farming is a balancing act at any time. The difference between successful harvest and starvation is dependent upon numerous factors. Bad weather and insect invasions may destroy the crops. Outbreaks of disease could remove enough manpower to make planting and harvesting difficult to impossible. Diseases among the livestock might kill off or debilitate enough animals to edge the farmers into starvation. During the Thirty Years' War, additional stresses were added when scavenging parties from one army or another would steal or destroy crops and animals. Farmers who fled the armies could not tend their crops, leading to losses. When the farmers did return to their villages, they often did not have sufficient manpower to plant or harvest.

A few things need to be made clear about German farming villages in the seventeenth century. Unlike the USA model of single-family farms, Germans farms consisted of a village—known as the *Gemeinde*—farming as a whole. Physically, the German farming community more closely resembled a fried egg on a plate than the USA model of neatly-laid-out individual farms of rectangular fields bounded by straight roads crossing at right angles. Consider the yolk to represent the village and the white to represent the fields and land around the village. Village land sizes ranged from roughly 640 acres to nearly six thousand acres with the average size around one to two thousand acres. This average village would have roughly two to three hundred acres in crops and about another one hundred acres in pasture and hay growing. Villages also had fishponds, forests, and meadows held and used in common. Villages normally ranged in size from ten to ninety households.

The village was run as a communal corporation, complete with elected officers. The farmers decided communally what to grow in which fields. Each farmer had a strip of land assigned to him from which he took his profits and food. The amount of land an individual farmer had the rights to could vary in size. Also, each farmer had the rights to pasture a certain number of cows on his share of the village commons. A farmer was by definition a person who held enough land in the village corporation to support himself and his family by farming, using a combined work-force of his own family members and a couple of hired men or girls. A farmer who held this kind of share in the lands had a full vote in the village *Gemeinde*, was expected to do his share in holding local offices, etc. The average farmer leased around forty to eighty acres of arable land. Finally, draft animals might belong to individual farmers but they were used communally.

The villagers were *not* serfs. The village lands were held by written lease from the landowners. A common lease ran for ninety-nine years or three lives, whichever came first. A village usually owed rents to several landowners, as land rights could and often were subdivided, leased, sold, inherited, etc. Think of it as somewhat equivalent to the landowners as shareholders of stock and the rents as dividends. Thus a village mayor and council would collect the revenue and send one sixteenth to X, one eighth to Y, three thirty-seconds to Z, and so forth.

The harvesting of the 1631 crop using up-time machines to replace the missing farm labor would have given the down-time farmers a glimpse of what mecha-nization can do for harvesting. The use of Grantville's machines to aid in the following spring's planting would drive the lesson home. Mechanization allows you to farm with fewer people and, as many of the machines do not require adult strength, you can now use younger family members. By the fall harvest of 1632 those farmers around Grantville know that mechanization does reduce labor requirements and costs. Some local down-time farmers may begin to see how Grantville's machines and knowledge also improves the yield per acre.

Grantville brings with it practical and theoretical knowledge, mechanized farm machinery, and up-time livestock. The introduction of Grantville's farm machines will bypass, to some degree, several centuries of slow development and mechanization of the farm which were required in our time line. ("Our time line" will be henceforth abbreviated as OTL.)

That does not, however, mean that farm mechanization will necessarily develop very rapidly or evenly. In OTL, mechanization of farms in the United States required around 120 to 150 years—and even now, in the twenty-first century, there are still large areas of the world where farming is not mechanized at all or is only minimally mechanized. Before galloping off with grandiose ideas about how fast mechanization will spread in the 1632 universe, we should look at why it took so long in OTL and why it has not completely spread even in the twenty-first century OTL.

One reason OTL mechanization did not spread faster was that the equipment itself developed slowly. As Grantville has examples of fully developed draft animal– and tractor-powered mechanized farming equipment, this developmental phase will be bypassed. Time factors on the machinery side will primarily be how fast the horse-drawn equipment can be copied and adapted for manufacture with available resources. Tractors must wait until the tools and materials are available to manufacture engines. Still, farm machinery at least to an OTL 1930s level should be available by 1650–1660.

Aside from availability, the major factor retarding mechanization was the cost of the new farm machinery. To a single farmer, the OTL model in the USA, cost was often the biggest problem in mechanizing. In modern OTL examples of non-mechanized farming it appears that cost remains a major factor for the lack of mechanization.

Usually the speed of mechanization comes down to costs, infrastructure problems, and some social factors. Farm costs, regardless of the time period, include the cost of the land, of labor, of livestock, of the farmer's subsistence, and the purchase and upkeep of any implements or machines. Against these costs are the profits from each crop or animal raised. Profits must exceed the operating costs or the farmer loses. Farmers tend to be very fiscally conservative because of these factors.

The cost of the land is something our down-time farmers obviously already know. The farmers have been able to produce sufficient crops and livestock to pay their land rents. Without sudden increases in rents, the down-time farmers have no incentive to mechanize from land costs.

Land costs can be considered as a neutral factor for mechanization. Labor costs, the number of people required to raise and harvest a crop using down-time methods, are also known.

Infrastructure costs include those concerning the initial machinery costs, maintenance and repair costs of the machine, the power source and its fuel, maintenance, repair, and upkeep cost, and costs associated with storage and shipping of the crops.

Social factors tend toward the universal desire to not be seen by neighbors and relatives as backward and unfashionable. This factor has led OTL farmers into financial trouble and will undoubtedly ruin some down-time farmers also.

Farms are businesses and you cannot afford to farm at a loss. A money trap OTL farmers encounter is when that shiny new tractor costs $100,000 and raises gross profits by 15 percent but, between the cost of the loan, fuel, and maintenance, it costs 25 percent more to use it. A net loss of 10 percent will quickly put a farm in a financial hole. To quote a farmer cousin, "People romanticize the family farm and forget it is a business. You must at least break even and the idea is to make a profit. It's easy to only count the money in your hand at the end of harvest and forget what it cost you to make that harvest—at least until the bills come due."

Grantville, under the direction of Willie Ray Hudson, is developing granges to help with the spread and utilization of up-time knowledge and technology. Granges are basically cooperative groups of farmers who pool knowledge, machinery, labor, and money. As the German farming villages were already communal farmers, the granges should fit in nicely.

Where a single farmer might not be able to afford a new piece of farm machinery, the farming village can; and if the village can't afford it, the grange can. Cooperative arrangements for the use of these machines will be negotiated along with the repayments of the loans required to obtain them. The machinery manufacturers will also extend credit in some places and perhaps lease equipment to those who can not afford to buy. This cooperative buying should make farm mechanization occur more rapidly than in OTL. Still, there are some potential bumps. Unfortunately, due to the nature of farming this cooperative sharing of equipment can only go so far. The limited time period for successful planting puts limits on the sharing of some farm machinery.

The cooperative nature of the early modern German farming villages can be both more and less conducive to a rapid adaptation of mechanization. On the more conducive side, there is the factor that the village farms will be better able to afford the new machines. However, conservatism on the part of the villages' governing councils may retard rapid adaptation. Farmers tend to be very conservative; it is their livelihood and homes that are on the line. Once it becomes clear that the reluctant farmers will have to adopt machinery or be satisfied with considerably lower profits and higher labor rates than neighboring villages, this should change. Here the granges should help not only by spreading the cost of machines out among several villages but also by persuading reluctant farmers to mechanize to some extent. In part, this last involves social as well as economic pressures.

OTL mechanization began with the development of horse-drawn farm equipment, firstly in plows, reapers, and seed drills. Once the inventions began to show promise they were adopted as they became available and affordable. Similarly in the 1632 universe the first wave of mechanization will be animal powered. Power will be provided by horses, mules, and oxen. As a note, the switch in draft power from primarily oxen to primarily horses or mules occurred for social and status as well as economic reasons. Horses could pull greater loads faster and longer than oxen but they cost more to purchase and maintain. By the seventeenth century, European farmers overwhelmingly preferred horses to oxen for draft purposes. The use of oxen in farming seems to have been equated with backward and poor farmers. Oxen can be used with horse-drawn machinery, and given the shortage of draft animals in the war zone any draft animal available will be used.

Steam-driven tractors were first introduced in the late nineteenth century but were not practical or truly economically viable for most farmers. It was with the development of gasoline engines that tractors became both practical and affordable. Grantville most likely will totally bypass the steam phase of tractors. Once internal combustion engines can be built in numbers, farm tractors will became available. Probably the first tractors will not be easily affordable and we may see the rise of specialty companies such as the OTL harvest and threshing crews. Because these companies lease their labor and machines the costs can be spread amongst numerous villages.

[A side note here: In Grantville there exists a steam engine hobbyists' group who have the knowledge and practical experience to build better steam engines than were available in the nineteenth century. They will build such engines and these engines will be useful on farms as stationary power sources for threshers, balers, loaders, etc. It is their use as power sources for tractors that is unlikely to occur.]

Let's look at affordability as it applies to all mechanized farm equipment. Availability is important, but affordability is critical. The problem is not the just the initial cost of the farm machinery, but also the cost of upkeep—repair, maintenance, and fuel. These same costs have driven the spread of farm mechanization throughout its OTL history.

A major driver in the slowness of the OTL adaptation of tractors was not just the initial cost of the tractors but was the infrastructure cost. The first nonsteam OTL tractors were very expensive but they also had new requirements for fuel, fuel storage, maintenance, and repair. These new requirements added up to new costs to the farmer. In addition, switching to tractors generally meant having to either alter or scrap existing horse-drawn equipment. For some of the later tractors there was no way to adapt horse-drawn equipment so the farmer was forced to buy new equipment, driving the costs of tractor mechanization even higher.

Grantville may be able to sidestep this incompatibility if they decide from the start to produce tractor versions of farm equipment and introduce the use of a fore cart. A fore cart is just what it says; a cart that sits between the gangplow or seeder and has a team of horses hitched to it. OTL fore carts vary between those that simply adapt the tractor hitch system to horse-drawn and those carts that carry a motor and/or a hydraulic pump to operate the tractor version equipment.

Down-time farmers will have the same concerns about the costs of the machines as the OTL up-timers had. It isn't just the costs associated with tractors. After all, the repairs, maintenance, and fuel required by draft animals are also costs. The biggest difference between the competing power systems is that the down-time farmers understand the costs and problems involved with draft animals but will view the first tractors as carrying many unknown costs.

Mechanization, however fast or slowly it occurs, will quickly bring benefits. Mechanization can be as simple as a better tool. The walking plow has no moving parts and is not radically different from the old heavy wooden plow. Better yet, someone familiar with using a heavy wooden plow will be able to quickly learn to use the walking plow. The walking plow alone decreases the time it takes to plow an acre of land. Those farmers who adopt only the walking plow will experience a decrease in the labor (man-hours) required by their wheat crop. Farmers using a walking plow with their old harrows, hand broadcasting of seed, harvesting with scythe, and threshing with flails will find that their wheat crop takes 50–60 man-hours per acre and yields 20 bushels per acre. This results in 2.5 to 3 man-hours per bushel. The same fields plowed with the heavy wooden plow generally took 100–120 man-hours per acre or 5–6 man-hours per bushel for the same 20 bushels per acre yield.

The motive power—horses, oxen, or mules—are available and the farmers know how to feed and maintain them. Better yet, the down-time farmers usually already have these draft animals and the walking plow requires fewer animals, oxen or horses, than the heavy wooden plow. While suitable draft animals are in short supply due to the war, they are being bought outside the war zone and brought in.

Another factor in favor of starting with the simpler up-time equipment is that what little maintenance is required by the walking plow can be done by the farmer. The local blacksmith can do any repairs the farmer can't handle. Here the supporting infrastructure for the mechanization already exists. Overall the costs for a walking plow are low and will be familiar to the farmers, which makes it a good first step.

The next step up in mechanization is introducing the sulky or gangplow, seed drills or mechanical seeders, binders, and bull threshers. Each piece of equipment can be added without need for the rest. Thus, a village can pay for the next piece of equipment with the profits from the last. The increases in yields and drop in labor requirements are great enough to justify moving to this level of mechanization. The complete package, gangplow, mechanical seeders, binders, and bull threshers drop the labor rates down to 8–10 man-hours per acre and 0.4–0.5 man-hours per bushel for a 20 bushel per acre yield.

This increase in productivity does have additional costs. A sulky or gangplow is quite a bit more expensive both to buy and to maintain. On the sulky plow the farmer had two, three, or four plowshares or bottoms and he rode on top of it instead of walking behind. Upgrading from a walking plow would not require extensive retraining. The seed drills and mechanical seeders also fall into the mechanically more complex and expensive category. They improve the yield of the crops by making planting more uniform. Their use was faster and less labor intensive than planting by hand, especially for row crops such as beans and corn.

To achieve the low man-hours above, the farmers must use a binder and thresher. Here things get more complicated. Because Grantville has the advantage of being on the end of the development phase for horse-drawn farm equipment, it is likely that they will skip over reapers and go directly into binders and eventually combines.

A quick look at reapers still is useful.

When the first reapers appeared on the scene they revolutionized harvesting. No longer was the grain cut by hand. With the reaper the cut wheat still would be raked and hand stooked for later threshing. The binder took the next step and, as the name says, bound the stooks and dropped them neatly behind it, ready to be tossed on the wagon and taken to the thresher. No longer were stooking teams needed to hand bind the wheat, eliminating one of the most labor intensive and backbreaking jobs on the farm. The mechanical thresher was another quantum leap forward over using flails and hand winnowing, processing in one day what had taken weeks to thresh before. Once more a time-consuming and labor-intensive operation was replaced.

The price for this massive increase in productivity was both monetary and increased mechanical complexity. Reapers and later binders and combines were the single most expensive piece of farm equipment. Early on it was not uncommon for the wealthiest farmer in the area to own the reaper and rent it out to other farmers. In OTL, machinery costs led to the development of specialty harvesting crews and farmer's cooperatives to purchase and operate the harvesting machines.

Binders are more mechanically complicated than sulky

plows and seed drills. Repair and maintenance require greater mechanical skills and a bigger toolbox. The farmers, having learned to maintain their other farm equipment, should still be able to do some of the repairs themselves. The local blacksmith can make other, more complicated repairs. However, additional players come on the scene now.

Mechanical complexity has its own costs. Farmers who have not had to deal with anything beyond pulleys and wagon wheels now are going to have to deal with slipped belts, jammed gears, twisted chains, and remembering to lubricate the moving parts. The farmers will have to learn not just what an open-end wrench is but where it is used. As with any advance in technology some people will adapt easily, others will struggle, and some will fail. In OTL, this advancement occurred over several generations and when mechanization was entering into all aspects of life. Because of the accelerated mechanization Grantville is promoting, the down-time farmer may find himself unable to decipher the inner workings of a reaper. Exposure to the machines will mean that our poor befuddled farmer's children will find mechanisms easier to understand and fix. Thus the second generation of farmers should be both more mechanically savvy and inclined to further mechanization.

The accelerated mechanization also means that the farm machinery manufacturers will have to not just briefly demonstrate the new machines but really teach the farmers how to operate, maintain, and repair them. These jobs fall to the manufacturers' representative or dealer who sells machines, trains farmers in their care and operation, and handles replacement parts. In OTL, some manufacturers also began providing for repair work that was beyond the farmer's or local blacksmith's abilities. This was the introduction of the factory-trained mechanic. The factory-trained mechanic's services were usually available through the manufacturer's representative or dealer at a price. Because of human nature and the need of manufacturers to charge higher prices to cover overhead, there should also arise the independent mechanic and his repair shop.

In OTL, along with the reapers, binders, and combines a new category of worker appeared: the mechanical specialist or mechanic. Sometimes these were blacksmiths, sometimes farm boys, but they were always young men who were fascinated by machines and how they worked. With the ever-increasing complexity of machines, these mechanics began to be necessary parts of the infrastructure. A mechanic could afford to own the specialized tools necessary for uncommon repairs. He had the arcane knowledge of how linkages and pulleys worked and why you really needed a washer under that nut over there. OTL farmers still did most of the maintenance of their equipment themselves, but when they were stumped by a problem they could call in the mechanic. In Grantville, these mechanics will be even more critical for the beginnings of farm mechanization.

While the motive power for the farm machines discussed above remains draft animals, the reaper or binder requires larger teams. This adds the costs of buying and maintaining the additional horses and harnesses to the cost of the binder. The additional horses usually mean some additional farm laborer(s) to tend them. Due to the seasonal requirements for these draft animals, the OTL farmer might make arrangements to lease the teams or work cooperatively with other farmers. In Grantville, with the communal farming and the establishment of granges, it is likely that there will be cooperative ownership and use of binders.

The introduction of tractors and all things motorized in OTL took the mechanical complexity level beyond what many horse-drawn-era farmers were comfortable with. When OTL motive power became tractors, the farmer needed a new set of skills and knowledge in addition to what was needed to run the horse-drawn farm equipment. It was usually the next generation that took up the use of tractors. The farmers' children learned to deal with the mechanical complexities of tractors while growing up around them. With the introduction of the tractor, repairs or replacements that a farmer could not do himself were also introduced. These repairs had to go to the equipment dealer or an independent mechanic and that added to operational costs. Additionally, the introduction of the tractor meant that fuel had to be purchased and stored. A horse might up and die on you but he wouldn't quit working because you forgot to check the fuel storage tank. Tractors meant the farmer had new costs and requirements to deal with for his motive power.

The farmers in the USE will have similar problems adapting to tractor use. We know that oil production is starting up and eventually there will be gasoline available, but the infrastructure for distribution and on-farm storage of the gasoline must also be developed. Perhaps fortunately,

Grantville will not see new internal combustion engines being manufactured in great numbers for several years to come. This delay should allow for other necessary elements of infrastructure to catch up.

Going to full tractor-driven mechanization allows for an incredible leap in productivity. Using a tractor, a 12-foot plow, a 14-foot drill, 14-foot self-propelled combine, and trucks, should give the farmer labor rates of 1.5 man-hours per acre and 0.05 man-hours per bushel for a 30 bushel per acre yield. Remember these same fields plowed with the heavy wooden plow took 100–120 man-hours per acre or 5–6 man-hours per bushel for a 20 bushels per acre yield. Add in that laborers will be in short supply due to the accompanying increases in industries, and the down-time farmers will be forced to adopt some level of mechanization.

This will not come without a price. The first price is the cost of the farm machines themselves. The second price is the need to understand and deal with the increased mechanical complexity of that machinery. The third price is the need for supporting technology infrastructures. To accomplish such a leap in farm mechanization requires equal leaps in many other industries. Bringing seventeenth-century farming up to OTL 1930's levels cannot be done unless the supporting industries also are brought up to those same levels. Among the required supporting industries and infrastructure are:

Steel plants
Foundries
Mechanical design engineers

Electrical design engineers
Machine shops
Bearings
Gears
Gas engines
Batteries
Spark plugs
Farm machinery factories
Trained mechanics
Refineries and fuel distribution systems

My own estimate is that it will take until 1640 to begin to produce the simpler horse-drawn farm machines in any numbers. As discussed above, these machines will make a great difference in the productivity of the down-time farms. The major problem once the farm machines are available will be how much the machines cost to purchase and operate and the availability of mechanics to maintain them until the farmers learn to do their own maintenance. Some time in the decade of the 1640s, I can see the development of traveling mechanics who spend the year going from farm to farm working on the new horse-drawn farm implements and teaching the farmers how to use and maintain them.

There are other means of increasing farm productivity besides mechanization.

Along with the new farm equipment there will be modern tillage methods taught and the introduction of a few new crops and new livestock strains. Some of the tillage methods will increase crop yields even without the new machines.

The up-time livestock such as dairy and beef cattle also have the potential for greatly increasing yields without any new machines.

We know that beef cattle exist in sufficient numbers around Grantville to keep twentieth-century breeds going. Not all the up-time breeds will have enough breeding stock to remain pure but an aggressive breeding program should see results in general beef cattle. This happened in OTL, with the size of cattle brought to one meat market for slaughter doubling in weight over a century. With the up-time cattle as a start and the up-time knowledge of genetics and nutrition it should be possible to duplicate the OTL gain in size faster. Dairy cattle are more problematic as there are fewer of them around Grantville. Again, the various breeds may not have enough numbers to remain distinct but there should be enough to breed dairy specific cows. With greater milk yields the farmers have not only better family nutrition, but also can sell surplus dairy products such as cheese and butter for profit.

Beef is raised for both sustenance and sale. Doubling the slaughter weight of cattle increases both and may move some marginal farm villages and farmers out of mostly sustenance farming and into mostly sale farming. In some of the areas where farming is marginal due to the land types, these beef cattle may cause a switch to cattle-raising-only farms.

Dairy cattle also provide sustenance and some profit. A dairy cow provides milk and calves. The milk may be used by the farmer or sold. The cow's calf can either be slaughtered for the family's meat, sold for slaughter, or sold for breeding. With dairy-specific cows there can be extra milk for making cheese for sustenance and sale instead of just subsistence. Research has not come up with any milk yields for seventeenth-century cows but we could safely say that yields will at least double.

In the seventeenth century there was not the distinction between beef and dairy cattle that exists now. Cows gave enough milk to support their calves and have some left for the farmer's family but the amounts were small. Similarly, when slaughtered the cow did not yield the masses of meat found on modern beef cattle.

Also, as the power sources for most of the farmers are going to be animals for quite a bit yet, Grantville's veterinarians and their knowledge will also contribute to farm productivity.

Tillage methods and theories will also help along with the specialized tools to accomplish them. A fairly simple tool that certainly should be available in Grantville is a hillside plow—which is a plow especially designed for contour plowing on hillsides and slopes. As to the various theories, well, those arguments should make for interesting grange meetings.

Fertilizers and their use will be a great boon as will the pretreatment of seed to prevent fungus. Even without up-time chemical fertilizers, the knowledge the up-time farmers have of using natural fertilizers will be a great step forward. The down-time farmers do know about resting fields and letting their livestock self-fertilize the resting fields, but they do not know why it works. Another useful up-time knowledge set is just which crops should be planted in what order to restore nutrients to the soils. The spread of this knowledge should spark some lively debates and new and different answers to farmer's problems.

In the end, I'll quote my farmer cousin again. "Farmers are conservative. If what they are already doing works, they aren't going to jump on the next new thing just because it is new. Most of them will wait until somebody else shows that the new gadget works better than what they have. And it has to work a whole lot better or a whole lot cheaper to get them to change." Admittedly he is just one farmer, but the same philosophy has run his family farm for over a hundred years and run it at a profit.

Appendix 1: A Single Day's Work

Assuming a well-conditioned team, equipment in good repair, and ten hours in the field, with two 1,500-pound horses, in one day you can expect to:

Plow	1.5–2 acres
Cultivate (single row)	7 acres
Harrow	8–10 acres
Mow	7 acres
Seed drill	8–10 acres
Rake	14 acres
Plant	8–10 acres
Haul on a wagon	1.5 tons 20–25 miles

Four horses could accomplish twice as much with the same human labor, but would require implements twice as wide. Where the draft horses are smaller than 1,500 pounds, three horses may be needed to accomplish the same amount of work.

Appendix 2: Team and Manpower Requirements

These requirements assume modern-size draft horses of 15.5 to 16 hand and 1,400 to 1,600 pounds. This is the size horse known today as a "chunk." The use of smaller draft horses would require an increase in the number of horses per team. This is only a partial listing of farm equipment.

- One bottom wooden plow: Oxen team of 2–8 oxen, 1 oxen driver, 1 person to handle the plow
- Walking plow: Horse team of 1–2 horses, 1 driver/plow handler
- Sulky plow, two bottom: Horse team of 2–4 horses, 1 driver
- Sulky plow, four bottom: Horse team of 3–8 horses, 1 driver
- Drag harrow: Horse team of 1–2 horses, 1 driver
- Disc harrow: Horse team of 4–8 horses, 1 driver
- Seed drill: Horse team of 2 horses, 1 driver
- Two-row corn planter: Horse team of 2 horses, 1 driver
- Hay mower: Horse team of 2–4 horses, 1 driver/operator
- Buckrake: Horse team of 2–4 horses,

1 driver/operator
- Stationary hay baler (200–250 lb. 3-wire bales): 2 horse–driven treadmill or sweep
- Stationary hay baler (125–150 lb. 3-wire bales): Tractor belt driven
- Wooden pull grader (or snow plow): Horse team of 4–6 horses, 1 driver
- Grain binder: Horse team of 3–5 horses, 1 driver/operator
- Bundle wagons (carrying shocks to thresher): Horse team of 2 horses, 1 driver
- Farm wagon (hauling sacks of grain): 6-horse team, 1 driver
- Spring wagon (light hauling): Horse team of 2 horses, 1 driver
- Manure spreader: Horse team of 2 horses, 1 driver

Bibliography

Gladitz, Charles. *Horse Breeding in the Medieval World.* Four Courts Press, 1997. Dublin.

Hyland, Ann. *The Horse in the Middle Ages.* Sutton Publishing Limited, 1999.

Langdon, John. *Horses, Oxen and Technological Innovation.* Cambridge University Press, 1986. Cambridge.

Telleen, Maurice. *The Draft Horse Primer.* Draft Horse Journal, Inc., 1977.

Online References

www.ruralheritage.com
  Recommended site to start with. Lots of good information on four-legged farming.

www.history.rochester.edu/appleton/a/agmac-m.html
  History of agricultural equipment. A very good site for those interested in horse-drawn farm equipment and the nuts and bolts of using it. This site uses illustrations from the nineteenth century to explain how things work.

www.farmerbrownsplowshop.bigstep.com
  Lots of good stuff and pictures of modern farming and logging with horses.

http://ag.smsu.edu/cweq72a.htm
  Pictures of many horse-drawn implements from Southwest Missouri State University.

www.erm.ee/pysi/engpages/kyla.html
  Pictures of an Estonian farm whose buildings are similar to those of Germany in the seventeenth century.

www.science-tech.nmstc.ca/english/collection/
  Canadian Museum of Technology. One should read this entire marvelous site.

www.ikisan.com/machine/cache/ma_tillageequipments.asp
  An "everything you ever wanted to know about farming" site.

www.grange.org/
    Information on granges and their development in the USA.

Flint's Lock

*Part one of a series devoted to firearms in the
1632 universe*

｛◎★◎｝

Leonard Hollar, Bob Hollingsworth,
Tom Van Natta, and John Zeek

*[Editor's note: The Grantville Firearms Roundtable
is a group of experts on firearms whom I asked to
develop a series of articles for the Grantville Gazette
on the issue of firearms as it bears on the series. The
members are Leonard Hollar, Bob Hollingsworth,
John Rigby, Tom Van Natta, and John Zeek. Rick
Boatright edited the article.]*

In *1633* Eric Flint and David Weber give us our first
glimpse at the type of firearm Grantville introduced to
arm its allies. Many fans of the series were surprised that
more advanced weaponry was not produced. To better
understand why a muzzle loading flintlock rifle was

421

chosen, rather than the pet design of every fan, requires a look at many problems faced by the Grantvillers and their understanding of those problems. What weapons would they face on a 1633 battlefield? What materials were available? What thought might have gone into developing the features that are to be found on the weapon now called the SRG?

To understand the reasoning behind the adoption of a flintlock rifle when other designs are available, requires starting with a brief discussion of the weaponry arrayed against Grantville when the town was dropped into the middle of the Thirty Years' War.

Most of the European army units had more men armed with pikes, long wooden poles with metal blades on the end, than men armed with firearms. These units were pike heavy. The ratio of pikes to muskets was in flux and some units might have had as few as one pike per musket, but others might have had as many as four pikes to one musket.

The range of the pikes was the length of the pikes. The pikes served to keep mounted troops from riding down troops armed with muskets and to keep skirmishers armed with blades out of the musket ranks. The pikes tended to be organized into large square or rectangular formations and smaller squares of musket-armed men formed to either side. When threatened by a cavalry or dismounted charge, the musketeers retreated within the pike squares.

This is necessary because the musket of this time has a very low rate of fire and a very short effective range.

The matchlock musket is the most common firearm on

the battlefield facing the Americans in 1632. A "lock" in firearms terminology was the system that ignited the gunpowder. Locks may actually have been associated with locksmiths. A gun lock had as a major component a flat metal plate with holes bored in it for the passage of small metal parts and bore some vague resemblance to door locks of the time. Locks might be described as the trigger mechanism in modern terms. Other types of ignition systems existed, but the matchlock is far and away the most common. A matchlock system used a piece of smoldering cloth cord to ignite the priming charge of a musket. The cord was soaked in a solution of saltpeter and allowed to dry. This cord then burned when lit, with little danger of going out. In small arms, this burning cord was called "slow match." A matchlock musket without slow match or some other source of flame was merely a clumsy club.

The matchlock action held the burning cord on an arm that was lowered into a small cup on the side of the barrel near the closed end called the priming pan of the musket. A hole from the priming pan led inside the barrel to the main propelling charge. This priming pan was filled partially with a fine grain of gunpowder and when the match was applied, a small explosion occurred. Some of the hot gases from the explosion of the "primer" flashed through the hole in the barrel and set off the main charge, which then launched the bullet on its way.

The bullet was usually a round lead ball. In 1632, muskets in the hands of infantry could range from .52 caliber (.52 inches) to over .80 caliber or 13 to 22mm in diameter. The muskets were smooth-bore and the balls were undersize so as to drop easily down the barrel. The diameter of the barrel or size of the round lead ball were often expressed as *bore* in the 1600s. This was the number of round lead balls that fit the gun that are necessary to make one pound. Roughly speaking a 28-bore was .58 caliber, a 20-bore was a .62 caliber, a 16-bore was a .68 caliber, and a 12-bore was about .72 caliber. Those measurements tended not to be exact.

Most of the military muskets of 1632 weighed between twelve and sixteen pounds. There was some move to standardization, but guns of different lock type, length, weight, and caliber could be found in the same formation of most armies.

The musketeer wore premeasured charges of gunpowder in twelve or thirteen wooden bottles, often called *cartouches*, on a bandoleer worn over one shoulder and across to the other hip. The cartouches hung on cords and swung about as he moved, reportedly clacking together and making a racket. He also carried a powder horn to prime his musket with, and a powder measure he could make more loads of powder with or reload his cartouche with, in the unlikely event that the battle progressed beyond thirteen shots. Although muskets were lighter in 1632 than they were only a few decades earlier, he might very well have carried a stick with something like an oar lock on the end to steady his weapon while he pointed it. This steady was often metal-clad near the ends and might feature a stub blade on the end resting on the ground to act as a short jabbing spear in case the pike men failed at their mission. He might also carry a rapier, or short sword, or large dagger, or some combination of such cutting and stabbing weapons. He also needed a ramrod that was most likely carried on the musket by 1632, but might be carried separately.

To load his musket, he removed the burning match from the holder and placed it someplace handy, like his hatband. Next he placed the butt of the weapon on the ground and held it by its muzzle end in one hand. He then pulled one of the cartouches from his bandoleer and poured this powder down the barrel of his musket. Next he reached into a pouch and pulled out a lead bullet, which he dropped down the barrel on top of the powder. He used a ramrod to force the ball down on the powder to compress the powder and to ensure that there was no air space between the powder and bullet. When in a big hurry, he might have simply dropped the bullet down the barrel and pounded the butt of the musket on the ground and hoped the ball seated itself via inertia. He risked damaging his musket and himself by doing so, for an air space between powder and bullet could be trouble, but it might have seemed less of a threat than the approaching enemy. No patch or wadding was generally used. Now the gun was raised and set upon the steady. The powder horn was used to prime the pan of the musket and a small cover was shut over the pan. The burning slow match was recovered, the ash flicked from the end, the coal blown on to be sure it was good and hot and it was placed back in the jaws of the match holder. When ready to fire, the pan cover was opened and the match lowered into the pan.

Gustavus Adolphus had recently improved this system when Grantville arrived in the seventeenth century. Many of his musketeers on his campaign in Germany had adopted paper-wrapped cartridges. Both the Dutch and the Poles claim to have originated this system, but it was not yet common in other armies. The powder, and in some cases the ball, are wrapped in a sheet of paper rolled into a tube. The soldier could carry twenty or even thirty of those paper cartridges in a pouch rather than the cumbersome and noisy wooden cartouches on a bandoleer. To use the paper cartridges, the end without the bullet was bitten open and the powder poured down the barrel. The bullet was then taken from the pouch or, if it was packaged in the paper cartridge, was squeezed from the cartridge and dropped down the barrel by itself or with the paper, and was then forced down into contact with the powder by the ramrod. Some of Gustavus' men figured out that one could prime the pan by pouring a bit of the powder from the paper cartridge into it and closing the cover before loading the main charge and bullet, slightly increasing their rate of fire.

All those activities involved in loading took a good bit of time. Around one minute between shots would have been considered fast shooting. Each musket produced a huge cloud of smoke when it fired. Musketeers were arrayed in ranks and each rank fired all together on order in a volley. This allowed the entire rank to see what they were shooting at. Most military muskets had only a simple front sight, much like is common on a modern shotgun. The musket was merely pointed at its intended victim rather than carefully aimed.

There are variations in the locks. Many were a simple S-shaped lever that, depending on the design, one either pulled or pushed away to lower that burning cord into the priming pan. Some were spring-loaded with a mechanical release, a trigger, to allow the spring-driven match holder to snap into the priming pan. The triggers might have been designed to be pulled by a finger or pushed by a thumb and could have been on the bottom, side or top of the stock depending on who made it, where it was made and when.

Armies of the day considered any firing of the common musket from beyond seventy-five meters to be pretty much a waste of powder and shot.

Some of the skirmishers to be faced would have had specially selected smoothbore guns of lighter construction that used a greased cloth or leather patch to make the bullets a tighter fit in the barrels. These generally were of relatively small bore, around .50 caliber or 12.6mm. That tight fit generally gave them a higher velocity and greater accuracy than could be had with the common musket. It might well also have had sights and a more advanced form of lock, up to the snaphaunce, an early form of snapping flintlock, or a wheel lock, a system much like the spark wheel on a modern cigarette lighter. The improved locks, sights, and the patched bullets made it possible for the skirmisher so armed to reach out as far as one hundred meters or even occasionally to 150 meters with some expectation of hitting an individual standing man. These weapons were slower to reload when used in that accurate manner, but were faster than a matchlock when a bare ball was dropped down the barrel and musket accuracy and range were expected.

A few people on the battlefield were armed with rifles. A rifle had grooves in its barrel called rifling. The rifling imparts a spin on the bullet when fired and made rifles much more accurate weapons. Rifles of 1632 might have had matchlocks, but were more likely to have a mechanical lock such as the snaphaunce or wheel lock. Some used an oversize ball that was hammered into the barrel and down on top of the powder and might take several minutes to load. Other rifles used a greased patch of cloth or leather and were not as slow to reload, but were still far slower than smoothbore muskets. Even those often required a mallet or an iron ramrod to seat the bullet after a few shots because of the fouling left by black powder when a shot is fired. Reload times on 1632 rifles were frequently three minutes or more. The rifles were also more expensive than a matchlock musket. There were rifles and riflemen capable of reliably hitting a man standing at three hundred meters, though they were rare on the ground.

Cavalry in 1632 was armed mostly with handguns or light carbines of smaller caliber in addition to a sword. Some were still using matchlocks, but mechanical locks like the wheel lock and snapping locks like the snaphaunce were becoming common. There were even attempts at making multishot guns, such as double (or more) barreled pistols and even primitive revolvers, though neither was common at this point.

For Grantville, the threatening infantry look like two kinds of soldiers that work together, one with basically medieval blades and a long pike and the other with a sixteen-pound matchlock musket. Besides his main weapon, the musketeer carried a bandoleer of thirteen loads of powder, a bag of lead balls, a powder horn and powder measure, a sword and dagger, a steady and a ramrod, plus his personal gear. They had to get within seventy-five meters to be a real threat.

The opposing infantry had some support. There was cavalry with advanced for the time handguns and horses. On the 1632 battlefield before Grantville's arrival, cavalry could close with an enemy over open ground in less time than a musket could be reloaded. There were also some little cannon, called battalion or regimental guns as a class, which fired either a solid ball or a multiple projectile load like buckshot with effective accuracy to two hundred meters. Those were typically set up before a battle in front of a formation to harass and reduce the enemy before the advance of the infantry. The guns were small and light enough that their two- to four-man crews could move them ahead of the advancing infantry until just out of range of an enemy's musket fire.

Given these factors, what Grantville needed in 1633 was a basic weapon that could be made with existing resources, cheaply enough to field in numbers, that could outrange the little cannon, reload fast enough to get multiple shots at the calvary and both outrange and have a higher rate of fire than musket armed infantry.

When Grantville made its appearance, there were many examples of late twentieth-century firearms available. Even a belt-fed machine gun was put in use by the Grantvillers early on. In a small, rural, fairly poor American town like Grantville, it would have been likely in 2000 to find representative pieces of nearly every type of firearm action available to civilians without special licensing that had been in large-scale production in the past hundred years. There would be scores of books available that show drawings of the internal parts of those and other gun designs, even machine guns and artillery. Unfortunately, there was no source of all the modern materials needed to manufacture and operate such advanced designs. There was a limit on what projects could be undertaken by the machine shops of Grantville.

In 1633, no one in Grantville could have known whether sufficient zinc necessary for combining with copper to make large numbers of cartridge cases would be available even for decades. No one knew when the chemical industry might produce reliable and safe percussion primers for firearms. No one knew how soon they would be able to make improved steels for reliable coil springs. No one knew when they would ever develop smokeless powder. No one knew how long it would take to increase the abilities of Grantville's machine shops and how they would replace worn out tools. What the leaders of Grantville knew with a certainty was that they needed small arms that would be better than an enemy's on the 1633 battlefield and that they were needed immediately and in considerable numbers.

What was needed was a weapon that would give the Allied soldier the advantages sought on the battlefield and that could be manufactured mainly by existing 1633 gun manufacturers from existing supplies and materials.

Enter the SRG . . .

In 1632, the French were secretly producing small numbers of a new and better gun lock. By the end of the century it would be the most common lock in use by infantry. It was a vast improvement over any lock then in service in terms of reliability of spark, being weatherproof, and cost per unit all taken together. It was the modern flintlock or French flintlock still in general use up until just before the American Civil War. When Grantville relocated to the seventeenth century, the modern flintlock was still in use for sporting black-powder firearms and Grantvillers had several as models on hunting rifles, reenactors' guns, or wall decorations. The flintlock required no advance in chemistry over what was already available. It did require quality flints, which were already being cut for fire-starting and for two other more primitive types of striking lock, the Dutch snaphaunce locks and the Spanish miquelet locks.

Rather than a burning cord, the modern flintlock depended upon spring power from a flat leaf spring to drive a piece of sharpened flint at a piece of hardened steel. This produced a shower of sparks that fell into the priming pan of a firearm. The piece of hardened steel was shaped so that its lower edge covered the priming pan full of powder until the steel was struck to produce sparks. This system freed the shooter of the burning match, gave him a much more weatherproof system and greatly reduced the amount of time between the decision to shoot and the bullet leaving the barrel. This latter meant that switching to flintlocks from matchlocks alone would make a more accurate musket.

Both for reasons of rapid loading and for their ease of use, a breech-loading gun was desired. The two systems that would work with a flintlock that were best known to the Grantvillers were the Fergusson and the Hall rifles.

The Fergusson was a rare gun used by a small unit of

Germans in the British Army during the American Revolution. There was very little chance that one existed in Grantville to act as a model for new production. It used a screw that was perpendicular to the line of the barrel to act as a breech. A half turn of the trigger guard exposed the chamber for loading. Despite wonderful things written about it by some, it was a failure as a design as no other nation produced it and the few hundred that were produced were withdrawn from service. Even the private manufacturer soon dropped the design and adopted a tipping breech much like the later Hall rifle.

The Hall rifle served the U.S. Army for a few decades before the American Civil War. The Hall started life as a flintlock and was easily converted to a chemical percussion primer when they became available. They allowed a soldier to load his weapon while lying down behind cover or more easily while on horseback. They had problems such as shooting loose and then spitting hot gases out around the breech. They looked very attractive as a potential rifle for Grantville. They also took far more machine time to make than a muzzle-loading rifle. It appeared that for the machine time, two or more muzzle-loading rifles could be produced for every breechloader. Was the Hall rifle worth giving up two muzzle-loading rifles for? Further, it began to look like a muzzle-loading rifle could be produced with minor tweaking of 1633 technology. The weapons makers of Suhl were already making thousands of muzzle-loading muskets annually. They would be able to make a muzzle-loading design to Grantville specifications, but for the immediate future lacked the machine tools and gauges to make something like the Hall rifle.

It was decided, then, that a muzzle-loading flintlock would be the basic design and a rifled barrel would be desirable. Many reams have been written about the American long rifle. That rifle grew from the very rifles the Grantvillers would face in 1633. The American versions were longer and lighter and usually of smaller caliber, but still depended on a patched lead ball for accuracy. They were as slow as the muskets of 1633 as well. What was needed was a type of bullet that could be loaded fast and that still gave the needed accuracy.

Such a bullet and rifles for it were common during the American Civil War. Again, Grantville had examples of both bullets and rifles of this type. Minié bullets have conical-shaped noses and a conical-shaped hollow in the base. (NB: Minié bullets are named after their inventor; they are not, as many assume, based on the name, small.)

Rifles give the bullet a ballistic spin, much like a well-thrown American football, resulting in bullets that tend to go straight and in a predictable trajectory. The 1633 rifle was accurate, but slow to reload. What the minié bullet does is make a rifle as fast to reload as a musket, or in the case of matchlocks loaded from wooden cartouche, much faster. The minié bullet was smaller in diameter than the size of the gun barrel's bore, just like the musket ball. It is loaded bare or with part of a paper cartridge, just like Gustavus' men are already using, into the bore of the rifle and rammed home. Firing the rifle expands the base of the bullet, thanks to the hollow, and drives the back half of the bullet into the rifling, which spins the bullet. When loaded as part of a paper cartridge, and when part of the powder of that cartridge is used to prime the pan, the minié ball can be loaded and fired for several minutes at a rate of three rounds per minute by trained soldiers standing in formation. Before the American Civil War, it was found that a .58 caliber minié ball weighing about one and one quarter ounce could be fired from a rifle by a kneeling man at the belt of a standing man and the bullet would strike him if he was anywhere between the muzzle and almost 250 meters. This would give any Grantville ally a rifle with three times the range of a 1633 musketeer and 25 percent greater range than enemy battalion guns (the little cannon), with only one sight setting.

The Enfield Pattern 1853 three-band "musket" was the second most common rifle of the American Civil War and most common with Southern forces. Reproductions of that rifle were available from Grantville's small group of reenactors as guides for the production of a minié rifle. The Enfield P53 was also among the longest of rifles of its type and can mount a long socket, or ring, bayonet, giving it some reach as a sort of pike if need be. The rifle could be loaded and fired with the bayonet in place. While the Pattern 53 used a percussion lock dependent on chemical production, it was easily adapted to flintlock action by Grantville's Ollie Reardon and initially produced by the Struve gun works of Suhl where it was called the Struve-Reardon Gewehr, or SRG in common use. (*Gewehr* is the German term for "rifle.")

Thus the SRG was basically a flintlock equipped Enfield Model of 1853. Like the P53, there are shortened models available for use by cavalry and support troops or marines. These are the basic rifle with shortened barrels, stocks, and ramrods.

Some basic characteristics of the SRG are as follows:

Standard Infantry Model

Overall length	55.25 inches
Weight	10.5 pounds
Ignition system	Flintlock in 1633
Rifling twist	One turn in 72 inches
Sights	Front: fixed post on bayonet lug Rear: stepped tangent and ladder to 800 yards
Ammunition	Paper cartridge with lubricated .577 caliber 510 grain minié bullet and 60 grains of black powder

Musketoon or Carbine

Overall length	40.25 inches
Weight	7.25 pounds
Ignition system	Flintlock in 1633
Rifling twist	One turn in 48 inches
Sights	Front: fixed post Rear: stepped tangent and ladder to 600 yards (Note, some models were made with simple fixed rear sight for 200 yards and flip-up sight for 400 yards as an economy move)

| Ammunition | Paper cartridge with lubricated .577 caliber 510 grain minié bullet and 60 grains of black powder. |
| Special notes | Some models featured a carbine ring and bar on the left side for use with the carbine strap and snap while mounted. |

Another consideration for adopting the SRG was that as percussion caps become available, the SRG could be easily converted to use the new caps. The production lines might be altered easily to produce new percussion lock guns and existing guns could be returned to depot to be converted. At a later date, as fixed and self-primed cartridges are produced, the SRG, both flintlock and percussion models, could be converted to a single shot breechloader such as the British Snyder or American Trapdoor series rifles, either as a frontline rifle or as an economy to provide more modern rifles to reserves such as militia.

The design for the SRG was chosen because it was the best that could be produced in large number within the first couple of years that also provided some hope of updating at small expense in the future.

Could a more advanced design have been adopted? Absolutely. But at what cost and at what levels of production?

The SRG was a rifle that was doable, could outrange the known potential enemy small arms, as well as the small battalion guns used in the open field, and load fast enough to get repeat volleys at advancing cavalry. It takes a long ring bayonet, a weapon not seen until the SRG's introduction, to allow SRG-armed soldiers to operate without supporting pike men. The SRG's efficiency as an arm allowed Grantville's allies to field smaller, easier to supply, more mobile and yet harder hitting armies than its potential enemies.

The SRG was not a modern assault rifle or machine gun or even a World War I–era bolt action, but it would serve well until better could be built.

Alchemical Distillation

《◎★◎》

Andrew Clark

[A Short Treatise of Spagyrical Preparations of Hope performed by way of Distillation, Being taken from a Study of the new American science wedded to the Proven Methods of the Ancient Chemists and in keeping with Christian Learning, Composed by Doctor Erasmus Faustus.]

Rejoice as at the break of day after a long and tedious night to see how this art of Alchemy begins to shine forth out of the clouds of reproach which it has for a long time undeservedly lain under and engender Hope to the people of our times. There is a glut of chemical books, but a scarcity of chemical truths. Nature and art afford a variety of spagyrical preparations and the American knowledge allows us to discover many without the three hundred years of trial and error. I can do no better service than to present some of these truths.

Of the creation of all things, matter exists by God's wise and powerful will to produce things which are light, heavy, wet, dry, cold, hot, and otherwise endowed with form for God may be all in all. With a holy flood were a few saved from the taint of the rest of the world. With holy fire will the souls after death be purged of evil and thus will the dross be separated from that which it is alloyed.

We know the Lord can clean by destruction, whether that is flood or fire. Either in flood, the antapokatastasis in Capricorn, or fire, the apokatastasis in Cancer, we have methods to transform matter ourselves. But too easily have we assumed the transformative processes would not work together. See that Fire and Flood are not Exclusive, but may be combined as in the Art of Distillation.

Distillation is the long known art of extracting the humid part of things by virtue of heat and being first resolved into a vapor and then condensed again by cold, but among the wide details of distillation, allow me to examine two. First is stratification, the separation of vapors prior to precipitation. Second is calcination, the reduction of a solid although humid mass into a calx while collecting the vapor.

Although we practice stratification, little has been heeded of the precision allowed. From the same process that allows us to extract the Spirit of Wine to yield Brandy, we can separate the spirit of many other fluids. Care to the heat applied to the menstruum will drive the most volatile spirit first while restraining the phlegm. Instruments can be used to measure the exact heat of the solution. Even the greatest dullard will understand how the color of iron in flame can be used to measure the heat of a preparation over fire. Such it is that we may stratify products at different heats, allowing in some cases a single distillation where multiple passes of rectification might have been required in the past.

By stratification we extract the spirit of vinegar, or acetic acid as the Americans say, from common wine vinegar. As Nicholas Flamel has taught us to employ spirit of vinegar as a solvent in many vegetable tinctures, we also should know it is also a fungicide and explore it as a product itself. The American texts imply it can also be used to make glues and paints.

Production of one particular subsequent potion using spirit of vinegar has immediate applications. Slowly add chalk to spirit of vinegar just until saturation, then dry and crystallize the resulting "Salt of Spirit of Vinegar" or "Sodium Acetate". Next slowly add oil of vitriol. Allow to cool and separate the liquid. The collected crystals are a form of the original spirit of vinegar, but with additional water removed in this most curious fashion. This "water-less spirit of vinegar" is called "acetic anhydride" by the Americans and the crystals desperately desire to react with water. They should be sealed away. The pulverized form is a potent weed killer and easily burns skin. It has been suggested the violence with which these crystals can desire water is employed by the Americans to make explosives.

Calcination has long been employed to extract interest-ing fluids from a solid. Large quantities of pine tar are produced in Sweden by calcination. By applying this process to the bark of the common birch, also known as the Black Birch, we can produce birch tar. Be aware this is different from the tar resulting from Silver Birch or White Birch and different yet again from the tar of the American's Canoe Birch.

Another pass of simple distillation of wood tar will separate the volatile Oil of Tar, or turpentine, from the *Resina Nigra*, or pitch. The Oil of Birch, or *oleum betula,* has a peculiar penetrating yet pleasing odor and can be used as a flavoring agent if used in small quantities. Americans confirm the Oil of Birch as the concentrated active component of willow bark used in so many healing potions. Birch tar yields less product, but a much purer form than willow tar however as the willow bark contains many other undesired elements that pollute the *oleum salix*. Starting with birch bark and twigs, we can easily generate large quantities of *oleum betula,* or methyl salicylate as the Americans call it. They also warn that while the concentrated nature has healing properties, it is very irritating to the skin and too much will kill. They suggest a different preparation.

Take then into a glass vessel, one part caustic soda and into this add one part Oil of Birch. Observe that a white gum is formed. Wash then this gum with settled water before scraping. Of this white gum then with an equal part add waterless spirit of vinegar and a half part oil of vitriol. Immerse the vessel in a bath of boiling water for a short time. Remove to cool and allow crystals to form, but first you may mix an addition of a little water to hasten the cooling. After which time you will add enough hot water to just dissolve these crystals. Repeat the operation to cool and see that crystals reform. Remove these white crystals and allow to dry overnight.

The white powder resulting from pulverizing these crystals is a most potent and secret pain relief as revealed by the Americans. They call it Aspirin or maybe Esperan, from the hope it offers. Besides drinking potions with this Esperan, poultices can be made and directly applied to aches of the body.

Arise, O Sun of truth and hope, and dispel the fogs and mists of ignorance and suspicion, that the Queen of arts may triumph in splendor! I desire not to be mistaken as if I did deny Galen his due, or Hippocrates what is his right for, indeed, they wrote excellently in many things, and deserve well thereby. That which I cannot allow of is assumption that only these ancients held genius and that the men of today and tomorrow have nothing to contribute.

As the Lord told Matthew, "Seek and ye shall find" and note well the words of Saint Paul, "Attend to reading, Timothy, my son." Mysteries may be hidden, but God desires us to search them out. It must therefore be possible to determine truth through such a search and long have we been on this quest. Our faith and knowledge show us Hope.

Images

❧◆★◆❧

There are various images, mostly portraits from the time, that illustrate different aspects of the 1632 universe. In the first issue of the *Grantville Gazette,* I included those with the volume itself. Since that created downloading problems for some people, however, I've separated all the images and they will be maintained and expanded on their own schedule.

If you're interested, you can look at the images and my accompanying commentary at no extra cost. They are set up in the Baen Free Library. You can find them as follows:

1. Go to www.baen.com
2. Select "Free Library" from the menu at the top.
3. Once in the Library, select "The Authors" from the yellow menu on the left.
4. Once in "The Authors," select "Eric Flint."
5. Then select "Images from the Grantville Gazette."

Submissions to the Magazine

If anyone is interested in submitting stories or articles for future issues of the *Grantville Gazette*, you are welcome to do so. But you must follow a certain procedure:

1) All stories and articles must first be posted in a conference in Baen's Bar set aside for the purpose, called "1632 Slush." Do *not* send them to me directly, because I won't read them. It's good idea to submit a sketch of your story to the conference first, since people there will likely spot any major problems that you overlooked. That can wind up saving you a lot of wasted work.

You can get to that conference by going to Baen Books' Web site www.baen.com. Then select "Baen's Bar." If it's your first visit, you will need to register. (That's quick and easy.) Once you're in the Bar, the three conferences devoted to the 1632 universe are "1632 Slush," "1632 Slush Comments," and "1632 Tech Manual." You should post your sketch, outline, or story in "1632 Slush." Any discussion of it should take place in "1632 Slush Comments." The "1632 Tech Manual" is for any general discussion not specifically related to a specific story.

2) Your story/article will then be subjected to discussion and commentary by participants in the 1632 discussion. In essence, it will get chewed on by what amounts to a very large, virtual writers' group.

You do *not* need to wait until you've finished the story to start posting it in "1632 Slush." In fact, it's a good idea not to wait, because you will often find that problems can be spotted early in the game, before you've put all the work into completing the piece.

3) While this is happening, the assistant editor of the *Grantville Gazette,* Paula Goodlett, will be keeping an eye on the discussion. She will alert me whenever a story or article seems to be gaining general approval from the participants in the discussion. There's also an editorial board to which Paula and I belong that does much the same thing. The other members of the board are Karen Bergstralh, Rick Boatright, and Laura Runkle. In addition, authors who publish regularly in the 1632 setting participate on the board as ex officio members. My point is that plenty of people will be looking over the various stories being submitted, so you needn't worry that your story will just get lost in the shuffle.

4) At that point—and *only* at that point—do I take a look at a story or article.

I insist that people follow this procedure, for two reasons:

First, as I said, I'm very busy and I just don't have time

to read everything submitted until I have some reason to think it's gotten past a certain preliminary screening.

Secondly, and even more importantly, the setting and "established canon" in this series is quite extensive by now. If anyone tries to write a story without first taking the time to become familiar with the setting, they will almost invariably write something that—even if it's otherwise well written—I simply can't accept.

In short, the procedure outlined above will save *you* a lot of wasted time and effort also.

One point in particular: I have gotten extremely hard-nosed about the way in which people use American characters in their stories (so-called "up-timers"). That's because I began discovering that my small and realistically portrayed coal mining town of 3,500 people was being willy-nilly transformed into a "town" with a population of something like 20,000 people—half of whom were Navy SEALs who just happened to be in town at the Ring of Fire, half of whom were rocket scientists (ibid), half of whom were brain surgeons (ibid), half of whom had a personal library the size of the Library of Congress, half of whom . . .

Not to mention the F-16s that "just happened" to be flying through the area, the army convoys (ibid), the trains full of vital industrial supplies (ibid), the FBI agents in hot pursuit of master criminals (ibid), the . . .

NOT A CHANCE. If you want to use an up-time character, you *must* use one of the "authorized" characters. Those are the characters created by Virginia DeMarce using genealogical software and embodied in what is called "the grid."

You can obtain a copy of the grid from the Web site, which collects and presents the by-now voluminous material concerning the series, www.1632.org. Look on the right for the link to "Virginia's Up-timer Grid." While you're at it, you should also look further down at the links under the title "Author's Manual."

You will be paid for any story or factual article which is published. The rates that I can afford for the magazine at the moment fall into the category of "semipro." I hope to be able to raise those rates in the future to make them fall clearly within professional rates, but . . . That will obviously depend on whether the magazine starts selling enough copies to generate the needed income. In the meantime, the rates and terms I can offer are posted below in the standard letter of agreement accepted by all the contributors to this issue.

Standard letter of agreement

Below are the terms for the purchase of a story or factual article (hereafter "the work") to be included in an issue of the online magazine *Grantville Gazette,* edited by Eric Flint and published by Baen Books.

Payment will be sent upon acceptance of the work at the following rates:

1. a rate of 2.5 cents per word for any story or article up to 15,000 words;
2. a rate of 2 cents a word for any story or article after 15,000 words but before 30,000 words;

3. a rate of 1.5 cents a word for any story or article after 30,000 words.

The rates are cumulative, not retroactive to the beginning of the story or article. (A story of 40,000 words would earn the higher rates for the first 30,000 words.) Word counts will be rounded to the nearest hundred and calculated by Word for Windows XP.

You agree to sell exclusive first world rights for the story, including exclusive first electronic rights for five years following publication, and subsequent nonexclusive world rights. Should Baen Books select your story for a paper edition, you will not receive a second advance but will be paid whatever the differential might be between what you originally received and the advance for different length stories established for the paper edition. You will also be entitled to a proportionate share of any royalties earned by the authors of a paper edition. If the work is reissued in a paper edition, then the standard reversion rights as stipulated in the Baen contract would supercede the reversion rights contained here.

Eric Flint retains the rights to the 1632 universe setting, as well as the characters in it, so you will need to obtain his permission if you wish to publish the story or use the setting and characters through anyone other than Baen Books even after the rights have reverted to you. You, the author, will retain copyright and all other rights except as listed above. Baen will copyright the story on first publication.

You warrant and represent that you have the right to grant the rights above; that these rights are free and clear; that your story will not violate any copyright or any other right of a third party, nor be contrary to law. You agree to indemnify Baen for any loss, damage, or expense arising out of any claim inconsistent with any of the above warranties and representations.

Grantville Gazette

An electronic-only magazine of stories and fact articles
based on Eric Flint's 1632 "Ring of Fire" universe

The *Grantville Gazette* can be purchased through Baen Books' Webscriptions service at www.baen.com. (Then select Webscriptions.) Each electronic volume of the *Gazette* can be purchased individually for $6, or you can purchase them in discounted packages, as follows:

- Volume 1. This volume is free, and can be obtained from the Baen Free Library. (Once you're in the Baen web site at www.baen.com, select "Free Library" on the left hand aside of the menu at the top. Then, select "The Books" and you'll find *Grantville Gazette Volume 1*.)
- Volumes 2–4, $15.
- Volumes 5–7, $15.
- Volumes 8–10, $15. Volume 8 is already available, with Volumes 9 and 10 in production.
- Or, you can purchase a single package of the entire series thus far, Volumes 1-10, for $40.

All editions can be downloaded in a number of formats, several of which are unencrypted and DRM-free.

1634: The Baltic War
by Eric Flint & David Weber
1-4165-2102-X ◆ $26.00

1634: The Galileo Affair
by Eric Flint & Andrew Dennis
0-7434-9919-0 ◆ $7.99
New York Times bestseller!

1635: Cannon Law
by Eric Flint & Andrew Dennis
1-4165-0938-0 ◆ $26.00

1634: The Ram Rebellion
by Eric Flint with Virginia DeMarce
1-4165-2060-0 ◆ $25.00

Ring of Fire edited by Eric Flint
1-4165-0908-9 ◆ $7.99
Top writers tell tales of Grantville, the town lost in time, including David Weber, Mercedes Lackey, Jane Lindskold, Eric Flint and more.

Grantville Gazette edited by Eric Flint
1-7434-8860-1 ◆ $6.99

Grantville Gazette II edited by Eric Flint
1-4165-2051-1 ◆ $25.00

Grantville Gazette III edited by Eric Flint
1-4165-0941-0 ◆ $25.00
More stories by Eric Flint and others in this best-selling alternate history series.